CRADLESONG

JESSICA PALMER

POCKET BOOKS

New York   London   Toronto   Sydney   Tokyo   Singapore

This book is a work of fiction. Names, characters, places and incidents are either products of the author's imagination or are used fictitiously. Any resemblance to actual events or locales or persons, living or dead, is entirely coincidental.

An *Original* Publication of POCKET BOOKS

POCKET BOOKS, a division of Simon & Schuster Inc.
1230 Avenue of the Americas, New York, NY 10020.

ISBN: 0-671-73421-0

First Pocket Books printing May 1993

10 9 8 7 6 5 4 3 2 1

POCKET and colophon are registered trademarks of Simon & Schuster Inc.

Cover art by Lisa Falkenstern

Printed in the U.S.A.

WHAT THE CHILD SEES . . .

Jason raced from the living room. He paused at the study door, pressed his ear against the wood for a moment and listened.

In the living room, his mother was picking up the throw pillows from the floor.

Turning from the door, he heard a squeak and muffled laughter.

"William?" the little boy said hopefully.

A creak, and Jason turned terrified eyes on a decomposing Tommy Erwin dangling on the end of a noose which hung from the second floor landing. The body swung in a lazy arc, back to the frightened toddler.

Suddenly, it turned to face Jason. A blackened tongue protruded from a pain-contorted face. Rocking gently, back and forth, back and forth. Hypnotic.

Then the eyes opened, and Jason fell to his knees. . . .

———————————————

"Jessica Palmer is set to take over the V. C. Andrews crown."

—James Herbert

For my friends:
Molly Brown, Ron Chetwynd-Hayes, Colin Greeland, Stella Hargreaves, James Herbert, Mary Scott and a host of others, with special thanks for their continuing moral support.

With an additional thanks to Dr. Ian Goodman at Northwood Medical Clinic in Northwood, Middlesex, for his medical expertise.

CRADLESONG

Prologue

White noise.

Tom Erwin stopped writing and threw his pencil down on the desk in disgust. His homework could wait. He rubbed his forehead and looked out the window. The old Graves house—backlit by the setting sun—stood out in stark relief. The ghostly, decaying edifice was made all the more surreal by the celestial golden glow, like a demon with a halo.

Children's voices, sibilant whispers like so much white noise, echoed throughout his mind. With them came visions of the long-dead little girl, Sara Graves.

Her voice rose above the rest. Dissonant, strident, it called him: "Tommy?"

He looked briefly over his shoulder.

No one there.

The hiss inside his head turned into a roar. Young Erwin covered his ears, trying to shut out the sound, but it only increased in volume. For years the voices had taunted him—haunted him—but they were getting worse.

"Sara?"

No response.

He pushed away from his desk, too distracted to work, and stared at the Graves place.

"Sara?" Again he whispered her name.

Furious, he turned his back to the window as a final ray of sun burst from behind the house—a fiery nimbus.

Inexplicable rage blinded him. The room, which he had shared with his brother for so many years, spun around him, and anger was replaced by a choking terror. The teenager ran through the house and into the yard beyond—followed, as always, by the continual static.

White noise.

Hands stuffed in his pockets, he sauntered aimlessly up the street to stand on the dilapidated front porch of the old home. Between loosened floorboards he could see a ghostly image, the diaphanous tracer left by the young toddler who had died by suffocation beneath these same steps a couple of years ago.

"Tommy?"

He shuffled back to the stairs where he could look up at the second story window. Sara stared down at him, her face pressed against the glass, mashed and contorted by the filthy pane. A golden cloud of hair surrounded a normally cherubic face, its features flattened and twisted, pink lips spread wide to reveal white teeth. He shook his head to clear it, and she vanished.

Tom strolled around the house several times as the sun slipped below the horizon and evening turned to night. The eastern sky was a deep indigo while the west was shrouded in bloody crimson. He completed another circuit and stopped near the back door.

It creaked slowly open, a squealing invitation.

As the last rays of the dying sun slipped behind the trees Tom went inside. He leaned against the kitchen counter, waiting for his eyes to adjust to the darkness, ignoring the soft, skittering patter of unseen feet.

When he had last been on the other side of that door?

The answer came all too easily to him. The night the

2

remaining members of the family had been wiped out . . . the angry squawk of a police radio followed by garbled, static-ridden chatter.

White noise.

Bleary-eyed neighbors collected in the streets outside the Graves home.

Sara dead. Gone . . . forever. Dead, gone . . . is no more. Killed by her father, and now this.

Then the child, Tommy, had struggled to comprehend the incomprehensible, watching as someone pushed a mottled human hand inside a plastic bag and zipped it shut. Elliot Graves, Sara's father.

Two men, blue-clad ghouls, hovered over a pasty-faced technician.

"All through?" one said.

The technician nodded, stood up with a sigh, and led the grim procession from the room.

"There's more in front. This guy's pretty in comparison —at least there's something left of the head. The one in living room, hm," the officer smacked his lips. "The entire back is gone . . ." The voice dwindled as the men moved off.

Tommy crept silently through the door, skirting the bag and its gruesome contents only to be arrested by the chalked figure of a man sketched on the floor around a bloody pool. The boy slipped through the side door into the dining room. From his hiding place, he watched as the technician scraped a viscous red-and-gray substance from the far wall into a baggie.

A camera flashed and a hand fell onto his shoulder from behind. Tommy stifled a yell.

"Hey! What the hell are you doing in here? How'd you get in?"

A flashlight beam centered upon the child's face, and the officer pulled him roughly into the living room.

"You wanna see, huh? Well, look!" The man clasped Tommy's neck and forced him to look down at Jane, Sara's mother, with the cold black barrel of a gun extending from blue lips, a gaping hole where the back of her head should be.

"Christ, Bob, get that kid outa here!"

"I didn't invite him, found him hiding in the dining room. Musta slipped in the back."

Tommy heard his mother shriek his name. The policeman dragged Tom onto the porch and shoved him toward the stairs. "This yours? Well, take him home. I betcha he's gonna have real bad dreams tonight."

His mother pulled him across the yellow-ribboned barrier while another staccato burst of static followed.

White noise.

The promised dreams came, and they never went away.

Somewhere outside, someone turned on a porch light, which washed the kitchen with sickly illumination. Tom Erwin levered himself away from the counter to walk cautiously through the kitchen, half expecting to stumble across Elliot Graves's supine form, enclosed in an oversized plastic bag.

Pushing the kitchen door open, he gasped and took an involuntary step back. A little boy with pale luminescent skin awaited him. The young Sara beckoned from the foyer. For once the voices in his head fell silent. The boy took Tom's hand and pulled him into the front hall. His eyes took in the noose without a second glance. It seemed almost natural, hanging from the second-floor landing.

Sara prodded his side, urging him toward the steps. Every fiber, every nerve ending screamed in protest as he placed his foot upon the stair. Sara floated beside him, staring deep into his eyes, her expression peaceful and angelic.

Her specter drifted toward the second floor. Mesmerized, Tommy followed. She gestured, and Tom bent over the railing to grasp the rope. She smiled her approval, and he placed the noose around his neck, tightened it, and climbed over the banister.

She bowed her head, her lips twisted into a feral grin, and

her skull collapsed, her specter mimicking the fatal wounds her father had inflicted upon her so many years ago.

Horrified, Tom let go of the rail, stepping away from the landing. His body hung suspended in space for a second, then plummeted. His plunging descent was roughly arrested by the rope. He swung, gagging.

Poorly made, the noose crushed his larynx but did not snap his spine. Each rasping breath became a burning agony as he tried vainly to get air to his tortured lungs.

Too late. Tom Erwin recognized the insanity of what he had just done. He battled hopelessly against the bond, clawing at the rope around his throat, but his desperate action only drew the noose tighter around his neck and sent him into a spin.

The room whirled around him. Brief broken pictures, like disconnected snapshots, burned upon his retina. The hall. The wall. The front door. The stair. The study. Followed by the hall again.

He swung again in a cavorting, capering jig. *The hall . . . the wall . . . the front door . . . the stair . . . the study.*

Faster! *The hall, the wall, the front door, the stair, the study.*

And faster! *Thehallthewallthefrontdoorthestairthestudy.*

Again and new images began to appear.

The hall . . . Jane's mangled body twitched to life under his kicking feet . . .

The wall . . . splattered with blood and gray matter . . .

The door . . . Elliot's corpse struggled to sit up in the kitchen . . .

The stair . . . Sara's leering visage, her battered head and shattered skull . . .

The study . . . a girl, which he knew to be Sara's sister, with her charred, bubbling skin appeared . . .

The hall again . . . and a little boy stepped into view beside Jane.

Tom's tongue rolled out of his mouth; his eyes bulged. He

jerked, his feet kicking spastically. His lungs filled with molten iron. Sara swooped down to join the little boy. His eyes glowed red as he picked at an open sore on his leg. Sara's sister joined them from the study. Undisturbed, the children regarded Tom Erwin's strange, jittering death dance.

His vision began to fade, and the last thing he remembered was the sound of their lilting laughter.

1

Splashes of blood!

A blood-red shaft of light from the dome atop the ambulance pierced the crepuscular afternoon sky. A Saab fishtailed around another corner in hot pursuit. Scott McDowell crammed the stick shift into fifth gear as the image of blood seeping into the cracked dry wood of the porch rippled across his consciousness.

Strapped together in the front seat, his sons, Adam and Jason, clung to each other. One of them let out a cry of mixed terror and glee. With a dangerous three-quarter turn the car glided through an intersection. A horn sounded, and the Saab barely missed a delivery truck as the rear tires again drifted out of Scott's control.

A light drizzle had begun, wetting the oily surface of the streets. Scott fought with the steering as the tires spun on the rain-slicked roads, his eyes still trained on the pulsating ambulance lights as they receded in the distance. The tread found purchase, and the car darted forward.

Berating himself for not getting the name of the hospital, Scott punched the accelerator as the signal ahead turned yellow. He must not lose them. He couldn't believe he hadn't thought to ask, but when he saw the growing puddle of blood, his mind had switched off. Scott had grabbed the boys and thrown them into the car, never thinking to ask the name of the hospital until the ambulance leapt away from the curb.

All that blood.

Another blood-red flash pierced the dreary sky as Scott's mind replayed the scene again in agonizing slow motion . . .

The proud young couple pausing to beam with pride at their new home. Their first home. The boys cavorted on the porch. Allison's hand touched the railing and she yanked it back as if burned. She wore an unreadable expression, and Scott couldn't tell if it was pleasure, surprise, or pain.

Her foot hovered over the first step and then descended to make contact with the wood. Her jaw went slack and she teetered up the next step. Her hand went protectively to her stomach as she stumbled up the next two risers. She crumpled, folding eternally, as Scott bounded up the stairs on legs gone suddenly rubbery to catch her before she hit the boards. As Scott lowered her to the porch he saw the blood seeping from between her legs and felt the tremulous ripple of muscles beneath his hand.

Contractions! And she wasn't due for another four months yet.

A horn blared; another car slid past in a blur, and Scott forced his attention back to the ambulance which he pursued in a high-speed chase in the best of Hollywood traditions. Images came and went. Frames frozen in time. A stop sign ignored. Another blaring horn. A street light. Squealing tires. A sign subliminally registered. Cars skidding in a deadly metallic dance. A montage bathed in blood-red light.

All that blood!

It wasn't supposed to happen like this, Scott thought. The first day in their new home and Allison hadn't even made it through the front door.

The ambulance careered through an intersection. Jason's mewling and the siren's shriek melded to form a single high-pitched keen. Scott tried to follow, only to be cut off at the last minute.

His eyes trained on the disappearing taillights, he put the car in reverse, backing up a bit before he nosed it around the next car and into opposing traffic. A self-professed cynic, if not an agnostic, Scott prayed fervently to whatever God happened to be listening at the time as he floored it, swinging around the next car and careening through the intersection.

The ambulance turned left. The Saab skidded around the next corner into the hospital zone. The ambulance pulled up before the squat, utilitarian building. Ignoring the sign, Scott slid the Saab into a place marked "Emergency Vehicles Only—No Parking Anytime."

He plunged from the car just as they lifted Allison from the ambulance. Balancing the two-year-old Jason on his hip, pulling Adam by the hand, Scott bolted for the door before it closed behind his wife.

The waiting room was furnished with couches and chairs, the upholstery dirty and worn to a grey gloss by a thousand bottoms. The institutional white walls were relieved by colored stripes that were apparently both decorative and functional. A blue stripe pointed to X-ray, a green to the Pharmacy. Yellow to some other place Scott didn't quite catch as an attendant grabbed him, propelling him toward the desk.

Allison's cart disappeared behind a flutter of curtains.

"My wife," Scott indicated the room.

"We'll need some information from you, sir." The attendant said, giving Scott his most professionally sympathetic smile.

Blinking in the cold, blue fluorescent light, Scott placed Jason on the reception desk and reached into his pocket for his wallet.

A voice came over the loudspeakers and intoned: "Code blue. Emergency Room. Code blue in Emergency." The speaker crackled, spitting its deathly message.

Someone burst from another curtained alcove to dive into Allison's. White-clad men and women appeared, with studied nonchalance, to converge at the nurse's station for instruction.

Color drained from Scott's face and he stood dumb as his shock-fogged wits took time to react. Shoulder down, he leapt, ramming the attendant who hovered nearby, slamming him against the wall. Scott launched between two chairs, deaf to Jason's loud cry and the groan of the orderly.

"Code blue. Emergency Room."

Before Scott had made it ten steps, four men were on top of him, pulling him back. The people in the waiting room turned to stare at the group with dull, bovine faces.

"Hold it. You can't help her. You'll only get in the way. You wouldn't want that, would you?"

Scott deflated as the five-year-old Adam launched himself at one of the attendants and Jason attempted a clumsy tackle of another man's kneecap. Sanity returned, and Scott mumbled an apology while he loosened Jason's grip on the attendant's shin.

Three of the men left to cluster in the hallway between Scott and the curtained partition. The largest escorted Scott to the desk. A myopic clerk with an annoying nasal twang asked for name, age, insurance numbers.

Scott shuffled through the cards in his wallet: credit cards, social security card, driver's license. They all looked the same. She shoved a seemingly unending stream of papers under his nose. Admittance forms, release forms, insurance forms. Scribbling his name with a flourish on the last, he shoved his wallet and the loose cards in his hip pocket.

A hand touched his arm, and Scott looked up at the ambulance driver.

"You're gonna have to move your car, buddy."

* * *

The faint hiss of oxygen. The pressure of the cuff inflated around her upper arm. The prick of a needle and the scream of the siren. Allison was aware of these things, but what she saw—what she remembered—was the terror in Scott's eyes and his pinched mouth as they lifted her into the ambulance.

Allison had wanted to assure him that she was all right. She wanted to reach out to him, but her body refused to respond to her mental commands.

After the initial twinge, comforting darkness like the indigo velvet of early spring twilight wrapped itself around her. Someone or something had joined her. *She was not alone!* Warm arms embraced her. No pain. She was suffused with the glow of welcome and love that seemed to penetrate from the wood of the porch itself.

The feeling of wood grain—satiny, rich and aromatic—surrounded her. A titillating current ran through her body. The unknown, unnamed force eagerly examined her, concentrating on the small life within her womb. She felt the hot rush of blood from between her legs and the unrelenting undulation of a contraction. Allison became detached from herself, as the presence clenched at her frantically, fighting for her life and for that of her unborn child.

Something held her, and Allison knew she was going to be all right.

Two words echoed in her head—*The Key*. Then Allison succumbed to darkness.

When next she opened her eyes, her senses seemed particularly acute, although the perspective was somehow skewed. One minute she was staring directly into the tight, drawn face of the nurse only inches from her own; the next she viewed the commotion from above.

People as ephemeral as shadows flitted around her. Out of the corner of her eye Allison thought she saw a little boy dressed in odd old-fashioned clothing, and she wondered idly what he was doing here.

From a distance not far away, Allison heard the mechanical rasp of a loudspeaker.

"Code blue, Emergency Room."

The unearthly voice sounded breathless and agitated. Then her attention was drawn to furious activity below her.

"Board!" someone shouted with the voice of command.

Two people lifted her flaccid figure from the bed while another shoved a hard board underneath it.

"Bag."

A white-clad figure moved around to the head of the bed, holding what looked like an oblong balloon with a long tube attached. She forced the patient's jaws open and pushed the tube past clenched teeth.

The Allison who floated above the chaos found herself gagging and the next thing she knew she peered into a green-cast face, half-obscured by the black balloon. Only then did she realize, with a shock, that the life they fought to save was hers. For a moment she resisted their efforts until she looked into the angry face of a little boy who hovered above the congregation of flustered nurses and orderlies.

She would have gasped, but the tube prevented it. Allison choked instead, and the oddly dressed child disappeared from view.

Scott paced in the waiting room between rows of tired, worn chairs and sagging sofas. Jason slept, curled up in his brother's arms, while Adam watched his father guardedly. With as much enthusiasm as he could muster, Scott smiled at the child. It didn't work; Adam peered at him with flat, dead eyes, and didn't smile back. Wincing an apology, Scott spun to march rigidly away from his sons.

He had been warned, more than once. The thought came unwelcome and unbidden. Snatches of conversations drifted to the surface, along with the self-accusations, and Scott could not push them away. No, it wasn't as if he hadn't been warned. Sam Holloway, the former owner had spoken the loudest and longest about the house.

"... *nine, ten dead. Three murders, at least, maybe more, two suicides! That can't be coincidence. Good God, man, what further proof do you need?*"

Holloway had done his utmost to dissuade Scott from the purchase, and his words echoed like a premonition. "*I swear to God, the house has a taste for blood. It warps. It instills madness. It destroys. And it's growing stronger every year. . . .*"

Scott's complacent reply seemed a mockery now. "A house is plaster, wood, mortar and stone—an inanimate object. It can't be held accountable for what has occurred within its walls." Scott frowned. "People die. There's nothing magical about it—no ghosts, no drama or romance except in people's minds. Once the bodies are gone, nothing's left to reach through the floorboards and grab your ankle."

The builder also had warned him, his booming basso intruded on Scott's consciousness, answering the young man's rebuttal. "*. . . In my work you learn there's good buildings and bad buildings. Buildings, like people, have personalities. This building is bad—so much has happened here—just seems to me that buying a place like this is like sittin' down to play poker when you know the deck is stacked against you.*"

Holloway's final words sounded prophetic, indeed. "*If you are so dead set on your own destruction, who am I to interfere?*"

Under the harsh, glaring light of the waiting room, their warnings rose to haunt Scott. He made another circuit around the emergency room, listening to the sound of muffled coughs and soft rustles of human rumps on sagging seat cushions.

Words fluttered around in his mind—like moths never alighting so he could grasp them and examine them.

Bad . . . Code blue . . . This house is bad . . . kills . . . Code blue, emergency room.

Clenching his fist, Scott paused, midstep, to bring his

13

hand crashing down on his thigh. Enough, he thought, a home reflects its occupants, and it doesn't sound like this home has had too many happy people living here. Bad things have happened, but it's what the people did—not the house itself.

His gaze went to Jason and Adam sunk low on the torn leather couch. They were a happy family—or had been—and the boys needed him now. Scott strode over to his sons and pulled them into a crushing embrace, staring over their heads at the treatment room. The curtain parted, disgorging white-clad personnel. A sob caught in his throat as he noticed that they were . . . smiling.

Scott clutched the boys' hands, plunged toward the alcove. A young intern stepped from behind the curtain, turning to speak to someone inside the treatment room.

"Nurse, I believe we have a couple of customers out here who could use lollipops. Do you think you could scare some up?"

A young woman emerged and managed a crisp smile before she took both children by the hand. Jason started to wail. Adam moved protectively closer to his brother.

The older boy resisted as she tried to lead them away. His chin resting on his shoulder, Adam watched his father with dark, hollow eyes. Scott nodded, and the child acquiesced, allowing himself to be herded away from the treatment room.

"We're moving your wife to Intensive Care. We gave her Ritrodine to stop the contractions, but the fetal heart tones are dangerously high."

The doctor guided Scott away from the curtain. Someone scurried through the partition, and Scott's eyes fixed on Allison's feet through the opening. Her legs, feet, and hips were raised above her head. An IV dripped into her chalk-white arm. The bellows of some monstrous machine wheezed open and closed.

A respirator!

The curtains closed again, and Scott felt his legs give out

under him. That machine was the only thing that stood between her and death!

Scott huddled forlornly next to Allison's bed. Suction cups with two serpentine wires connected Allison to various monitors. The electrical cords snaked along her chest and stomach. The monitors—one wall mounted, the other portable—revealed the ragged lines of two divergent heart beats.

Oblivious to Scott's presence, Allison slept the sleep of the dead. Her chest rose and fell, artificially aided by the respirator, and her lips had a bluish tinge. Scott bent to kiss her good-bye. His hand brushed a clammy forehead, and he went out to collect the boys and take them to the house that would not be a home until Allison could return with them.

2

Eclipsed in darkness, the sleeping Jason in his arms, Scott sat in the room he had chosen for his study. Moonlight filtered through the windows to cast hulking shadows along the floor. Boxes lined all four walls and were stacked in front of the built-in shelves. They sprouted like mushrooms on the desktop and in the office chair.

His expression bleak, Scott stared down at his son, then stood up sighing. With the boneless fluidity of cats and the very young, his son draped himself loosely over his father's arm without so much as a groan.

Scott turned on the single desklight, rummaged a bit, before extracting a scrapbook from a box of files. He returned to sit, and Jason readjusted his loose-limbed position, molding himself to fit in his father's lap again.

Tall but willowy, Scott was not the kind of man to attract attention at a gathering. His coloring was light—hair somewhere between insipid blond and nondescript brown, his complexion pale. He wore thick, thick glasses that grossly magnified his deep green eyes. His eyesight was so bad that he couldn't even consider the idea of contacts, and he

16

doubted he'd be able to recognize his own children in a crowd without some kind of corrective lenses.

His hand groped along the box-clad desktop until he located the old wire-rims and placed them on his nose. Scott was a cerebral man. Other people would have considered him mellow, patient and easy-going, and that wouldn't have been an entirely inaccurate description. He'd learned patience of a sort. He was tolerant and could tolerate a whole lot before he blew, but when he did . . .

Jason's thumb found his mouth, and Scott removed it, scowling and wondering when his son had picked up that habit. He leafed through the pages, his gaze falling on newspaper clipping. A single photo dominated the page under a banner headline.

ANOTHER BODY FOUND IN DEATH HOUSE

Oswego, Illinois—The body of a high school student was found in the notorious death house at 413 Elm. The young man apparently hung himself. The police found no evidence of violence to suggest foul play. . . . The cause of death was listed as asphyxiation by strangulation.

The house takes its name from its most infamous inhabitants, the Graveses. They moved into the Elm Street residence after their former home had burned to the ground, killing their eldest daughter, Shelley Graves. The entire family died within six months of moving. Their story is a bizarre tale of family tragedy and revenge.

Elliot Graves, a musician and teacher at a local parochial school, killed his seven-year-old daughter, Sara, and buried the young girl's body in her late sister's grave. Jane Graves, the mother, subsequently bailed her husband out of jail and allegedly shot her husband and then herself.

The house was built at the turn of the century by Mr. Wilhelm Van Clausen, a land speculator of doubtful reputation and character. It is generally believed that he killed his own son. The child's body was unearthed from the basement many years after Van Clausen's death. The father, too, died violently—trampled by his own horses.

The youth's death is the second "death by asphyxiation" at this address within two years—an unusual record for a place that remains unoccupied. A toddler was found dead there last January, and the most recent death has the neighbors up in arms. They would like to see the house torn down.

Most are convinced the place is haunted and complain of strange sounds and lights appearing in the night. No few swear the house is cursed. They say that small animals and pets that wander over the boundary line inevitably die, and this reporter, when investigating their claims, did find the remains of a squirrel and a rabbit. To look at the house and the surrounding homes, mostly deserted, one would have to agree . . .

The house featured in the picture was their own, before they had completed the remodeling. Even in this dim half-light the photograph looked grim and foreboding.

Curiosity piqued, Scott had researched the house and the family for a possible book. His inquiries had revealed one horror after another. His curiosity became fascination, and his fascination obsession, which had been fired even more when he first arrived on the doorstep of the old Victorian home.

With blistered paint and a dingy grey exterior, gingerbread men did a tortuous shuffle along the eaves. Even from the opposite side of the cul-de-sac, the house loomed overhead, looking like a misshappen parody of a human face. Bay windows flanked the front door like protuding eyes around a nose. The slightly warped porch was a toothy mouth, twisted into a sneer. With one of the front shades pulled up, the house appeared to wink at him.

Scott fell immediately in love with the much-maligned house. It had staying power. It stood secure despite what had taken place within its walls, apart from and above its human occupants. Suddenly, the leer seemed more like a smile, and the wink a friendly gesture as if Scott and the house shared some secret. He had contacted Sam Holloway right away to make an offer.

Jason shifted slightly in Scott's lap.

"It'll be all right," he breathed into the child's ear. Scott patted Jason's back, realizing the movement was meant more to comfort himself than his small child.

Liar! A voice within his brain shrieked its derision. Scott shook his head. He could not argue. He had heard those words often enough as a child—*it'll be all right*—and the statement had almost always been a lie resulting from adult desperation. Parents said it only when they could think of nothing else to say.

The house pressed down around him. Despite his sons' presence, the place felt empty. Allison's absence was palpable. She wasn't around. He could feel it. There was an emptiness, a void where Allison should be. A blackness, blankness, where there should have been warmth. In seven years of marriage they had developed a bond, a rapport, so close that Scott could feel her lack even when she went no farther away than the store. Even on those days when they rarely spoke—when each was busy with their separate tasks, he with writing, she with the boys—he could tell she was *there,* as though she imparted something of herself to him merely by her existence.

There was no desperation in the bond—no sick-love feeling of adolescent dependence, more akin to nausea than emotion. Their relationship was a comfortable one, not confining. If Allison was there, all was right with the world. Hoping to capture that special feeling, Scott conjured a picture of Allison in his mind. Dark, nearly black hair. Ivory skin and a square Slavic jaw that lent a bit of sturdiness to her petite, fragile frame. Her best feature—her eyes. Blue, but not blue, almost too light for blue, the color of ice. His arm asleep, Scott rearranged Jason's limp body on his lap, sliding the child's head up to rest on his shoulder. Jason groaned softly and Scott suppressed the urge to repeat the fatal words: *it'll be all right.* Jason snuggled deeper into his arms, and Scott rocked the child. The boards beneath the rocker screeched in protest.

This wasn't at all how he had expected to spend their first night in their new home.

She *had* to be all right. If something happened to her now . . . Scott glared at the phone: it wouldn't be connected until Monday.

Nothing would happen to her, and he set his jaw as if he could will her return to health. She hadn't even seen the place since all the furniture had been delivered and set in place. As a matter of fact, she hadn't seen the place since they completed the remodeling. Not since the workmen died.

She wouldn't know what it looked like or how it had been transformed, the home of their dreams . . . his dreams. The kind of place they had always talked about. The dream come true. And now a lumbering machine was the only thing that kept her alive. She might never see it.

The formerly forbidding countenance had been lifted. He had turned the ugly house into a beautiful home he wanted to share with her. The foyer was papered in new medallion-rose wallpaper. The living room was an eggshell white, with one mirrored wall to give the illusion of more space. Upstairs, Disney characters paraded gaily across the walls of Jason's room. Adam's room was decorated with his chosen bright tartan plaid. The smallest bedroom had been converted to a gaily-colored nursery, and the once dingy master bedroom, also white, seemed palatial, with the black-lacquer furniture and the gilt Oriental screen. Scott could not imagine anyone approaching this house with the same fear and trepidation they may have felt before.

The rhythm of his rocking picked up a pace. The shadows in the study swelled, flickered, and shrank again. Scott sat up, peering into the inky recesses, and he thought he could sense movement. Scott glanced furtively into the darkened corners of the room.

Sleep stole over him in barely perceptible stages. His head drooped, and Jason slid down until he was curled in a fetal position, his head tucked in Scott's crooked arm. Scott drifted, lightly, in and out of sleep.

. . . his parents stared at him from a wreath of flames. Their scorched lips parted, peeling away from their teeth, moving continuously as they called to him with a soundless plea for help. Then he saw Aldo surrounded by the fiery sheath, motioning for his nephew to join him.

Scott awoke with a violent start and nearly jostled Jason from his lap. Shaken, he pulled his son into a more secure position before leaning back to try and recall the gruesome images.

In waking life, Scott remembered little of his childhood. Even his parent's faces were fuzzy—his mother no more than a pair of scarlet lips that kissed his cheek, and his father a loud, booming voice. What he did recall came in flashcard images: birthday parties, little league, boy scouts, a best friend—the name long since forgotten—so he supposed he had not been a loner. Everything changed after he lost his parents.

Like roman candles in the sky.

A blinding flash, a fireball, and all memory had been seared from his mind. He couldn't even remember how they died. Scott groaned, rubbing his eyes with the heels of his hands.

Their death had ripped his world apart. Scott was sent to live with his mother's sister, whom he had met only once, on her rundown farm in the Texas panhandle. Aunt Delores had tried to make him feel welcome, but Scott had never been accepted by his cousins. They formed a tight phalanx against the strange older boy, and considering their father, it wasn't surprising. The unwanted Scott was housed in the barn by his Uncle Aldo where any hired hand should sleep.

Aldo was a drunk who reasoned with his fists, beating anyone and anything who got in his way. Each member of the family lived in the private isolation of personal pain, shrinking from Uncle Aldo and from one another, and daily life was a precarious peace which had to be maintained at all costs. What remained of Scott's innocence was not so much lost as it was torn from him physically. His turbulent upbringing left him with a hair-trigger temper coupled with an oddly plodding patience.

By the time Scott had reached his teens, he had learned to answer Aldo's rage with rage and match violence with violence. The already tenuous family situation exploded, and the final blow-up had, unlike his parents' death, been seared indelibly in Scott's memory. A timeless photograph etched in caustic, cremation colors and finished in a fiery frame. Uncle Aldo had, in fact, died in a fire.

Scott buried his face in his hands, trying to blot out the memory.

That night all the years of abuse had suddenly coalesced. The throbbing fury rose like a *tsunami,* unstoppable. Out of control. When Aldo had attacked his aunt with a kitchen knife, Scott had fought back, breaking a chair over the man's back. Bellowing in rage, Aldo had chased Scott into the barn, brandishing a kitchen knife. Wildly, Scott searched for a weapon as Aldo lunged through the barn door. He sprang and the knife arced down while Scott dodged and backhanded his uncle, who reeled from the force of the blow. The blade fell harmlessly to the straw-covered floor.

Then Aldo came at Scott with his fists. Scott circled, spied a loose board and seized it, but not before Aldo extracted a pitchfork from a bale of straw. He rushed forward to impale his nephew against the wall. The younger man stepped swiftly aside. Aldo came on, driving Scott before him with short jabs. Scott batted at the pitchfork with the plank as he backed through the door to his small room.

He tried to close the door between them, but Aldo rammed it with his shoulder. The flimsy wood gave under his weight, and the door sagged in its frame. Aldo overbalanced, tripping over the kerosene heater Scott used to warm his drafty cubicle. Pink fluid sprayed across the room followed quickly by flames.

Using the two-by-four, Scott pushed his uncle away. Aldo whirled, the pitchfork's tines caught Scott's shirt. The cloth offered little resistance, and Aldo fell, sprawling helplessly at Scott's feet. And Scott lost all control. He brought the board down upon Aldo's head. Aldo groaned and attempted to roll away, but Scott didn't stop. He couldn't. Panting, he swung again, and again, and again.

There was an audible snap over the sound of the crackling flames. Throwing the two-by-four to one side, Scott straddled Aldo to pummel him with both fists, oblivious to the fire which nearly surrounded them. Aunt Delores had dragged him off Aldo, her cheek still bleeding from the knife wound Aldo had inflicted.

Backlit by the burning barn, she begged him to leave before the authorities arrived. Behind her, his uncle, his neck hopelessly awry, lay unconscious on the barn floor. Scott's rage ebbed from him as she pleaded. Like a sleepwalker he started to pull his uncle away from the fire. Delores stopped him.

A timber in the loft overhead popped and fell with a shower of sparks. Coughing and choking, they ran to the barnyard. The straw exploded in a brilliant flash. The southern sky glowed red in an impossible dawn. And Aldo—what was left of him—was no more.

Responsible for his uncle's death, Scott spent two years on the run—a fugitive, drifting from one farm to another, from one job to another—he had become a confirmed misanthrope. His eighteenth birthday freed him. By then the attitude of distance and aloofness was firmly ingrained. Then he had met Allison, and she had had patience. She had seen past the anger to the frightened child within, and she had made him whole. He didn't know if he could make it without her. He didn't want to try.

With the move, Scott had hoped he could give Allison and the boys all those things his own childhood had lacked, and now this. Jason's heartbeat thumped against Scott's chest, and Scott knew he'd have to make it somehow. He had the boys to think of.

But if something happened to Allison . . .

Death was an integral part of Scott's being as it had been an integral part of his life. It seemed to stalk him, and today, it had come too close. Scott knew that he never wanted to be alone again. He sighed, hugging Jason to his breast he stood to take him to bed.

And somewhere miles away, the respirator forced oxygen into her lungs one more time.

The ringing telephone woke Scott from a sound sleep. He groped for it without thinking. A high-pitched whistle greeted him as he put the receiver next to his ear. Letting it drop from nerveless fingers, Scott was suddenly wide awake.

The phone hadn't been connected yet. Even with the receiver two feet away, lying on the bed, he could still hear the piercing skree. He picked it up and jammed it into the cradle.

Waiting a few seconds, Scott lifted it and listened.

Nothing. The line was dead.

3

Clouds scudded across a sky of the deepest royal blue. Something flickered with sun-dappled orange. A butterfly lay still and silent on the blacktop. Its wings, caught by the breeze, fluttered. Adam advanced slowly, afraid that he might scare the tiny creature away and entranced that it had let him get this close. The bright splashes of brilliant carnelian quivered in the September sun, but it did not flee as Adam crouched down beside it.

It was dead.

Jason swooped in on Adam, interrupting his examination.

"Pretty." Chubby fingers clutched the fragile wings, and they crumbled.

"Jason!"

The toddler opened his hands to stare wordlessly at the pieces.

"You've ruined it."

Jason gulped. "I . . . I sorry."

Adam glared at his brother, and the child extended his hand to his elder brother, offering the tattered remains in a

25

conciliatory gesture. The wind picked up a few of the fragile fragments and sent them off in swirling iridescent orange.

"That's okay. You keep it." Adam turned away, disgusted. He didn't want it now that Jason had broken it.

"Oh boy," Jason said, thrilled at the gift, and shoved the colorful pieces into his pocket.

Hiding his smile behind his hand, Adam decided he couldn't stay mad at his little brother. There he was grinning over a broken butterfly like it was a princely present. Jason, Adam concluded magnanimously, couldn't help it. He was just little, that's all.

Shrugging out of his windbreaker, Adam dumped it on the porch steps, and Jason did the same. Adam put his hands in his pockets, and Jason put his hands in his pockets too. Like a shadow, the toddler mimicked Adam's every movement.

Adam stopped to look back at the house, disgruntled and scared. Jason glanced back at the house and then turned to face his brother.

Everything was wrong this morning, all wrong, Adam thought. Breakfast had been cereal with powdered milk—bluck—and his father hadn't served it in his favorite bowl, the one with Peter Rabbit on it, like his mom always did.

Adam crossed his fingers against evil. He knew all about hospitals, more than his father would have given him credit for. Hurt people went there. Sick people went there. *People died there.*

Several boys rode their bicycles toward the cul-de-sac in a thin, straggling line. Jason ambled up the driveway to greet them. The largest of the boys slammed on the brakes before entering the circle, sending his bike into a rubber-burning skid. He swung his leg over the crossbar and stood—one hand resting on his hip, the other supporting the bicycle—gazing disdainfully down on the toddler. The others halted, arranging themselves in a semicircle around the first boy who—judging by his size and their deference—was evidently the leader.

"So what do we have here?" The big boy indicated Jason with a jut of his chin. "A baby."

Jason stopped, dismayed by the ignominious salutation.

"Am not!" He stuck his thumb in his mouth.

"A baby, and he sucks his thumb, too!"

The children snickered as Adam moved alongside his younger brother.

"Am not!" Jason countered.

"Baby! Baby! Baby!" they chanted in unison.

Jason began to pule while Adam interposed himself between his kid brother and the jeering boys.

"Leave him alone!" Adam said.

"Who are you? The baby's brother?" The boy slammed the kickstand into position, leaving his hands free, and swaggered toward the brothers.

"That right, and I want you to leave him alone. He ain't hurting you," Adam said.

"Well, he's a crybaby."

The other boy took another few steps, and Adam pulled himself up a little taller.

"I bet when you were that age you cried, too," Adam said.

The big boy stiffened at the infeasible notion before advancing another two paces towards Adam. They stood nose to nose.

The other boy was two inches taller than Adam, but Adam held his ground.

"You're crazy," the leader said, more to his audience than to the two brothers. "Anybody that lives in *that* house has gotta be crazy."

"Nothing wrong with the house," Adam interjected.

"It's haunted."

And behind him the other boys nodded to each other sagely.

"Says who?"

"Everybody knows that. People have died there."

Jason wiggled, edging a little closer to his brother.

"So!" Adam challenged, his voice rising a note.

"It's haunted!" The leader hooked his thumbs into his belt loops and rocked back on his heels.

"S'not," Jason said. "Only stoopit people think so."

Adam cringed when Jason repeated what they had both heard their father say on more than one occasion.

"Stupid, huh?" The leader stepped around Adam to poke Jason with his index finger.

"The baby's callin' me stupid," the boy shouted over his shoulder.

"Stupid, huh?" Another jab, and Adam's face flushed red.

"Stupid!" He gave Jason a two-handed shove, and the toddler tumbled backwards, landing on his butt so hard his teeth clicked shut with an audible clack.

Adam launched at the larger boy, both fists lashing great swathes in the air.

Nobody could treat his little brother like that! Jason may be a dummy, Adam thought, and Jason may be a baby. He was certainly a pain in the neck. But nobody, *nobody*—besides Adam—had a right to push his little brother around.

Adam's fist connected with the other boy's ear, and the group's leader bellowed, springing a return attack. The next thing Adam knew he was knocked flat, and the other boys moved en masse toward Jason where he cowered on the ground.

"Jason, RUN!" Adam hollered just as the leader's fist was driven into his abdomen and sent the breath rushing from him with an ooph.

The house was as quiet as a tomb. Scott moved another stack of boxes to a more accessible location, pulled his shoulders back, and rubbed the cramped muscles in his neck. What should he unpack next?

"Daddy!" Jason's voice sliced the silence, and its fear slivered through Scott's perplexity.

He leapt through the door as his youngest son catapulted into the living room.

"Fight! Fight! Big kids. They're hurting him. They're hurting Adam!"

"Who? What?" He looked around, clasped Jason's upper arm, and hauled him to the window to look outside. A tangled mass of unrecognizable arms and legs rolled in the driveway. A circle of about four boys cheered the combatants on.

Scott plowed through the foyer and out the door.

"Hey, what's happening here?" His voice boomed across the yard, and the boys froze.

A couple retreated to the safety of the cul-de-sac and mounted their bikes, poised and ready to ride away.

The battling pair still squirmed on the pavement. Arms swung high and wide, rarely hitting anything. Scott raced down the steps, lifted the larger boy by the seat of his pants and the scruff of his neck and set him down, hard, on the blacktop.

"What the hell's going on here?" Scott seized the front of the boy's sweatshirt in his fist. The child threw back his head. His eyes fixed Scott with a defiant glare.

Brushing dirt from his jeans, Adam stood up with an amazing amount of dignity and pointed at the older boy.

"He was pickin' on Jason. He said the house was haunted, and he started pushing Jason around."

Scott's fingers closed tighter on the boy's sweatshirt, drawing the neck line taut across the boys throat. Scott felt a narrow band of hot iron riveted to his skull, and everything turned the color of blood.

A screen door squeaked open, and an old woman peered out; a cat wound its way between her legs.

Embarrassed, Scott loosened his grip on the child's shirt.

"What's your name, and where do you live?" Scott demanded.

The child's eyes rolled back wildly, resting for a second on a particular house. Scott followed his gaze and noted the open garage door and empty drive.

"There, huh?" Scott let go of the child, giving him a little push for emphasis. "Pick on someone your own age. If this ever happens again, I'm going to talk to your parents. If they don't do something about it, I will!"

Scott straightened, and Adam gazed up at him with awe and apprehension. With a nervous gulp Scott looked down at his hands and from them to the spiderweb of wrinkles on the front of the boy's sweatshirt where Scott had held it. The child scrambled for his bike.

Jason barreled up the walk, nearly knocking Adam over with a big bear hug.

"You okay?" Scott asked.

"Uh-huh." Adam looked nervously at his feet.

"You want some cookies before we go visit Mom?"

"Sure," Adam said, and Jason was off like a shot, running just as fast as his fat little legs could carry him up the walk to the front porch.

"Dad?" Adam stared into his father's eyes.

"Yes, Adam," Scott said.

"Is our house haunted?"

Straightening Adam's collar, Scott glanced at the children playing at the end of the street before he spoke. "Now, Adam, you remember your mom and I talked to you about that. Remember how we explained that something bad happened here a long, long time ago, and how some people are superstitious."

"Yes," Adam said uncertainly.

"That doesn't mean that there's anything wrong with the house. Does this place look haunted to you?" His hand swept in a large circle, taking in the entire lawn.

Adam wrinkled his nose, considering, as Jason struggled up the front steps. "Naw."

"Good," Scott said. "Let's go get some cookies."

A heavy drizzle had begun. Scott helped Jason into his jacket in preparation for a trip to the hospital. The rain dampened the road's surface, and it glistened in the hazy light. The photosensitive streetlamps came on in the early dusk, and drivers turned car headlights on. Their brilliant colors were caught and reflected by the oil-slicked streets, which blazed in rainbow colors.

He strapped the children into the car before traipsing across the street to thank the neighbor. Scott pondered the pools of amber and red light, glancing from the idling car to the house. He thought he sensed a flicker of movement, and he concentrated on the second floor window. He saw nothing, only a dark, empty window framed by crisp white curtains.

Scott knocked on the neighbor's door and waited. Jogging from foot to foot, he contemplated the neighborhood, and again he was struck by the empty cul-de-sac. Their Victorian towered over the circle, like a spider squatting in the center of its web. Only one other dwelling dared to encroach upon its domain, and this interloper was deserted. It leaned precariously, a large crack in its foundation creeping up the demi-brick exterior.

Even this still occupied tract home, which stood right next door and just outside the Elm Street circle, seemed decrepit, as though it and the neighboring houses dwindled while the McDowell house thrived. Definitely, their two-story house with its gabled roof and gingerbread eaves looked out of place among the other homes, and he didn't wonder that it had gotten a reputation.

A hand twitched at the blinds and a shrouded face peered out at him. Scott put on his best Pepsodent smile and waved. The blinds twitched shut. He heard a heavy clip-clopping shuffling noise, and the woman appeared at the door, supported by dual canes. The screen banged open. The old crone hobbled out the door. Dark eyes protruded from a wrinkled face—her lips twisted into a sneer. A cat trailed at her feet.

"I just came by to thank you for letting us use the phone the other day." His eyes fastened on her wizened features, her crepe-paper skin.

She sniffed at him.

"You see, our phone hasn't been connected yet, and well, you have been a real lifesaver. I mean it. I can't thank you enough," Scott said, but the stony face remained unmoved.

He grinned, showing a few too many teeth, shrugged, and turned to go.

The woman snorted, finally deigning to speak. "Some people don't know when to leave well enough alone."

"Pardon?"

"Look at what you've already stirred up." She indicated the house with the wave of a cane as the cat wound itself around Scott's ankles.

"I'm not sure I understand," he said.

The woman gave him an appraising look and nodded. "I'm not surprised."

Muttering under her breath, she withdrew into the house as Scott felt the hot flash of anger burning his face red. Schooling his features, he turned to face the boys.

"Witch," he murmured as he climbed into the car.

A small skeletal hand pushed the curtains aside. A face appeared at the second-floor window to watch the man talking to the old woman across the way. The man got into the car, slamming the door, and the curtains shivered shut again.

In the living room, the stereo popped on, with a blast of static and a blaze of lights. The serpentine equalizer band bounced, matching sound for sound the sporadic sizzle, hiss, and pop of the speakers. Beneath the crackle, other sounds began to emerge.

A soft sigh. A hushed conversation—like the background noise on a movie set from which no words could be distinguished. The volume swelled, and the equalizer lights jounced in response. *Pop, crackle, crackle, hiss!*

Bees swarming. A murmured voice. The mew of a cat that stretched and elongated until it became the cry of a child. A cat spitting, and the unmistakable sound of two cats fighting. The bark of a dog. Panting. A snarl. The spine-chilling howl of the coyote.

The snaking line of the equalizer dipped and rose.

The hoot of an owl. The whisper of wind, and the sound of a thousand birds—chirping, warbling, twittering until it became a deafening screech. The equalizer band reached maximum output and stayed there.

"Help me! Let me o-o-u-UT!" A disembodied voice shrieked in agony.

The hiss of a snake. The slither of scales of sand. Pop! A single voice that screamed which was joined by others, blending, meshing into a single note that rose, and rose, and rose. Sirens. Clanging bells.

Pop!

Something flashed briefly, and sparks flew from the equalizer as the red band went first flat and then dark. There was a mechanical click and a soft whir, and the arm on the turntable moved up and over to drop onto the album below. It scraped across the plastic surface. The words of the song came out tinnily . . . *I won't let no bad dreams come and bother you. Just put your trust in me . . .*

Barely audible now that most of the internal electronics were soldered into a single lump, the words of comfort emerged as little haunting scratches that played to an empty room.

4

Sorry I screwed up the housewarming," Allison whispered through dry and cracked lips.

Her jet black hair lay lank and wet against the hospital sheets, and Scott's eyes were drawn to a single strand of gray he had never noticed before. Her normally ivory skin looked ashen, and when she peered at him, her eyes seemed soft and unfocused. She reached out to clasp his hand.

"It'll wait." He shuffled distractedly before he leaned over to bury his face in the damp hair.

Scott straightened, aware of the doctor's eyes upon them. "The doc says you're going to be all right, sweetheart."

"Yes, I know."

"What happened?" he asked.

"I don't know. I just stepped onto the porch and something, uh, gave."

Scott winced. "He said the baby's going to be okay too."

"I hope he's right."

"If it's a choice between you and the baby, you know who I'd choose."

"Me, of course. Who else do you have to clean that big barn of yours?" She chuckled weakly.

"Pretty crappy way to get out of unpacking, if you ask me."

Allison laughed again and flinched as something in her abdomen caught.

"You okay?" He asked.

"Just a little sore." She yawned. "And sleepy."

Doctor Greene moved in between them, taking Scott by the arm. "Let her sleep. Her body's had one helluva shock, but there's no reason why she shouldn't recover. Tomorrow or the next day, with your permission, we'll do some more tests—ultrasound and an amniocentesis—to make sure the fetus hasn't been damaged."

Awake for the first time in what they said was days— forty-eight hours to be precise—Allison watched the jagged lines on the heart monitor and those of the fetus, with its double-time beat. Two for every one of hers, the tiny heart worked twice as hard to nourish the yet-unformed body.

Forty-eight hours. The nurse said Scott had visited her. She had spoken to him, but she couldn't remember his being there much less what he had said.

Intensive Care? Allison couldn't believe it. She was as healthy as a horse. Carrying her other two children had been a breeze. She had had no problems at all with this pregnancy until today.

Two days ago, she reminded herself.

She felt tired. In truth, she felt *exhausted,* and sore—like she'd been run over by a truck.

Plucking at a miscellaneous wire, Allison tried to think back to what she could recollect. If she thought hard, Allison could recall Scott's worried face hovering above her own and the blood-red flash of ambulance lights. She remembered trying to talk to him, and she remembered strange faces. The rest of the time was a blank, as if the last two days didn't exist.

The last thing she remembered clearly was standing there on the curb, arms linked with Scott. Feeling pride, not only the pride of ownership—pride all couples must feel when they buy their first home—but also pride in Scott. This was his accomplishment. He had made this happen. His success had made it possible. All his work at night and on weekends had paid off. He had found the home, and he had seen to its remodeling, overcoming all obstacles.

Never having known his parents or a real home, this was more than the realization of a goal. It was the fulfillment of a dream. She also felt his pride. It accentuated her own.

As though he were reading her mind, his eyes sparkled as he waved toward the house and said, "Well, what do you think of the Leave-It-to-Beaver dream home?"

"If you think you're going to get me to run around in a fifties skirt, high heels, and pearls as I clean house, you're crazy."

"That's all right. I prefer you barefoot and pregnant." He nuzzled her neck.

Allison's gaze turned back to the house, and she thought that the Cleavers would probably have had better taste, but she liked it. Her initial reluctance to the move had more to do with her fear of change than with the house itself.

Built during the Victorian era by or for someone of Scandinavian background, the house combined the worst features of each structural style. Despite the new paint, something about it still seemed skewed, not ominously so, just a bit off. As if it had been built by an architect who used too much laudanum.

It was eclectic enough, eccentric enough, to appeal to Allison's taste. The place had personality. She was, as Scott was always reminding her, an old-fashioned girl. Raised by second-generation immigrants of stolid eastern European stock, she revered all the old values, even the illogical.

Changeless.

The word echoed through her mind. The house itself was changeless.

The Allison upon the bed scowled as she mentally re-traced her steps up the path and grasped the wooden railing of the porch. It had felt alive and warm to the touch, and for an instant it had seemed to move under her palm. She pulled her hand hastily away.

Allison moved up the first step, and she had the fleeting impression of vibration, a pulling, a draining sensation. Heat radiated from the porch, and her stomach did an anxious flip-flop inside her abdomen. She faltered a bit and then placed her foot upon the next stair. She felt like she was being drawn through the wooden risers into the concrete foundation and then into damp earth below.

Her surroundings swam in and out of focus. Scott ran to her in slow motion. Her head spun, and he seemed to recede as she reached for him. She felt wetness spread between her legs, and Allison collapsed where she stood. A slight twinge. And she was being sucked through the floorboards into the space beyond. She paused, and the external world receded, and she retreated into the comforting arms of darkness.

Frantic voices eddied and flowed around her as something moved inside her body, questing, searching. The alien presence meant no harm. Allison felt only eager curiosity and a trill of joy when it found the fetus.

The line on the heart monitor did a quick jitterbug. Somewhere an alarm went off. A nurse hurried to Allison's bedside, in a flutter of white, like an avenging angel.

Nurse Kelly lifted Allison's slack wrist, one eye on the monitor and another on her watch. She counted and then placed the woman's arm across her belly. Allison smiled at her.

"I'm fine," she said.

"Of course," the nurse replied. She bent to check the wires and connections. When satisfied that things were as they should be, Kelly bustled off, returning to the desk to catch up on her notes before the next shift.

The nurse eyed the dark-haired woman opposite her. Kelly didn't like it. The intermittent arrhythmias, the brief periods of apnea. Like the woman forgot to breathe. Something about this case bothered her. It was more than the instinctive reaction one had when one saw a young person—a mother and a pregnant woman at that—with everything to live for, fighting for her life.

The whole thing just didn't make sense. They could find nothing physically wrong with her. She was, for all practical purposes, a healthy woman. Yet Mrs. McDowell's heart seemed to go on holiday every once in a while.

With a quick glimpse of the monitor the nurse bent back to her notes. Although she didn't agree with the doctor's decision, she was going to be glad when McDowell moved out to the medical-surgical unit tomorrow.

Three children sat cross-legged in the attic. Two girls sat side by side, clinging to each other, their expressions forlorn, fearful. Their pupils were dilated, reflecting their fear. With golden hair and catlike eyes, their images were flimsy, filmy, as vague and soft as smoke on the breeze. The filthy sunlight that filtered through windows was unable to combat the gloom, but it pierced their bodies easily enough.

They floated, hovering somewhere a few inches above the unfinished "floor," thick studs stuffed with pink, foil-wrapped insulation. One girl leaned into the other, and, at times, they overlapped—bits of one getting mixed with pieces of the other.

They shrank away from a third child, a small boy, probably two years younger than the youngest girl. He appeared more solid, if no less odd with his big floppy bow-tie and torn shorts. His eyes glowed in the darkness. The boy played with a dead rat—the body stiffened by rigor mortis. He waved it at them, and the girls' images thinned, thin fragments of figure and form floating away from them in tatters.

Downstairs a door opened and closed, and they paused from their silent mime before they faded into darkness.

5

*B*eneath the house something stirred. A prescience, an intelligence that was anything but human, yet intelligent all the same. Older than old. Ageless. Dormant except when disturbed. Reviving then to consume all who dared trespass on its domain. Sentient. Silent. Man had known it by many names.

Living only to destroy, it grew stronger. With an almost human gluttony this presence fed on hatred and despair, and there was more than enough hatred in the human psyche— and despair in the human condition—to nourish its evil always.

Pleased, it hummed below the building where a man and two children settled into their new home. The father and his sons were appetizers. Their roiling emotions already fed it. The ultimate feast, however, was lost. The woman and the child she carried.

With prehensile intellect it tested the occupants, finding their weakness, extending its control. Playing with them and winding each of them up like a child's top. A flex, a nudge, that's all it took. The creature stretched, purred, and waited

—calling upon those hapless souls who had already fallen to act as its hands, its eyes, its ears.

In the basement, two men—dressed in workmen's blue— jerked to life. They shuffled across the floor with twitching movements, like marionettes operated by an unskilled hand. The skin around their lips was blue. Their loose jaws clenched and unclenched in unison. Two pairs of hands clutched spasmodically. Eyes stared out from faces suffused in red— the white sclera expanded and bulging from their sockets.

One man—his long hair tied neatly back, his face bleeding and torn—shambled clumsily across the lineoleum. A rosary dangled from the pocket of the other, who took a stumbling step forward before he folded to his knees, his face caught in an expression of surprise and terror.

Another psychic flex, and the specter shot up to jig and dance, with frantic, almost birdlike movements. The younger workman flipped onto his back, his arms flailing, and his body arched; his back impossibly bowed. His heels drummed against the floor. The other peered mutely from dead eyes surrounded by waxen flesh. Further dark shapes appeared in the background. Childish giggles echoed about the chamber. A shrill whisper became intensified as it bounced from hard surface to hard surface.

Both workmen pitched forward, forgotten, and the other shapes dissolved as the creature's attention was drawn elsewhere . . .

At the age of two and a half, the world's a magical place expressed in sights, sounds, smells, and, more recently, words. Magic was everywhere when the sun shined and the sky was blue—and even when it wasn't. Where fat white clouds can become animal faces, or soaring dragons. Where there were buttercups, daisies, and dandelions. Where "butters" fly in dizzying colors, mothers hugged, and the toddler frowned at this last thought.

For Jason, everything was fresh and new. Each day a new experience, and anything could happen. Pigs can fly, at least

his father had said that once, and overgrown turtles were
good guys. On television, he'd seen elves and hobbits, and
witches who twitched their noses twice a day and made
things appear or disappear. So he knew the world was a
magical place. Thus, he wasn't very surprised the first time
he saw the little girl.

But life is also made up of routines—like his Mommy
getting him up in the morning was routine, a ritual. That
was the way things were, should be, and always would be.
But not now, Mommy wasn't here. She was in the hoss-
spittle, and everything was all wrong. Jason glowered at
Goofy on the bedroom wall.

In this world of routine, the people Jason knew came into
a room through the door, but this little girl didn't. She sorta
stepped outa the wall, pushing her way through the cartoon
characters. First an arm, then a leg, then a golden head.
With the world turned upside down, Jason was only mildly
disturbed by this new breach in the normal routine.

Yet in a world full of magic, and in a world gone suddenly
awry, anything was possible. So Jason played with her, and
he liked her. She knew all sorts of neat tricks. Jason was
surprised, though, when he realized Adam couldn't see
her . . .

Standing in the study, Scott surveyed his work. Books,
rather than empty shelves, stretched from floor to ceiling.
This was the last of them.

With a weary moan, Scott straightened, a stack of books
held to his chest. He kicked aside the empty box before he
slid the last books into place and ticked off another room
from his mental list. The lights dimmed, and Scott paused,
head cocked, listening to hear if the refrigerator or some
other large appliance had kicked on. His face clouded. It
shouldn't do that. He had had the place entirely rewired, an
absolute necessity. The old Victorian home had not been
built with modern conveniences in mind. Now most of the
major appliances had separate lines to avoid even minor

disruption in current to the rest of the house. Another necessity. He couldn't afford to lose current to his computer while he was working.

Scott wondered if he should dig up the old surge protector from the box in the basement. When he'd set up the computer he hadn't included it, thinking it was no longer needed.

Sure, he thought, if he could only remember which box it was in. Grabbing the empties, Scott moved through the house toward the kitchen.

The house was beginning to have the look and feel of home if one disregarded the growing mountain of cartons on the back porch.

Surprisingly, Adam and Jason had done their share—each unpacking the toys and clothes in their respective rooms—although Scott had had a hard time convincing Jason that there was any better place to keep his toys than the middle of the floor. After they finished, Scott inspected their work. More often than not he had to rearrange a portion of it—smooth the clothes they had crammed into drawers or hang up things they had piled in the closet—but all in all, he was proud of them. At the ages of two and a half and five, they had done well.

Sometimes, they would work together as a group. Scott made the chore into a game whenever he could. In the kitchen they had formed a long line from box to cupboards, his sons handing him things upon request. The results had been hilarious and an education for all of them. Jason knew few of the utensils' names, passing a spoon when Scott had asked for a spatula. Even Scott had been baffled by the purpose of many of the items.

Organization eventually dissolved and everything became a doohickey, a thingamabob, or a whachamacallit. Adam discovered an ingenious use for the baster, and Scott responded with the Waterpic, which he had unearthed from one of the bathroom boxes. The resulting water fight had left them breathless and soaked. They rewarded themselves with an entire box of Ding Dongs for lunch as they mopped up the mess.

There had been only one casualty, a glass. The procedure took most of a day between hospital visits, but had done much to relieve the emotionally charged and gloom-laden atmosphere that had hung over the house since their arrival.

The interrupted days, the trips to the hospital, were taking their toll. Each night, Scott went to bed bled dry, but with nerves still stretched taut and tingling, and he'd lie awake staring at the ceiling until he was driven downstairs to prowl the house or play with the computer.

Now that he had acquired her job, Scott marvelled that Allison had been able to keep up with everything. His sons, he discovered, were in fact filthy creatures who could attract any stray dirt in any room—which would immediately attach itself to their tiny persons—and Scott wondered if Allison changed their clothes five times a day in order to keep them looking tidy.

To get them out of his hair Scott had sent them to put the last of their toys and games away in the basement. He figured the boys could handle the job without his supervision. He cupped his hand around his ear and listened. They were awfully quiet.

With a shrug, he returned to foraging through the cupboards and extracted a can of pork and beans, another of Viennese sausage, and still another of tomato soup. Scott was getting damned tired of cooking. Not that what he did could really be called cooking. His meals made the hospital food—with its pasty consistency and lackluster flavor—look good.

He emptied the contents of the cans into the saucepan and gave the mixture a quick stir.

"Boys, come up and wash your hands. It'll be lunchtime soon!" he yelled over his shoulder as he pulled plates from the cupboards and slapped them down on the table.

What was taking them so long?

Scott stirred the beans.

They boiled viscously, a bubble burst through the lumpy surface with a liquid burp. He turned the burner down and headed for the basement, pausing at the top of the stairs to survey their work. The games were stacked, after a fashion. It was easy to tell who had done what. Jason's pile was precarious, Adam's meticulously neat. Mostly, though, their toys were strewn across the floor. Each child absorbed in a separate game.

The many balls—the baseball, the Nerf football, the basketball, volleyball, miscellaneous tennis balls (with the all bounce bounced out of them), Ping-Pong balls and paddles—were piled in a jumbled heap, evidently a joint effort and the type of engineering feat only a child could accomplish. Only the ping-pong paddle held the whole tenuous structure in place, acting like a keystone.

"Lunch, kids."

Jumping slightly, Jason jostled a paddle with his elbow, and the whole sloppy composition came cascading down. Balls bounced across the room, scattering.

A sharp stab of pain hit Scott right between the eyes. The irritation communicated itself to his body, nerve endings jangled and tingled. His jaw snapped shut, his fists clenched, and Scott had to count to ten to calm himself.

Easy does it, he thought, *just a bunch of balls. No big deal.*

The pain receded and Scott's vision cleared. With a carefully controlled voice, he said, "Pick those up, boys, and then wash your hands. Lunch should be ready in a minute."

Shaking his head, Scott moved over to the utility room. Too many things had been bothering him lately. Little things. Things that normally would have passed unnoticed. Big things too—a lot of big things that made the small annoyances seem somehow worse.

The thin veneer of his control was cracking, and his reactions didn't seem his own. It was as if they had an external source, coming from outside of himself. His moves choreographed and manipulated by a paranoid puppeteer going through DTs.

Scott's hands shook.

He examined them as though they were alien, detached from his body. His eyes took in the fine lines, the blue veins, blood pulsing just beneath the flesh.

Fury was part of him, as much a part of him as the color of his hair or the color of his eyes. It found outlet in his books, and his books sold. Fascinated by the dark side of human nature, his obsession powered his work.

The old rage had remained repressed, lurking just beneath the surface, and rarely put in an appearance until now. Until recently, there had been no cause. Scott didn't welcome its reappearance.

Without Allison, he became stuck in the black morass of his mind. Adam and Jason had borne the brunt of it. He snapped at them, growled and commanded when he should have tried to comfort them. After all, they were going through a hard time, too.

And Scott promised himself that he would make it up to them. "So what have you two been up to?"

"Playin'," Adam said.

"L'il girl," Jason added.

Adam elbowed Jason, shushing him.

Scott mumbled a preoccupied uh-huh and fiddled with the washer's buttons and knobs. "What little girl?"

"Uh, dunno." Jason hung his head, inching away from Adam.

Scott winced, heaving himself from the floor. His head reared, and he sniffed the air. Smoke! Their lunch was burning. Scott swore and raced across the basement toward the stairs.

Billowing clouds greeted him as soon as he stepped through the door. The pan on the stove glowed with the intensity of the heat. As Scott made a frenzied search for a hot pad the pan caught fire.

Spying the fire extinguisher in the corner, he seized it and glanced over his shoulder at the boys.

"Stay back!" he ordered.

Shielding his eyes, he let 'er rip. A stream of fluffy white foam landed on their beans flambé, and the flames died.

Jason squealed and jumped up and down. Adam advanced toward the stove, rose up on tiptoes, and looked inside the blackened pan.

"Wow! Can we do that again?" Adam said while Jason stared in fixed fascination at the last curl of greasy brown smoke.

Scott removed the pan from the burner and checked the heat setting before turning it off. He had set it on medium heat. Not high enough to start a fire.

"No, we cannot do that again." Scott snarled. "That was lunch. Look, we've done enough work for today. How about pizza?"

"Pizza, all right!" The boys clapped each other on the back in congratulations.

6

Scott stood at the head of the stairs and saw the house as it once had been. Large sections of the faded wallpaper had been stripped from the wall. Bubbled and wrinkled, what remained intact revealed telltale splotches of blood.

Glowing outlines of chalked figures marked where Jane Graves's body had once lain. A saxophone played a mournful tune in the background. The music had awakened him.

Scott didn't know what time of day, or night, it was. The walls seemed to absorb the light. A low, bluesy note floated past him, and his soul wept, as though the musician had discovered Scott's own note of sorrow and was playing it on his horn.

Mindlessly he followed the sound down the stairs and into the study. The walls were lined with books as they should be, but the shelves were wrong. Made of concrete blocks and boards, they canted at an angle—as though they had been improperly stacked, with none of the boards quite straight. The books had been placed on the shelves haphazardly. One, a Bible, fell to the floor as Scott stepped into the room.

His computer and the rocker were gone. The musician sat

47

in an overstuffed easy chair, his figure just a light discoloration in the darkness. The saxophone gleamed silver in the moonlight. Scott recognized the song, a lullaby, "Dolphin's Song." He hummed along.

A shimmer of gold, and Scott's eyes were drawn to a moving shadow. A girl, about ten years old, stood next to the solitary musician. She placed her hand on the man's forearm. Her head swung eternally toward Scott. It seemed to keep turning and turning, always in motion, but with the face remaining just beyond his field of vision.

The song ceased, and with it the motion halted, too. She faced Scott, smiling. Her expression anything but innocent. Savage, even cruel, hinting at a yet-unclaimed victory. Her eyes glinted, cold, hard . . . *red!* Her hand slipped from the man's forearm to his side and from there to his thigh. She clutched the inside of his thigh near his crotch and squeezed. The girl leaned over, her tongue flicking out to caress the spot where there should have been an ear as the picture began to fade.

The waterbed sloshed as Scott jerked into a sitting position. He shivered in the cool night air. His eyes felt like two hot coals in scorched sockets, and his eyelids rasped like gravel when they closed. Wiping his forehead with the back of his hand, he got up shakily, sure he wouldn't be able to fall asleep again.

When he had gone to bed that night Scott had been exhausted. Every muscle in his body ached from all the lifting and sorting. He would have sworn nothing short of an earthquake would have roused him before morning. He had been wrong.

Slipping into a pair of jeans, Scott moved toward the door. His dream had been so vivid that he was afraid to look out into the hall, afraid he might discover that his dream had come true, and the house would be the same as it had been before the investment and remodeling.

Cautiously, he peeked out the door and let out a long, low

breath. The wallpaper was fresh and new. No blood dotted the wall, no chalk-drawings interrupted the oak floor to mark the place where a former resident had died.

The empty house pressed down around him, weighing his spirit, his soul.

Abandoned. The word coiled around his spine like some poisonous serpent, touching a primal cord.

"No," he groaned.

Abandoned and alone. Allison *had* almost died, and the reality of his own mortality pressed down on him.

How many people had died right here in this house? For Scott, the murders, the deaths had added to the house's appeal rather than detracted from it. The murders didn't frighten him, but death did. His death or Allison's, when all that humanity held dear was to be wiped out in a single second. What was the point?

Abandoned. That word again; it touched the secret chord of his terror and set it vibrating.

Allison had abandoned him, deserted him, like everybody else in his life. His mother, his father . . .

Logic and reason told him no, but unreasoning emotions said otherwise, and they had the louder voice. Allison gone. Not in his time of need, no. She had disappeared from him during his moment of triumph, and his accomplishment was diminished by her absence.

And Scott couldn't quite repress the feeling of betrayal. Childish, foolish, he berated himself, but the feeling remained, and the anger was easier to cope with than fear.

The familiar band of hot iron tighten around his skull—a sure sign that his temper was teetering on the brink. He pushed away from the door and rubbed his clammy palms against his pantlegs. It had been one helluva week, and he was tired—sullen, irritable, and tired.

Scott felt a slight pressure against the base of his skull, like a cold finger prodding his neck, and his anger grew. The band tightened more as he descended the stairs to the foyer and moved through the living room to the kitchen.

The bright overhead light reflected harshly off the polished oak cupboards. The fluorescent tube buzzed, and the clock's minute hand clicked to the next number.

This should have been a time to celebrate, to relax and be lauded for the lovely home he had managed to create from the former's unlovely shell. A night to nestle in front of the fire with the aroma of a good meal still wafting through the air. Instead, cardboard cartons from the local Chinese carryout cluttered the kitchen table, the food's remains congealing on paper plates. Scott picked them up and tossed them on the trash.

It wasn't fair! He had worked hard for this. He *shouldn't* be pacing restlessly through the house—his nerves stretched taut like a clock spring wound too tight—unable to sleep.

His eyes fell on the small bar sink and liquor cabinet. He moved across the room and opened the cupboard door to stare inside, mesmerized by the gaily colored bottles.

Milky white, amber, brown, green. Chivas Regal, Tanqueray, Drambuie, crème de menthe, crème de cacao, Bacardi, and a multitude of mixes. He had not stinted on the bar.

He licked his lips. The image of Uncle Aldo drinking himself legless night after night popped into mind, and Scott rubbed his lips with a gesture characteristic of his uncle once the thirst was upon him.

Perhaps, the man hadn't been wrong after all, Scott thought. Those four whining kids and a cringing wife would have been enough to drive any man up the wall.

Allison should be here now! The finger on the back of his neck became a hand that squeezed. Scott reached for a bottle while his mind buzzed a warning. His temper, never good at the best of times, was not improved by drinking.

The well-stocked liquor cabinet was, for him, another symbol, like the house. A symbol of success. When they had bought the place Scott had imagined himself and Allison entertaining friends in their new home.

Friends. A luxury he had never had time for in the past.

Too much of his life had been spent working—teaching school during the days and writing at night and on weekends. Allison had never complained about how many hours he devoted to his work. She seemed to understand what drove him. She took care of the kids without complaint, sharing his time when he had it to share and leaving him alone when he did not.

She had been more than understanding. When Scott had gotten his first short story sale and a sizable check from a prominent men's magazine, it had been Allison who insisted they spend the money on a computer rather than a winter coat for her—despite the fact that hers was threadbare.

This house was as much her accomplishment as his. She had earned it. Dammit, she should be here!

After he poured himself a stiff drink Scott went to the living room, where he approached the stereo with caution, the equalizer so recently replaced. Scott checked the wiring, shrugged, and rummaged through the CDs. Phil Collins . . . Whitney Houston . . . McCartney. He picked one and went to hunker down on the sofa as the first climbing notes drifted through the living room. A few minutes later his glass was empty, and Scott hefted himself wearily from the couch and went to pour himself another.

What the hell! This was the only housewarming party he was likely to have, Scott thought sourly. Might as well make the most of it.

With the fresh drink in his hand Scott moved restlessly through the house, stopping occasionally to stroke a wall, a fixture, or the satiny, smooth wood with a loving caress. Then he returned to the kitchen to refresh his drink, grabbed the bottle, and walked to the basement stairs.

Here Scott had placed his stamp most indelibly on the house, tearing out the old heater, tearing out walls. The new fluorescent lighting in the modern rumpus room chased all the old shadows away.

Once dark and dank—with its antiquated furnace, which

resembled the mutant offspring of an illicit union between a dumpster and an octopus—the cellar was now a bright, open room. Nothing remained of its former fusty, sepulchral appearance.

Scott marched down the stairs to stand next to the pool table, set the bottle down on an old TV tray, and rotated on the ball of his foot to appraise his handiwork. A pool table stood in the center of the room. Their old worn couch was pushed against the south wall. The bricks, blocks, and boards from their old apartment had been set up as shelves to house the boys' many toys and games. Scott planned to create a permanent sewing nook for Allison—something she had always said she wanted.

The Joker's leering face peered at him from the shelves. Suddenly the faces of the dead electrician and his helper were superimposed over that of the doll, their expressions that of frozen horror. Their faces appeared, only to be quickly replaced by others. A girl with golden hair which shriveled and burned right before his eyes. Then she was gone. Another surfaced, who could have been her twin, and like the girl before her, she was transformed, her head imploding as he watched.

This was replaced by first one image and then another— each visage twisted in agony—each coming more rapidly until he had scarcely less than a fraction of a second to take in an expression or features. They merged into a single shrieking face as he was held spellbound. He forced himself to look away, shuddering, and the colored pool balls on the felt tabletop blinked into focus. Sesame Street characters peeked out from behind Adam's turtle chair. Their button eyes somehow sinister. Adam's old rocking horse—now Jason's—stood poised in the corner, waiting for a small boy to bring it to life.

A sound, little more than a whisper, came from behind the partition that separated the utility area from the game room. Upstairs, the stereo switched off.

The room had attained a nice fuzzy glow. Scott took a sip

of his drink, and the sharp pain sliced through his skull again like a knife. The room began to fade and dim, starting at the periphery of his vision. The blackness grew, creeping inexorably through his consciousness.

The alcohol was muddying his thinking. Aldo appeared with his bloodshot eyes and his ragged breath, swaying eternally in a drunken swagger, and Scott quickly slammed the door shut on that area of his brain where Aldo lived before he poured an unhealthy portion of gin into his glass.

After taking a hefty swallow Scott racked the pool balls, grabbed the cue ball and bowled it down the center of the table to break the neat triangle.

Clack! Balls scattered, hitting the soft felt sides of the table and bouncing back.

It wasn't fair, Scott thought, catching one of the balls on the rebound. He sent it crashing into the clustered balls at the opposite end of the table.

Clack.

"Allison should be here now!"

Clack! And Scott sent another ball spinning across the table.

"Abandoned."

Clack!

Just as his mother had abandoned him.

Clack!

And his father. Everyone. . . .

Scott grabbed two balls and thrust them blindly across the table. She should be here now!

Frantically, Scott twirled the eight ball into the corner pocket. He grasped another rolling ball and spun it across the pool table. It bounced over the side and fell with a crack to the floor. Scott winced.

Meanwhile, the balls set in motion continued their dizzying, clicking path, picking up speed.

Click, clatter, clack. The balls darted helter skelter across the green felt.

Scott took a deep breath, willing himself to be calm. His

head spun. He had had too much to drink. He wasn't used to it. The colorful whirling orbs on the pool table gained momentum beside him, taking on a life of their own. Faster and faster they went as Scott wandered away from the table no longer interested. His glass was empty, and his head light. Scott lurched for the stairs, humming a tune.

The balls continued their darting dance.

Halfway up the stairs he heard a loud smack as a ball rebounded off the floor. Scott stopped, turned, and stared at the ball as it skidded toward the utility area. The remaining balls bounced into each other and the sides of the pool table.

Fuddled, he shrugged, unconcerned by the unnatural motion, and shambled up the remaining steps to the kitchen.

Bang, crash!

Something fell to the floor in the basement behind him as he made a stumbling progress through the first floor to the foyer.

The walls reeled about him, and he, in turn, reeled from wall to wall, fending himself from them, barely able to make it to the second floor. Scott paused outside Adam's door. He wove slowly back and forth. His stomach rolled rebelliously, and Scott launched himself toward the bathroom, hand clapped over his mouth.

His head hanging over the toilet, his stomach emptied itself of its unfamiliar liquid contents. The hard bark of his vomiting completely drowned out the sound of footsteps overhead.

Jason cowered in the darkness. He was not alone. With a whimper, he dragged his body across the floor toward the thin line of light coming from beyond the closed door. His fingers hurt and, pausing, Jason stuck them in his mouth to taste the coppery tang of blood. He began to cry.

Something brushed against his face, with a soft caress, and he batted it away, cringing. Clothes. He was in the closet.

Pulling his legs under him, Jason leaned against the wooden doorframe. "Mommy?"

A husky female voice came from the other side. "Be quiet, honey, you'll only make it worse."

"Mommeeee!" Jason wailed.

His fingers hurt, and his tummy hurt. His stomach grumbled loudly. Jason was *so* hungry. He had never been this hungry before in his life, and it seemed he hadn't eaten for days. He stuck his fingers in his mouth again.

"Hush, William," the voice said.

Jason rocked back to rest on his heels. *William?*

"Mommy?" he asked again, questioningly.

A dark shadow separated from the blackness behind him with a soft rustle. Jason flinched and tore his gaze away from the safe line of light to stare into the yawning umbra behind him. Something had moved.

Panicking, Jason began digging at the door. "Lemme out!"

Another whisper of movement, Jason shot an anxious glance over his shoulder and two red eyes stared back at him. He clawed at the door, using fingers already worn raw with the effort.

"Mommeeeeee!"

The eyes advanced toward him, and Jason heard a scraping as something started to slither across the floor. And that's when Jason woke up screaming.

A high-pitched scream penetrated the drunken fog of his dream. Scott lifted his head from the cool tiles as a board squeaked overhead. He heard a gentle sobbing.

Jason. Scott recognized the soft whimper. He placed his hands under his shoulders to push himself from the floor. The world spun around him, and his head followed a swirling path around the bathroom. The sobbing stopped, and Scott lowered his throbbing head slowly back to the cool floor. He was *so* tired; he'd check the boys in just a little bit, and he descended into a spinning slumber.

7

Adam hung onto Jason as the front door swept slowly closed, shutting them out of the house. They wore light jackets against the morning chill—the grass still damp with dew.

Great play! Adam thought sarcastically as he swung to scan the strange surroundings. Play? Play what?

A curtain swished in a window across the way, a hand flicking it aside to observe the two puzzled children on the porch. The woman's seamed face was a dusky smudge in a black background surrounded by wisps of dirty white hair. She leaned forward to stare at the boys, her lips pursed in a perpetual frown.

Something rattled in the background, like a leaf skittering across a concrete walk. Adam dropped Jason's hand and kicked at the air. He shouldn't hafta baby-sit for his little brother, and he didn't want to *play* with his little brother. Adam was too old for Jason. After all, Adam had just started kindergarten.

The rattling increased, becoming a steady buzz. Adam flopped down on the porch steps, limp hands dangling between his legs.

This was stupid. Everything was wrong, and this was stupid—like finding his father this morning sprawled on the bathroom floor.

Adam pushed the memory away, not ready to confront it.

A cat wound a leisurely path across the street. Jason squealed, made a beeline for the unsuspecting creature, and picked it up by the throat. Adam gave a short cry of exasperation as he scrambled down the steps to rescue the cat from his brother's clutches.

"No, Jason, not like that. Put the kitty down," Adam instructed. "You pet a kitty cat like this."

Starting at its head, Adam traced a line to its tail. The cat arched into his hand, purring. Adam petted it again.

. . . finding his father this morning . . .

A buzz like a thousand insects swarming rattled in his brain, and he thought of static on the radio, hissing snow on TV, or spiders pattering across glass.

Adam's hand found the furry back, putting a little bit more pressure into the stroke. The hiss increased, and he found himself remembering the morning whether he wanted to or not.

Waking up, his bladder crying urgently to be emptied, he had stumbled into the bathroom and found his father half wrapped around the toilet. Sleep-fogged, Adam had stared at the improbable apparition.

Dead? The word surfaced, bringing with it niggling fear.

Adam fuzzily recalled often repeated lectures about calling nine-one-one in case of an emergency, but his bladder was screaming to be relieved. His anxiety only made this need worse. He had to go! Adam skirted his father. He smelled funny—sour, stale.

Almost around his father's prone figure, the toilet only two steps away, Adam cast a sidelong glance at Scott before he moved forward and unsnapped his trousers.

A hand clutched his ankle, and Adam let go. He felt the wet, warm urine running down his leg and scalding-hot shame burning his cheeks.

Scott sat up.

"Daddy?" he croaked.

Scott peered owlishly at him. He took in the soaked drawers and blinked, his face contorting with mirth. "Scared the pee outa ya, huh?"

The child blushed, the flush descending to Adam's neck and chest. His skin turned blood red. Scott took another look at him and roared with laughter.

Even now, Adam felt the blush rising to his face. The buzz became a crackle, and the crackle a roar. It sizzled throughout his head, filling his mind. Static.

Adam's hand closed convulsively around the cat's tail, and he pulled. The cat let out a loud yowl which Jason mimicked, slapping at Adam's hand to make him let go. Adam glared at Jason, and his fingers closed tighter on the cat's tail to drag it across the pavement toward the house. The cat clawed at the concrete.

Adam heard a heavy knock at a window. He looked up. The old woman glared at them. Her straggly wisps of hair were snow white, but it was the white of snow much grimed by exhaust and fumes. She was shrivelled and hunched. The knotted fingers turned in on themselves, curling off to the side like twisted claws. She extended one nobbly, crooked finger and shook it at him, and he let go of the cat with a final yank.

Free, the creature streaked across the street to hide among the border shrubs of the neighboring house. The woman hobbled from the back door.

"Wicked little boy. I saw you. I saw you." And she waved a cane at him as if, with a flick of an arthritic wrist, she could make him disappear. Then she picked up the cat, stood contemplating them a moment, turned, and walked back into the house.

Scott stuck his tongue out at his ashen reflection in the mirror—his red-rimmed eyes looked like twin road maps of downtown Chicago—the whites lined with jagged red capillaries. Scott rubbed his hand over his eyes and splashed water in his face. He ran a comb through his hair and a brush over his teeth.

It didn't help. His mouth tasted like formaldehyde.

Hung over. What the hell was wrong with him? He didn't like to drink. How had the Pandora's box where a drunken Aldo lived—weaving permanently, fists balled and voice perpetually raised in inebriate ire—popped open? Scott lifted a shoulder in a shrug of dismissal. He missed Allison; that was it. He wanted her here. Nothing was wrong with him that having his wife home wouldn't cure. There was nothing wrong with that.

Slipping out of his wrinkled shirt and replacing it with a fresh one, Scott leaned within a few inches of the mirror and rubbed his chin. He should shave, and he glanced at his watch. No time.

Scott bounded down the stairs, his head pulsating with each step. Outside the boys crouched on the sidewalk. Scott looked from one son to the other, ducking from view when Adam looked askance at the window. He should apologize to Adam, but something within him rebelled at the thought.

"Boys!" Scott shouted out the front door. Adam and Jason walked slowly up the stairs to stand on the porch and stare at him expectantly.

"Time to come inside. You're going to have to put your toys away. We want to keep the house all pretty for Momma."

Noting the false cheer, Adam shot his father a wary look.

"Do we hafta?" He eased a few steps away from his father.

"Yes, but don't worry. Daddy's going to have to put away his toys too. We'll make a game of it. It'll be fun."

Both boys stared at their father as though he had lost a considerable number of marbles, turned to each other, and grimaced. They would humor him, but not for long.

The boys started to bicker before they had shed their coats. Each word echoed through Scott's already aching head.

"STOP!" Scott roared. Both boys flinched.

"That's better," Scott said. "I don't care what you do, just do it quietly, okay, fellows?"

The last four boxes lay open at his feet. Scott stared in dismay, sifting through the contents of one. Shoes apparently without mates. Jars of nails, thumb tacks, screws. A hammer with a wobbly head. String, twine, ribbons, rubber bands, and copper wire. Another contained mysterious papers, phone numbers without names, loose coupons, scraps of newspapers, scribbled recipes. And he wondered why Allison kept these things.

The contents of the third, at least, made some sense. Scrapbooks, envelopes filled with pictures, and letters tied up in ribbons, some written in his own hand, and the children's first baby shoes. The final box contained miscellaneous nicknacks and bric-a-brac. Book ends which were no longer needed now that they had real shelves.

With a grunt he plopped down to sort through the mess. Scott had no idea where to put these things. They must have had a home in their old Blue Island apartment, and he was sure that there was room somewhere in this house, but he wasn't sure where.

Puzzling over a glass figurine, Scott tried to remember in which room it had once resided. The living room? Kitchen? It was no use. He wrapped it again in the old newspaper and returned to the box. He'd had enough. This much he could save for Allison.

Scott extracted a scrapbook and leafed through the pages, pausing to look at a particular photo of some well-remembered and much-loved event. Adam grinned a toothless, infantile—and most likely gaseous—smile with the soft, fuzzy look all babies had before they were able to focus, adjacent to a photo of his equally toothless, equally bilious younger brother.

Setting the book aside Scott walked through the house to the back door where he watched the boys play unnoticed.

Trailed by his brother Adam paraded proudly around the backyard with his Ninja turtle lunch bucket, and Scott smiled. So unusual to see Adam, normally so serious, actually behaving like a child. Scott was glad that his young scholar enjoyed school. Too soon it would become drudgery, something boring inflicted by heartless adults to spoil the fun of youth.

Although Scott doubted if Adam would ever feel that way. Of the two, Adam had always been serious, with a well-developed sense of responsibility, even as a toddler. The little professor. A learned scowl marked his face as often as a childlike grin. Any reprimand or scolding was taken to heart, and few mistakes were repeated. Adam had taken over the burden of a younger brother, easily, almost zealously. Forever ready to guard, protect, and teach Jason, with his vaunted three-, four- and five-year-old wisdom, as soon as the toddler exhibited a willingness to learn.

With his cherry-apple cheeks Jason was the exact opposite, more like one imagined a child should be. Chirpy, beaming, not always happy, but almost, and as transparent as glass. When scared or hurt, he cried, even sulked; but the tears soon dried, and the smile would come, lighting his face like the sun bursting out from behind a cloud. Scoldings given to Jason weren't ignored exactly, simply forgotten two minutes later as he immediately repeated the same behavior for which they had been given.

Sometimes Scott thought Adam had gotten the short end of the stick. He wondered if Adam reflected his and Allison's insecurities in childrearing or if this seriousness was inborn, inbred, for Adam resembled Scott. While Jason—with his enthusiasm and open-hearted trust of everybody and everything—was like his mother. Scott didn't believe in favoritism. Still he was more drawn to the exuberant Jason than the dour Adam. However, he was proud of Adam and secretly glad that if such differences must exist between brothers that it had been the compliant Adam who came first.

With a quick look at his watch Scott returned to the living room to hide the boxes—along with their confusing contents, in a closet—before collecting the boys to take them to the hospital for a visit.

Frank Gibbons paced between his desk and the picture window of the real estate office. A wiry, little ferret of a man, his movements were sharp and quick. Normally, Gibbons displayed the typical little-man's attitude—belligerent and bellicose—but that didn't show through today. He was nervous.

It wasn't that he couldn't believe that a paper had gotten lost, things like that happened when closing a deal, but why did it have to happen on that particular house? Not that Frank believed in any of that supernatural bullshit, at least not until recently. The signatures were a formality—the house was sold and the McDowells had moved in—but they were a formality he couldn't afford to ignore. There was no way around it. Frank was going to have to go to get those signatures.

"Damn," he muttered to himself and slammed out the office to the parking lot.

The sky was cloudy and grey, but the clouds did little to relieve the oppressive heat of early autumn. The air was muggy, and the atmosphere charged with the sense of impending storm. A Mercedes turned the corner on to Elm Street, and the children parted to let it pass.

Tall, stark, and grim, the large Victorian touched an atavistic fear in Gibb. Frank shivered despite the eighty-plus temperature. The soft patina of sweat across his forehead belied his sudden chill. Last time he was here, he'd sworn he'd never set foot in that place again, and here he was.

His body began to shake. Gibb was thrust back in time to the spring day when Frank had first shown the home to the McDowells.

* * *

CRADLESONG

The young couple had just left, and summer sun splashed over the wooden cupboards in the outdated kitchen when something crashed in the basement. There had been the soft patter of footsteps on the stairs.

Gibb would have sworn he heard the tumblers click and fall as the door unlatched to open on rusty, creaking hinges. Arms crossed, he had leaned against the wall to wait for some neighborhood brat to emerge. No shamefaced child had appeared.

Then Gibbons poked his head inside the door. "All right in there, come on up before I lock you inside and you have to spend the night here without supper," he growled.

The only response was the twitter of childlike laughter.

"Crap!" he muttered to himself and then shouted down the stairs. "I'm coming down, and when I catch you, I'm gonna give you what for."

He stamped down the stairs, trying to sound as big and scary as possible. Before Gibb had gone two steps, he knew something was wrong. The giggling stopped, and the hair on the back of his neck stood on end. Feeling his way, he moved cautiously forward.

"Look, kids, I don't have time for games. Now come on out!" Hesitantly, he let his foot dangle a few inches above the next riser.

"DO YOU HEAR ME?!" he shouted while his scrotum tried to withdraw into his pelvis. Gibb took another reluctant step, and another—bravado gone—until he stood at the foot of the stairs. His pulse raced, bounding, leaping through his veins, and he broke out in a cold sweat—totally engulfed by claustrophobic fear. The walls closed in around him.

In the insipid light, he saw no one. He advanced slowly across the basement floor—hands outstretched in front of him. The shadows thrown by the old gravity furnace danced and moved, creating the illusion of imaginary attackers.

That's when he saw them—two glowing eyes which stared at him from the cellar's far corner.

"All right, dammit! I see you now. Don't make me come get you." He took a menacing step in that direction as clammy hands grabbed him from behind. He shrieked and whirled around, arms flailing.

An emaciated boy in shorts and a ridiculously frilly shirt smiled up at him. Dark, hollow eyes stared out from a gaunt face, imploring. The child clasped Gibb's hand, who in turn pulled away, repelled by the slimy touch.

The boy's bony legs were ripped and torn, the open sores running from his knees to his ankles. No blood flowed from the tears. They had festered, suppurating a thick, purulent discharge. A rank, fetid stench enveloped the child, and he opened his mouth, revealing sharp teeth.

Gibb recoiled, coughing. The boy lunged—landing on Gibb's back. Gibb screamed and beat at the child who clung to him with formidable strength and tenacity. The miasmic odor enveloped Gibb, and he felt himself going under. Instinct kept him conscious as he fought a wave of nausea.

"Holy shit!" Steeling himself, he pulled at the thing on his back. Gibb, a confirmed skeptic, suddenly found himself a believer, and he started to pray as he reached around to grab the apparition and throw it down. Wheezing and panting Gibb had clambered on all fours for the stairs and then darted up to the kitchen without looking back.

Inside the house a silent presence watched the car below with mild interest. From within its shaded confines, a distraught face stared up at the house and looked directly into the eyes which gleamed hungrily. The face behind the windshield blanched and disappeared from view.

The house was preternaturally quiet. Gibb peered up at it inquiringly, paled beneath his fading summer tan, and gasped. The curtains fell shut.

Sweat rolled from Gibb's forehead down his cheeks which he wiped away with an impatient gesture, making no move to get out of the car. Screwing up his courage, he pulled himself from the car, strode toward the porch, and eyed the closed garage door.

A loud crash emanated from somewhere in the house.

Good, he thought, at least, someone is home. Breathlessly, Gibb bounded up the steps—the paper to be signed, crushed in his grip. He knocked and waited. Something moved behind him. Alarmed, Gibb shot a nervous glance over his shoulder and laughed timorously.

He knocked again.

Something scrabbled away beneath the porch, scratching at the boards beneath his feet. Gibb swallowed and knocked again. The slight susurrating scratch became a heavy digging noise as though something were trying to claw its way through the wooden porch.

"Mr. McDow—uh," Gibb hollered as he knocked on the closed door, his panic rising.

He heard the loud, ripping crack of breaking wood—as if something behind him had broken through—and the name died on his lips. Gibb swung away from the door, his expression frozen, eyes wide and mouth half-open. He swallowed, hard, and his adam's apple bounced up and down convulsively. A child's laughter penetrated the fog of his terror—and Gibb couldn't tell whether it had come from the house, the children down the street, or the boards directly beneath his feet—but he wasn't going to hang around and find out.

Relaxing against the upraised bed, Allison let the sounds of hospital activity wash over her. The woman in the next bed chatted on the phone about her surgery. Her gallstones, her red badge of courage, floated in a jar that sat on the overbed table. Bells rang and horns sounded as a game-show participant won the grand prize.

People wandered up and down the halls, trailing IV bottles on stands and plastic bottles filled with various bodily fluids like dogs on leashes. With an explosive exhalation Allison contemplated her room. She wasn't used to being in the hospital; her only other stays had been in the maternity ward, where the air was charged with subdued jubilation. The medical section was depressing, but it was better than Intensive Care, which was permeated with the ominous, brooding silence of impending doom.

She was ready to go home to her family—her sons, her husband. To rooms that didn't smell like disinfectant, where the atmosphere wasn't one of quiet despair or desperate hope. To halls that didn't echo with: "maybe if they remove this bit or that bit, I'll be all right."

Any resistance Allison had to the move was gone. She had known all along that she was rebelling against change, any change. Unlike Scott, Allison had a strong need for stability, and an equally strong sense of home, of community, of continuity, of established family and service to others. Where he had known none of these things he had created them. She, however, had had them all her life.

Her childhood had been quiet, filled with warmth and understanding. The same kind of warmth and understanding that she had come to associate with the house, for some odd reason. Yes, she was ready to go home.

Allison disliked disruption of any kind, but after a week in the hospital, she realized that there were changes and there were *changes.* Moving wasn't so bad after all.

Her objections, her fears had nothing to do with rumors and had everything to do with her opposition to change. Her personal superstition. For Allison, change had meant death. Her father's death. Her mother's death.

Her father's death had rearranged her life. Until then they had been a happy family, a strong, close-knit unit. Tight within their own circle, and secure. They had been happy but poor, as cliché as that sounds. Success had never been as important to her father as it was to Scott. Oh, her parents had believed in the American dream. Second-generation Americans, their forefathers had worked in the stockyards or railyards of Blue Island back when Chicago was in its heyday, the commercial and transportation hub of a nation. Her parents were proud of what they had been able to achieve. From the stink of the stockyards to shop owner and shopkeeper.

Allison's family had lived above their little corner store, which had been bequeathed to her father by his father, and they were a success, when one considered it against the backdrop of starvation in the old country and mucking around in cowshit.

Then came supermarkets, and the shop couldn't hope to compete. But her father and mother kept the store open out of a sense of duty and service to the community. There was old Mrs. Williams who couldn't walk all that way to the supermarket. And the Joneses with the new baby that needed supplies at all hours of the night. They had twenty regulars, people who, for some reason or another, preferred the corner grocery to the anonymity of the supermarket. And hundreds of people who wandered in during off hours, when the bigger supermarket was closed.

They squeaked by. Then came Seven-Eleven and that had killed them. Not only the store, but also her father. He died that same year.

Her mother said, "Money killed him."

Allison knew now that her mother meant money worries. Money was a metaphor, but to her still-malleable mind the message sent shock waves that rocked her life and to which she responded still. The gap in her life left by her father's death was filled when she married Scott. With him she had recreated the family life that died with her father. Her mother's death a few months after Jason was born had created another gap—nothing as drastic, but both created empty places in her heart, in her life.

But Scott was different. Their backgrounds were different. Their reactions were different. He was always ready to move ahead. She had always felt: why move if I'm comfortable where I am?

Scott wanted to control the fates. He believed he could. He had the ambition, the desire, and the drive. Allison preferred to make herself as small as possible and hope the world would pass her by on its unrelenting march to self-destruction. She neither wanted to conquer the world nor to save it, only keep her own little corner neat and tidy.

She feared change and, she had to admit it to herself, she feared their sudden success. Something about their new-found riches seemed wrong, as though they were somehow dirtied by wealth. With her staunch Catholic background, to want more than was needed was greed, and greed was sin.

The entire concept was alien. Allison couldn't comprehend Scott's ambition, his overwhelming desire to achieve, but she would not begrudge him. He walked a little straighter now that his books sold well, stood a little taller.

The fire of Scott's ambition had always gleamed in his eyes. Their differences, rather than their similarities, had been what attracted her to him in the first place. Like a wild animal, he was skittish about people. Distrustful, he guarded himself and his feelings, bristling every time someone tried to get close. At an over-enthusiastic and naive nineteen, Scott was a challenge. It had taken a while before she had convinced him that she wasn't going to evaporate and blow away.

Sounded a little sick now, when she thought about it, but the Scott that had emerged from the bristling beast was well worth the effort. Allison picked at the sheet. Scott was a good man—a good person. His temper remained a distant memory, present in his sarcastic wit, but usually smothered before it had a chance to flare. Some of his wit, usually directed at the children, could have drawn blood if they had been old enough to comprehend.

But after they started work on the house Scott's temper had gotten a little shorter. His manner gray and gloomy— like he used to get after a rejection letter—but it was understandable that he should be impatient when he was so close to the realization of a dream and things went suddenly awry.

Allison heard a gruff bellow in the hall, recognizing Scott's voice. She put away her glum thoughts. Flustered as a new bride, she smoothed her hair, patted the tangled sheets to some semblance of order, and waited anxiously for Scott to appear at the door.

8

Jason watched the shrinking sliver of light. He didn't want to be left alone in here, but his father had been in no mood to listen to his pleas.

"Daddy?"

The sliver shivered to a stop for a moment, and his father said: "Good night, Jason. You sleep in your own room tonight. You'll be all right. There's nothing in there that can possibly hurt you."

Jason lay still, and he heard the soft click of tumblers and a susurrating whoosh! He sat up, looking hopefully at the bedroom door—reprieve!—but no corresponding light appeared from the hallway.

He wanted to sleep with Daddy, or Adam. Jason wasn't ready to face this huge house alone, this house that had swallowed them whole. Jason glared at the far corners of the room where the meager illumination of the Snoopy nightlight would not penetrate. The shadows yawned and stretched while Mickey Mouse smiled benignly down on him.

The piping chime of children's voices came to him, as

though from far away. He scrambled to his knees, listening. A squeak. Jason turned back to the door, clutching the bed's rail in a chubby fist.

Eyes narrowed to slits, Jason squinted, willing his bedroom door to open.

Another creak, and Jason knew which door was opening. He didn't want to look, but his eyes were drawn inexorably from the bedroom door along the wall.

Donald Duck capered with Daisy. This creature didn't look nearly so benign as his friend Mickey. Like the bad Donald in the cartoons, he seemed to have developed horns and a tail, and he grabbed Daisy's dress, tearing it, and knocked her down. Donald pulled up his sailor's coat and leapt on top of her.

Jason blinked. Donald had returned to his old position, but his smile was oily and evil. Jason continued his scan—ignoring the antics of the other small creatures on the wall, who were doing all sorts of naughty things—until his gaze lighted upon the open closet door.

As though aware of his attention, it responded by swinging out another two inches. Jason gasped. His mind readily supplied a hand with squishy, ooky skin that was going to reach out and grab him. He crawled, whimpering, to the foot of the bed. A shrill screech, and the gap widened. Two eyes glowed out at him. One slowly winked and Jason scampered across the room, only to freeze when he heard a sound coming behind him.

A small cry escaped his lips. Back rigid with fear, Jason spun.

An old woman, her limbs twisted and contorted like a spider's, floated a few inches above the window seat. Her mouth was little more than a knife slash in her seamed face until it opened in a silent scream.

Standing stock still with a concentration unusual for a toddler, Jason was caught between the spiderlady at the window and the monster in the closet. Jason didn't know which way to turn, which was more dangerous—the dried stalk of a woman with her twisted limbs or the eyes, the unblinking red eyes.

The woman straightened one crooked limb and motioned for Jason to come. Jason took a reluctant step forward, as if compelled. Above his head he heard the steady creak of boards.

Footsteps!

And he was released from the spell. Jason darted from the room.

The bell rang, and the children exploded from the classroom. Recess!

Adam sniffed his disgust, shoved his hands in his pockets, and wandered off to the furthest corner of the playground to separate himself from the rest of his classmates.

Such babies, playing baby games, he thought as he watched the girls skip rope and the boys chase a ball around the schoolyard.

He was different. He had a little brother to take care of and a mother in the hospital. He was responsible; he had to be. His father had told him time and time again. Adam picked up a stick and prodded the bushes along the fence.

Being responsible was no fun, and Adam looked enviously at the other children in the playground. He bet that they didn't have a little brother to take care of. They didn't have to be strong, or responsible, or spend long hours in the hospital. He bet that they had both parents at home, a father to lecture them and a mother to kiss the hurts away.

His mother's absence, the loss, the confusion, and his father's irascible temper—so unlike him—bubbled to the surface to bring stinging tears. Adam brushed them away. Only babies cried.

The idle prodding became an angry swipe, and he noticed his teacher, Ms. Courtney, staring at him curiously. Adam began to draw something on the ground, while still keeping her well within his line of vision.

The branches rattled behind him. Adam glanced back, startled, and heard a soft whimper. Another teacher joined Ms. Courtney. With a rapid sideways step Adam receded into the shrubs.

A puppy hunched at the base of a tree, whining. A chewed-through rope tangled in the brush held it fast.

"Aw, poor puppy." Adam reached out to untie the rope, and the dog bit him.

He yanked his arm away, examined the livid teeth marks and stuck his sore hand in his mouth. He glared at the whining mongrel, contemplating it before grabbing a stick, which he raised above his head to strike.

"Bad!" he yelled.

His arm dropped leadenly. *Thwack!*

The twig broke on the puppy's back with a satisfying crack, and Adam immediately started searching for a larger, sturdier branch.

"B-r-r-room, rrhm!"

Jason pushed Adam's batmobile across the living room floor as he waited for his brother's return from school. School seemed a strange and glamorous place. Jason equated it with new shoes, new clothes, boxes of brightly colored crayons, pencils, and books filled with pretty pictures.

Behind him his father glared at the computer, stopping at disjointed intervals either to bark at Jason, when the toddler got too noisy, or to grasp his own head and groan.

Collecting Leonardo, the Joker, and Bart Simpson, Jason retreated to the foyer to play somewhere well away from his father. A line of concentration painted between his brows, Jason scrunched over the imaginary battle. He wanted Adam home. War wasn't no fun unless you had someone to fight against, Jason thought. He wanted Momma home, too.

The furrow between his brows deepened. Mom had been gone *forever,* it seemed. Now Adam was gone, and Jason was alone. Jason peeked anxiously over his shoulder.

His father growled at the computer, and Jason, who had rearranged the troop deployment on the foyer floor, was glad that his father had found something else to yell at.

One force, which consisted of Big Bird, Glo-worm, and Adam's Autobots, drew a meandering line in front of him. A toy troll, some Matchbox figures, Jason's "Little Pony" and a Care Bear made up the opposing force. The Joker and Bart were discarded off to the side, a couple of war casualties.

Jason picked up one of the toys and dropped it bomblike onto the battlefield. The figures scattered.

He wanted his mother home. He wanted Adam. Jason didn't want to be left alone in this big, empty house. He didn't particularly want to be left alone with his father.

A loud smacking noise came from the study as his father hit the computer for some supposed misbehavior. Jason scowled. It wasn't right. A lot of things weren't right, and Jason sprawled on the floor to be in a better position to thump his Bart Simpson soundly.

Momma gone. Chubby forefinger flexed behind his thumb. Thump!

The toy scooted across the floor a bit.

Adam gone. Thump!

Dad gone. His forefinger froze at the thought. Gone? Gone where? His father was in the study, even now swearing at the computer.

That man wasn't his father! The idea surfaced from somewhere, rising like an evil dragon, to wrap itself around the child's psyche, and somehow it seemed to fit.

Thump! He hit Care Bear.

Around him, the house was menacing and quiet. Small sounds like his marching the Joker across the wooden floor were picked up by the walls and returned to him, louder. His own breath sounded harsh to him in the huge, open foyer.

Big. That's what it was, big! Too big! Jason felt small in this new home. From Jason's diminutive perspective, everything seemed harsh, too new, cold, and unfriendly. The ceilings towered overhead, and the walls stared down at him watchfully.

Everywhere Jason went rooms opened up on to labyrinthian rooms. A kitchen, a dining room, a living room, a playroom and laundry, a study, a bedroom for each of them, a nursery for the baby that lived in mommy's tummy, and the grand wide-open foyer, like an entrance to a castle.

Grand, he thought, like the ballroom he had seen in Cinderella. But empty and hollow.

The hand which held Big Bird swooped down on the unsuspecting villain, a toy troll, to batter it relentlessly. He missed their home in Blue Island. This wasn't their home. This was . . . this was . . . Jason groped for a word to explain his feelings.

Scary.

He picked up the troll and threw it across the foyer. It bounced against the far wall.

"Jason? What are you doing?" His father's voice floated from the study door.

"Just playin'."

"You be good. Daddy's trying to work."

"Yes, daddy." Jason waited until he heard the soft clicking of the computer keys before he stood up to kick the assembled toys savagely.

It wasn't fair, the little boy thought.

He grabbed Leonardo and stabbed at the Glo-worm.

Adam was at school; Mommy was in the hospital, and Jason was here all alone in this bad place.

It wasn't fair.

Jason definitely preferred their cozy two-bedroom apartment. Here, he could get lost and not be found for days! He could starve to death, and an icicle of terror was thrust into his tiny heart.

"But it was great for hide and seek." A small childlike voice spoke within his head, and Jason sat up straighter listening intently.

A bad place, he thought.

"Hide and seek . . ."

Jason started, looking around for the source of the whispering voice inside his mind. He scanned the foyer before his eyes darted apprehensively upstairs.

Three children stood on the second-floor landing. A boy, flanked on either side by two little girls, stared down at him. The boy was dressed in funny clothes like a girl's. His face lean and gaunt. The girls looked identical to each other, except that one was slightly larger.

They moved woodenly at first—motions stiff and saltatorial—stumbling into each other. Jason clapped at their antics. They sorted themselves out and turned to him. The boy lifted his hands, in which he held a single noose.

"Jason, it's time to go pick up your brother from school," Scott called from the study. Jason scrambled to his feet. His father poked his head through the door.

Jason peered up at him impatiently and then spun back to search for the children. They were gone.

"You've made quite a mess in here." Scott stood over his son, jingling the car keys in his hand. "You will have to put your toys back in the basement when we get back. Are you ready?"

With another quick search of the second-floor landing Jason shrugged and followed his father out the front door.

"I don't know why you don't play in the basement more," Scott said as he held the door open for Jason. "Why do you always have to drag your toys up here to the foyer?"

Strapping his sons firmly into the backseat with a stern warning to keep still, Scott pondered the crumpled piece of paper in his hands.

Angrily he tossed it on the dash and concentrated on the complicated system of belts which held the kiddy carseat in place. A futile effort since Jason was better at unstrapping himself than Scott was at anchoring him into position. In five minutes the child would be bouncing around in the back of the car, wreaking havoc.

When Scott opened the door on the driver's side the paper glided across the dash. He picked it up and deposited it in his pocket.

"I don't suppose you can tell me what this is about." Scott slid into the car seat, extracted the paper and waved it under Adam's nose. Playing nonchalantly with the seatbelt buckle, the boy did his best to avoid his father's penetrating gaze.

Less than a week in school, and Adam had gotten into enough trouble that Scott was being summoned to talk to the teacher. Irritated, he put the car into gear, and Adam sunk a little lower in the car seat. They drove home in silence. Even Jason's normal ebullience was suffocated by his father's scowl. When he pulled into the driveway Adam didn't move. Annoyed, Scott helped Jason from the car, walked around to Adam's side to yank the door open impatiently, and twisted the seat belt off with a deft tug.

"Come along, young man, we have to talk about this," Scott said, and Adam tried to shrink back into the car.

Using more strength than he had intended, Scott dragged his eldest from the car. Adam stifled a small yelp as his arm was wrenched from its socket.

"Inside!"

"Gotcha!"

The jubilant cry penetrated Scott's contemplation, if, in fact, contemplation is what it was. He jumped slightly, blinked several times, and then took off his glasses to rub his eyes before looking at the computer screen.

Blank except for the C-prompt.

His eyes swung wildly in his sockets until they alighted on the clock. Nearly two hours had passed since he had sat down at the keyboard. Scott stared suspiciously at the computer.

The cursor pulsated on the screen, and his fingers rested

lightly on the keyboard, ready for typing. He pulled his hands away as though burned. Two hours gone. Scott pinched his nose.

Gone. Gone where? How?

His gaze again sought the clock. Surely, that much time could not have passed. He stood, and his muscles—caught in the same position for too long—protested. His joints popped. His feet were asleep, and Scott almost plunged head first to the floor. Using the desk as a support, Scott shook one leg and then the other before mincing gingerly over to the window.

Lecture forgotten, Adam frolicked with his little brother in the field. The overturned earth had hardened into rock-like clods. Fallow, it had a sad, ragged look. Dying weeds ringed the plowed ground like tattered fringe around a shabby rug.

Scott watched them race. Adam split away from Jason, leaving him alone. Distracted, Jason clambered over broken dirt. He shouted and started to chase something—or many things, because suddenly he would halt and change course. The movement wasn't random, or didn't appear to be. There seemed to be some intent and some purpose. Jason appeared to be playing tag but made no attempt to find his older brother. Instead he pursued something that Scott couldn't see.

Jason dodged and darted until he slapped at empty space and shouted a triumphant, "Gotcha."

The computer whirred, a reminder that Scott was already behind schedule, and he turned from the window, wondering if his little talk with Adam had done any good at all.

Adam had remained adamant. He didn't know why the teacher had summoned his parents to school. Nothing that Scott said about lying and teachers-don't-just-do-that-kind-of-thing-for-fun-you-know seemed to make any impression. One son's getting in trouble at school, and the other's chasing shadows, Scott thought sourly.

With a grunt he went to sit before the screen and resisted

the impulse to switch to the games directory. He must work, but his mind refused to follow instructions. His thoughts kept returning to his son's antics in the field.

Scott would have sworn that if he had concentrated hard enough, he would have been able to see Jason's invisible playmate. Scott closed his eyes. There it was, shimmering just beyond the range of consciousness, a shape, a human shape. Everything started to fade as he focused on this mental picture, and he sat—seconds melding into minutes. Minutes became an hour as the light outdoors dwindled.

Chattering to his brother, Jason flung himself through the front door into the foyer. Scott, jolted out of his reverie, got up from his desk, chiding the boys for their muddy feet. Then he bent to help Jason take off his sweater.

9

The teacher bent over a chest as she put away the toys left over from class. She heard rather than saw the family walk into the room. Ms. Courtney straightened.

"Mr. McDowell?"

"Yes."

"Is your wife going to join us?"

"No, she's in the hospital. We'll go visit her after we are through here."

"We usually prefer both parents to be present."

"It can't be helped unless you want to postpone this till later." He lifted one arm in a shrug, pulling Adam's arm with it.

Ms. Courtney frowned. "No, I don't think we'd better."

"What is this about?" Scott dropped Adam's hand and put Jason down next to his brother before he crossed the room to tower over the teacher.

"Yesterday your son was found, uh, torturing a dog." She watched him assimilate the information. His features darkened, and his lip curled up into a sneer.

"Dog? What dog? Since when do they let dogs in school?" He glanced sharply down at Adam.

"It was a puppy, actually, that just wandered on to the school grounds." Ms. Courtney backed a few inches away from McDowell. "We found your son beating it with a stick."

Scott stiffened. "This is ridiculous. Adam loves animals. He's always on to his mother and me about getting a pet."

"Well, I wouldn't recommend it," she said.

"Are you sure you have the right boy?" he asked. He eyed the teacher sceptically.

"Quite sure."

"He hasn't been in your class all that long. I can imagine at first it's hard telling one child from another."

The teacher paced in front of shelves laden with books, construction paper, and paste. She was no good at this kind of confrontation. No parent took kindly to these revelations. She, like the parents, would have preferred to believe that all the children in her class were angels.

"It *was* Adam! And whether it sounds like him or not, he did tie some poor creature up and beat it with a stick. I was not mistaken."

Scott paled, and he paused briefly before he responded in measured tones, thrusting the words one at a time through clenched teeth. "You *must* be mistaken. *My* son wouldn't do that!"

"Why don't you ask him?"

"Look, I don't have time for this now. We're on our way to visit my wife in the hospital. All I can say is that you're wrong." He left no room for argument—his face hard, like a closed fist—and she recoiled from his barely repressed rage.

His reaction seemed extreme. Ms. Courtney looked him up and down—noting the bunched cords in his jaw and neck—and wondered if the father was the root of Adam's problem. She had seen it before. She stopped and turned to face him head on.

"I'm sorry, sir, but it is true. It happened."

"Adam!" Scott swung on his son. "Front and center, young man!" He pointed to a place before him.

"Did you tie up some poor little puppy dog and beat it?"

Adam shook his head no. His eyes had a wounded look that was difficult for a child to fake.

"There, you see," Scott said to the teacher triumphantly.

"He's lying."

"My son doesn't lie."

"I assure you, Mr. McDowell, it did happen," she said, turning a sour eye on the child.

"My son doesn't lie! He knows I'd tan his hide if he did."

"I don't think spanking will solve anything."

"I've never spanked the boys in my life!" His nostrils flared, and the teacher shrank away from him.

"You just said . . ."

"It was a figure of speech," he informed her. "You have the wrong boy," Scott said, "I'd recommend you get to know your students a little better before you go calling their parents into school.

McDowell grabbed his sons by the hand and marched them to the door. Courtney's eyes followed his abrupt movements suspiciously as the man lifted the toddler to his hip.

When they appeared outside her window, Ms. Courtney watched as the father gave Adam a rough shake. His animated voice carried through the plate glass. She folded her arms across her chest. Never spanked his sons, indeed! Having met the father, Ms. Courtney would have to keep a special eye on the son.

Tummy full with heavy cafeteria food, Jason sat at the kitchen table, regarding his father carefully. Daddy was mad! Sliding from his perch onto the floor, Jason moved away, glad that his father's anger was directed at Adam.

Sheepishly, Adam showed his workbook to his father, proud of the gold star he had gotten for successfully matching triangles with triangles and squares with squares.

"Congratulations. Now if you can just try getting along

with the teacher . . ." Scott frowned at his son over the rim of his glass.

"Come play." Jason tugged at Adam's hand.

"No, Jason," Scott said. "I have to talk to your brother. Why don't you go outside and play by yourself? It shouldn't be dark for a while yet."

Lower lip extended in childlike pout, Jason scrutinised his father and Adam. He snorted and looked down at the page. His lips formed a small O, and the gold star sparkled and shone. Jason eyed it covetously. He wanted a star like Adam. He was wanted *that* star.

Slipping the paper into his pocket, Jason went out the back door. The late evening sun filtered through the trees. The toddler clambered onto a swing, squinting at the kitchen window. Jason sniffed a little and took the crumpled paper from his pocket to gaze at the star. It caught the dying rays of sun and gleamed a dull red. When he held the paper away from himself and pointed it in the right direction, the reflected light of the sun stained the grass crimson.

The toddler fingered the star. The night was summer warm, and Jason let his feet dangle a few inches off the ground as he redirected the scarlet stain to another section of lawn and across a pair of feet. The paper fluttered to the ground as Jason looked up at the familiar boy who stood only a few yards away.

With a wide grin of welcome Jason stared into the child's huge and shadowed eyes, wondering where his friend had come from.

The little boy smiled at him.

"Hi. Wanna play?" Jason chirped.

The boy nodded a silent yes and then pointed to the paper, which had begun a windy jog across the yard. Jason jumped from the swing as it blew against the other boy's legs. He reached down and picked it up.

Excited, Jason motioned for the older boy to join him.

* * *

Scott drifted gently. His head waved and bent like a flower in the breeze, keeping fluid time to the music. The ice-filled glass moved back and forth to the soulful strains of Whitney Houston. The only light in the living room came from the bright, bouncing band of the stereo receiver. It had been one helluva day. He seemed to be having a lot of those lately.

His head drooped to his chest. The notebook he had been working on slid from his fingers. He dozed. A small tongue of flame darted across the empty log rack. He let out a gentle snort just as the crisped images of his mother and father coalesced in the flames.

Scott awoke with a start. Swallowing hard, he turned to the cold, dark hearth. He must have been dreaming. The album ended with a quiet click, and Scott glanced at the clock.

"Adam, Jason, it's time for bed."

Adam peered up from his picture book.

"Where's your brother?"

"Outside," Adam said.

"Outside, at this hour! Why didn't you tell me?"

Adam regarded his father coolly.

Scott frowned. "Is he in the backyard?"

Adam shrugged.

"Go get him. It's time for the two of you to go to bed."

His hand tapping a rapid rhythm on his leg, Adam slid from his chair and went outside. He loped down the porch steps to the driveway. "Jason!"

He stopped to let his eyes adjust to the darkness.

"Jason?"

Muffled voices murmured to his left. Adam followed the sound. Jason stood near the swing, his back to Adam.

"Dad says you gotta come in," Adam shouted at his brother across the yard. "It's time for bed."

Jason made no move. Adam clenched his fists at his sides. Little brothers were such a pain! He strode across the lawn, seized his younger brother's shoulder and swung him around to face him.

"It's time for bed! Did you hear me?"

Jason poked his thumb in his mouth. Adam spotted the faint flap of paper clasped tightly in Jason's left hand. The spectral glint of a star held Adam's attention, and he grabbed for it.

Recoiling, Jason stuffed it into his pocket. "No, mine!"

"Is not! That's mine! I saw the star." Adam reached into Jason's pocket as he pushed his younger brother away. Jason flailed, caught off balance and off guard. He clutched at the paper, now in Adam's grasp, ripping it in two.

Adam's head was filled the sound of crinkling papers. Or a rattling buzz . . . static . . . and he struck his younger brother without thinking. His brand-new paper, his homework assignment with a gold star, destroyed. The slap echoed loudly across the backyard, and Jason let out an unearthly howl.

From his vantage point on the back porch Scott heard the loud snap of flesh against flesh echoing across the hushed yard. Everything dimmed slightly, and all the frustration and irritations of the past week came boiling up. Scott was off, bounding across the lawn to where his sons stood.

Jason bawled, a shrill screech, as Scott flopped onto one of the swings, lifting Adam off his feet and pulling his pants down to his ankles, before laying the child "face-down" across his lap.

"Don't you dare hit your brother!"

Jason's weeping subsided into stunned silence, his eyes following Scott's hand as it rose and fell to crack against Adam's bare bottom.

Smack . . . "Do" . . . smack . . . "you" . . . smack . . . "hear" . . . smack . . . "me!"

With practised hands Allison swept her hair into a ponytail before putting down the hairbrush. Her finger traced the streak of solid gray, and she sighed. At least the olive undertones had returned to replace the sallow pallor.

"It happens to all of us eventually," the nurse said sympathetically. Allison's eyes sought and found the other woman's reflection in the mirror.

"The gray, I mean," the nurse added hastily.

"It wasn't there before . . ." The sentence died, the thought unfinished.

"I look awful. I'm probably going to scare them to death" Allison patted a stray strand back into place. "It would help, I suppose, if I could wash it."

The nurse scowled.

"Okay, a bath then, a *real* bath, not one of those bedside affairs."

"You can do that when you get home. If you want to do that here, we'll have to get doctor's orders."

Allison grunted. "Doctor's orders? I have to get permission for a bath?"

"When you're on complete bed rest, you do. We had to get special permission for this visit. I suppose we could stretch the rules at bit, since you'll be going home tomorrow. I'll see what I can do." The nurse pulled the wheelchair away from the small sink. "Let's not keep those two lovely children of yours waiting. They're getting anxious to see their mother."

"Heigh-ho, Silver, away!" Allison pointed toward the hall.

Nurse Melkoweitz grinned at the young woman's reflection in the mirror before she turned the chair around and pushed Allison out the door.

At the far end of the corridor, Allison could see Scott's tall figure silhouetted by the late afternoon sun. He stood next to Jason. His hand rested lightly on the toddler's head. Adam sat slouched in a chair a few feet away, looking lonely and forlorn.

She leaned forward in the chair until the nurse put a restraining hand on her shoulder.

"Adam, Jason!" She called to them and was rewarded by their simultaneous shrieks of jubilation.

Adam hurled himself from his chair and lunged full-speed down the corridor. Jason broke away from his father's grasp and barreled, elbows out and plump legs pumping, through the waiting room door. Scott followed at a more sedate pace.

Adam plunged into her outstretched arms. "Mommy!"

He clung to her, arms tightly squeezed around her bulging midriff. The nurse sighed and tried to pry the older child off his mother's lap. The woman gave the nurse a look of sharp reproof. Chastened Melkoweitz stepped aside.

Jason hit next, climbing over and around his brother until he lay half-sprawled on Allison's already occupied lap. Allison blinked rapidly to keep the tears away. She reached down and tousled Jason's blond head.

"You'll never know how much I've missed you two imps."

Adam mumbled something into her stomach that Allison didn't quite catch.

"What was that?" She peeled her son from her side and was surprised to discover that he was crying. Adam was fast approaching the age when he would spurn childish tears. She dried a tear with a corner of her robe. "What was that, honey?"

"I miss you, too, momma." He sniffled, wiping his nose with his sleeve.

"Hey, got room for one more," Scott stooped to kiss her cheek.

"I don't know. Do you think you can fit?"

Scott eyed her lap and said, "I don't know. Looks a little crowded."

Melkoweitz stepped in and scooped Jason from Allison's arms, handing him to his father.

"Now, you can all go down to the cafeteria for lunch. You have to be back in half an hour." The nurse wagged a finger at her patient.

"What happens if I don't?" Allison asked defiantly. "Do I turn into a pumpkin?"

"No, but I turn into a rat and squeal to your doctor." Her

expression softened. "Most of the staff have eaten by now, so you should have more than enough time."

The lunch passed quickly with Adam and Jason, each vying for her attention. Scott ate in constrained silence. Even with her attention split between her two children, she couldn't help but notice that Adam avoided looking at his father. Jason, too, seemed guarded, shying away from both brother and father. Their bodies canted slightly away from the other, leaning instead toward her like flowers toward the sun. Neither child talked to him, and when Scott spoke to them, they recoiled. Concerned, Allison tried to act as a bridge between them, drawing first one and then the other into the conversation; but all her attempts fell flat.

With Jason riding on the back of the chair and Adam walking beside her, they returned to the second floor. Allison asked about school and Adam sidled away from Scott before he muttered a sullen, halfhearted reply. Allison shot Scott a sidelong look.

Nurse Melkoweitz greeted them at the elevator doors. "I thought I was going to have to come get you. Mr. McDowell, I'll see your sons are settled into the waiting room if you'll take her to the room. That will give you two a chance to say good-bye. Come along, boys, the doctor's orders are that each of you gets a piece of candy for being so well behaved."

She winked at Scott as she popped a licorice stick into Jason's open mouth before he could let out a howl of protest at the separation.

Scott wheeled her into her room, aligning the chair carefully next to the bed. He bent over her to lock the wheels and then straightened.

"So what's up?" Allison said.

"What do you mean, what's up?"

"What the matter? Something happened between Adam and you. That's obvious."

Scott put his hands in his hip pockets and walked to the window, his back to her.

Allison unlocked the wheelchair and steered over to his side. She placed a tender hand on his wrist and peered into his face. "Scott?"

He looked down at her, expression clouded. Their eyes met, and he glanced nervously away to stare out the window.

"I guess I've been a little hard on him."

She waited for him to continue.

"He's the oldest, and I suppose I've been expecting too much from him." Scott turned to her. "Christ, Allison, I'm no good with the kids."

Allison chuffed. "Nonsense, you've always been good with them."

"Not now that you're not there. Let's face it, I'm just no good without you." He kept his voice even, but Allison could hear a small child's anguished wail beneath the carefully controlled monotone. "I'm so glad you're coming home tomorrow."

Tugging at his hand, she drew him down to her. "You're worried about nothing. I know you; you wouldn't hurt a fly."

Scott's body grew rigid in her embrace. Extracting himself from her arms, he stared down at her hands. "Oh, wouldn't I?"

"Look," Allison caught his eyes and held them, "I know they're a handful, but you're doing fine. I'm sure."

"Visiting hours are over Mr. McDowell, and time for us to get you back into bed, Mrs. McDowell," Melkoweitz interrupted. "Your sons are waiting for you in the waiting room. I managed to interest them in 'Gilligan's Island.'"

Scott kissed Allison good-bye and joined the boys. Adam looked dully up at his father as Scott entered the waiting room. He rose to leave, but Scott motioned him back to his chair.

"Let's finish the show."

Adam nodded. Scott sat in the chair next to Adam, and the child squirmed slightly, his torso slanting away from his father.

"Adam?"

"Uh-huh?"

"Adam, I'm sorry." Scott put his arm around Adam. "I'm sorry I spanked you. I shouldn't have. Oh, and I didn't mean to scare you like that the other day. That was wrong of me. Can you forgive me?"

For the first time in several days Adam met his father's gaze, eyes glistening. He shook his head in silent affirmation before he buried his face in Scott's shirt.

The two sat for a while, entwined, as Jason uttered a screech of delight when a clumsy Gilligan tripped over something and spilled goop into the fuming Skipper's lap.

The morning sun crept into the kitchen. A playful beam danced gaily across Scott's hand as he scrubbed at the greasy smear left by the several-day-old beans. The pan was a write-off. He had thrown it out days ago and had judiciously avoided the kitchen ever since, but Allison was coming home today.

His head throbbed dully as he surveyed several days' accumulation of toys and dishes that littered the kitchen and the living room.

"Thank God for dishwashers," he whispered to no one in particular, and he shoved a few more glasses into the already full machine.

Grabbing the empty McDonald's cartons from the kitchen table, Scott deposited them in the wastebasket, feeling a stab of guilt at his own laziness. The beans had been his last attempt at cooking.

Adam and Jason didn't seem to object to peanut butter and jelly or whatever he could drag home in a carton or a box. The boys had loved it. McDonalds, pizza, Chinese. For them it had been a real treat.

He scooped up the toys from the living room floor and then puzzled over whether they were Adam's or Jason's. He solved the problem by pulling an empty box from the porch, pouring them all into the carton and hiding it on the basement stairs. Then he threw another load of the seemingly eternal pile of dirty laundry into the washer.

Back upstairs, Scott made one last unhurried search through the house. When it passed inspection, he went to the second floor to get the kids ready for one final trip to the hospital.

Something slithered beneath the house, following the ripple of Scott's passage with intent interest and reaching out with a tendril of its consciousness to touch him. The man paused in his progress and shivered. The father zipped up his jacket and urged his sons to hurry. The door whispered shut behind the group, and the entity trilled its triumph. The woman was coming home!

A nudge and a chuckle.

Inside the darkened basement, the washer began a jittering, jarring dance, an ungraceful boogaloo that sent it clanging against the dryer with a loud crash. It jiggled—its alarm buzzing stentoriously.

In Jason's room, the closet door opened, and the boy, once known as William, scampered on all fours from its confines. The apparition lifted its head to reveal hooded eyes. Somewhere deep inside, if one chose to look, one could have seen the hurt, confusion, and pain of the mortal child who had been the house's first victim.

The specter appeared now as it first appeared in death. Through translucent clothes, a non-existent heart battered against a bony ribcage. Dripping sores from old rat bites ran up and down its legs. The expression, forlorn, starved— starved as the child starved to death in this same closet with rats gnawing on its body.

A shudder ran the length of the childlike body. The lids dropped slowly shut, only to reopen and uncover eyes that gleamed the dull red of the house's first minion. The specter smiled and cocked its head. From deep with the house came a rhythmic thumping as the washer bumped against the wall in its clattering jig.

*Bang, bang, **bang!***

The washing machine wobbled a few more times and stopped. Its alarm buzzed for a while before it, too, sputtered and died.

10

A slow tremor slid up her spine and settled at the base of her skull as they drove into the cul-de-sac. The tingling thrill spread outward, and Allison was sure every hair on her head must be standing on end. Next to her Scott was chattering with false animation and cheer, talking a little too much a little too fast.

"Everything's unpacked—well, almost. The toys—Adam's, Jason's, and mine—all the clothes. I think I unpacked it the way you would have. I put your underwear and lingerie in the top drawer. Your blouses in the second, and slacks 'n' things in the bottom. Is that okay?"

"Sounds fine," she said.

"And the kitchen, too." Scott frowned. "You may not be able to find anything for six months, but," he said, brightening, "I'm sure everything will surface eventually. Wait'll you see the house. Damn, you never even made it inside the door."

He parked the Saab next to the cobbled walk, got out, and strode around the side of the car. He fished through the keys and opened the trunk to wrestle out the rented wheelchair.

Making a show of it, Scott fought the mechanical demon into position while Adam and Jason giggled at his charade.

Allison contemplated his performance and said, "This is ridiculous. It's not all that far!"

"You stay seated!" he ordered.

"Yes, sir!" Allison saluted.

"I didn't get a chance to carry you across the threshold last time. Well, this time I will. I had to bribe the doctor. It cost a mint; that doctor's not cheap. So you better just sit there!"

For the boys' and Allison's amusement, Scott proceeded to bounce the wheelchair around, saying magical words like "Abracadabra!"

He finally pronounced Allison's chariot suitable and safe for transport, and then he pranced proudly around to the front of the car to help Allison, with much bowing and scraping, from the passenger seat into the chair.

They pushed, pulled, and tugged her along the cobbled walkway. Her teeth rattled as they jostled her over the uneven surface. All three were winded and Scott's forehead was beaded with sweat by the time they reached the bottom of the stairs.

"You see, if you'd let me walk, I'd probably be in bed by now," she said triumphantly.

"Hush, woman," Scott said from his position towering over her chair.

"Yes, my lord and master." She gave him her most demure grin, and he snorted. Scott carried her to the porch and set her down on the topmost stair.

Allison's flesh, even the muscles of her buttocks, seemed to withdraw as soon as it made contact with the wooden slats, as though her musculature wanted to retract into her bones. A mild shock ran though her body—no cramping, no pains, no dizzy spells, only a slight vibration as the house thrummed beneath her, stirring to life. The feeling was warm, comforting.

Allison patted the porch step beside her. The house was welcoming her.

Scott propped open the screen and unlocked the inside door. Then he backed the chair up the porch stairs and rolled it into the foyer. He paused to lock the wheels and returned to pluck Allison from her perch.

"Welcome home, Mrs. McDowell." Scott gave her a wet, sloppy kiss.

The boys moaned, "Mushy stuff."

And Scott carried her over the threshold.

Allison didn't know where to look first. Her gaze darted from room to room at the fresh medallion wallpaper in the foyer, the antique coat rack. She saw little to remind her of the dreary domicile they had bought with its dingy, peeling paper. If anything, the house seemed to have come alive, and she gave a delighted cry.

"How about the grand tour?" Scott suggested.

The boys trailed behind as he wheeled her into study. "Not much to see in here, except that everything is set up and ready to go. I haven't had much time to work, though."

Scott pulled her from the study and steered around toward the back of the foyer.

"And here we have, ta da!" He opened the door. "A bathroom."

Allison stuck her head inside the door.

"It's nice, though it doesn't look like it was built for a wheelchair," she said ruefully.

"Nope, I'm afraid not. This"—Scott tapped the back of the chair—"was not part of the plan, but then neither was this." Scott indicated the bathroom. "We found lots of wasted space. After we pulled out the old heating vents we discovered there was enough room left over after the bathroom here"—Scott knocked on a wall—"for a walk-in closet. I even toyed with the idea of a sauna, but I decided that could wait. I had them line it with cedar. So, we can go either way—sauna or moth-free closet."

Stepping over to an adjacent door, he opened it. "I know, the house was modified through the years as all old houses are, but even to my unpracticed eye, something seems off, askew, as though the walls are slanted and don't meet at the proper ninety-degree angle. Things don't seem to match even now. I wouldn't be surprised if we didn't have a hidden passage or two."

"Oh, boy!" Adam whooped. "Jason, let's go find a secret passage."

The children ran off, and Scott looked at Allison, chagrined. "Great. They'll probably tear down the walls."

Adam returned, hurtling across the room to slide to a stop in stockinged feet. "Daddy, how do you find hidden passages?"

"Carefully, Adam, very carefully," Scott answered. Allison and Scott looked at each other and laughed.

Grumbling and grousing good-naturedly, Scott lugged Allison through the house. The boys watched, hiding smirks and twitters as Daddy huffed and puffed his way from one room to another, setting Allison down and then dragging the folded chair behind him through the door.

The change in the place was nothing short of miraculous. Gone were the water spots and the many generations of finger marks. Each room blazed with light. Allison marvelled, oohed and ahhed. Scott preened under her praise.

Bored with the tour, the boys returned to rapping on walls and testing every miscellaneous knob or piece of molding.

Caught in Stygian darkness, the presence quivered in anticipation. The woman had returned. It scented the abundant life within her, and it scented its own release. Retribution and release. The key . . . So it hurled, through the walls and floorboards of the home, strands of welcoming thoughts, humming a sweet comforting lullaby. Gentle, sweet, caressing.

* * *

The stairs creaked and groaned. The wind blew around the eaves with a hollow whistle. Each rattle, each wooden scream, seemed to emphasize the underlying silence. Jason slept contentedly beside Allison where she lay awake in the huge waterbed. Adam played outside, and Scott worked in the study.

With the curtains drawn the bedroom was gloomy. Only a wavering light penetrated from outdoors. The leafy shadows, like dark fairies, did a flittering dance within the thin quadrangle.

The building pressed down on her with its years and its tales, told and untold. Restless and unable to sleep, Allison quivered, reacting to each individual noise. Another gust of wind hooted in the eaves, and she turned. Catching her reflection in the mirror she jumped slightly to let out the air in a rush when she realized that it was her own reflection she saw.

Allison forced herself to relax. She had nothing to fear. If anything, she felt safe, and she sensed a welcoming presence, watching and waiting, as if someone, or something, stood guard over her and her sleeping son. Inhaling deeply, Allison was reassured by the baby-soft smell of Jason's freshly washed hair. The house seemed happy, glad to have a family living within its walls, and Allison smiled dreamily.

Around her, the house hummed in contentment. It embraced her in warm, welcoming arms. She drifted, lulled by the motion of the waterbed and by her relief at being home. She sank into a light, gently rocking doze.

The humming increased, and she thought she caught the refrain to a familiar melody and beneath that the words to a song. The house crooned to her, telegraphing feelings of content. Wordless comfort—a thing heard, yet unheard—subliminal.

The song wove through her, its slow measured rhythm matching the sluggish beat of her heart. The sweet notes teased her thoughts like flitting butterflies. She tried to move, but something weighed on her hands, her chest. Allison sank deeper, offering no resistance.

Her body felt heavy, heavier. Languid, lethargic. A warm relaxing heaviness. She had neither will nor desire to move. Her legs held fast, pinned to the yielding surface of the waterbed.

Something caressed her thighs, her stomach. Allison twisted sinuously as unseen hands ran up and down her belly, stroking it tenderly as Scott sometimes did to help her sleep.

The impression of weight grew until she felt gargantuan, of almost elephantine proportions. As she gained mass, she also seemed to gain density, sinking lower into the bed. Allison's eyes fluttered open, and she looked over the mound of her stomach.

She was forced deeper into the mattress, and Allison had the impression of something cold as her body penetrated the plastic mattress of the water bed. She smelled the faintly sweet smell of newly manufactured polythene. Then she was surrounded by water, drifting peacefully through blue chemically treated water with its sharp bite of chlorine.

Next she sank through the honeycomb of plywood at the base into the wooden floor beyond. To revel in the silken texture of its grain. Even as she settled another part of her seemed to expand, to disperse. As though, in her slumber, she could defy the laws of physics, and her molecular structure was somehow altered. This part of her began to drift, floating. Allison felt herself drawn up to the ceiling and outward to the walls. The altered Allison flew until she was driven through the coat of fresh paint with its oily tang to find herself immersed in the chalky dust of the sheetrock. It tickled her nose, and below her on the bed the corporeal Allison sneezed. Still she moved deeper, penetrating through the walls, until she got lost in the scratchy, pink fiberglass insulation between the wooden siding and the plaster.

A portion of this new and atomically rearranged Allison

continued to plunge into darkness between floors, while another of part of her got lost in the musty, tenebrous attic. Arrested finally where rafters met overhead, she'd become part of the house—one with the house.

Alien feelings rushed in as the house opened itself to her, revealing itself to her, its surprisingly animate hopes, needs, desires, and fears. Allison knew how it felt to be violated, to be raped. The indignity of having one's outer shell torn open and its wire-bowels exposed. Allison clenched her fist, lashing out in adopted anger.

She settled. *The feeling of wood grain.*

Changeless, timeless.

And she knew how it felt to be more than a century old, to watch humans—so fragile, so transitory—living within these walls, and Allison caught a brief flash of disdain at such puny mortality and futile human hopes. She thrashed on the bed.

As Allison hovered in this dream state she understood the house, as a living entity—not the belligerent, malignant thing of neighborhood myth—but something welcoming, loving, and warm. The house was pleased to have her home.

Allison sighed, rolling over on her side to stroke the wall, before she descended deeper into the empty space of the cellar and then pierced the unyielding concrete below the house.

The smell of earth, like a freshly opened grave, and Allison started to writhe upon the bed.

". . . mommymommymommyMOMMEEEE!"

Jason's quavering screech pierced the fog of pink insulation, and Allison was jolted from sleep.

". . . mommymommymommyMOMMEEEE!"

She slid over to Jason where he slept beside her on the bed.

"Honey." She shook him softly.

Jason threw himself into her arms, sobbing. "The monster's loose. The monster's loose in the house."

Allison lifted him on to her lap and cradled him.

"Shush-sh. There's no monster. It's just a bad dream. Shush."

Scott appeared at the doorway. "That old monster again."

"He's loose, mommy; the monster's loose in the house." Agitated, Jason beat at her shoulders. She had to catch his little hands and hold them tight.

"Come on, trooper." Scott scooped Jason from her lap. "I'll show you there's no monster loose in the house." He flicked on the light. "No monster here."

They moved over to the closet. Scott swung the door open with a dramatic flair. "No monster in here."

He took the child across to his own room, grabbed the He-man light saber from a stack of toys, and stabbed at the air.

"Onward, young man, we're going to rid yon castle of the dread beast." Jason looked unconvinced as Scott charged out of the room with the toddler bouncing on his hip.

Allison followed Scott's voice as father and son made their way through the house. Scott's pronounced "No monsters here" accompanied the opening and closing of doors.

The bathroom door; the door to Adam's room. The rhythmic thumping as Scott beat under the bed for monsters. The linen closet. Down the creaking stairs until they reached the distant kitchen. Scott thudded through the pantry, the cupboards, and—her forehead creased in concentration—the drawers!

Most of the time, Jason would be satisfied after Scott had opened the first door. Other times, though, he wouldn't be satisfied until they revealed every room, every closet, every nook, cranny, and hidey-hole. It all depended on the intensity of the dream. This one must have been bad.

Allison supposed all children had bad dreams, some of them recurring. She saw no reason for alarm. At that age, all dark corners held danger. All shadows were potential demons. For one so young, the smallest shadow became a yawning chasm where something evil lurked, and for Jason, the demon was an unknown, unnamed monster.

Adults weren't all that different. Only usually life's evils had names. Taxes, death . . . money.

The monster is loose in the house.

This was the first time the monster had ever gotten loose. Usually it resided in the closet or under the bed, content to stay put.

"See, Jason, no monsters." Scott carried Jason back into the bedroom.

Eyes round and a little fist tucked in his mouth, Jason looked doubtful, as if his father might have slipped one little beastie past him somehow.

"All secure?" she asked. She took Jason from Scott's arms.

"Nary a monster, a goblin, or even a hobgoblin anywhere within this domicile." Scott bowed with a flourish, the flat of the plastic sword against his forehead.

"You see all's safe." Turning from Jason to Scott, Allison said, "I'll sit with him a while and see if he can get some more sleep."

"I'll try and get some work done if you don't mind, madame." Scott walked over to kiss her on the cheek. "Jason, you protect your momma, okay?"

Wide eyed, Jason only stared. Allison pressed his head against her breast and crooned a lullaby. The small body's trembling ceased, and she felt the tense muscles along his back and neck begin to relax.

She scanned the room. Bright and open, there were few places for a monster to hide.

With a quivering yawn Jason's tight muscles loosed a bit more, and he molded himself to her body. She switched off the light and leaned back.

Every shadow leapt back to life, but Jason, with his nose nestled into the nape of her neck, didn't notice. Somewhere down below her Scott started to swear. She heard the heavy clump of his footsteps on the stairs, and he appeared at the door.

After a quick glance at the clock he scratched his head.

"Well, I'll be damned."

"What?" she asked.

"Every single clock in the house has stopped," he replied.

A swift check over his shoulder confirmed that the neighborhood children planned to keep their distance. They huddled in a group, eyeing him suspiciously.

The old witch-lady across the street withdrew into her house, and the cat scrambled from her arms, darting out the front door.

Extending a hand Adam called to it. "Here kitty, kitty, kitty."

With a flick of its tale and feline snoot in the air, it turned its back to him and stalked away.

"Stupid cat," Adam glowered.

Then he, too, turned, heading for the backyard, past the clinging fecal odor surrounding the septic tank, past the swing set and the tetherball pole into the stand of trees beyond.

The boughs formed a lacy canopy above him. Sun filtered through the branches and thick foliage, bathing everything in a guipure of yellow-green light. The interstitial shade fell in delicate patterns across the dying underbrush of gilt filigree.

The trees seemed to hold the late September heat, and Adam shed his jacket. The wind rose, and the golden patterns moved, alternating dark, light, dark, light. Somewhere behind him the children played with noisy high spirits. Their joyful shouts rose and fell in the same rhythm as the shadows. Adam bent over to pick up a stick, pretending not to notice their exuberance. Although he would have liked to join them, he doubted he would have been made welcome since his fight with their leader. Shoulders drawn up to his ears to block the sound, Adam hunkered down to draw a shaky figure of a cat on a bare patch of earth. He leaned back to examine his work and decided he didn't like it. He drew an X over the figure.

A soft rustle.

Adam reared up, using the stick like a cane. Its sharp point sank into the moist dirt, driven through center of the X and through the cat's heart.

Whoosh. The barest whisper of movement.

Adam wheeled around to confront a little girl with large, sad eyes and golden hair. She seemed somehow familiar, but he couldn't connect her face with a name or place. He *hadn't* seen her playing with the other children in the neighborhood. Nor had he noticed her in the schoolyard.

Sizing her up as a potential playmate, Adam turned away to yank the stick from the damp soil.

As far as Adam was concerned girls were dumb. Besides, she was probably three years older than himself.

"Go away," he said with a dismissive shrug and stabbed savagely at the earthen heart of the sketched figure.

Around him the woods darkened. The golden light faded and the shadows emerged. Each leaf, twig, and bough was etched in black fretwork along the ground.

With a hard gulp he looked back; the girl was gone. Adam shivered and went to grab the windbreaker he had discarded earlier.

For a moment he contemplated the place where she had stood. Something about the spot was mildly disturbing, but he didn't know what. He sauntered over to examine it more closely, then looked back from where he came.

The weeds, where he once stood, were crushed and his footprints deeply impressed into the dirt. Here, though, there was nothing, no dent, no bent twig to mark her fleeting passage.

Something hissed in his ears. Static.

His eyes fell on a book of matches, and he dropped to his

knees to pull them from the undergrowth. Then Adam rose and took a few halting paces backwards to stare at the proof of his passage, next to the blank spot where the girl's prints should have been.

The hiss turned to a roar, and the green-gold light faded, the sun hidden behind a cloud. Pocketing the matchbook, he fled from the stand of trees toward the house.

11

With a faked growl Scott chased the squealing boys up to their rooms. Allison scowled to herself. Many of their antics and their good humor seemed feigned. During the day the children had remained conspicuously out from under Scott's feet, and once, when Scott had raised his voice in jest, Jason cringed like a kicked puppy.

Her hospital stay must have been more of a strain than she had realized. Normally Scott's roared instructions were met with childlike complaisance, but today both children moved as though dancing on eggshells, trying to anticipate his commands before they were voiced.

A few minutes later, Scott returned. He bent over and kissed her cheek before he settled on the couch. "I've missed you." He ogled her. "It's good to have you home. I don't like being deprived of my favorite bed warmer."

She scooted over a few inches, closing the gap between them, and ran playful fingers through his hair.

"It hasn't been easy for you, has it?" she said.

"What do you mean?"

"Oh, the move, the boys, my being put in the hospital."

"No, I confess it hasn't. I've been a real bear lately, and I'm afraid I took it out on the boys more than I realized," Scott said.

"They'll live. Kids are resilient." She snuggled into the warmth of his side. "Don't worry, love, I'm home now, and it'll take an earthquake to dislodge me."

Scott put his arms around her and gave her a hug.

"I'm proud of you," Allison said. "You have done wonders with this place. I'd hardly recognize it as the same house. You were right."

"Right? Right about what?"

"All this place needed was a good coat of paint and a happy family to bring it to life."

His expression clouded, and he tugged nervously at his lower lip.

Allison peered anxiously into his face. "You don't agree?"

"I didn't say that, did I? No, I'm glad you like it. I was hoping you would like what we'd done to fix it up." He snorted. "Took long enough for you to see it."

"Well, I approve of everything—the remodeling, the work you've done, the unpacking, and the house." She turned and nuzzled his neck. "Especially the house. I've never felt so welcomed, so at home."

Snapping his fingers Scott stood up and marched out of the room. Allison sniffed, slightly miffed.

When he returned he was juggling four boxes, holding them by the open folds. He grinned at her sheepishly. "Speaking of which, I couldn't find homes for these things."

After kneeling on the ground and placing the boxes at her feet, Scott held them open so she could peer inside. "The other stuff was easy. Books go on bookshelves. Kitchen items go in the kitchen. The kids' clothes and toys go in their respective bedrooms. But these?" He waved a hand over all four boxes.

The junk boxes. They contained a motley assortment of mismatched shoes, nails, and thumbtacks; rubber bands, two different kinds of twine, and clipped pieces of speaker wire all tied in a single Gordian knot. Another consisted of collected mementos, a shoe box full of old letters, some from him and some from beaux who predated Scott. Old scrapbooks and both Adam's and Jason's first baby shoes which they always said they were going to get bronzed one of these days. Wedding pictures, baby pictures, slides—even though they had no slide projector. And lots of loose papers.

"Ah," she said, "the unmatched shoes we throw, unless you happened to stumble across the mate. Did you?" She looked up hopefully.

He shook his head no.

"Toss it, then. And the rest?" Allison dug around in the empty box for a while and extracted a scissors, a screwdriver, and a hammer from one to put them into another with the many screws, nuts, and bolts.

"Do you have an empty drawer in the kitchen? Please tell me you have an empty drawer in the kitchen."

"We have a couple of them," Scott said.

"Great. The box with the papers goes in one. It"—she peeked into the box—"should all fit. And the one with the tools you can dump in the second free drawer."

"Is any of this junk of any use?" he said as he picked up the boxes.

Allison shrugged. "Sometimes. It's handy to have a few tools close by, and the papers. Heavens, I don't know. It's doubtful. They're old telephone numbers which we never put in the book, research clips for stories that you cut but never filed, miscellaneous recipes that I use every once in a while. Coupons. Some of it's useful; some of it's not. If you feel energetic, you can sort through it.

"Uh, no thanks." Scott took the two boxes into the kitchen.

A few thuds, a clatter, and one 'ouch' later, he returned. Allison had the scrapbooks and pictures spread out before her.

"These, I don't know. I used to keep them in the closet. It was the only place we had room."

Scott brightened. "That's great. That's just where I put it. I'll put it back."

Allison scowled at him with mock severity. "It seems in a place this size we can find a better place than that." Picking up a wedding picture and showing it to him, Allison smiled. "I'd like to get a frame for this."

Somewhere underneath the house, something moved. Scott could feel it through the soles of his shoes. A slight vibration, that grew and grew into a rumble, and Scott thought of an old man grumbling in protest.

His gaze dropped to the floor, and it stopped. Bemused he turned to Allison, but she, still looking at the photograph on her lap, hadn't seemed to notice.

"What space," she asked, "like shelf space or cupboard space, either up here or down in the basement, haven't you used?"

Scott took a deep breath, then held it before exhaling loudly and shaking his head from side to side. "I don't know. I can't think of any."

"Did you put anything besides the china into that lovely built-in china hutch in the dining room?"

"China hutch?"

"Yes, the china hutch. You know, that thing we put china in."

Screwing up one side of his face, Scott winced. "I forgot about the china hutch completely. The china is in the kitchen."

Allison nodded. "As good a place as any for it now, as long as it fits. How about the drawers?" She noticed his bemused expression and added: "In the china hutch, I mean. Did you use those?"

Again Scott shook his head no.

"Voilà! We can use the drawers to store our keepsakes until they become so full of fancy linen that they"—she indicated the photos—"have to be moved."

"Great! I'll be right back." Scott disappeared into the dining room.

When he reappeared she asked: "What else?"

"Just that." Scott pointed to the box of bric-a-brac and whatchamadoodles.

"Those I'll put away myself after I've got more of the feel of the place. Well, good, you managed so well without me I was beginning to think I wasn't needed anymore."

Scott, who had bent over to slide the box to one side, swung on her fiercely. "Don't you believe it. Don't you believe it, ever!"

"That's nice to hear." Looking out of sleep-shrouded eyes, Allison stretched and yawned. "God, I'm sleepy. I shouldn't be; all I did this afternoon was rest."

"Well, you're not supposed to tire yourself. Let me go get your hot wheels." He pointed to the wheelchair in the corner.

Allison groaned. "It's only nine o'clock."

"You sound like Jason. Don't fuss." Scott wagged a finger at her. "I may have to spank you."

"Sounds kinky," Allison commented with a sigh, "but I don't think I'm up for it."

"I know, so I have every intention of making sure you rest. Just like the doctor ordered. Then maybe you will be ready for it."

"Tyrant!"

"I'm just doing what's good for you," Scott said.

"Like spinach?"

"Like spinach."

"Yuck!"

Scott chuckled as he picked her up from the couch and placed her on the chair.

The study blazed with light, and Scott walked around his desk to lower himself into the chair. With Allison and the boys in bed, maybe he'd be able to get some work done. He was behind schedule. The idea for his book, once fresh, seemed vague, muddy. He switched on the computer and propped his chin on his hand to stare at the screen.

Allison was happy with the house, but now Scott wondered, unsure if he had made the right move. Funny how things developed. Scott had decided over a year ago that the house would make a good backdrop for his next novel, but since he was in the middle of another book he'd simply filed the idea for later use.

When the time came, he dusted the old idea off, and the minute he laid eyes on the house, he had been enthralled. Something about it got to him. He felt a kinship with the house. It seemed to represent the darkness he carried inside himself. The house had a presence. It was obvious that few dared trespass on the property. No neighborhood child dared to throw an idle stone through its windows. No litter accumulated in the garage, or out back, an area which would have made a perfect dumping ground or hiding place for neighborhood adolescents who wanted to get away from prying parental eyes for a quick pet, cigarette, an indiscreet drink, joint, or whatever the current teenage craze was now.

About that same time Allison found out she was pregnant, Scott went to interview the owner, a Mr. Sam Holloway, and made an offer. Things just fell into place. After the foreign rights sale, the sale of the movie option, and the next book contract, suddenly they could afford a home. And they needed to move. No way could five of them fit into their little Blue Island apartment.

Scott felt no superstitious dread about the house or its history. After all, he wrote about that kind of thing, and he had discovered both in living and in writing that the worst horrors were found in the human imagination. And fleeting images rose to mind—Allison collapsing on the porch; the nightmare ride to the hospital; pool balls scattered around the basement floor; smoke pouring from a pan; the boys bickering; and the hard eyes of the teacher as she explained Adam's alleged transgression.

Scott grunted and the computer beeped. Hunching his shoulders, he peered at it.

Del file? the prompt asked.

No. He replied, trying to remember when he had given that command.

The computer whirred. *File deleted.*

"No!" Scott bellowed. His fingers tapped out D-I-R, and the directory appeared on the screen. Nothing appeared to be missing. Neither were there any new documents.

The dream may have come true, but now that he was here he couldn't seem to write. Indirectly, his work had brought him to this house, and once here, his work had ground to a creaking halt. During his few abortive attempts in the last week he'd been able to do little more than review his data file and his outline.

The computer directory glowered at him, and Scott realized that to truly get into the swing of things, he'd better start from scratch. He pulled his old file from the drawer.

Then as if to emphasize his quandary, Scott suddenly recalled the load of laundry he had put into the wash earlier that day. It didn't look as though he was going to get much writing done tonight either. Dirty laundry beckoned. Since they moved, Jason seemed to have lost all bladder and bowel control, just when they thought he had mastered it. His constantly soiled pants had nearly doubled Scott's work-load.

Scott picked up a pen, jotted down a few notes about where best to start, and then headed for the basement. The stench hit him as soon as he stepped through the door. Covering his nose and mouth with his hand, Scott peered incredulously into the fluorescent-lit game room. He loped down the stairs to poke into corners and look behind furniture for the malodorous source. It smelled like something had crawled into the basement and died. He crunched a stray G.I. Joe action figure underfoot and cursed before peeling the partially flattened toy from his shoe.

Engrossed with air currents and probability factors, Scott moved over to pull the laundry from the washer. An odor that powerful should have permeated the door into the kitchen, not simply stopped here. Or it should have blasted him when he opened the door and not waited for him to walk through some invisible barrier.

Snapping his arm back to his chest, Scott squinted into the cylindrical compartment. He'd found the source of the smell. He jumped away from the machine, dropping the lid shut with a clang.

"Christ." Scott couldn't remember exactly what he had stuck in the dryer before they left to pick up Allison from the hospital, but it hadn't been brown.

With a hard gulp he ran for the small half bath.

The stench was worse here. His stomach lurched. Scott slammed the toilet seat up to stare in shock at its contents. The stool, too, was full, almost to overflowing, with sewage. The septic tank had backed up.

Scott lost it, turning to retch his dinner, compliments of Colonel Sanders, into the sink.

Newspaper clippings littered his desk; a open file folder held a disarrayed pile of notes. Scott shifted in his seat, becoming suddenly aware of his surroundings.

The silence had awakened him.

Silence? Awakened? His thoughts jumbled, bouncing against each other. But he hadn't slept! His being unable to sleep is what had brought him down here in the first place to stare myopically at scribbled notes.

Glancing down, Scott could see that he had sat as he had sat before—some, he looked at the clock, thirty or forty minutes ago. His pupils dilated with shock. He moved and his joints cracked with a loud pop.

His eyes were wide open, and his head ached. Yet, like before, time was lost. How many minutes did he lose each day? The time gone never to be retrieved from the never-never land to which it had escaped.

Not noticeable at first, but then little by little the loss crept up on him. Scott would look up and discover that several minutes had passed. Only a few, at first, then more and more. And nothing, no memory of what he had done in the intervening time.

Always the same. Like awakening from an unremembered dream. Time gone, and its loss unaccounted for. The lost time nagged at him. If one counted the minutes, Scott supposed it wasn't all that much; but any loss was disconcerting.

What was wrong with him? What the hell was going on? All these questions flitted through his mind in an instant as the late hour registered. Half the night was gone.

Scott blinked and peered from the papers to the computer screen as if he could divine the answer in the nether world beyond the C-prompt. His memory as blank and as empty as the computer screen was now.

With as little writing as he'd been able to accomplish, Scott couldn't even comfort himself that he had gotten involved in the typical mental chase searching for just the right word or phrase because his work wasn't going well.

Groaning, he lowered his head into his hands. His headaches had been getting worse lately. Scott had always been prone to them, but recently it seemed he always had one. Sometimes severe. Sometimes not so severe just an annoying pressure behind the eyes. Tonight a fist clenched around his skull and the world went black again.

A big growling truck marked, R-O-T-O-R-O-O-T-E-R, pulled into the drive in the morning. Impressed, Adam had gone out to watch. The man had seemed glad of the company. He talked a lot, telling Adam that his dad must be rich. Being a Sunday and all, this job was going to cost a "pretty penny." It didn't sound like much money to Adam.

With a huge hose, the man raised an even bigger stink that drove Adam inside the house until the job was done. Much to Adam's surprise, Scott didn't give the man a bright, shiny new penny, but rather a check. Adam didn't know exactly what a septic system was, but it must be pretty nasty. The smell still hovered over the backyard despite the mild weather, nauseating and oppressive.

Adam wandered around the side of the house, pausing to inspect the work. Turning to look back at the stand of trees, Adam caught a faint shimmer of gold. He followed it, his fingers fondling the book of matches in his pocket.

Once out of sight of the house, Adam gathered loose twigs and leaves. Maybe if he built a big enough fire, the little girl would come out and play.

12

Space ships swooped against Scott's defensive position. He hit the arrow keys to dodge the bright yellow rays that threatened to blow him out of space. Each movement was marked by a computerized clack. Then he hit the space bar, and the alien ship disintegrated with a mechanical crackle.

Scott glanced guiltily toward the foyer, praying the kids wouldn't hear. The sound of the games always sent them pell-mell into the study to climb on Scott's lap so they could "help Daddy." Scott wasn't in the mood to share his solitary activity.

A little voice in the back of his brain told him he should be working. His deadline hung over him like the sword of Damocles. But the still louder thud of a headache drowned out conscience's voice.

That morning, he had awakened with a headache that felt for all the world like a hangover, although he'd had nothing to drink the night before. Scott hit the space bar—hard. The ray missed the enemy saucer, and Scott's ship exploded with a sizzle of dazzling colors.

Wearing his favorite Cubs cap, carrying a plastic baseball

bat, Jason burst from the kitchen and flew through the living room into the foyer. "Fry ball!" he squealed, skidding on his bottom along the floor.

After he slid to a halt Jason sat, his back rigid. His poised body canted a little to the right, as if he were listening to a whispered conversation from that direction. His eyes focused, not on the distant television nor on the bat that lay forgotten on his lap, but on a specific point only twelve inches away.

"Okay," the child said. Sticking his well-padded rump into the air and then pushing himself off the floor, Jason got up and toddled into the living room. Shouts came from the tube. The Care Bears battled with a dragon, a wizard, warlock, or some other baddie, but Jason's attention remained fixed elsewhere.

A cold finger ran down Scott's spine.

Near the door he flopped back to the floor, spread-legged. An Old Maid deck filled the gap between his legs. Jason had his own special version of Old Maid, which consisted of each participant grabbing cards from the heap and the first to extract the Old Maid won.

Perfect for Jason's short attention span, but it required two players. The blond head bent, tongue stuck out of the corner of his mouth, he mixed up the cards between his splayed legs.

Then he lifted his head and spoke to a space directly in front of him: "Okay, your turn!"

"Jason?"

"Yeth?"

"Who are you playing with?"

"William."

"William who?"

Jason stared straight across from him, as though questioning. "I don't know."

"Could you and, uh, William go play someplace else? Daddy's trying to work."

With a quick flick of his eyes toward his imaginary companion, Jason clumsily stood up, brushed his bottom with two-year-old-dignity, and tottered off.

Scott's gaze returned to the computer, reminded again that the days weren't the only things that would be growing short. His deadline seemed to loom just over the horizon. He switched from the games directory to the word-processing program.

"Adam! Mine!" Jason yowled.

"No, it's not, it's mine!"

"Not again," Scott muttered. He couldn't understand it. The boys had had their share of squabbles in the past, but now all they seemed to do was fight.

Taking a deep breath, Scott waited, hoping that Allison would intercede from her eyrie in the master bedroom.

Instead, Jason's voice took on a more strident note. "ADA-YAM!"

"Okay, you two, behave," Scott shouted through the study doors.

"Jason's got my coloring book, my alphabet book!" Adam's head popped into the study.

"Jason give the book back to Adam. You've got coloring books of your own."

The toddler wandered into the study, trailing the book behind him. He walked around the desk and stared up at Scott with blue-eyed innocence.

"Mine," he insisted.

"Let me see," Scott leafed through the pages and immediately recognized the book as Adam's. Jason's artistic abilities consisted mainly of keeping the crayon marks within the page, while Adam had, with five-going-on-six-year-old wisdom, mastered coloring within the lines.

"Sorry, old fella, this one's Adam's." Scott passed the book to Adam and Jason let out a wail.

"Enough!" Scott roared.

Jason teetered two steps backward.

"Jason, you go watch TV, and I don't want to hear another peep out of either of you until it's time for dinner."

The shortening day rushed into premature dusk as though someone had splashed indigo ink across the sky. Adam looked up from where he sat, bent over a book. Scott glanced down at the page: A is for Apple. Adam was coloring the outlined apple blue.

"Apples are red, or green, or yellow, not blue," Scott informed Adam.

Ching, ching, chink, thunk! Jason pounded on his toy piano.

"Can't you bang on that thing elsewhere?" Scott snapped irritably. "I didn't know that cooking could be such a pain in the neck," Scott grumbled into the cupboard. "I'm tired of cooking. I damn near killed myself today."

His eyes flicked to the still boxed microwave next to the pantry door, a replacement for the one that had blown a fuse, or something, in a spectacular pyrotechnic display this afternoon.

"Mealtime has been something of an event around here," Allison mused. "How about stew? We've got a big can on the top shelf."

"Canned stew? Always tastes like dog shit," he said.

Allison winced and shot a hurried glance at the boys.

"You can doctor it," she explained with exaggerated patience. "It doesn't take that long."

"If I've got to doctor it, why bother with canned? Why not make the real thing?"

"Are you feeling up to it?"

"No," he answered petulantly.

Grabbing a can of soup and a box of macaroni and cheese, Scott stood looking from one to the other indecisively.

"I can't believe that in all those years without me, you never learned how to cook." Allison said.

"All right, dammit, so I'm not perfect!" Scott exploded,

"I was a farmhand, fer chrissake, then a student. When I finally got to be a teacher, I figured I could afford to eat out."

Adam and Jason turned up from their play to stare at their father.

"Well, we really should have a salad," Allison suggested. "All you have to do for salad is a little chopping. That's simple. Besides, if we don't use it soon, all that stuff will spoil."

Fishing through the refrigerator, Scott discovered a suspicious-looking green lump with limp, browned leaves. The head of lettuce. The celery drooped sadly in his hand as he lifted it from the shelf. The tomatoes were still good, and he was pretty sure he could salvage enough for a decent salad.

He trooped over to the sink, dumping the vegetables into it. Spying the new food processor, he snapped his fingers. "Aha, I know what I'll do. I'll use the food processor."

"Uh, are you sure you want to do that?" Allison glanced up from her magazine.

"Why not?"

Allison shrugged, skeptical.

Scott peeled the wilting leaves from the lettuce and washed the carrots and tomatoes. Then he piled the vegetables next to the food processor, pausing to dig the instruction manual from the shelf with the cookbooks. He inspected the many blades, picked one, and locked the mechanism into place.

The processor grinned at him, the blade forming an evil half smile. Evidently it, too, had heard of his cooking skills.

The tomatoes followed the lettuce into the clear plastic gullet. Scott studied the various speeds and punched the button marked slice, and the processor sprang to life with a vicious growl. He stuffed two limp celery stalks down its throat, and a carrot.

The processor began to clatter and shake, skipping along the countertop. Green-orange liquid spewed from the top, splattering vomit-colored splotches against the wall. The processor snarled for another minute and then died. Ozone drifted up from the jittering mechanism, followed by the unmistakable smell of burning rubber. Scott grabbed the cord and yelled as molten black insulation stuck to his hand.

The processor continued its drunken waddle along the countertop, and Allison jumped from the wheelchair. It rolled back, hitting the wall. Orange and green slop spilled over the sides of the processor, oozing onto the floor.

Waving her back, Scott wrapped his unburned hand in a towel and yanked the plug from the wallplate. The room fell silent. Scott examined his hand for bits of insulation. A large red weal was beginning to form.

Cautiously, Scott looked inside the chamber, and the blade grinned back at him, bits of carrots coated in green slime clung to its teeth.

"Can I help?" Allison asked. He ignored her.

With barely controlled movements Scott cleaned the counter and the wall before pulling a few more towels from the roll to wipe the mess from the floor.

He poured the contents into the garbage disposal and dropped the plastic container in the sink.

"Well, that was exciting. What should I do for an encore?" Scott quipped.

"How about pizza for dinner?"

Allison settled back into the wheelchair, pulled her magazine onto her lap, and began to peruse the knitting patterns, trying to look unconcerned. "Pizza sounds fine."

Grumbling under his breath, Scott extracted a coupon from under a magnet where it kept company with menus from Colonel Sanders, Domino's, Pizza Hut, and the local Chinese. He walked over to the telephone and lifted the receiver.

Static sizzled in his ear followed by the eldritch hollow-sounding crackle one might get with a bad connection. An electronic buzz like the steady drone of somnolent summer bees. A slight rapping, as subtle as that of a moth batting against a screen, was replaced by a chattering clatter. The crackle became a roaring hiss. The hiss, a banshee wail. His ears pricked because underneath the cacophony, he detected a murmuring voice, and Scott struggled to pick out the words.

There was the creak of Allison's wheelchair as she advanced toward him slowly, but Scott's ear was riveted to the receiver. Someone was on the other end of the line. He could swear he heard breathing.

A squeak. A soft screech. Squawks. A raucous cackle, like the twittering of a Shakespearean witch. Hoots. Whistles. Howls. A snarl of anger which dissolved into a squeal of pain. Screaming. Many throats trilling in torment. One voice rose above the rest, that of a child, a trembling falsetto which cracked and broke, descending into sobs.

Scott swallowed and the line went dead, only to be followed by the mechanical clicks of a connection. Pulling the receiver away from his ear, he stared at Allison and grimaced. "Phone's out. I'll go pick something up."

Three pairs of eyes followed him as Scott slammed out the back door.

"A lotta things have broke." Adam turned to his mother. Her expression was blank; her mouth dropped open. Her hand stroked the wall absently, as if she were trying to give or receive comfort from the house.

Plink. Plink. Plunk. Jason pounded on his tiny piano, and with a scowl Adam wandered from the room.

After a dinner of cold, soggy pizza Scott carried the gaily wrapped Jason up to his bedroom, wondering if tonight the child would manage to sleep in his own room. The afghan-cocooned body was only a light weight against his chest, and the child's breath that of sweet slumber.

With a graze of his father's lips against a downy cheek Jason awoke and pointed at the window seat. "Spiderlady."

Scott glanced at the corner, half expecting to see some ghostly apparition materialize there. Nothing.

Shuddering, Scott turned back to Jason, playing with the toddler for a while before insisting Jason lay down to sleep.

Back in the living room he told Allison about Jason's newest friend. The boy's world, it seemed, was cluttered with unseen people.

"Spiderlady. That doesn't sound like the kind of friendship that you cultivate," Scott mused. "And why William, I wonder. Why that name of all names?" The name made him shiver. He lowered himself onto the vacated couch and stared down at the discarded Old Maid deck upon the floor.

"William was my father's name," Allison suggested.

"Yes, but Jason wouldn't know that. Your father's been dead all these years. Long before Jason was born, and the name hasn't come up."

"I don't know what you're talking about. Of course, we've talked about him. We must've talked about my father sometime and Jason probably heard us talking."

"Of Grandpa Woititz, maybe, or we may have referred to him as your father, but not as William."

"Who knows," Allison shrugged. "After my mother's death, we had all those papers to work through. The name could have come up then."

Scott looked at a place above her head, thinking of the then six-month old Jason. "Perhaps, but he was so young . . ."

13

*W*ith form, yet formless; changeless, but ever-changing, it pulsed and throbbed. Bubbling to the surface of its subterranean tomb, the entity sent fluid filaments seeping through the concrete foundation and from the concrete into the wooden studs of the home. Soon portions of its evil had invaded every molecule, every atom of the Victorian home. From the ceiling, the walls, the molding, it observed the occupants.

The youngest child tossed fretfully in the bedroom while the rest of the family sat in the living room watching television. It reached out—poking, prodding, and probing. The woman's jaw loosened, her eyes dull and glazed. The older boy squirmed uncomfortably on the floor. He reached into his pocket, seeking and finding a matchbook. His fingers curled around it tightly. The man's head drooped slightly, and when he looked up again, it was through fire-streaked eyes.

Searching for individual weaknesses, it delved through each individual's subconscious to match the victims to their vehicles of destruction which stood ready in the kitchen, the foyer, the hall.

In the upstair hallway, Sara Graves and her sister, Shelley, appeared. Twin apparitions, sometimes whole, sometimes *not. Shelley began to bubble, the skin charred and blackened. The ghostly Sara, meanwhile, went through a similar transformation. Her skull folded in on itself, revealing torn muscle, tendon, and bone.*

Tommy Erwin clutched the rope which held him forever suspended in the foyer. The decaying flesh of his fingers clung to the rough hemp as he pulled himself hand over hand to the landing above. The phantom William helped Erwin climb over the railing, his lips twisted in a wicked grin.

Tentatively, the presence stretched—testing its strength. In the kitchen, Elliot Graves slipped in spectral blood while Jane sat up in the foyer to watch Erwin's sloughing progress with apathetic eyes.

Each moved to pre-set positions, as though by command, and waited. Shelley hovered between Adam and Scott; William fluttered next to Allison. Elliot floated above Scott, sinking slowly, so that for an instant the two merged. Sara drifted through the door to Jason's room.

The presence withdrew. Bodiless, it traveled around and through the wall, into the pink fiberglass insulation. Dispersing itself, it blended into the chalky sheetrock. It telegraphed through the copper wires faster than electrical power back to its prison of darkness, causing no interruption in service unless it chose . . .

The television picture turned to snow. The living room lights flickered. Adam and Allison looked up from the television.

"I'll go check the fuse box," Scott said.

The TV cleared, and the lights flared briefly before they settled to a nice, steady glow.

Scott went into the kitchen and rummaged through a drawer until he found the flashlight. Carrying it, he returned to the living room.

"Seems okay now," he said, and he strode to the window to see how the rest of the neighborhood fared.

Outside all was dark. Shadows slunk over the ground until light shattered the darkness and power returned.

"Seems like the entire street is having problems," Scott said. "Maybe I should call the power company."

Jason listened to his parents' voices. He rolled over on his side and glared at Mickey Mouse. He just hated to be put to bed early. Adam was downstairs now, looking important over his Big Chief pad and his book, which contained magical pictures of the letters of the alphabet. Jason reviewed the pictures in his mind. An "A" and a bright, shiny red apple.

Adam got up to stay late. Adam was big. Adam was in school.

Envy filled him. A child's voice whispered in his ear, and Jason bent his head to listen.

Jason wanted a book like Adam's. Jason wanted to go to school. Jason wanted to stay up late, but no, he was little, and he had to go to bed before everybody else. Peevish, Jason dug down deeper into his bed.

A slight creak brought him from his sulk. Adam's voice was raised in querulous protest.

"But Dad, my homework . . ." The voice trailed off.

"You've been staring at that book for two hours. You already know the entire alphabet. You just want to stay up and watch more TV."

Their voices got louder as they moved up the stairs. Their footsteps passed his door, Adam still arguing weakly. Jason slid back down into his bed to listen as his brother and father discussed Adam's impressions of school.

"Good night, son," his father said, and a few quick steps brought him to Jason's door.

Jason scrunched his eyes up tight as his father walked to stand over his bed.

"Still awake, I see."

Jason opened his eyes. How did his father know, the boy wondered.

Scott mussed his hair and left the room. Jason relaxed; Daddy hadn't yelled at him for not being asleep.

Then he felt it. Someone, or something, was in the room with him. It began as a crawly sensation on his skin, and Jason was sure he could hear a rasping breath, a steady hiss.

The sound reminded Jason of a movie he had seen once where some man had fallen into a room full of snakes. Snakes crawled and slithered over everything. They coiled on a sand-covered floor, and they fell from above. Snakes. That's what this sounded like: snakes sliding over sand—like in the movie—and the flesh on his arms crept. The noise grew louder. Whistling hollowly to drown it out, Jason searched the hovering shadows the small night-light didn't reach. Before his gaze had completed the circuit of the room he knew he wouldn't find anything except . . .

The closet door, once closed, had opened slightly. *Just like before.* If he waited long enough, there would be glowing monster eyes. Jason pulled his blanket up so only his nose and light blond hair were in view and tried to find a word to describe the way it felt.

Stubby fingers pulled the blanket down, and he peeked at the closet.

Nothing.

Bad. He flipped through words that, with his limited vocabulary, could explain the feeling.

Creepy, naughty, nasty, wrong. *Bad.* Badder than bad. Baddest. Evil. He went through this mental list.

Dead. Jason turned this word over in his mind cautiously like one would turn over a stone to discover squirming insects. The reality of death was beyond his comprehension. For Jason it meant gone. Like Granny was gone. Jason remembered his mother sitting in the living room crying after his grandmother's death. And anything that could make Mommy cry had to be bad, the baddest, worstest thing in the whole world.

Dead. Yes, that seemed to fit. Jason ignored the closet and turned to the comfort of Goofy's benevolently idiotic image upon the wall.

Jason gasped. Goofy's pee pee was out and hard, like Jason's got when he had to GO, and Goofy fondled himself.

Naughty!

Jason slapped Goofy's paper nose, and he crawled down from his place on the wall, hissing, and ran gibbering into the closet.

A cat's paw of fear touched the nape of his neck and the base of his spine simultaneously. Horrified, Jason looked away from the wall. Stifling a cry, Jason climbed over the baby rails of his bed and scuttled toward the hall door.

Something rustled behind him, and Jason halted midstep.

The monster's loose in the house!

His hands still outstretched, he turned to see the spiderlady curled up in the window box.

His shoulders were hunched up around his ears, and his fists bunched up as he stood ready to flee. The spiderlady watched him with rheumy eyes. Jason tilted his head to peer at the twisted figure in the window seat.

The toddler took a cautious step forward. The woman hovered an inch or two above the cushion, as though her limbs were too contorted to sit with any comfort.

He took another step, and another, advancing slowly. The spiderlady didn't move, except to drift slightly higher, then lower above the seat.

Jason stopped, eyeing her curiously, but afraid to get any closer. Would she leap down on him and devour him now that she had drawn him into her web?

Their eyes met. A large tear rolled down the runneled cheek and dropped to the cushion below her floating form. Amazed, Jason followed the course of the tear and watched the dark stain with fascination as the droplet was absorbed into the coarsely woven cloth.

The spiderlady smiled, her lip curling up over toothless gums. Jason reach tentatively toward her.

Her image began to waver, and she looked at him sadly. Jason watched as she faded in and out of vision, and a rattling began in the closet.

As the noise grew louder, she grew dim, weaker. Jason's hand fell and he touched the wet spot on the cushion, left by a single tear.

The closet door flew open, flung by such force that it banged against the wall.

The spiderlady vanished. Jason scurried from the room.

Loving hands stroked her legs. Allison twisted sensuously under their feather-light touch. Insistent fingers traced lacy patterns along the inside of her thighs. Languorously, Allison opened her eyes to stare through the heavy veil of her lashes at . . . *the little boy from the hospital.* Repulsed, she tried to push away from him, but something held her fast.

She drifted in a world of soft, pink insulation. The feeling of wood grain. The chalky dust of the sheetrock tickled her nose and she wanted to sneeze. She looked down at the boy again, feeling no fear this time. He smirked at her; his probing fingers crept up her thigh to the dark thatch of hair between her legs.

Out of the corner of her eye, she saw a girl, oddly familiar, materialize to fiddle with the drawstrings of Scott's pajamas. Young, too young, her breasts as yet unformed.

The impression of infinite space, and she observed the two of them from all angles at once. The density of hard, compressed earth—the impression of infinite evil—and alien desire like red-hot magma erupted. The girl straddled Scott. Nubile young thighs gripped Scott's waist. Golden hair fell in her face as the girl rocked. Faster, faster, and faster! Scott moaned, and Allison was catapulted from sleep.

Bolting upright, Allison scanned the room, searching the inky corners and finding nothing. She sagged against the pillow and was again surrounded by warmth and suffused with a sense of welcome. Scott tossed and turned next to her, caught in his own dream. Allison's hand crept over the surface of the bed to the head board until it touched the wall.

The house hummed contentedly, and Allison descended again into seductive slumber.

Adam felt the comforting warmth of Jason's body, and for once didn't mind the intrusion. He floated close to the surface of sleep, his eyes half-closed. The moon's light formed a distorted square, dissected into quarters, on the floor. The branch rattled against the glass. He put his arms around his brother who squirmed deeper into Adam's embrace. He heard a gentle whispering breath next to his ear that was not Jason's.

Hisss-s-s.

Adam tensed at the familiar noise. Static. Like the TV when it was all snow or the radio between stations.

Jason writhed in his brother's grasp. Adam looked up and a large-eyed girl stared back at him. Her blond hair a beacon in the ill-lit room. Her expression was one of indefinable sadness as she watched the older boy cling to his brother.

Sorrowful blue eyes faded, becoming hollow, empty sockets. She leaned over; bleeding lips touched his ear. She spoke, and the words she said made his blood run hot and cold.

The hissing increased until it became a silibant ululation.

Quivering, Adam reached out to the wavering image, and she was gone. Vanished in shimmer of gold dust. Still nestled in his brother's arm, Jason moaned.

The static had become unbearable. *Z-Z-isss-s-s!* Adam pushed Jason out of bed.

. . . the girl Shelley floated above Scott. Golden hair blazed like a sun, forming a rippling nimbus around an innocent face. She smiled, and the face was transformed from vulnerable to predatory. Long canines dimpled her bottom lip, and she drifted closer to where Scott lay spread eagle on the bed. Her mouth opened and pink-tinged saliva fell onto Scott's exposed leg. Closer. Scott looked down at his flat torso and realized he had an erection. Lips closed over his penis, and the ceiling above turned to flames from which his parents stared . . .

A wail pierced the darkness.

Scott's eyes popped open to peer at the ceiling, disoriented. No child hovered over him and no dimly recognized parents stared from a funeral pyre. He heard a soft whimper, a few muttered words, and a squeak as weight shifted in the attic above his head.

Flinging the covers away, Scott looked down over his naked body to stare at his erection. The digital clock clicked, another number flipped over, and he deflated. Another muted whisper, and Scott got up, slipped into his pajama bottoms, and crawled to the edge of the bed. Feeling in control of himself again, Scott went to check the boys.

Jason sat in the center of the room, mewling. Eyes still fogged with sleep, Adam watched him, blearily.

"What's the matter?" Scott inquired.

"He fell," Adam stated flatly.

"Come on, fellow. I thought you were going to sleep in your own room tonight." Scott lifted Jason from the floor and carried him from Adam's room to his own. Lowering Jason to the bed, Scott sat and ran his hand through the toddler's damp hair. So far Jason had yet to spend a full night in his own room, and Scott wondered why his younger son was so resistant to staying here.

The room was cheery enough, with the full complement of Disney characters to watch over him. His eyes rested on a blank space above Jason's head. The wallpaper was designed so that the characters were irregularly but evenly spaced. Mickey and Minnie, Donald and Daisy, Pluto, Snow White and the seven dwarfs, Bambi, Flower. No one character was any more than six inches from the next, except for the glaring white spot above Jason's head.

Jason followed his father's gaze and seemed to understand his father's quizzical expression.

"Goofy," he said.

"Oh, yeah? And where did Goofy go?"

"He ran away."

Jason's simpering silenced. Adam swung his legs over the side of the bed and planted his feet on the floor.

Tap. Tap. Tap.

The bough scraped the window. Adam dug through his pockets until he found the crumpled matchbook. Only a few matches were left.

He pulled one, flattened the book against the floor using one hand to hold it in place, and struck the match against the emery. It flared briefly. His fingers, too close to the match head, were burned, the phosphorous embedded in his fingertips.

Putting his fingers in his mouth, Adam began to cry soundlessly.

Voices made too loud by alcohol droned in the background. The young couple said good-bye to the last of their guests, leaving the door unguarded. Just the opportunity Skipper had been waiting for, and the terrier darted out the door—no more than a white blur—careered across the lawn at full gallop and leapt the small border shrub, turning back to run past the neighbor's house. Fear and exhilaration powered his short, stubby little legs to another burst of speed. Somewhere behind him a voice called his name. Skipper ignored the call as he slowed to a stop to sniff a particularly tantalizing bush and urinate on a child's toy. A conqueror of the night, the dog paused intermittently to lift his leg and claim a lamppost, a fence, a carelessly discarded bicycle as his own. Moving in fits and starts up Elm Street Skipper nosed each plant, each decaying dog pile. The street widened into a large concrete circle. Skipper paused at the last house looking into the inviting expanse of open field beyond. Something flashed golden, and a shadow fell across his path, obliterating the feeble light of the moon.

Canine senses alert, Skipper did a sideways dance until he backed into the base of a huge oak. Skipper snuffled and wagged his tail. The child advanced slowly, hand extended in a gesture of welcome. The dog took a uncertain step forward. The child crouched to pet the white back. Skipper tried to wriggle away and the hand brought more pressure to bear against his back. His stomach scraped the ground. The hand seized him, and he was hoisted into the air, to hang suspended above the earth. Skipper opened his jaws to bite, and that night's dinner erupted from his stomach in a sour, curdled stream.

The large muscles of small body twisted as he snapped at . . . nothing. He thrashed, straining in a death dance and trying to reach his attacker, whom—blinded by his pain— he could no longer see. In his confusion he bit his own haunch, and his body's agony was such that he didn't notice. Instead he bit down harder. Every instinct told him to attack, to kill, or if that was not possible, to inflict some kind of pain. The coppery taste of blood filled his mouth, and his teeth sank further into flesh. Skipper had a brief moment of triumphant satisfaction before there was a loud snap and a tearing sound, and his anguish ended. With a thump Skipper landed on the ground—his back horribly awry, his jaws still locked on his haunch.

The small terrier twitched a few times. His jaws relaxed. Blood flowed from the wound, soaking into the roots of the old oak next to the house. The branches and autumn gold leaves began to tremble and shake in the windless night.

The computer hummed behind him. Unable to concentrate Scott paced agitatedly across the study, as if he were being chased by hell's demons. Reaching one end of the room, he walked around the rocker to head back in the opposite direction. Goofy, for Chrissakes. Where had the wallpaper figure gone?

An agonized yelp penetrated from the outdoors, the anguished cry cut prematurely short. His step faltered and Scott halted before the window to swing back and forth a few times, indecisively—drawn, yet afraid what he would find—he looked outside at the blank night sky.

Nothing there.

He pressed closer to the glass to survey the vicinity immediately surrounding the house.

Nothing at all.

His gaze returned to the field. With last year's harvest plowed under, the field had a ragged, motheaten look, made even more macabre in the insipid moonlight. Large strips of dying brown straw were folded over clumps of earth. The result was a crazy quilt design of irregular rows, the reverse of its summer face. Something like a photographic negative where dark was light and light, dark. The image was unsettling.

Scott rubbed his eyes. Sleep. He needed sleep. Scott marched resolutely across the study, pausing to let his hand rest on the door jam. It angered him that he couldn't sleep. Everyone needed to sleep sometime. Body and mind must have sleep or they would crumble. The dreams didn't help. Each night he would bolt out of sleep as though ejected bodily from a dream. But the images—be they horrifying or tantalizing—dissipated the minute his eyes opened, except for that of his parents staring at him through a sheet of flames.

Why did he dream about his parents, he wondered. Aldo made sense, but his parents?

His waking mind couldn't begin to conjure their features even now, but his sleeping mind could. He wasn't sure how he recognized them, but somehow he knew always it was them.

And the saxophone that played in the background? Scott

was no fan of jazz. Much of the modern stuff seemed too strident, dissonant. Often written on a minor scale, to Scott's plebeian ear it seemed totally devoid of harmony, melody and form.

The significance of the instrument wasn't lost on him. The last residents here had been a husband, wife, and young daughter. The husband was a musician—a live musician when he'd moved into the house, a dead one when he left.

These last few days Scott had been able to refresh his memory about dates, names, events that had occurred right within these walls. Although with something that gruesome, it was a little hard to forget the big things, but little things—like the saxophone—he had forgotten. Not now. Elliot Graves had played alto sax. To dream about a book wasn't all that unusual. Once he got involved in a project the involvement was total, but why pick up on the saxophone, of all things?

Scott grunted and paced back toward the window. He had been working hard lately—not that he had been getting a lot done. He cast a sidelong look at the computer. Long days and even longer nights undisturbed by sleep.

Insomnia had been a lifelong companion. Sometimes it seemed that he'd spent the better part of his life lying awake while others slept. Awake as he pondered the loss of his parents. Awake as he waited for Aldo's bellow of rage. Awake as he waited for violence to erupt. Then later, awake as he waited for the police to come and take him away.

After his eighteenth birthday he'd hoped that insomnia would become a thing of the past, but he still maintained vampire hours. Until recently, though, sleeplessness was more often associated with inspiration than worry, as he chased a story from beginning to end, as much a captive of his work as its creator.

When they were first dating, Allison had asked Scott what made him write, and he had quipped that all authors were pathological liars with a strong sense of morality. In truth, he had started putting pen to paper to fill the dark void between dusk and dawn.

Older and a little wiser now, he realized there was another stronger factor in his need to write. Writing was solace. As a child he had been able to transport himself anywhere, be anything, and life's pain and its questions would recede, vanquished by the strength of his stories. At the farm he'd often spin little yarns for his young cousins, to entertain them as Delores and Aldo battled in another room. And after he left, his stories helped keep the loneliness at bay.

Writing gave him a sense of control he had never been able to achieve in life. So much of life was beyond human manipulation. *Most* of life was beyond human control, either ruled by an indifferent monetary system or by societal and cultural dictates. Death, poverty, prejudice. Once one ran up against those impenetrable barriers, a person soon gave up any delusion of control.

But in his stories, long or short, Scott had control. In this illusionary world he found security from whimsical fate and from the futility—no, cruelty—of life. With his work Scott could manipulate plot, story line, themes, character to his delight and satisfaction. If he didn't have control, he at least had the pretense.

Such illusion was all too soon shattered when the manuscript left his hands to be critiqued, applauded, accepted, or rejected by a publisher and mangled by a frustrated writer turned copyeditor. However, for that brief moment while he wrote, he attained divinity. If a character doesn't work, kill it off. A problem arises and the hand of God (alias Scott McDowell) descends to save the day or really muck up the life of the protagonist.

To be honest, Scott had to admit he would have preferred life if he could control everyone as easily as he did the characters of a book, and Scott tried to imagine Jason with an on-off switch and volume control. He snickered.

In some ways the concept was frightening. It revealed a

sad similarity between himself and his uncle. Aldo had used his belligerence and his fists to achieve this same control. Scott funnelled his belligerence through a computer and called it art—a marked improvement over beating his family into submission, but the basic need to control was still the same.

With a grim laugh Scott meandered slowly back to his desk. One thing over which he had no control: when inspiration, if one could call it that, would strike. Tonight it had left him cold.

"Damn." Scott flopped into the chair and stared at the last paragraph he had written.

14

Autumn had painted the trees with devil's colors. The once-yellow leaves had deepened to brilliant fiery orange and blood red which would all too soon fade to rubiginous browns and the dun colors of russet and roan. Scott pulled up in front of the cobbled walkway and killed the engine before reaching across to Allison to hug her. The house leered down at them.

"So next week you get out of the horseless carriage, huh?" he said, thumbing back toward the trunk to indicate her wheelchair.

"Yes, thank God."

"Let me turn the holy terror loose first and go unlock the door, then I'll come back and get you."

Whistling, Scott got out of the car, moved to the rear door, and opened it. Jason sat still as his father removed the seat belt, ready to be released from an afternoon of restraint during his mother's weekly visit to the doctor's office.

Trailing a nearly deflated balloon behind him, Jason wriggled past Scott and ran for the backyard.

"You be careful," Scott called after Jason. "I want you to stay in the yard."

Once he had unlocked the house and propped open the door Scott returned to the car for Allison, grunting when he lifted her from the seat.

"I'll be so glad when you're finally up and around again," he said.

Wheezing dramatically, Scott lugged her up the porch steps and into the foyer. Adam's and Jason's toys cluttered the floor, and he had to pick his way carefully through the debris. He lowered her to sit on a riser at the base of the stairs.

"Back in a minute."

Allison pulled one of Adam's dirty shirts from where it hung on the banister while Scott left to get the wheelchair from the trunk.

As he tussled it through the door, she commented: "You think *you're* glad; I'm ecstatic. I'm so damn sick of the horseless carriage. I wish he'd released me this week. If he thinks I'm healthy as he says I am, why wait?"

"Well, I prefer him to be cautious." Scott plucked her from the stair, put her in the chair, and steered it into the living room.

"I'm actually rather surprised that Dr. Greene let you get up in the wheelchair," Scott said, "I thought delicate patients shouldn't be moved. *At all.* Think of "M*A*S*H." How many episodes were built around patients that couldn't be moved? Great in terms of serial drama as the enemy advances across the forty-eighth parallel, but there must be some logic in it."

"Maybe I'm not all that fragile."

"Still, it doesn't seem like all this bouncing around, up and down stairs, in and out of chairs can be good for you."

"You're just wishing you didn't have to haul me around," she chided.

Scott stretched and placed a hand on the small of his back. "It has been a little hard on the old sacroiliac, but actually I'm glad to have you around, even if it is in a wheelchair."

"So I can keep track of the boys?" Allison raised a questioning brow.

"There's an element of that." He surveyed the messy living room. "It can't be your great housekeeping ability."

With mild exasperation she asked, "What do you expect me to do? Their toy boxes are either upstairs in their room or down in the basement. Unless you install an elevator, I'm stuck."

"Only kidding, honey." He patted her cheek. "You'll never know how happy I am that you are all right. For a while there, it didn't look like you were going to be."

He shuddered before continuing in a lighter vein. "Although if Greene hadn't told us today that this was the last week with your hot wheels, I might have considered installing an elevator. One of those old-lady affairs like they had in *Gremlins.*"

"Great, so I can be shot through the roof."

"That creates a rather interesting visual image," Scott chortled. "Unidentified flying blimp lands in Oswego."

Allison pulled one of the throw pillows from the couch and threw it at him.

He ducked into the kitchen, shouting over his shoulder: "How about some coffee?"

"Sure."

He came back a few minutes later to hand her a steamy mug.

Peering at him over its rim, she said in all seriousness, "Well, all I know is if I had been stuck in bed for an another month, I would have gone stark raving mad. You think this place has history now. Keeping me confined longer would have made me mad as Alice's hatter. Lizzie Borden would look like a Girl Scout compared to me."

Scott had gone to pick up Adam from school and exchange another of the many self-destructing appliances. Nearly electronic gadget in the house had broken. Every new appliance they had purchased before they moved had had to be replaced, or repaired. Today, it was the blender. Tomorrow, who could guess?

Waiting for his return, Allison lounged on the recliner, the wheelchair in easy reach. Jason played at her feet, chattering happily to his imaginary friend. Allison slipped the knitting into the bag next to the chair. She leaned back, her hands folded across her stomach. The fetus seemed to rebel against the additional weight and gave her a sharp kick in the abdomen.

"Well, excuse me," Allison said, dropping her arms to her sides.

Allison felt the familiar thrumming she had come to associate with the house. A comfortable sensation, relaxing, soothing. Never had she felt more at home, as if the building rejoiced in her presence.

Lolling somnabulently, Allison patted the living room walls. The gentle humming increased slightly, becoming recognizable, the now familar tune of a lilting lullaby. She let it wash over her, through her, its pulsing rhythms ran through her veins. And she began to sing along.

Allison shifted to a more comfortable position, and her reflection in the mirror did the same. A bulge, too large to be an arm or a leg, rippled across her belly—visible despite the thick terry cloth robe. A fragile fetal skull butted her flank.

"Ouch! Calm down in there, kid. Give Momma a break."

Her eyes grew more focused, and she scanned the room again, critically. It was a mess. Jason's and Adam's toys were a perfect complement to the several days' accumulation of dirty dishes.

The chair rested next to her, a silent challenge. Clumsy, it allowed only limited access to the first floor. With sudden resolution Allison lifted herself to the wheelchair. She looked at the clock. Eleven-thirty. Scott would be gone an hour; she might as well help out.

Unlocking the wheels Allison started along the tortuous

path to the kitchen, jamming her feet into first the couch and then the end table. Jason scampered out of the way.

After a series of backward and forward motions she got the chair facing the right direction and at the proper angle for a frontal assault on the kitchen door.

The counter was covered with crumbs and dried spills. Allison circumnavigated the kitchen table and chairs with a minimal number of bruises. She pulled up next to the kitchen cabinet to dig out the cleanser. She tried to open the door, and the wheelchair rolled backwards.

Cursing softly, Allison pulled herself forward and locked the wheels into place before digging out the cleaning supplies. Jason eyed her cautiously.

Her scalp tingled as if electrical current were running through her. The sensation coursed through her body, down her spine to her fingertips.

The doorbell rang. Her fingers fumbled with the wheel lock, and she spun around to face the front door.

"What now?" she grumbled.

The tingling stopped.

"I'm 'round the back." Yelling as loud as she could, Allison wheeled herself to the window, where she could see a small portion of the porch and the cobbled path at the base of the stairs. Pressing her cheek against the glass, she tried unsuccessfully to bend the laws of optics and physics so she could see who stood at the door. Then she waited.

"Jason, will you go see who's at the door?"

He toddled back to the living room.

A minute passed, and no one trod down the front steps to the path. Allison tapped on the window and shouted again, "I'm over here."

No one emerged from the sheltered porch.

She couldn't have missed anyone. She couldn't! Anyone who had knocked would have been immediately visible to her as soon as they reached the bottom of the steps.

* * *

On tiptoes, stretching about as far as he could, Jason was just barely able to reach the doorknob. He twisted it, and the door swung open to reveal an empty porch. He skipped back to the kitchen.

His mother's face and hands were pressed against the glass as she strained to peer out the window. Jason looked again. They weren't exactly flattened against the glass. Instead they were a part of it. The palms of her hands had become fuzzy, blurred. They blended with and sank into the window. Her cheek was indistinguishable from the frame, a portion of it gone. She was disappearing into the wood, as if the house were eating her alive.

Glancing from the window to his mother's face, Jason saw the same slack expression he had seen many times before. She'd be talking or working, and suddenly she'd become quiet, her eyes empty, and he knew she was *gone*. He didn't know where she went when this happened. He only knew she wasn't home. It was a lot like looking at the TV before Daddy put in a tape. Empty. Blank. Dead.

Clearing his throat, he said, "No one there, Mommy."

She twitched and pulled away from the window, her hands withdrawing from the glass, and the skin on her cheek detached from the frame, to stare at him.

"Whah?" She stuttered.

"No one's home," he muttered, and Allison eyed him speculatively.

Evading furniture with acquired skill and patience, Allison carefully continued her tortuous trail through the house to the front door. Although she knew Jason was telling the truth, she had to see for herself.

The porch was empty. No salesman or overzealous Jehovah's Witness waited to sell her unwanted magazines or argue the covenant of God.

A basket of dirty laundry had been left at the base of the stairs. She leaned over and sorted through the pockets for pens, loose change, or the more mysterious items her sons collected. Allison pulled the basket onto her lap and started toward the basement stair. She could save Scott a few steps, at least.

Retracing her path with more confidence now, Allison maneuvered around the last turn to the cellar. The door was ajar. She couldn't remember it having been open before. Suddenly cautious, Allison rolled forward slowly and peered into the inky darkness. A chill ran up and down her spine.

She chided herself. What did she expect to jump out at her, the dryer gnome? The invisible little man who stole single socks from the drier to leave only mismatched pairs behind?

Laughing at her own jangled nerves, Allison dropped the basket of clothes near the door. Then she returned to the living room to gather the morning's accumulation of cups and glasses. The Saab pulled into the driveway, and Jason raced from the living room toward the back door. Picking up odd items as she went and restoring them to their original location, Allison listened as the screen door slammed, followed by Jason, who caromed into the room brandishing a shiny Woodstock lunch box.

"Mommy, lookit!"

"That's nice, dear," Allison said absentmindedly.

"Figured he deserved it," Scott said between sips of water. "Thought maybe it would take his mind off other things." He stared moodily out the window.

"See, Adam, see." And he thrust it in Adam's face, "like yours."

"No, not like mine. Mine's Ninja Turtle; yours is Woodstock."

Jason nodded sagely. "Woodstock's better."

Jason burst from the front door with an exuberant shriek. Stubby legs pumped hard as he descended the stairs, arms akimbo, precious lunch pail held before him. Adam followed calmly, hands stuck in his pockets. He hopped from one step to the next, giving Jason plenty of time to run ahead.

When he reached the path he took swipe at a shrub. He resented being sent out to play with his little brother. He had more important things to do with his time. After all, Adam was big now. He was in school.

"E-e-e- e-E-E!"

Screaming, Jason tore across the adjacent vacant lot, which Daddy had told them was their property, toward the empty fields. Dressed in a red hat, yellow parka, and green cords he stood out like a stoplight against the flat, gray horizon. Adam shuffled after him.

The wind had dropped to an almost leaden stillness. The moisture-laden air was chilly, and the sky overcast. The once-colorful leaves hung heavy and damp, clinging with stubborn ferocity to the tree boughs which drooped glumly in the deadened air.

His brother frolicked in the dirt, a bright spot in the muddy brown background.

Adam moaned. If Jason got dirty, Adam was going to get it. Adam kicked Jason's tricycle where it lay discarded on the lawn.

It wasn't fair. Adam thought.

Jason dumped a fistful of dirt in his metal lunch box.

It just wasn't fair. Jason had gotten a brand new lunch pail, and he hadn't done anything. He wasn't even in school. Adam's lunch box was *old*. He'd had it for . . . for a *whole month*.

Adam kicked the tricycle again. The cuff of his pants got caught in the pedal, and Adam tumbled over the bike and sprawled on the wet ground. He sat up, nursing his bruised shin, and eyed his brother jealously. Jason didn't even know what to do with the thing, he thought angrily. Look at him; he was filling it with dirt.

"Jason!" Adam yelled, and Jason looked up innocuously from his play to wave a muddied hand at Adam.

The older boy untangled his pant leg from the tricycle pedal and climbed to his feet, muttering under his breath.

"You're getting all dirty," Adam said, as he limped toward Jason over clumsy clods of broken earth. "Stop it."

Jason said something over the growing mound of dirt that Adam didn't catch.

"What?" Adam closed the last few yards between them breathlessly.

". . . William," said Jason. Then he peered up at Adam and smiled beatifically.

From his position towering over Jason, Adam glared down with dismay at the mud-slimed jeans and caked hands. Large brown smears decorated the front of his parka where he had wiped his hands against his jacket.

"You're not supposed to put dirt in there." Adam bent down, reaching over Jason, and seized the box.

"It's supposed to be for food." Adam turned the box over and dumped the dirt on the ground. Jason's face fell.

"Now it's all dirty, and you can't play with it anymore," Adam concluded.

"It's mine!" Jason grabbed a handful of mud and flung it at his brother. Adam dodged. Jason jump to his feet and lunged at his brother, arms pinwheeling wildly.

"Mine, mine, mine, mine!"

Adam planted the heel of his hand on Jason's forehead and held him at arm's length. The toddler swung futilely, fists striking at empty air.

Adam threw back his head and laughed, a cold, mirthless chuckle. Jason relented, falling back a pace.

"Mine! Gimme. Meanie!"

"Not yours now. It's mine. You don't need it; you don't go to school. You're such a baby you can't even sleep in your own room, you always come crawling in to me. Baby!"

He leapt away from the confused toddler.

"Baby, baby, baby!" Adam trotted in easy circles around Jason, chanting, "Baby, baby, baby . . ."

Jason followed his progress, pivoting, swiveling his torso,

and shuffling his feet quickly to keep up with his brother's loping circle.

"Am not!"

"If you're not a baby, then sleep in your own room tonight!" Adam taunted. "Betcha ya can't."

"Can too."

"Prove it!"

Adam stopped, and Jason lurched dizzily, stymied. Adam scooped a handful of mud and threw it at Jason, missing him by a mile.

"Baby," he hissed.

"Am not," Jason murmured, less confidently than before.

Adam threw another handful of mud. Closer this time, and Jason began to whine.

Morning's sun had faded to leaden clouds by noon. As afternoon progressed the clouds darkened to steel and early dusk.

Fading . . .

Scott wrenched his gaze back to the computer. With a shake of his head he jerked his attention back to the novel. The words came with such difficulty. Each had to be torn from him. His thoughts so easily drifted of into nothingness.

Enough! Scott roared, using the same bellow on himself that he used often with the boys. He turned to the file, extracted the cassette with Sam Holloway's interview, and put it in the tape player.

Every attempt to write returned him to the same hopeless tail-chasing reverie, the boys fighting, Allison drifting farther and farther away. Sometimes, Scott wondered if any of them were playing with a full deck. At one time or another, he had noticed every member of the family fall into the same semi-trance. The boys, Allison, and himself.

The hesitant movements followed by the vacuous look, with the head cocked as though trying to catch something no one else could hear.

Hitting the play button, Holloway's voice—the anxiety

palpable—filled the silent room, telling Scott about the house.

". . . the Graveses and young Tommy weren't the only ones to die in that house," he said. "The first was a child, my second cousin, named . . ."

"Baby, baby, baby . . ." The words drifted in to Scott from out of doors, interrupting Sam's monologue.

Glancing out the window, Scott saw Adam throw a dirt ball at his brother.

"Damn!" He turned off the tape and left the study to intercede in their quarrel.

"Adam! Jason!" His father's sharp tone penetrated, and its meaning was not lost on Adam. They'd been seen. Adam's eyes locked on Jason with a hot stare.

"If you tell on me . . ." He let the threat dangle unfinished.

Jason straightened, aware that somehow he had gotten the upper hand.

"Gimme, mine!" he said sullenly, reaching out with tiny hands raking the air like claws.

Adam looked from Jason to the dirty metal box. "Sure, you can have it. It's dirty. I don't want it anymore."

Then he executed a perfect one-hundred-and-eighty-degree turn and drop-kicked it further into the field.

"ADAM!"

The boy's gaze shot to his father where he stood on the porch. Scott cupped his hands around his mouth, but the only word Adam heard was "instant."

Jason teetered precariously over mist-slickened earth to pick up his lunch box and started toward the house. Adam toed the dirt below his feet, unwilling to return to the house. His father's figure loomed menacingly at the door, one hand resting on his hip.

The damp air had thickened to swirling mist. Small patches of low-lying clouds gathered in the field's shallow valleys. Patches of ghostly white against the black soil. The unseen sun was setting, and the sky darkened perceptibly. Beyond a nearly skeletal stand of trees Adam could see the round turbine of a factory.

"Adam . . . in," Scott yelled.

The child grimaced and began the long trek across the field. Lunch pail in his hand, Jason had preceded him to caper about in the yard. His father said something inaudible to Jason and went into the house, satisfied that Adam would follow.

Adam shrugged. No point in putting off the inevitable, and it was all Jason's fault, anyway. Adam heard a short, sharp, anguish-filled cry, and all anger was forgotten. He broke into a run.

Jason stooped next to the oak tree. The lunch bucket fell from nerveless fingers. Adam ran up, breathless.

"What's wrong?" Adam panted.

Jason straightened, goggle-eyed with horror. Adam peered over his shoulder at a small white dog. It was curled in a tight, little ball, a position of rest and repose; but it did not sleep. Its teeth were clamped on its own haunch, and the grass below was stained a dull ocherous red. Empty eyes stared blindly into the branches of the oak.

His face grim, Adam followed the dog's blind gaze and saw the single bough that grazed his window. He took Jason by the hand and led him away from the grisly sight.

Scott greeted them at the door, ready to scold. The lecture died on his lips after one look at his sons' frightened faces. Allison rolled into the foyer, and Scott frowned at her.

"What's happened?" she prodded gently.

Jason threw himself at her. "There's a dog. Ooh, it's awful." He burst into tears.

Scott turned to Adam. "What's all this about? What dog?"

"A dead dog, around the side of the house near the oak," Adam replied.

"Jesus."

* * *

148

Inside the kitchen Allison peeled the dirty clothes from Jason, dumping them unceremoniously on the floor. He wept, and she tried to comfort him without success. Adam changed upstairs and helped his mother by bringing a pair of Jason's pajamas and silently picking up the clothes from the floor and putting them in a basket. She asked him a few questions about the dog, and he answered in uncommunicative grunts. Scrubbed and clean, Jason showed her his dented lunch bucket, but its importance had paled, overshadowed by death.

As darkness descended Scott came in from the garage. He stood stocking-footed and with muddy hands, waiting patiently while Allison wiped the last smudges from Jason's tearstained cheeks.

"What did you do with it?" she asked.

"Buried it in a stand of trees," Scott said, stopping further questions with a shake of his head. Allison backed away from the sink and locked the chair's wheels, allowing Scott to get clean. Scott washed his hands and the lunch pail before moving to sit at the kitchen table across from his eldest son and beginning the long-postponed lecture.

Banished to his bedroom, Adam sat with his hands resting on his thighs.

The familiar buzz grew louder. A scratchy sound. Static . . . White noise. It hurt his ears. Adam's slim fingers dug around in his pocket and closed around the wooden sticks with their fat red tips. Matches.

Adam pulled them out and examined them one by one. He didn't quite know why he had taken them from where they were kept in a jar upon the shelf. He had just grabbed them when no one was looking.

With his right hand Adam dragged the red phosphorous tip down along the wall like he had seen Daddy do when he lit their small barbecue.

Nothing happened, although the match had created a scratch on the bright tartan wallpaper. Adam stared at the match, wondering what he had done wrong. It worked for Daddy.

Again.

Nothing happened.

Adam remembered the liquid that Daddy would pour on the charcoal to make a really neat fire. A look of determination on his face, he decided that next time he was outside he'd find the lighter fluid so he, too, could make a big fire.

One final time Adam raised the match to strike the wall. It lit with a flash, and Adam almost dropped it. Round eyes were drawn to the flame, and he noted the fine gradations from blue to red to orange to yellow. Adam didn't think he had ever seen anything so pretty.

Hearing voices on the stair, Adam's eyes darted nervously from the door to the match in his hand. He waved the half-spent match in the air like he had seen Daddy do. It flew from his grasp to land on the floor near the closet. It flickered and went out.

15

Free at last, Allison stood on her own two feet and luxuriated in her newfound independence and mobility. She stared down at her toes and wiggled them, marvelling how much one took for granted having two good legs and feet, and she promised herself: "Never again."

The coffee-maker light winked invitingly at her like an old friend. The coffee would taste like mud by now, so Allison turned it off and waddled back around the table to the sink. Ignoring the new food processor, she peeled the potatoes by hand, cutting them into chunks, which she shoveled into the colander in the sink. The stew meat already simmered on the stove. She pulled a carrot from a plastic bag. Jason's piping voice interrupted her.

"I want the purple one!" he chimed.

Swinging to stare at him where he sat coloring in a book Allison watched him slap at the air. His eyes focused on a spot somewhere about two feet from him, slightly above the empty chair to his right.

She turned back to the carrot.

"No, gimme, Sara," he shouted. "Give it back."

She stiffened, recognizing the name. Uncontrollably her irritation began to rise.

Couldn't they play outside? she thought angrily.

A tingle. Each hair on her head stood on end. The current shot throughout her body to her fingertips. The synapses rocketed from nerve-ending to nerve-ending.

The feeling of wood grain. Warm. Hard yet yielding it embraced Allison in satiny smoothness. Rich. She wandered, through the pattern of the grain, following each ripple, each fold, tracing it to its source . . . knowing it.

The coffee pot belched to life, gurgling. Her fingers fumbled with the knife, and she almost cut herself. Allison spun around to face the coffee maker. A few weak spurts of mud-colored fluid dribbled from what should have been an empty chamber. With a shrug, Allison sidled to her left to unplug it. The coffee maker burped a final time and fell silent. The tingling coursed through her body, and she returned to the sink.

As soon as she had picked up another potato the skin on her scalp began to crawl. Expectant, her head swiveled on her neck, her eyes frantically searching along the counter. The overhead light came on, and Allison's head snapped up. The bulb sizzled, flashed, and then popped. Slivers of shattered glass showered down over her head and shoulders.

Allison jumped and raised a tremulous hand to brush the glass from her hair. A few splinters pierced her flesh. She snatched her hand from her hair and examined it. Blood oozed from the wounds. Leaning against the counter, Allison stared at the blood, squeezing her fingertip to watch it well from the cut and run into the sink, only dimly aware of Jason watching her from the corner of his eye.

Staring at the tape player Scott felt the chill inside him spread. He stopped it, rewound a bit, and hit the play button so he could replay that particular portion of the interview over again.

Holloway: "Ah, now here's someone you should meet. This is Critter, Elliot and Jane Graves's dog."

Scott: "You're kidding. How old is he?"

Holloway: "Near as we can guess, about fourteen."

A rustle as Scott scooted forward in his chair.

Holloway: "This might interest you. Critter won't go into that place—can't be bribed, cajoled, or coerced into setting foot on the property."

Scott: "Maybe he remembers . . ."

Holloway: "After what, ten years? Perhaps, but I doubt it. The night it happened he was found hovering over Jane's body, barking and snapping at the air. Yet when the police arrived, Critter backed off. He seemed happy to let them take over. However, if they left the corpse alone even for a moment, he stood guard, snarling and growling, until one officer or another returned. Even the police found Critter's behavior odd."

A dog whined in the background.

Impatiently, Scott hit stop, fast forwarded the tape, and punched play.

Holloway continued. "Another thing that was of only mild interest to the media was the recent death of Jane's mother. She had a stroke only two days before the murders. The poor woman was an invalid. She'd had a series of strokes that had left her totally incapacitated. After years of being bedridden, her limbs were so twisted she couldn't sit upright."

The spiderlady? Scott chewed nervously on his lip.

There was an unidentified rhythmic thumping from the tape player, and Scott tried to recall what had been happening in the background as they spoke.

Holloway: "There have been other deaths, too. About eight in all. Although it's hard to keep track, people lose pets and I'm always stumbling across the body of a squirrel or a racoon. Certainly, there's more than enough skeletons in the old family closet. That clip mentions my second cousin,

William. Few people know the real story. It's a well kept family secret. The child was murdered by his father, although no one will ever know if the death was intended. The elder Van Clausen locked the boy in a closet as a punishment. For a week. The child starved to death. My aunt, Emma Van Clausen, never spoke of it until after her husband died, and some believe that his death was no accident. She was stark raving mad by the time she died years later, reputed to be the neighborhood witch."

Something popped somewhere in the house, and Scott leaned forward to turn off the tape.

"Honey, are you all right?" he shouted and then waited for a reply.

"Fine . . ." She said something unintelligible.

Slumping back into his chair, Scott pulled on his lip and contemplated the tape player.

William and an old lady with limbs so twisted that she couldn't sit. Was that the spiderlady Jason talked about?

These people had existed once, here in this house. How could Jason possibly have known?

And his eye darted about the room, as if he expected some contorted apparition to materialize from the walls before he called his son.

"Jason! Jason, could you come here for a minute?"

Sara cheated, and Shelley did too. Jason stuck out his lower lip and pouted. Dwarfed by the kitchen chair, he rocked from side to side, considering the girls.

"Gimme." He seized a handful of crayons. "Burple one."

The sisters looked at each other and began to waver and fade.

"Sorry," he mumbled into his fist.

Their images coalesced and hardened, outlines sharp and clear. Sara and Shelley smiled their approval. Jason let go of the crayons and huffed back into his chair, expelling air from pursed lips in a loud raspberry, his stubby arms folded across his chest.

Let them steal the crayons. Sometimes they were no fun, and no fair! *He* couldn't move the crayons without touching them.

Jason ducked his head so that he appeared to be staring at his lap and examined the sisters through a fringe of gold hair.

Friends. *Jason's* friends, and Jason felt a certain sense of proprietary pride. No one else saw them, not the way Jason could see them.

His friends, not Adam's. At least Jason didn't think they played with Adam. He never mentioned them, and Adam was so full of himself, if he made new friends he would have said so. He was *always* bragging about school.

A crayon flickered a bit and reappeared next to Shelley.

Unfair. They could do things, special things. Tricks like he saw on TV, like being able to pop in and out of any room, or to fade away.

Jason didn't question their abilities. If TV people could do them, he thought, then why not his friends?

No, he didn't question them. He wanted to learn how to do the things they did. They did real neat tricks. He liked them. They played with him and didn't call him baby.

Sara and Shelley were here—unlike Adam who was away in school and Daddy who was always working on his computer—and his mother who, he realized, wasn't quite "all there" and hadn't been since she came home from the hospital.

Some of their tricks weren't fun. Like when they were mad at him, they would go away, and they wouldn't come out and play until he apologized, even though Jason didn't even know what he was apologizing for. Or when they went all funny. Like the people he had seen in that movie where all the bad guys melted.

Jason remembered the movie. Some guy was looking for an ark. And Jason waited for him to find a boat like Noah had, all full-up with animals, but the guy didn't find a boat. He found a box, this big gold box, and when he opened it, the bad guys had melted. They just melted clean away.

Well, Shelley did that, made her face all runny like a Halloween witch candle.

She did it to scare him if he did something bad. Something she didn't like—like trying to tell his parents about the house. Then her face would start to droop, and her skin peel away, leaving a nasty looking skull.

But if he behaved, they were fun. They told him things. Lots of things. Things he wasn't supposed to know. Like about Adam and the matches. Secrets. Funny things. Bad things. His brow creased as he tried to remember these bad things. They got all fuzzy in his head when one of the children was around.

They had told him about the house. They told him about Mommy. One time Shelley told him about how babies were made. Like when Donald grabbed Daisy, knocked her down, and . . . Jason knew she lied. His mother and father wouldn't do *that!*

He might be a baby, but Jason wasn't stupid. He didn't believe it any more than he believed that his mother had a baby growing in her tummy. Jason's eyes rested on his mother's stomach.

When his parents had explained it to him, all proud and beaming, they made him put his hand on her tummy. It had bounced and jiggled under his hand, and Jason knew something mean and nasty was gonna come bursting from her belly button.

He eyed his mother. It was no baby, but something ugly, nasty, slimy. His parents were wrong, all wrong. They had to be. Jason had thought and thought about it. He was a baby—everyone always told him so—and no matter how he folded himself up, he couldn't fold up small enough to fit in Mommy's tummy.

Uh-uh, no way. They must have gotten it wrong—like Shelley was wrong about how babies were made—and it was an earth-shattering concept to think that his parents were wrong. Jason didn't know who or what to believe anymore.

No, Jason didn't like to think about the baby. He didn't like to think about what might be growing in Mommy's tummy. Not at all.

The house? After all, Daddy said Mommy would get as big as a house.

Uh-uh, not the house. It was *too* big.

Yes, Sara, Shelley, and William told him secrets. Secrets like the house. Things he wasn't suppose to tell anybody else. Cross his heart and hope to die.

Sometimes when he was alone he wanted to tell his mother, his father—to warn them about the house—but William, Shelley, or Sara would always appear. Then thought would get all muzzy, and Jason couldn't remember what he was going to say.

Sara spoke, and Jason grumbled back at her.

Sara and Shelley vanished. Poof!

Jason's gaze went to his mother's stooped shoulders as she picked up a carrot. Then he looked at her feet. They had *grown into* the floor. No longer separate, her feet were part of the wood. He could see neither soles nor bony uppers—her feet sunken deep below the floor line to her ankles.

Jason had noticed this before, the first time when she was in the wheelchair and her hand seemed to go through the window. After the doctor had taken the wheelchair away and she was up and walking around the house Jason saw it more often. Most often it was her feet. He'd glance down and realize that her feet would sink through the wooden boards. He couldn't see the bottom part at all. Sometimes her hand, when she'd touch the wall, would fuse with it, and she became part of the house.

Each time it happened Jason would look at her face, and he knew she was gone. And each time it happened more of her foot would disappear until he couldn't see her feet at all. They would be gone, the wood coming up to the ankle.

A rain of tinkling glass, and the wall next to Allison

bulged, oozing outward. Hands seemed to grow from the surface, reaching for her.

She took her hand from her hair and stared at the blood. The wall bubbled and boiled, all shiny and gleaming.

She put her hand to her mouth, and it leapt at her. She squeezed blood into the sink, and the wall subsided back into place and was just a wall again.

"Fine." She paused long enough to look at the slivered glass in the vegetables and swore softly.

Her feet rested on the top of the floor again, and she bustled around the kitchen to collect the broom.

Jason wondered how she did that. Everybody in the house could do tricks, except Jason. Glaring, he slumped lower in his chair.

"Jason. Jason, will you come here for a minute?" his father called from the study. The toddler cocked his head to listen and opened his mouth to speak.

William appeared, standing next to Jason's mother, his hand on her stomach, and her face went all loose and floppy again. Jason's mouth snapped shut.

"Jason." Scott shouted as he strode into the room, plucked Jason from his chair, and set the toddler down, hard. Jason's teeth clacked shut inside his head.

"Hey!" Allison roused herself and intervened on Jason's behalf.

Noticing her for the first time, Scott observed the sprinkling of broken glass.

"Jesus, what happened?"

"Just a broken bulb, that's all. Dinner's ruined." Allison grimaced.

Scott looked overhead at the jangled ends of the shattered bulb still screwed tightly into the socket, and all other thoughts were chased from his mind.

"That's going to be fun to get out," Scott said.

Allison glanced up. "Yeah, you'll probably need to turn it off at the mains.

Scott's attention returned to Jason, whose tiny arms were

still tightly clenched in his fists. Scott dropped them, wheeling away, while Jason rubbed at the red marks his father had made on his arm.

A cold, blustery wind blew around the corner of the house, lifting dead leaves like spiraling dust devils. The air was charged with impending storm. Autumn's warmth had fled too soon, and his father was predicting an early snow.

Back pressed against the outside wall, Adam listened to the muted thunder of his parents' voices as they argued. His mother sounded agitated, and his father was mad. They were talking quite excitedly about Jason's imaginary friends and had been since Adam came home from school. Daddy didn't like their names, and Mother thought Dad was just being silly.

Sure that they would be busy for a while, Adam slipped away from the wall through the porch down to the driveway and headed for the garage to find the lighter fluid.

"Aren't you worried about this William thing at all?" Scott's voice dwindled as he got lost in his own private thoughts.

"Why should I be worried? Lots of little boys have imaginary friends," she answered peevishly.

"Named William?"

"Lots of people are named William. Think of *Willie Wonka and the Chocolate Factory.* He could have picked it up anywhere." Allison mused for a moment. "William's just a name, and William gives Jason an outlet. William only seems to appear when Jason's feelings are hurt or when he's angry."

"Hurt! Angry?" Scott snorted. "And what does Jason have to be angry about?"

"I don't know. The move. The fact that Adam's in school, and Jason's left alone. There's a new baby coming, so there's the threat of the next in line." Allison smoothed the sweatshirt over her stomach. "Any number of things. Maybe

William allows him to voice these things. William's convenient. I suppose in a pinch he can take the blame if something gets broken."

"Where'd you get that? Dr. Spock?"

Allison bridled but said nothing.

"Maybe we shouldn't let Jason play with William anymore," Scott said.

"Right. How do you suggest we do that? I'm sorry, Jason, you can't play with that little boy any more. Which one? You know, the one that doesn't exist. Or maybe we should tell William that Jason can't come out and play," Allison said sarcastically, adding: "I don't understand you. Our little boy is so lonely that he invents another little boy to play with, and you want to take that away."

"Come on, Allison," Scott shouted over her words, "you were never one for that child psychology crap. Neither am I. You're saying William is an outlet for Jason's two-year-old rage. Next you'll be telling me that the spiderlady is a manifestation of his anger at his separation from you because of the baby. My child prodigy is getting through his Oedipal complex early. The precocious pup."

She flared and said: "Have you got any better explanations?"

Scott grimaced. He did, but he didn't like to think about them.

After dinner, they settled around the television set. Jason fiddled with the remote. Like most children the boy had mastered electronic gadgetry almost as soon as he learned to walk. With adept precision the toddler pressed one button and then another, and the VCR sprang to life.

Scott started to scold and stopped himself. The credits for *Snow White* rolled onto the screen after the standard copyright warnings and dire threats, and for some odd reason Scott found himself thinking about the tags on pillows.

Nestled between Allison and Scott, Jason snuggled against his flank. The tiny heart beating against Scott's ribs was a comfort. Scott stared down at his son, thinking about the revelation this afternoon. He had gotten little sense from the child when Scott had tried talking to the boy about William. All Jason would say was the walls were trying to grab his mother, and then he had shut down, refusing to speak any more.

Distracted, Scott turned back to the television. Snow White ran through a dark and ugly forest, pursued by the wicked huntsman.

William? Scott hadn't been able to get a description of the child from Jason, but he'd try again when the toddler wasn't so upset.

Whistling while she worked, Snow White cleaned the house.

Things were getting a little frayed around the edges, Scott thought. The seven dwarfs arrived home to discover the princess asleep upon the bed. Scott waited for the usual consternation as they discussed the intruder, but the dwarfs didn't pause predictably as they should have. Instead they crept stealthily toward the sleeping woman. They leapt, grabbing her wrists and ankles so she lay spread-eagle upon the bed. While four held her thrashing body, one tore the dress away and another dropped his baggy tights to climb on top of Snow White and grab melon-sized breasts . . .

Scott bolted, seized the remote from the end table, and turned the television off.

Twisting to face Allison, one hand still holding the remote, he said, "Jesus Christ, did you see . . ."

The question died on his lips. Her eyes were dull and glazed, her expression drained of all animation. Her muscles, loose and limp, seemed to hang on her face. Slack as they were, he realized with a shock that she was losing weight. His eyes were drawn to the gray hair that hadn't been there until the move, and he shivered. Staring at her, Scott sensed the same lifelessness he had seen before, noting also the same feeling of blankness he had had when she was in the hospital. Like she wasn't there.

Wherever she was, she wasn't paying attention to what was going on in the room.

"Allison?"

She blinked. "What?"

"Did you see that?"

"See? See what?"

"The television?"

Her eyes focused on the television. "The television was on before. Why'd you turn it off?"

Scott sagged into the couch before turning to Adam. "Adam, did you see that?"

Adam averted his eyes. Scott swung toward Jason. The toddler didn't seem to be paying attention; he was staring at his mother's feet.

"How about if we listen to the radio for a while?" Scott said.

"Fine with me." Allison pulled her knitting from the bag.

The one-time bootie had been torn out so she could make a sweater. She spread the large square across her lap. It was too big for a sweater, and he wondered what she planned to make now.

Scott stood up and strode over to the radio.

A jazzed-up version of "Jingle Bells" bounced gaily across the room, and Scott gave Allison a wan smile as he turned it up so they could hear the lyrics.

Jingle bell, jingle bell, jingle bell, fuck . . .

Horrified, he switched it off. "Now you can't tell me that you didn't hear that."

Peering up from the flying needles in her hands, Allison said, "What? Hear what?"

16

Two hearts beating as one. The lyrics of an old song came to her as she felt the regular rhythm of his heart beneath her palms. Scott's embrace was warm and reassuring. Despite her advancing pregnancy, they still managed to meld to each other, with him molding himself around her body, leaning over her stomach, and swallowing her in his arms. And for a brief moment she could pretend that things were all right, that things were the way they had been before they moved and things had gotten all crazy.

They had argued for much of the afternoon. He had apologized, and she had forgiven him, after a fashion. But Allison wouldn't listen to such nonsense. Scott said their son was picking up ghosts from the house. Ridiculous! He'd spent too much time reading his own fiction.

First it was Jason sucking his thumb—and wetting his bed—then the spiderlady and his imaginary friends. The boys fought all the time, her boys who had once been so close. Adam—her Adam—had become secretive, almost furtive. And Scott was angry with her about the television. The television! He said that he saw the seven dwarfs gang-banging Snow White!

Well, *she* hadn't seen it. Her family was falling apart.

Allison sniffled a few times and stepped away to stare into his eyes. They looked moist, glistening in the soft glow of bedroom lamp. He lifted her chin with his index finger and peered deep into her ice-blue eyes. "You okay now?"

Allison nodded. Her gaze fell on the mirror, and her hand touched the hated gray with a careworn gesture.

She couldn't agree with Scott that something was wrong with the house. Scott was worried; she could tell, but there was no tangible reason to associate any current problems with the house.

Much of what they were undergoing was nothing more than stress. Their situation had changed radically. They were in a new house. Adam was in school, and Jason was separated from his brother for the first time in his short life. Many of the changes were positive. Scott's long-hoped-for success was finally a reality, bringing with it a sudden financial status. The new child. But even positive changes were stress-inducing. Frayed nerves, short tempers, bad dreams. All stress reactions, but Scott insisted on blaming the house.

For that matter, her dreams were pleasant, if a trifle naughty. Allison stirred.

No matter what her doubts before, she had none now that she had lived here for a while. She had been resistant to change; that was all.

The toilet had backed up. Inconvenient, yes, but nothing particularly frightening. A few small appliances had broken, appliances that were all under warranty. The clocks stopped. Lights flickered.

So what?

Lights had flickered all over the neighborhood. Who knows, maybe their clocks stopped as well.

The phone?

Well, that was Baby Bell all over again. Nothing had ever been the same since divestiture.

Nothing frightening. The worst had been what happened

on the porch. The swoon, for what else could she call it? The incident had grown dim and unimportant in her memory. After the initial pain what she remembered was being suffused with a sense of completeness, with the feeling that she was not alone, that someone was there with her, and the feeling had been a pleasant one.

Her worries and fears before the move had been silly, and Allison wouldn't let Scott him dredge them up again.

There was nothing wrong here. Nothing wrong at all.

Each human psyche, even the most healthy, had its gaps, its dark spots, and given enough time, each could be ferreted out. Such gaps were weaknesses which—if poked, prodded, and probed often enough—would widen, becoming gaping chasms through which evil could enter. The wise observed this, but the wicked used the information, and the entity had more than enough time to study this family.

Now it hummed contently beneath the house, intent on its goal, poking, probing, prodding . . .

Loving hands stroked her legs. Allison arched into the tender caress. Fingers traced light circular patterns along the inside of her legs, starting at her knees and moving higher and higher up her thighs. She let her legs flop loosely apart.

The dream. Allison didn't open her eyes. She knew what she would see: the little boy from the hospital. Insistent pressure forced her legs wider apart. The warmth in her groin spread.

The feeling of wood grain. The tickle of pink insulation. The little girl appeared at the side of the bed next to Scott.

Fingers probed, and she let them.

The impression of infinite space, of being everywhere and nowhere at all.

The girl straddled Scott, and Allison woke up . . . horny.

A light finger tickled the back of his neck.

"Wah . . ." Scott batted at her hand.

Allison giggled and nibbled his earlobe. He rolled over to look at her groggily. She knelt over him; her hair brushed against his cheeks, his lips.

"Wanton woman." Scott wrestled her gently back down and the waterbed responded with a slurp.

Scott covered her mouth with his own and felt her back bend slightly as she tried to press herself against him and still accommodate the round belly. Her fingers gave his hair a light tug, and her breathing quickened.

"I love you," she moaned. "I love you so much."

Scott propped himself up on his elbow and gazed at her exquisite eyes. "I love you, too."

She pulled at his pajama top. "Take this thing off." And her fingers traced feathery circles on his chest. "I want skin."

"Shameless, absolutely shameless," he admonished as he slipped from the shirt.

"How do you think I got this way?" Allison lifted her head off the bed and peered down at her stomach. "Christ, I can't even see my toes."

"I can, they're lovely toes." He slithered down to the end of the bed and started to kiss her feet.

"That tickles." Allison bent her knees, pulling her feet away.

"Just what I wanted you to do."

His hand slid under the cotton gown, caressing her calf, then her thigh. He pushed her legs apart, at the same time slipping the gown up over her knees. Scott got up on his hands and knees, fumbled with the drawstrings, and the pajama bottoms folded around his knees. Allison's eyes were closed to mere slits as she waited expectantly. Even pregnant, she was beautiful.

Scott got ready to mount her, carefully, a trick he had learned with Adam. His eyes feasted first on her face, made vulnerable with passion; next on her round tummy, with its skin stretched taut; and last on the open invitation of creamy thighs. Then he froze, his eyes drawn to the triangle of dark hair, and he felt himself deflating.

Dream images came to mind. A young childlike face, blond hair, and a groin covered with soft down—like peach fuzz. Scott looked down at himself. Limp.

"Jesus Christ," he said and flopped down to lie next to her. Allison looked up, confused.

"What's the matter?" She rolled over on her side.

"Ah, my body doesn't seem to want to cooperate."

"You mean copulate?"

"Either, or both, whichever you prefer," Scott growled.

Allison tried to smile, but Scott could see the hurt in her eyes, and he felt a sudden flood of emotions—from shame to rage. He wasn't a goddamn circus animal to perform on cue, he thought, and Scott crawled under the covers.

"We're both exhausted," she said. "Let's get some sleep."

Scott grunted, and Allison leaned over and tongued his cheek playfully.

"Mañana. I'm going to get you mañana," she said.

Turning his back to her, Scott pretended to sleep.

Sleep seemed to take forever to find him, but when it did, *she* was there. Shelley, sweet, young, and enticing. The erection, which refused to put in an appearance earlier, came.

Rock hard, so hard that it woke him up.

Scott glared at his betraying penis, reassured only slightly by the fact that it was normal for men to get an erection while dreaming—whether it was an erotic dream or not. His head swiveled on his neck, and he faced Allison to watch her sleep. A light sheen of sweat covered her face.

"I'm sorry, babe," he murmured. Scott groped among the covers for his pajamas. He dressed quietly and headed for the stairs. Perhaps he could get some work done tonight.

A stud creaked in the attic. The sound volleyed off the walls, ricocheting into silence. Scott froze.

A harsh whisper of voices followed by a short thud, and all was still. The boys?

Scott shuffled over to Jason's room.

The toddler slept, breath soft and even, his cheek and nose burrowed into his pillow.

Scott's gaze darted around the room, coming to rest first on the twelve-inch blank spot where Goofy used to be. His eyes lighted on one of Jason's toys—a doll, a little girl doll with blond hair and blue eyes.

Made of hard plastic, it sat stiffly against the head of the bed. Scott wondered what had possessed Jason to want such a toy. Not that he believed little boys shouldn't play with dolls. "Action figures" was just a fancy name thought up by some wise-assed marketing man. But this doll was too cumbersome to carry, too large to fit in with any of the games they played with the action figures. It wasn't even good for cuddling.

With a slight shake of his head Scott leaned forward to stare intently at the doll's face. Something dark seeped from the corner of the blank, empty eyes. Scott reached out and touched it.

Red and wet. He tasted it. Salty.

He looked from his finger to the smudged plastic cheek. Blood.

The goddamn doll was weeping tears of blood.

The day was crisp, clear, unseasonably cold, unreasonably quiet. The boys played outside. Their distant shouts had the brittle ring of frost, like brass bells, and the clear sky had grown infinitely tall. The delicate silver dusting of hoarfrost would soon melt, but for now it looked pretty. Sprawled comfortably on the couch, her legs covered with an afghan, Allison stared out the living room window.

In the study, Scott labored at the keyboard while Allison nursed her steaming cup of coffee. The dishes were done. Lunch was made, and the house was cleaned to an implacable high gloss that gave away no secrets. Each day, the ritual was the same. She would lovingly polish and clean every surface until she had very nearly erased all trace of human occupation.

Normally Allison would have enjoyed the rare luxury of a break and solitude; but her expression was clouded, worried. Scott had awakened her out of a sound sleep last night to drag her to Jason's room, all excited. He was going to prove to her that something was going on. He had then proceeded to shove a doll in her face. The big plastic doll she had bought for Jason a couple of weeks ago.

"Don't you see?" he had shouted, rousing Jason.

Startled, the poor child had started to cry. As she cradled him Allison had examined the doll, but saw nothing.

Agitated, Scott didn't believe her. He had taken the doll from her hands and tried to gouge out the eyes. He swore, absolutely *swore,* the doll had been crying tears of blood.

It had taken thirty minutes to get Jason back to sleep. Meanwhile he had shown her a blank section of wallpaper, an interruption in the pattern.

"Goofy," he said. "Goofy ran away."

Jason had agreed with him then, and *that* was when she started to get worried.

The faint rustle of movement, and Allison turned from where she stared out the window to Scott, who shuffled through the room, coffee cup in hand.

"What's up?" he asked.

"What do you mean what's up?"

"If looks could kill . . ."

Allison tried to smile. It looked more like a sneer. "Sorry, I was just thinking."

"About what?"

Allison caught his eyes with her own. What could she say? That she thought he was going nuts. That he and their sons were all bonkers.

"Oh, nothing," she said.

He cocked his head. "You sure?"

"Yes." She turned her back to him to survey the cathedral sky. Somewhere Jason squealed. A cry of joy.

"More coffee?" Scott offered.

"No thanks," Allison said. Scott continued through the living room and Allison sighed.

Sizzle. Hiss!

The continual static threatened to overwhelm him, and Adam shooed Jason away angrily. Adam had come here across the narrow isthmus of the cul-de-sac to be alone. Besides, Jason wasn't supposed to cross the street. 'Cuz he was mad, Adam made Jason go the long way round, and Adam watched his brother until he disappeared around the back of their house.

He surveyed the circle, their house, the two vacant lots, and then this lonely deserted house—the only other house within the cul-de-sac.

Satisfied that he was alone, Adam moved down the driveway toward the garage and hunkered down between the empty building on his left and the old woman's house on his right. Squatting in front of the garage, he was hidden safely from casual sighting by anyone along the street.

When he could break away from his brother Adam spent a lot of time over here near the deserted house. He was fascinated by this house with its flaking brick and by the other two houses just outside the cul-de-sac that were also empty. All three houses had been abandoned long before they moved in, and Adam wondered about that. They looked lonely and forlorn, and they seemed to squat like toads around Adam's house. All hunched over, as if they were leaning away from the Victorian.

Adam knew nothing about architectural styles, but he knew his house was *old* in comparison. Like the woman, and Adam glanced at her house to make sure she wasn't watching. He couldn't seem to escape her.

Good, Adam thought, no wrinkled face, with a black

smudge of a cat perched on her shoulder, peered from the murky windows.

Duck-walking to the house, Adam pulled the charcoal lighter fluid from its hiding place. He returned to his position over the anthill that had grown up sometime during the summer in a crack in the drive. The loose pile of dirt intermingled with little snowflake crystals.

Kneeling and closing one eye, Adam leaned as close to the tiny hole as he could, trying to look inside. Did ants still live there? Did they sleep when it got cold, like bears? Or did they die?

He upended the can, squeezing it with both hands to get a nice hard stream, and aimed it to get as much of the liquid into the hole as possible. The dry earth turned to mud and then the mud flowed away, carried by the pungent fluid. A small puddle formed, and Adam turned the can upright, returning it to the hiding place.

Standing well back, as he had seen his father do, Adam struck a match against the wall and threw it in the puddle. Then he ran just as fast as his legs could carry him to the far side of the house and scrunched down just as small as he could, and waited.

Despite the day's weak sunshine he could see the reflected glow of the fire on the side of the garage, even from here. A door opened and closed.

Tap, tap, swoosh, swoosh. Tap, tap, swoosh, swoosh. Tap, tap, swoosh, swoosh. Adam listened to the strange shuffling four-legged gait of the woman as she hobbled up the walk.

The glow along of the side of the garage wall dimmed, the flames having greedily consumed most of the fluid.

"Little boy." Her thin reedy voice was whipped and snapped about by the wind. "Little boy! I know it's you, little boy."

Adam pressed against the wall and giggled into his hand.

"And I'm going to catch you one of these days," she shouted.

The black cat walked around the side of the house, and Adam jumped at the sight of the slinking specter.

"And I'm going to tell your father."

Tap, tap, swoosh, swoosh. Tap, tap, swoosh, swoosh. Tap, tap, swoosh, swoosh. The voice receded as the woman moved up the path. The cat sat, extended a leg, claws outstretched, and started cleaning between its toes.

The phone rang, and Scott hesitated at the kitchen counter, his arm holding a bottle of Coke ready to pour. It rang again. He put the Coke down and walked over to the phone, catching it on the third ring.

Silence.

Pulling the receiver away from his ear to glower at it Scott cursed the phone soundly, then slammed it back into the cradle. He spun on the ball of his foot to face the counter, and it rang again.

He yanked the receiver from the cradle and yelled hello. Clicks and whistles. HissSS!

"Hello?" This time Scott's tone was questioning.

"Scott? Scott?" His agent's voice came through an ocean of crackling waves. "Hi, Scott, we've got a lousy connection, so I won't keep you long. Have you got a pen and paper handy?"

Groping for a pen, patting pockets, with the phone locked between his shoulder and his ear, Scott spied Adam's Big Chief pad on the kitchen table.

"Hang on, Ira, I'll go get some."

Extracting a pen from his breast pocket, Scott walked over to the table, picked up the pad, and leafed through the pages. On the first he found Adam's name, address and phone number scrawled in a child's shaky hand.

Idly he flipped to the next page. The writing there was neat and concise, definitely a more practiced hand. The address was the same, but the name and phone number were different, puzzling. It said, "Sara Graves."

With a sharp intake of breath Scott halted next to the

phone—his agent and his message forgotten—and flipped
to the next page. Shelly Graves' name, address and phone
number were written in rough, shakey script.

And to the next . . .

Tom Erwin's signature appeared in a clean cursive which
had now developed the first elements of a style.

Before picking up the phone again Scott tore the pages
from the pad and stuffed them in his pocket.

Back in the study Scott extracted the crumpled pages and
flattened them against the desk, side by side.

Four distinct writing styles, four different names and
phone numbers, and three separate addresses.

Three different addresses? Scott tried to force his mind to
work. Why three? The gears in the old brain, improperly
lubricated after drinking himself to sleep the night before,
refused to function.

Pinching his nose between thumb and index finger, Scott
tried to blot out the image of Allison looking at him as if he
were totally nuts when he'd showed her the doll. Shaking his
head, he returned to the rumpled papers before him.

Sara and Shelley Graves, and young Erwin. Of course,
Erwin had lived just up the street. His family had moved not
long after his suicide. Someone—he couldn't remember
who—had pointed out which house.

But why three addresses? Erwin's and the Graves's, which
was also their own.

Then, the pieces slid into place, like the pieces of a jigsaw
puzzle. The eldest Graves child had died before the family
moved into this house. Of course, her address would be
different from Sara's since she had never lived in this house.

Three addresses. It made a creepy kind of sense, but was
Erwin's old address four-o-seven? Scott had never thought
to look.

Shrugging into his coat, Scott strolled onto the front
porch. The sky was the brittle blue of late autumn. Yesterday's dampness had been replaced by a freezing frost that

had dried both the air and soil. The air seemed to crackle and snap around him with each step. The sudden cold had turned any remaining red in the leaves to a sodden brown. They carpeted the ground. Scott let his pace fit his mood and ambled slowly up the cobbled walk to the street. From there he turned left. The old woman appeared at the window. She followed his progress up the street.

Ignoring her, Scott went on, unsure why he bothered. He knew, didn't he? Or did he?

No, Scott decided, he had to check. He had to know for sure and, possibly, find a logical explanation. There *had* to be a logical explanation.

Perhaps Scott couldn't confirm the Erwin's old phone number, but he *could* check the address. Stopping directly in front of the Erwin's former home, he stared at the number and the autumn chill settled in his bones.

Erwin's address was a cinch, he told himself, not really convinced. Adam could have picked it up easily enough. The neighborhood kids obviously knew the history of the place, and they would probably know which house the Erwin boy had once lived in.

And what about Shelley Graves? What had the Graves's former address been? Did Scott have it written down and stuck in some miscellaneous file somewhere? Had Adam seen it?

And the phone numbers? Two of those phone numbers hadn't been listed for over ten years. There was no way Adam could have just picked those numbers up, unless he had picked them out of the air. But were they right?

With a final glance at the number Scott turned around and headed back for the house. It was beginning to look like he was going to have to talk to Sam Holloway again.

17

Sam Holloway stood at the base of the staircase. In his dream, he was small again. The little boy who was forced to visit his widowed aunt with her crepe-paper skin and sunken, haunted eyes.

He swallowed, unable to get the thick, stringy saliva down his throat.

Backing away from the stair into the door, Holloway fumbled blindly for the knob. He felt more than heard a dull, rhythmic thudding—like a human heartbeat, *BOOM, boom, BOOM, boom*—that came from the dark recesses of the house.

Something scratched against wood outside, and he reeled just in time to see a toddler clawing its way through the floorboards of the porch, erupting in front of the door. Even distorted by the etched glass, Sam could see that the child was bug-eyed, its skin a mottled, blue, and its face slightly decomposed.

He gasped and pressed the heels of his hands against his eyes before turning to edge away from the ghastly visage toward the living room. His muscles bunched, his adrenal glands pumped hormones into his veins, and Sam prepared for flight from terror.

Pale ephemeral images, strangely luminescent, formed before his eyes. One performed a palsied dance on the end of a rope. The second was little more than a faint outline of a partial human shape upon the floor. As he watched, the shape solidified and became recognizable.

Trapped!

Childish voices warbled, mocking. Jane Graves, the back of her head turned to cornmeal mush and her skin the consistency of goat cheese, sat up. She opened her mouth in a silent scream, and he could see the wall beyond through her parted lips.

With a whimper, Sam scurried away, only to freeze when Elliot Graves's bloodstained form emerged from the kitchen. He lumbered clumsily through the living room and swung slowly to gaze at Sam. Elliot's eyes filled with mute accusation, and he raised his hands in an imprecatory gesture.

And Sam looked down at his own hands to see that they were covered with blood.

Three children began a shimmering descent from the second floor while a dyspneic Tommy Erwin choked and gagged on his poorly constructed noose. Jane's now-erect corpse in the foyer jerked to a standing position and lurched toward Sam as his bowels turned to water and his sphincter muscle loosened.

Laughter echoed around him as Sam Holloway awoke from his nap, gasping, to discover that he had wet the bed.

Autumn had lost its tenuous grip upon the world. The heavy skies and all-too-brief days lay oppressive hands on the world. Days and nights merged, becoming one. The dark dreams of night had become nightmare days, indistinct, the change barely perceptible, differentiated not by character but only by content.

The needles clicked away in the living room as Allison

attacked her knitting with agitated fervor. The Autobats caromed across the television screen, and Jason huddled comfortably in a corner of the recliner in his blue Doctor Dentons, watching the television.

Concentrating on her stitches, Allison heard Scott pick up the receiver. Standing up, she inched closer to the door. A low mumble of voices, and she turned.

"How'd you like some hot chocolate, kiddo?"

"Yum," Jason said. He pushed away from the chair and trotted after her, pink apple cheeks glowing.

His mother put a kettle on to boil, and wandered around the kitchen nervously before she came to rest with her hand on the door frame.

Watching as her hand sank into the wood to the wrist, his gaze flicked down to the floor. No feet. No ankles.

The water began to boil. Jason eyed her guardedly.

She didn't seem to notice the simmering pot even after it began to whistle, and no spark of life glinted in her eyes. Instead they seemed to devour all light.

"Oh no." Allison mouthed the words rather than spoke.

The whistle changed in pitch, becoming even more piercing. Jason tucked his neck down into his shoulders and put his fingers in his ears.

Forehead propped on his hand, Holloway hunched over the papers he was grading. His brain was fuzzy following his nap. A flush spread across his cheeks as he remembered his wife's chiding as she changed the sheets. His head throbbed, and he couldn't seem to concentrate.

He stared at the paper before him, and the words blurred. Was it his imagination, or were children thicker than they used to be?

The phone jangled loudly.

His wife's voice rose an octave: "Who?"

"Just a second," she replied in a less excited tone.

Her head appeared in the door. "Phone call for you."

She mouthed something that he didn't understand. With

a sigh Sam picked up the receiver. A voice buzzed in his ear, and his spirits—already low—sank even more.

"No, that's all right," Sam said. "I was expecting your call."

He paused, and there was a distant buzz.

"What? Address? Gee, I don't know. It's been a long time. I'll take a look." Sam riffled through the pages of his address book.

"Here it is. I guess we don't know many people whose name begins with G." He examined the page that confirmed the numbers McDowell had rattled off.

"Let's see, yes, one-ten Second. The phone numbers? Yes, I have them." Sam gave Scott the phone numbers, both the one on Second and the old one for Elm.

"Mr. McDowell, is there anything wrong?"

Quivering in its chthonian niche the abomination roared its rage. Soon it would be free of its underworld prison, if . . . if only . . .

The entity had played with them, like a cat with a mouse. Nudging them towards the razor-fine edge of madness and withdrawing its control just before pushing them over the abyss.

Up until this time it had been patient, tolerant, even kind. If evil can be tolerant. If a devouring malignancy can be generous. If an abomination can be kind. The woman must remain happy. It must not lose her, the key.

No! A soundless shudder moved through the house issuing a warning.

Outside, the seedlings which would be the first soft shoots of summer. Grass withered. Trees dreaming of winter cold absorbed the blast of its fury through tangled roots, which shrivelled and died, while the small animals that made their dens nearby breathed their last and expired. All across the neighborhood, people tossed and turned in their sleep, their dreams gone suddenly awry. A child woke screaming, and one old grandmother gave up her tenuous grip on life, and still its fury rose.

He knew! The man knew! He must be stopped.

The entity roiled, twisting and turning, and the house overhead shook. Windows rattled and bric-a-brac danced around on tabletops. It sent the spearshafts of its rage through every atom, every molecule of the Elm Street domicile. Doors opened and closed. Anger transformed shot through the copper wires in ragged jolts.

The man was a liability. A threat to be removed. It summoned Scott's image, jittering in agony, his face a mask of pain. Concentrating, it imagined all that it would do to the man once it was free. Tearing at his tender scrotum to devour his essence, opening his rib cage to grasp the heart within and drink his blood. If only it had form and substance with which to act, and with a flick of a psychic finger, it sent these images to the house . . .

The numbers matched—both addresses and phone numbers. Scott regarded the pages as if by staring hard enough he could find the answer between the lines of the Big Chief pad. He buried his face in his hands. His headache pulsed. He wasn't ready for this.

As he arched awkwardly back in the chair, stiff from the mounting tension, Scott felt an icy hand clenched at his neck. Then he became aware of the slight pressure near the base of his skull. Gentle at first, but insidious, the pressure increased. It spread to merge with the throbbing of his head. Pain and fear pulsated in unison.

The sensation began at the nape and radiated outward. His spine tingled as though freezing fingers were brushed lightly against bare skin. Then they moved, touching, testing, electrifying the nerve endings and finding tender spots in Scott's psyche. His skin alternated between hot and cold, and he could smell the sour, acrid odor of his own fear. Every nerve in Scott's body was tingling now. Each excited end screamed in agony or ecstasy, he couldn't tell which. The excruciating pain within his head was matched by another in his chest. The pressure was unbearable.

Scott rose with a groan as a skeletal hand erupted through the floor to clasp his ankle. His jaw unhinged and his wild-eyed gaze riveted to the floor. The house around him began to shimmy and shake, and the hand vanished. Still, *something* clutched him, and he was held fast. Sinewy tendrils of panic found pathways to his brain. The tingle slid down his spine. His skin turned to gooseflesh, and he felt as cold as a polar bear on dry ice.

The papers he held fluttered to the desk, and belatedly, he reacted to jerk his foot away from the unseen hand. Scott overbalanced, and teetered back into the chair, eyes glued to the place on the floor where the hand should be—and wasn't. The oak boards there remained smooth, unbroken and unblemished.

"I'm losing my mind," he said out loud. "Certifiable. Soon they'll come for me with a butterfly net and one of those fancy jackets with the sleeves that tie around the back."

Sitting back in the chair, Scott tried to decide what he should do. Nothing. The word popped into his mind unanswerable, inarguable. What could he do?

The house echoed with distant thunder. The walls, the sheetrock, picked up the sound and threw it back to him. Below his feet the floor rocked. The windows rattled in their casings; the walls shook; the pencil holder and stapler on his desk performed a leaping, vaulting scuttle across its surface. The books in the most loosely packed shelves fell to the floor with a bang as loud as a gunshot. Elsewhere in the house he heard the tinkling of glass and the slamming of doors. Then it was over.

As Scott bustled hurriedly toward the living room, somewhere upstairs a door opened and closed with a bang.

* * *

A movement caught Jason's eyes as his mother pulled her hand from the door frame, and he swung away from her to confront a dark-haired man who lay sprawled on his tummy on the floor. His head was turned to one side, a shocked expression on his face, and glassy eyes stared blindly at the ceiling. His skin was a funny color, a splotchy blue, and blood pooled all around him.

"Ahhh." The breath was forced out of Jason's lungs as though a giant squeezed his chest with a brawny hand.

The man's eyes swiveled in his skull, and he turned his gaze upon Jason. The boy cringed away, running to clutch at his mother's hand. It was cold as ice. He tugged at her and shot a terrified glance over his shoulder.

The floor jigged below his feet, and she rocked back and forth above the teapot, moaning.

The man stood up. Jason seized her shirt and yanked with all his two-and-a-half-year-old strength. Her keening rose shrilly, and the man disappeared. Pop!

Things began to dance across the counter, and the child turned to consider his mother with eyes grown suddenly too mature. Ropy twigs snaked up her legs. He took both her hands in his—the sinewy vines fell way—and Jason led his mother to the living room, carefully avoiding the place where the man had disappeared only moments before.

"What the hell was that? An earthquake?" Scott yelled as he marched into the living room.

"I don't know," Allison said from her perch on the edge of the couch. She glanced at him, and Scott winced away from her distrustful stare. This woman was a stranger to him, as though someone had taken his wife and replaced her with this fey changeling.

Bewildered, he shifted his gaze to Jason. "You okay?"

Something about Jason's posture was mildly disturbing. He sat on the edge of the couch next to Allison, his body slanted away from her, staring at an empty space on the kitchen floor.

Scott followed his eyes, half expecting a gibbering apparition to appear.

"Jason?"

The toddler clambered down from the sofa and sped from the room, hollering. "SARA!"

Scott's head whipped around so fast it felt as though his brains sloshed around inside his skull. He turned on Allison.

"When the hell did that happen?" he said.

"What?"

"Sara."

"Oh, Sara's been around for a while."

"Sara?" Scott stared at the broken figurine, which had fallen from its position on the mantelpiece. A crack split the porcelain face.

"It's just a name," Allison observed.

"And when he did he stop playing with William?"

"He hasn't. William's still around," she said. An enigmatic smirk flitted across her lips.

Scott stormed from the house to pick up Adam from school. With hooded eyes, Allison stood at the window and watched as he stamped rigidly down the porch steps before she returned to picking up pieces of glass.

The figurine, one of her favorites, stared at her from a face that had been split down the middle. For an instant, part of her rebelled against the loss. A soft, sinuous melody wrapped itself around her, and the fleeting rebellion was squashed.

With a shrug, Allison placed the pieces in the trash. She couldn't understand why Scott was so upset.

Yes, Jason had an imaginary friend. Now he had three. So what of it?

She had kept silent about Shelley. Why mention it? Why add fuel to the fire?

Allison hadn't been particularly surprised when Jason introduced a Sara and a Shelley into his circle of imaginary pals. But she had been annoyed. With Scott jumping at every burnt-out bulb or temperamental appliance and attributing it to supernatural causes, Jason couldn't have chosen worse names for his newfound friends.

But it didn't take a great deal of intelligence to figure out where the boy had gotten them.

Scott was obsessed with the former residents, for Christ's sake. His room was filled with clips about the murder; and his thoughts were filled with their unfortunate demise. Scott had probably mentioned Sara Graves at one time or another. If Scott hadn't, then Adam or one of the neighbor kids had.

Children picked up these things, and they had an unnerving knack of picking up those things which most parents would prefer they left alone.

The problem was not with Jason, his imaginary friends, Adam. Or with the house. The problem was Scott. He was obsessed by this place. He always had been. Obsessed since the time he'd stumbled across that first article in the paper. Obsessed when he realized the place was still vacant and possibly for sale. The house had become a symbol for all he had lost in life. For everything that had been denied him. He had never been able to look at the place and see it clearly, see it for what it was.

This house was home. Their home. A delightful home. No more, no less. Why couldn't he see that? They were home. They belonged here; at least, *she* did.

Funny, Allison thought, when he'd first proposed moving she hadn't wanted to. She had resisted change as she always did and only agreed to the move because the house meant so much to him. This house, this particular house, had been his choice and not hers, but now that she was here, she liked it.

Here, she had found stability, security, continuity, and permanence . . . rootedness. As if she were able to connect with the earth below her feet through the house itself. The concept sounded ludicrous when she tried to describe it, even to herself. All very New Age, and Allison chuckled as she envisioned herself in full lotus position with some

California-style guru, Rama Dama Rubbadubdub, intoning a chant that would allow her to unite with their home.

Still, she was content. And the house was, too. Even now she could feel the happy vibration through the soles of her feet. Allison leaned against the wall to let the vibration envelop her, run through her, to let the house pull her until she was transformed, a part of it. Wood, stone . . . and she expanded in a thousand different directions, becoming something other than herself. Larger than life, ageless, timeless, and all powerful. She arched her back and moaned as some subtle presence penetrated her body—as if she had penetrated mortar and stone. Sensual, delightful.

Change, a voice hissed at her.

Everything changed, she thought. Even her relationship with her husband had changed, or was changing. Allison scowled. The shift was subtle, almost intangible, but apparent nonetheless. Nothing stayed the same, and Allison sighed, like a child greeting a sad truth. Only this house remained changeless, timeless, inalterable, like the earth beneath its foundation.

The rich scent of loam surrounded her. Moist soil, leaf mold, and sand. Allison twitched as she struggled to surface from the lip of a grave.

The Saab's engine idled as Scott watched Adam trudge up the cobbled path to the front porch. Scott waited until the door opened and closed behind his elder son, unsure why he did so. The boy was probably safer outside than in the house.

With a strained exhalation, Scott rested his head against the steering wheel. The new car smell surrounded him, calming, although Scott didn't find the aroma as aphrodisiacal as most men did.

The car, like the house had once been, was another symbol of success. Some smart-assed psychologist or marketing man could probably explain why, when he had had the opportunity to get any car he pleased, he had chosen the clunky-looking Saab instead of a sleek Jaguar, a phallic Ferrarri, or a sporty Porsche. He supposed it revealed upper–middle class aspirations. Or that he was a family man with no need to reclaim lost youth. Or an intellectual. Something along that line. But he didn't particularly care. He only knew that for now it was a refuge, a retreat, and he *wasn't* ready to go into the house yet. Not now.

Putting the car into gear, Scott swung around the cul-de-sac and headed up Elm, unsure of where he was going, only aware of the need to get away. A need to think. His mind seemed to clear, his mood lifted, and his headaches receded whenever he was away from the house.

Shell-shocked.

It seemed the perfect word to describe the family.

Numb, unquestioning. They moved through the day, unwilling to examine what had gone before. Too much had happened too fast to question or absorb. Too much to assimilate. No, it didn't pay to examine anything too closely right now, because it defied logic and reasoning. Yet examine it he must.

Shell-shocked.

Each member of the family withdrew from the others, each coping with the chaos in his own way. They had settled into a shaky routine, rotating in their own little circles of despair. Jason played with his imaginary friends, Adam went to school, and Scott hid behind his computer. Their lives intersected rarely—over meals, television, and their few other shared activities.

Shell-shocked.

The dream gone wrong, and his so-called success suddenly had the sour, coppery taste of terror. The fragile illusion of control it had given him was shattered. Things were out of control, and Scott was overwhelmed by a feeling of helplessness, a feeling he despised.

A person of action, Scott had never allowed himself to be

immobilized by obstacles. Any obstacle could be breached somehow, by either direct assault, or by strategic retreat and careful rerouting.

Driving past the old Erwin place without looking at it, Scott searched through his mind for a logical explanation, or at least a clue, sifting through memories like cards in a Rolodex, trying to decide when things had started to go bad. The truth was that things had been bad from the start.

Remodeling had been a nightmare. One worker broke his leg falling down the stairs, insisting he was pushed. Scott's ankle tingled where the unseen hand had clasped him this morning. Accidents caused, Scott assumed, by simple pubescent pranks that grew more menacing, more dangerous, as the work progressed. Their unknown saboteur tore apart the wiring and tampered with their tools. Two workmen had died—the electrician and his assistant. Cardiac arrest. Twin cardiac arrests, Scott reminded himself. The doctors thought they had been electrocuted, but they could find no burns. Electrocution seemed a logical explanation. More logical than the alternative: simultaneous heart attacks in two apparently healthy men who had no previous history of heart disease.

As if picking up Scott's thoughts from afar, two men appeared in the basement rumpus room, wearing blue cambric shirts and jeans, with tool kits that hung from their belts. Their actions were furtive as they moved around the night-black basement. The fluorescent lights sputtered a few times and then went on.

The younger man fiddled with a spotlight as thin and as transparent as himself. The two men talked wordlessly. Their lips moved but no sound emerged. They peered nervously to the corners of the basement.

Then, they bent. Their hands working a bizarre pantomime on invisible wires. Sara appeared followed by Shelley and William. They linked hands and started to circle around.

The younger man pitched forward, his cheek hitting the wall. He slid lifelessly to the floor, the soft flesh of his cheek sprouting sharp cuts as his descent tore non-existent copper wires from their intended place.

The older man froze, arm half-extended over the other as he sank to the floor. Then the other man flipped onto his back and clutched weakly at his heart. The young man's body arched; his back bowed, and his heels drummed against concrete.

The older workman moved, in slow motion, kneeling beside his partner. He groped for a pulse while the other jerked and writhed on the floor. The first workman bent to put his ear to the younger man's chest.

Then the grizzled head shot up—his eyes drawn to the corner of the room. Dark shapes moved toward him. Small shapes. Childish giggles echoed about the chamber. A shrill whisper became intensified as it bounced from hard surface to hard surface.

His eyes started out of his head, he shrank away. The skin around his lips turned a frightful blue. The white sclera expanded, bulging from the sockets, and he clutched at his chest. His face turned an ashen grey and the older man crumpled to his knees, his face caught in an expression of surprise and terror. The boy smiled at him; the workman's eyes rolled back into his head so only the whites were visible as he folded in slow motion over his partner's body.

Since they'd moved in, they had had more than their share of electrical problems. Scott stepped on the accelerator. Lights flickered on and off. Clocks stopped. Bulbs exploded. Maybe he should get the wiring checked by a professional. He'd checked the work himself—fiddling with fuses, examining master switches—but Scott could fit all he knew about electronics in a thimble and still leave room for a profound thought or two about the nature of the universe.

Faulty wiring, however, didn't account for Sara or William's sudden appearance in Jason's growing repertoire of friends. There was something decidedly creepy about watching Jason play with his imaginary pals. To peer into his eyes and know they were focused on a particular spot. Not the soft, unfocused look one gets when looking off into the distance—as Jason *should* look when gazing at something devised by his two-year-old imagination—but a definitely *fixed* stare at a *fixed* point in space. He wondered if at some future date Jason would remember Sara, Shelley, and William the way other children remembered little Jimmy or Amy up the street.

Faulty wiring and shoddy workmanship also didn't explain the headaches, the nightmares, and or those inexplicable blackouts which he had had. Neither did faulty wiring account for a wife who had become suddenly a stranger to him. For weeks, he had watched her change. The startling blue eyes glinted like sun off ice. Flat, dead, and lifeless. They were *ice*—cold, hard, and unyielding. Like any dutiful housewife, she puttered around the house, tidying, polishing—and Scott realized she was always cleaning or doing something to the house—but she didn't play with the children the way she used to.

The Allison he knew—the sturdy, strong, energetic woman—had become someone apathetic, dull, without human spirit or soul. A blank, an empty shell like a discarded husk with all animation drained from her body. Her expression would go slack, drained of all life, like a battery drained of juice, and her eyes, without spark, closed shut like a shuttered, darkened house. Scott shuddered at the analogy.

She wasn't *there*.

He saw it, was aware of it, but was unable to interpret what it meant. Until now he had assumed it was because she was unwell. The weight loss, the gray hair. As if the baby were somehow eating her alive from the inside out.

Splashes of blood.

A few fat flakes of snow began to fall. He drove on,

musing, sorting. Somewhere in the insanity there had to be a key.

Scott winced, pulled into a nearby driveway, and shifted into reverse, turning the car around to head back toward town, still unsure of where he was going. A cow standing next to a barbed-wire fence stared at him with bovine stupidity.

The snow fell harder, and Scott switched on the windshield wipers, their metronomic click hypnotizing.

Allison. The hospital. The night in the study, the night he thought she was going to die. The emptiness, the sense of absence that was almost palpable.

Deep in thought, he ran a stop sign just as a truck lumbered into the intersection. Scott swerved on the ice-slicked road. The truck's driver flipped him the bird, and the Saab skidded to a belated halt.

18

The first tentative flurry of snow turned to sleet. Ice coated leaf, limb, and wire indiscriminately. Under the street lamp each blade of yellowing grass stood out with crystalline clarity. The scene with its fairy coating of ice was deceptively beautiful. Glistening limbs bent heavily under the weight. As he drove, Scott saw broken boughs and snaking, sparking power lines by the roadside.

By the time he started driving home from Sam Holloway's house, Scott had a snootful. He pressed the accelerator, coaxing more speed from the Saab than conditions would permit or safety and common sense would allow. The car spun in an automotive pirouette, and Scott giggled like a little boy on a slide, too drunk to care.

During the long evening Sam Holloway had provided Scott with more than just a couple of drinks which dulled his reflexes. He had given a second recital of the house's history.

The older man's thinning red hair was flecked with gray. As if to make up for this bleaching of youth's color, his normally florid skin grew more flushed, but the poor man had paled when he saw Scott at the door. The splash of spider veins across his nose and cheeks became a scarlet mosaic standing out against the white skin. Corpulent with heavy jowls that hung down around a thickened neck, Holloway resembled a petulant bulldog. And he had looked like hell, like he hadn't slept for a month, but Scott was reasonably sure he didn't look much better.

Sam was none too pleased to see the younger man, yet he didn't seem surprised. Holloway seemed to be expecting Scott. The two men faced each other across the threshold like two wrestlers on Saturday night television, shoulder muscles bunched, bodies bristling, but it was little more than show. One look at the younger man's haunted expression and Holloway had opened the door with the bitter resignation of a harried housewife caught by a door-to-door salesman with his foot in the door.

Over a bottle of Chianti in the kitchen they discussed the house. Once again, Holloway repeated the tale of the Graves family, and Scott was able to pick up nuances that had eluded him before. He had known that Elliot, the father, was a batterer, much like Aldo, but had not known until now that the children may have been the recipients of a darker abuse than mere beating.

Scott blushed, remembering his dreams.

Other things he had not thought or known to ask came out. The eldest daughter Shelley had torched the family cat, and Scott remembered Ms. Courtney's accusations about the dog. She had died before they moved into the Elm Street house—perished in a blaze she had set herself. Something deep inside of Scott turned over.

His parents wreathed in flames.

They talked of the boy, William, and Sam was able to provide Scott with a photograph. Cracked, old, and sepia toned, it revealed a serious child dressed in the frilly clothes of the time. When Scott asked for a photo of the Graves family Sam simply shook his head. "We weren't that close; we didn't socialize all that much. The Graveses weren't easy people to be around."

191

Sam had been unable to say for sure in which room Jane Graves's invalid mother had lived and died, but he thought it was the old nursery. Jason's room where the spiderlady lived.

They stood before the door, saying good night. Scott turned to Sam and said: "You work at the parochial school, don't you? Are you Catholic?"

Holloway inclined his head in assent.

"Could you possibly talk to a priest . . ." Scott let the rest of the question dangle, expecting to be laughed at, but Holloway didn't bat an eyelash at the request.

"I don't know if they do that sort of thing anymore, but I'll see what I can do."

Now armed with the old sepia-toned photograph, Scott staggered up the steps and lurched in the front door. His welcome home was less than warm. Allison regarded him warily, as if he were a particularly virulent, and highly contagious, mutating virus. She tried to gather the boys to her, but Jason refused to get close. Neither would he come to Scott, staying equidistant from both of them. He kept looking at his mother's feet. Scott did, too, and for a moment they appeared blurred and indistinct, as if they had grown into the floor.

A fire crackled in the grate, and Scott winced, thinking of Shelley Graves. Adam lay on his stomach, his toys forgotten, watching the leaping flames. When his mother called softly to him, Adam went obediently to the couch, his eyes still fastened on the fire.

The gyrating flames seemed to turn her face into something deranged, like a picture drawn by a paranoid Picasso —all angles, harsh lines, and petrified planes. Again Scott was struck by her weight loss.

This wasn't going to be easy, Scott thought, and he went to the kitchen to fix himself a drink. Liquid courage.

Weaving slightly, Scott stood over Allison. "I went to visit Sam Holloway," he said with feigned indifference.

"How is Mr. Holloway?" she asked, picking up her knitting.

The needles snicked rapidly. Allison wound another loop of yarn around the foremost. The one-time bootie had evolved into blanket. Allison regarded Scott with hooded eyes as he flung himself into the recliner, drink in hand.

"Come here, Jason, I want to talk to you."

The toddler cowered away from him.

"Jason." His voice took on a warning note.

Clutching the blond doll to his chest, Jason took a step forward. Scott took a hard look at the doll's face, expecting to see twin runnels of blood running from its ceramic.

"I've got something to show you," Scott said.

The toddler's eyes lit up. "A present?"

"No, not a present, a picture."

"What picture?" Allison said.

"A picture of William."

"William?"

"A distant relative of Sam's. He died here," Scott informed her.

"Scott!" Allison hissed.

"I just want to know if it's the same William."

"Jason's William? How could it be?"

"Good question. How could it be?" Scott patted his breast pocket and withdrew the cracked, faded photograph.

"Look, Scott, I don't know what you have on your mind, but leave the child out of it."

A searing band of pain closed around his skull. This time his anger had the coppery taste of terror which soured in his mouth. He must get her to listen!

Slamming the glass down on the coffee table with a chink of ice, he shouted at her. "You may choose to be blind to what's going on around here, but I'm not."

Scott turned again to Jason, snapped his fingers, and pointed to the floor before his feet. "Come here, Jason."

Jason blanched and took another hesitant step forward.

"Now."

The toddler's face began to work up and down spasmodically. He opened his mouth once, twice, but no sound came out, only a strangulated gurgle. Then it snapped shut with a click.

Scott studied Jason. The child held his ground.

"Daddy?" he said.

The frightened tone tore at Scott's heart, but he had to know.

Allison stood up, her knitting falling from her lap. "I won't have you terrorizing the children. I don't know what's gotten into you."

The red of rage colored his vision, but beneath that he felt fear. And Scott could no longer tell who or what controlled his thoughts, anymore, but he had to know! Grabbing a hold of Jason's chubby arm, Scott wrenched the child, thrusting the photo under his nose.

With surprising agility for her size and advanced state of pregnancy, Allison lunged forward to seize the photo from his hand and retreated.

"No," she barked. "I will not have you infecting the children with your madness."

She threw the photo into the fire. Adam slid from his place on the sofa and scampered across the room to watch the picture burn. Jason sidled cautiously away from his parents. They glared at each other over his head. Then he scuttled across the room to look at the photograph.

As the cardboard caught and flickered Jason stabbed at it with a stubby finger.

"William," he whispered.

Scott neither saw nor heard any of these things, his attention fixed on Allison. The tightening band, the sibilant hiss of the fire as it eagerly lapped at the photograph. His expression contorted with rage, and his lips pulled into a cruel sneer.

"Quit blaming the goddamn house! Will you!" she shrieked at him.

In a single step he was beside her, grabbing her roughly. With a twist of his hand, Scott pulled Allison's arm behind her back. Just as abruptly he let go, and she reeled backwards, tripping on her own feet, falling against the wall.

He plunged after her, pinning her down. His hand closed around her throat, and he nearly lifted her off her feet by her neck. She flopped like a doll, her heels pounding against the wall as she clawed at his fingers to release their hold.

Jason screeched, and Adam shrank against the wall. Scott's fingers closed convulsively around her larynx and she gagged.

"Scott," she choked, and he slackened his grip, allowing her toes to touch the floor.

Then Scott released her and her hand instinctively went to her neck. Her breath came in short ragged gasps.

"You bastard. You're insane," she screamed.

Horses stampeded inside his head, and, out of control, Scott raised his hand to strike.

Allison watched, hypnotized, as Scott's arm swung upward in slow motion—rippling, eternally upward—packed with repressed fury. Adam sobbed and sprang, seizing Scott's hand before he could complete the downward swing.

"No," she begged, the word hardly more than a breath.

His expression hardened, and his eyes narrowed, snapping first to Adam's clutching his hand and then to her face.

"Let go," Scott said through clenched teeth.

"Daddy, please don't." Adam's arms dropped helplessly to his sides.

Scott spun. The violent action hurled Adam against the wall, and he folded like an empty coat. Allison leapt, catching him before he could collapse to the floor, but Scott was on top of her again.

Grasping her shoulders, he shook her.

"Can't" . . . shake . . . "you" . . . shake . . . "see" . . . shake . . . "what" . . . shake . . . "is" . . . shake . . . "going" . . . shake . . . "on" . . . shake . . . "around" . . . shake . . . "you?"

The television blared to life, and the VCR clicked on.

Allison's head rolled limply on her neck. Her eyes hazy, saliva dribbled from the corner of her mouth. She was gone, and her almost comatose appearance only fueled his fury. He shook her one last time, vaguely aware that Bambi, Thumper, and Flower were performing sodomitic acts on television.

Crawling over to Adam's side, Jason stared—not at his father or the tube, but at his mother's knees. Consciousness flooded back into Allison's face. Light sparked in her eyes once again. A series of warring emotions battled for supremacy in her face as something alien within her fled.

"There's nothing wrong with this house; it's you!" she shouted.

Scott stiffened for a moment, seeing a stranger looking out from her eyes. Just as quickly the impression was gone.

Ashamed, Scott escaped into the kitchen. What the hell had he done? The memory of those few seconds were a blur. He only remembered a sense of outrage and a need to punish . . . someone . . . something. Trying to recall what had set him off, Scott retrieved a bottle from the liquor cabinet.

The photograph was in ashes, and now he would never know. As he raised the glass to his lips with trembling hands, he wondered if he really wanted to know.

Tap, tap, tap, tap.

The lights were out, and his parent's voices stilled. The only sound in the house was the bare branch tapping plaintively at window in Adam's room. Jason knelt in his bed and then scooted around the raised rails to its foot. He got out of bed, moved to the closet door, and opened it.

"You can come out now," he said softly.

Sitting cross-legged on the floor, Jason waited for his friends to appear. He couldn't understand why his friends upset his parents so.

This house was *full* of people, not just the children, but

adults too. And bodies. Bodies that would suddenly come to life, like the man in the kitchen. They frightened him, but William would protect him. William was strong; William was smart; William sometimes seemed adult too.

Jason waddled over to his toy box and dug through the contents, scooping his toy soldiers from inside.

One of the trucks he had left on the floor began to move and Jason squealed his delight, clapping a hand over his mouth so his parents wouldn't hear. Another joined it, rolling across the room to come to a halt next to the closet door.

A small red fire engine leapt forward, rising to fly through the air, and the toy soldiers joined, swooping and whirling above his head.

Jason looked from it to Sara and then Shelley. Their images wavered, rippling. They smiled at him and nodded. William floated above them. His thin fingers twitched, and with each twitch, the toys responded with a frantic leap or a dizzying spin.

A neat trick! Jason mimed William's motions, hoping he could do it too.

You wanna learn? A voice sizzled inside his brain.

"Yes," Jason whispered.

Tap, tap, tap, tap.

Adam's face was pressed against the cold glass. Outside, the sky had cleared. Frigid stars glittered above the empty field, and a gust of wind harvested a few straggling leaves that remained on the nearby branch as the oak tree waved a gnarled greeting at him.

The security and peace of their old home in Blue Island was only a distant and tantalizing memory. He tried to remember the last time either his mother or his father had laughed and couldn't. Adam felt betrayed; but couldn't quite figure by what or whom. His mother's scream, his parent's argument. His parents *never* fought, until they moved here, and now it seemed they fought everyday.

Tap, tap, tap.

Time stretched and squeezed and stretched before him, and Adam wanted to go home. Home was Blue Island. Home was cracked ceilings and a stained sink, his mother singing in the kitchen, and a father who always ready to rough-house and romp.

The sizzling, hissing noise filled his mind. Buzzing like a thousand insects which gathered on a warm summer night. The high whine of a mosquito. Words, but not words that told him what to do.

Adam cocked his head. He scooped the matchbox from its hiding place behind his small desk. Pulling himself upright with spastic movements—a puppet on a string—Adam started toward the door of his room, still listening.

The rattling branch called to him, and Adam followed. A buzz of wordless commands directed him to foyer and he moved soundlessly down the stairs. The golden girl flitted before him.

Outside everything glistened, covered with a thin coating of ice. Chilled and yet thrilled, Adam scurried across the cul-de-sac to dive behind the vacant house and find his hidden treasure.

Brittle stars receded into the velvetine night.

Heart pounding in his chest, Adam cowered against the crumbling wall. Would it be here?

"Mew?"

"Here kitty, kitty."

"Mew." The old lady's cat wandered around the side of the garage, walked up to Adam and sniffed his cold-stiffened fingers, and Adam pounced.

His hand folded over the delicate feline skull. Holding it in place with one hand, he struggled with the charcoal lighter fluid's cap. It opened suddenly, almost toppling and spilling the precious contents.

Splash!

Fluid cascaded over the cat's body. It yowled and thrashed. Sharp claws raked his hand, Adam ignored the pain. Smiling beatifically, he lit the match. Holding it a moment, he contemplated the flames.

So pretty.

Then, acting quickly, he released his hold on both cat and the match. The flickering match fell on the saturated fur, and the flames exploded across its body. Adam stepped back, and the cat streaked across the yard like a flaring bottle rocket.

The harsh glare of the operating theater nearly blinded him. Scott could barely make out the forms of Elliot and Jane Graves. The two adults held Allison's legs pinned, while two girls, Sara and Shelley, dressed in surgical greens, immobilized her arms. The boy, William, floated above them, reaching out a bony hand, the nails dirty, ragged, and torn. One of the girls thrust an implement into his fist.

A butcher knife.

Other apparitions danced around her gleefully. Aldo. His parents encased in flames. A young adolescent, his neck twisted so that he looked at the ceiling. A bug-eyed toddler. And others, blurred forms, nothing more. Her belly moved in ever rapidly increasing undulations, keeping time with their demonic capering.

The operating room dissolved, and they were in their bedroom. Faster and faster, the phantoms circled the bed, slipping in and out of the walls to complete their circuit. Faster. *Faster. Faster.* And *FASTER!*

The child, William, yanked her legs apart. She shrieked and fought the hands which tried to force her knees to separate. Panting like a puppy, she kicked at the boy.

The phantom Elliot slapped her, ramming her shoulders against the bed. *Push!* he commanded.

Scott was rooted to the spot, helpless.

William caressed her thighs, poked at her peritoneum. The bag of water broke.

Her stomach seemed to take on a life of its own. The fetus clawed its way through the uterine wall. The skin split and two taloned hands appeared at the opening, and his parents disappeared behind a wall of flames.

Bathed in sweat, Scott wrenched himself from sleep. Sickly illumination came into the room through the crack between the drawn curtains. The light bore a single, thin, grey line across the floor. Morning.

19

Winter marched relentlessly on, goose-stepping across the calendar with blitzkrieg rapacity. The brief flurry of the previous night had returned with a vengeance sometime in the early morning hours. Big, fat clumps fell leadenly to the earth, coming not with the tearing winds of blizzard, but in a slow, gentle fall of fluffy white flakes. Silently, it fell, and by morning, the boys tumbled gaily in a snowy blanket. Neither parent had the heart to admonish the children, and Scott had taken Adam to school covered in a crusty, cold second-skin.

A loud knock at the door roused Allison from the pages of the cookbook where she was looking for the recipe for pumpkin pie. She marked her place with the empty matchbook she had found that morning on the kitchen floor and rose to answer the door, glancing out the window. The Saab's tire tracks marred the drive, and around the side of the house, the snow was trampled by the boys' feet, but the front yard remained unmarked except for shuffling footprints that straggled across the pristine surface. Something about the tracks were strange.

With another quick look around the kitchen Allison

bustled toward the door. An old woman leaning against an aluminum cane stamped the snow from her feet impatiently. Allison opened the door.

"Yes," she said as she studied the strange woman.

Cold eyes stared from a sagging face, surrounded by straggling hair more yellow than gray. Few of the lines around the pursed and pinched mouth were formed by laughter. This must be the neighborhood hag Adam complained so much about.

"Your doorbell doesn't seem to be working." The woman pointed a crooked finger at the button.

"We'll have to get that checked. May I help you?"

"I was looking for my cat. Have you seen him?"

"I? Why no. I haven't been out of the house all day."

The old lady eyed her distrustfully. "What about your son?"

Jason wandered into the room to cling to Allison's leg.

"Jason? Well, yes, he's been out." Allison looked down. "Have you seen a kitty cat, Jason?"

"Uh-uh." The toddler stuck a finger in his mouth.

"Not him, your other son. The mean one."

Allison's head tilted to one side in inquiry. "Adam? He's in school."

"Did he go out this morning?" the woman persisted.

"Of course he did. I told you, he's in school."

"I mean before school."

"For a little while, yes. Both boys were pretty excited about the snow," Allison said. "You know how children are."

The woman exhaled explosively.

"What's all this about? I can ask Adam about your cat when he returns from school, but I doubt that he's seen it either. Neither child was out for long."

Leaning heavily on her cane the woman poked at Allison with a bent index finger. "You'd better watch that boy of yours. He's a mean one."

"I don't know what you're talking about," Allison said frostily. "Adam's a very well-behaved child."

Hard eyes looked Allison up and down, and she harrumphed. "I don't expect you to agree. It's obvious you don't know your child. I'm reasonably sure he did something to my cat. He was always stalking her, and she didn't come in last night. I think"—and the woman paused—"that he's done something to her."

"You're wrong," Allison said, pulling herself upright. She glared at the harridan. "My Adam wouldn't hurt a fly. Now, if you don't mind . . ."

Allison started to close the door, and the woman stopped her by sticking her cane in the door.

"And your husband?" Her hard stare concentrated on the purple marks on Allison's neck.

"Yes, what about my husband?"

"Might he have seen my cat?"

"I don't know. He's at the grocery store right now. I'll ask him when he gets home."

With a shake of her head and an incomprehensible murmur the woman turned her back on Allison without even saying good-bye, and she hobbled across the porch.

Swoosh, swoosh, tap, tap and the sound of the sliding gait sent shivers up Allison's spine.

Closing the door Allison said, "And thank you, too."

Shrugging, she pulled Jason from her leg and herded him toward the living room. She planted him on the living room floor and gave him a pop-up book to look at before returning to the kitchen. She abandoned the cookbook and went to fill a bucket with water.

Allison bent to wash the woodwork, for the second time that week. Humming a lullaby, she lovingly stroked and caressed the wooden frame. Feeling at one with the house and with the earth beneath it, she soon forgot the old woman and her cat.

* * *

A weakling sun sank into a dreary landscape sapped of both life and color. Despite the unshriven gloom, the day had been a peaceful one—an island of calm in an ever-turbulent sea of madness. The snow continued throughout the day, turning the sky silvery white with huge, wet whirling flakes. It had obliterated the road that flattened into the curb and the yards beyond.

The house creaked and groaned under the increasing weight of the falling snow. Chin propped on his hand, Scott tried to recapture his lost thought. He snapped his fingers and returned to his work, typing faster and faster, as if speed could make up for lack of inspiration. He was rewarded when the story—so elusive before—also picked up speed.

A yawn, and a flick of a psychic finger, and the lights flickered.

"No!" Scott roared, his fingers skimming over the keyboard as he frantically gave the command to save his work.

Around him the room went dark, then light again, and Scott was plunged into darkness. The chapter vanished from the screen; even the computer main's light went out. In the few heartbeats that followed, Scott realized that the entire house was black. He pushed away from the desk, swearing. His empty coffee cup crashed to the floor.

Allison curled protectively on the sofa. She stared out the window at a blanched and blanketed world. A world of sanity, of safety, a world beyond Scott's reach. All its features were obscured, muted and softened by the same snow that smothered all sound. Curb, shrub, bush became indistinguishable, only one curve among many.

According to the radio reports, the entire state was crippled by nature's wrath. Only those driven by necessity went out on the treacherous roads. Allison was glad that they had picked up the Thanksgiving turkey early. All day she and Scott had avoided each other, hiding behind elaborate civility, trying to pretend that everything was all right. But around her throat, she wore a necklace of livid bruises as a reminder.

Her cocoa forgotten, Allison enjoyed the idyllic scene beyond the windows. The landscape was a single monochromatic blur without shadows, and the surrounding tract homes soared, white hillocks in the unbroken pallor. The sodium streetlights had blinked on nearly an hour ago, creating a glowing halo in the opalescent sky, and even minimal movement ceased.

The boys played war in the middle of the living room floor. Soon, she would need to fix dinner.

"Eh . . . eh . . . eh . . . eh . . . eh." Vocal gunfire rattled in Adam's throat.

Her gaze shifted from the scene outside to watch them, and she wondered why they never played in the gameroom. The few times she had sent them down there, they had dragged their toys back upstairs.

"Eh . . . eh . . . eh . . . eh . . . eh." Jason returned the barrage, and Batman went crashing into the motley collection of soldiers.

Light. Dark. Light. Dark.

"No!" Scott's bull bellow erupted from the study as the house plummeted into blackness.

A crash came from the study. Cursing, Scott rampaged into the living room, nearly tripping over Adam.

Allison heaved herself from the sofa. "I'll go get some candles."

"No wait."

"Wait? What do you mean wait? The lines are probably down; it'll be a while before we have power."

"I couldn't be that lucky," he muttered.

"Lucky?"

"Yes, I lost a whole goddamn chapter. It would be nice if, for a change of pace, it wasn't just because of some fucking fluke." His arms flung wide as if with his gesture he could encompass the entire house.

Light splintered the shadows.

"See?" he said. "Well, I suppose I'd better go see if I can resurrect the dead."

Still swearing under his breath, Scott groped for the switch, flipped it, and the computer began its mindless count of RAM, or ROM; Scott could never remember which. It booted, rolling automatically to his word-processing software. He stared at the amber screen, his face sallow in the yellow light.

Light. Dark. Light. Dark . . . Light.

Scott jumped.

His movement dislodged the software manual that lay open in his lap. It slid to the floor with a bang.

He cringed and fixed the computer with an accusatory glare.

The menu returned his glare with bland stare of its own.

Find a file.

Edit a file.

Copy a file.

Quit the program.

Scott rubbed burning eyes with his fingers. It felt like someone had stuffed ten pounds of grit underneath his lids.

To have lost a chapter to an irretrievable void. Impossible! He refused to accept it.

Only fifteen of thirty chapters completed. Fifteen, only if he could find chapter fifteen, Scott reminded himself. He had to be able salvage something. It must be hidden somewhere within the system. Scott stabbed at Q, and the computer switched to the central directory.

He typed D I R / W, and the computer responded, listing anonymous software programs that he rarely used. The database he had bought in the first flush of enthusiasm with his new toy. The database with which he could produce mass mailers for what and to whom, Scott no longer recalled.

The spreadsheet software he'd purchased in that same honeymoon period. That particular program, at least, he had tried to use, setting up rudimentary accounts before he realized that his accountant could do it faster and more efficiently. Stubborn, he'd continued to balance his checkbook on the computer until he lost interest. The games directory, which both he and the boys enjoyed, and the utilities software with which he hoped he could salvage his work, assuming it was salvageable.

Scott sat, trying to divine its secrets, and his eyes fell on bytes of hard disk memory. His heart leapt with both joy and trepidation. A big chunk of the forty-meg was gone, more than could be accounted for with his software and only fifteen chapters of text of about twenty-eight K each.

Scott's finger's fluttered over the keyboard, calling up the WP subdirectory but bypassing the menu.

D I R / W. Return.

And a long list of com-files, bat-files, and dat-files scrolled across the screen. Thriller.bin—the directory in which he kept the many documents that comprised his books—and one other.

Scott grabbed the software manual. Flipping through pages with semi-intelligible directions, Scott halted his search to chortle mirthlessly. He was making this a lot harder than necessary. Of course, if he were going to access it at all, it would be through the main WP menu.

He cracked his knuckles and twiddled the keys before typing in the required commands, suddenly unsure of himself. Shivering, Scott forced his fingers to move across the keyboard.

Find a file.

Filename: House15. Enter.

Nothing.

He switched to the subdirectory. His fingers crossed. It contained chapters one through fourteen.

"Son of a bitch," he muttered.

No good. The chapter was gone, chewed up along with that portion of the hard disk.

Score one for technology.

Arms crossed and resting on his stomach, he stared at the computer.

Technology, hell. He couldn't blame technology, not in a house where appliances, lights, even the telephone had taken on lives of their own.

Bending over, he picked up the pieces of the broken coffee cup. When he straightened, two words appeared on the screen next to the a-prompt: *Got you.*

The mouth-watering aroma of roast turkey circulated throughout the house—the steamy windows further blurred the hazy scenery outside. The sky was overcast, bleached of all color after divesting itself of snow. The white of the sky met the white horizon, and the eerie, reflected lightness made day of night.

Slowed to an occasional whipping flurry, much of the snow was still flawless. The town still hadn't dug out from under. Their little section of Elm, the portion leading to the cul-de-sac, had only been plowed yesterday, and then it was done at Scott's expense.

Tired of waiting and concerned about Allison, Scott had insisted they hire someone rather than wait for the township. The phone was out again, and Scott, after trudging to a neighbor's to call for telephone repairs, picked some name from the Yellow Pages. Two hours later some guy with a Jeep Cherokee and detachable blade arrived, like an L.L. Bean-clad knight riding a snarling stallion. The young man had been a breath of fresh air for the entire family. He gave both Adam and Jason a ride in his Jeep, and they, at least, revived for the holiday.

Scott listened to CDs in the living room. The mellifluous voice of Phil Collins competed with the cackles of the Wicked Witch of the West as the boys watched *The Wizard of Oz*—Scott's objections vetoed by Allison.

Allison paused to collect herself in the kitchen. Shadowed eyes swept the room. A crayoned turkey, signed by its kindergarten artist, decorated the refrigerator door. The counters were cleaned. Everything was neatly stacked, ready for serving. Allison ticked through a mental checklist. The turkey, with additional stuffing, was in the oven. Homemade muffins sat in the microwave, awaiting a final warming zap. The salad was chopped, diced, and tossed. The giblets and drippings simmered on the stove. Dessert had been provided by the local bakery, and the much-fondled pink box stood next to the dessert plates.

She moved leadenly from the kitchen into the dining room. The table was set with their best china. Allison rearranged silver, sliding it slightly to the side, only to return it to its original position.

Satisfied that everything was as ready as it could be until the turkey had finished its three-hour bake, Allison walked into the living room to join Adam and Jason. She dozed intermittently, awakening to a squawk of glee.

Scott glared at the television screen, suspiciously. Would Toto start humping Dorothy's leg? Or would the Cowardly Lion develop a brand-new four-letter-word vocabulary?

Jingle bell, jingle bell, jingle bell, fuck . . .

Scott slid down to the floor to play with Adam and Jason. They constructed something phantasmagorical with the boys' building blocks, borrowing a few black pieces from the domino set just to keep things interesting. Much to Allison's dismay, Scott showed the children a new card game, Fifty-Two Pickup, and they spent the rest of the afternoon chasing cards around the living room.

The oven timer buzzed, and Allison leered at Scott, who crab-walked to pick up the cards.

"Thanks," she said, as a card went fluttering over her head. "I needed that."

He grinned sheepishly and then thrust an arm under the couch for a hidden joker.

"Help me in the kitchen?" she asked.

"Is it ready?" Scott said.

"As soon as you've carved it and put it on the platter."

"Yum." Scott rubbed his stomach, and Jason picked up the refrain.

"Yum!" he mimicked his father, rubbing his round belly too.

"Adam, show your brother how to rub his stomach and pat his head while I go help your mother in the kitchen."

Allison fiddled with the microwave controls, her oven-mitted hands clumsy. It hummed to life, and she swooped to the refrigerator, extracting the salad and fruit platter, which she took into the dining room.

The boys traipsed in after them. Scott sharpened the knife, wearing a maniacal expression and doing his best imitation of Bela Lugosi's evil laugh. Allison returned from the dining room and glowered at Scott.

The family gathered around the table, and Scott said grace. Allison kept silent when the two boys echoed Scott's amen. She had yet to think of anything for which she felt thankful except perchance the house, but even that had palled recently.

The boys dived into their food, their appetite undiminished by the gloomy atmosphere that radiated from their parents. They fought over a drumstick until Scott tore the second off the bird and gave it to Adam.

Afterwards they ate in silence, concentrating on their meal. With a groan, Scott leaned back in his chair, stroking his distended stomach. Jason lifted his Batman T-shirt, exposing a pink-skinned belly, and Adam followed suit.

Scott chuckled. "It's hard to tell who's pregnant in this house tonight."

"You're lucky. Your big tummy"—and she patted first Jason's and then Adam's—"will go away tomorrow. Mommy's jealous."

Scott reached for her hand, and she pulled it away as though burned.

"Please, honey."

She grimaced. "I'll go get the pie."

Revulsion rippled throughout her body as he touched her

hand, an abhorrence that had been growing day by day. Revulsion at the soft texture and slight dampness of his skin, nothing like the silky, satiny feel of wood grain. Cool, rich, and inviting, and Allison lost herself as she sought the safety of the wood.

Before her the bony carcass of the turkey stood a proof of human savagery, so unlike the warmth and safety she felt emanating from the house. Dimly, she saw the hurt in his eyes as she recoiled, and part of her rebelled against her own revulsion, mourning the distance that had grown between her husband and herself.

Deep within she felt something fracturing, splitting apart, as she despaired the loss. The house around her held its breath. Allison began to sense evil in her place of retreat of wood grain and pink insulation.

The thunderous rumble started deep in the basement. The whole house shivered and shook. The cutlery rattled on dirty plates, and the light fixture danced above their heads. Scott bolted upright, looking wildly around him. His chair fell to the floor with a crash. Allison grabbed both boys, pulling them toward her to clench them tightly to her breast like a hen with her chicks.

A loud reverberating boom was replaced by preternatural quiet. They waited.

Aching silence.

Allison loosened her grip, and the day's fragile gaiety was lost. Adam hovered close to his mother's side while Jason ran to his father.

"Wha'z that?"

"I don't know, Jason." Scott watched his son's face fall. The fountain of wisdom dries up.

"I'll start clearing the table," Allison said.

"I'll help," Scott agreed.

They began a procession from dining room to kitchen, removing plates and platters. Adam stopped next to the window that looked out over the front yard.

"Dad?"

"What, Adam?" he said peevishly, balancing the gravy boat and handful of empty glasses.

"Look." Adam pointed out the window across the cul-de-sac. Scott put the glasses down.

"Oh, my God!"

"What?" Allison said as she entered the dining room.

"Come here." Scott motioned her to his side.

Curious, she came to stare into the bleached night.

The abandoned house across the way, where Adam often played, had an oddly bowed look, as though some unfriendly giant had come along and patted it a bit too hard. It had split down the middle—its roof collapsed under the weight of the snow.

The McDowells stood clustered around the window in awed silence. Besides an occasional gust, the hush extended throughout the entire neighborhood. Scott noted that several faces had appeared at the windows up and down the street.

Beside him Allison shivered, and Scott didn't know whether it was because for once something strange had happened somewhere else and not in their own home, or if she suspected—as he did—that the house's increasing evil now stretched far beyond its boundaries.

20

Even before she had opened her eyes her fingers were searching the other side of the bed for Scott. It was empty, and the sheets were cold. Allison groaned.

How many mornings now? She wondered how much longer he could continue like this. He'd slept little since the move. He'd never been a heavy sleeper, often up and around prowling the house late at night, but it had been literally weeks since she had awakened to find him at her side.

Allison tried to sit up in the waterbed and wobbled a bit before she had mastered the inertia created by her growing mass. Allison scooted over to the side of the bed where she rested, breathless from the exertion.

She hated it when she got this big. The bulk of the unborn child would press against her lungs, her bladder, and her bowels, making all bodily functions difficult or urgent. Allison felt like a beached whale. She could never understand why some people thought pregnant women were beautiful. To her they just looked fat and ungainly.

Rocking back slightly, Allison pulled herself upright with a mighty heave and an oomph. She waddled to the closet to get her robe and then went to Adam's bedroom to rouse him for another day. She clutched his shoulder and shook him gently.

"Adam. Adam, it's time to get up now."

Her eldest son batted at her hand, and Allison couldn't quite suppress a grin. Like his father, Adam wasn't a morning person. Her fingers tightened on his shoulder, and she shook him again.

"Come on, scoot." And she pulled him into a sitting position.

Adam mumbled a surly hello and stumbled for the door.

"Adam."

He stopped.

"Be quiet. I think your father's working."

He nodded mutely and headed for the bathroom. Allison rummaged through the drawers, looking for a semi-matched outfit. She was behind on the laundry. She dug out a pair of green socks, Adam's favorite Dracula T-shirt, and a pair of jeans.

Already mentally writing her grocery list, Allison headed for the hall. Adam joined her, more alert and less churlish than he had been earlier.

One hand resting on the door to Jason's room, Allison handed Adam his clothes. Dracula gave her a fanged leer. "Here. I'll go help your brother."

Dressed in faded blue pajamas, with one snap unsnapped so that his pale stomach protruded roundly, Jason sat playing pick-up sticks in the middle of the bedroom, wide awake. One fist stuck in his mouth, the other hovered over a pile of sticks. He chattered happily, grabbed one, and the whole stack shifted.

"Unfair!" Jason yelled at the empty room.

"Jason, time to get up."

"Am-mup, Mommy." Although he spoke to his mother, he eyed a space to his right. Spooky.

Marching over to the dresser, Allison pointedly ignored him. He continued his game, interrupting it occasionally to speak to Sara or to Shelley. Evidently William was not in attendance at this pick-up-sticks match.

Allison rifled through the drawers, searching for clean clothes. She wondered idly what Scott had done with the family's socks while she was in the hospital. Or had he only washed one from each pair in the load that had been ruined when the septic system backed up.

On her third drawer she resurrected a pair of Oshkosh B'gosh overalls and a Winnie-the-Pooh shirt. She collected everything from his training pants to his bunny slippers.

He didn't often need the additional protective padding now. He rarely had accidents. Only when he was scared. Her little boy was growing up. She glowed with parental pride when the young prodigy does something so apparently prodigal. Of course, she and Scott had learned a few tricks too. The first place they located during any outing was the nearest available toilet. And they planted him on the potty before they went anywhere and immediately upon their return. Their strategy kept accidents to a minimum.

Plucking him from the floor, Allison gave his rotund belly a wet, slurpy raspberry and unsnapped the remaining snaps on his pajamas in a single motion. She had his pants pulled down and his tiny bottom planted on the potty chair before he had the chance to squeal or object.

Knees together, ankles apart, one leg completely out of his pajama bottoms, Jason slouched on the potty. With his hands dangling at his sides, he continued to stare at the game.

With a shudder Allison turned her back on Jason and gazed longingly out the window. In times of peace she could almost forget everything. During quiet moments like this she allowed herself to be lulled by the routine little things that made up so much of an ordinary day, like trying to dress a child. Something about ordering and stacking his clothes was reassuring.

Mechanically Allison stooped, picking up toys. She went

over to the window box whose lid also functioned as a seat. Her fingers grazed the wood.

"Spiderlady," Jason was peering at his mother where she was stationed next to the window. Allison scanned the room, thinking it was getting pretty crowded in here, before she realized Jason meant that she had trespassed on the spiderlady's domain.

She snorted and grabbed the cushioned window seat, lifting the lid. Again Allison was struck by the soft, satiny texture of the wood grain inside the box. The feeling was strange and mildly narcotic.

"No, it moved," Jason chimed.

A pause.

"Did too!"

Allison's hands faltered in their practiced movements of returning toys to their proper compartments, and she had to fight the impulse to look over her shoulder, afraid that she might just see a stick moving all by itself.

Jason's warbling voice rose again to address someone unseen. Allison cringed away from the penetrating treble tone. It was getting on her nerves, and she had to squelch the urge to yell at him. Poised at the window, she vainly sought the calm his warbling voice had destroyed. Every element of her being was bent on ignoring the events of the last few weeks, as though such an avowal would make it real and denial made it somehow unreal.

Head draped over the rich smelling window box seat, she was surrounded by smell of wood, the soft and gentle feel of its texture, but she found no comfort there. Jason shrieked his delight, calling after Shelly, and something inside Allison snapped.

"Jason, stop that this minute!" she shouted, and he turned dazed eyes on her.

Sara, then Shelley, disappeared.

Lowering her voice, she said, "Please don't. It's time to get you cleaned up."

Jason's eyes flicked to his mother's and returned to stare

at the jumble of sticks on the floor. From the corner of his eye, and with infinite care, he examined her face—each familiar feature, trying to decide if she was really there.

The toddler cocked his head as he considered her; then the two-year-old eyes narrowed as he considered her distrustfully. Something sparked behind the glazed eyes. *She was there.* He had to tell her. They were gone, and she was *there.* All the warnings and fears—that went all mushy in his head when his friends were around—flew to the surface to be caught like a fly in a web of a two-year-old vocabulary unable to describe so complex a thought. He didn't have the words.

Allison swooped down on him and he was swinging, wet, cold rump and all, through the air to be draped over her lap. She wiped his bottom with a cloth. In that undignified position Jason tried to remember the words from the other night, when he'd seen Donald do the bad thing that Shelley said made babies. The words he had thought of then: bad, worst, worstest. Her gentle love tap on his bare bottom resounded like a crack throughout the room, and all the words blew away.

Jason thought of dry leaves on a windy day, and Allison urged him to step into his panties. Words did that sometimes, just blew away. Especially when he had dire need to communicate.

Allison pulled the shirt over Jason's head.

Like when he had to go pee real bad. The words disappeared to that place where words go. Someplace dark and spidery. Scary.

"Jason? Are you okay?"

Squirming anxiously, he pulled at the Winnie the Pooh emblem on the pocket. He wanted to tell her, but would she listen? Momma hadn't listened when he told her the monster was loose in the house. She wouldn't listen now. She didn't want to hear about . . . bad things. Scary things. Like the hand that grabs you from behind or the nasty stuff that gathers in shadows. Bad things like you see on TV.

Jason leaned against his mother's knees as she tugged the overalls into place.

The house wanted her. It took her sometimes. At first it had been Daddy, but when Mommy came home from the hos-spittle—he sounded the word out and decided he didn't like the sound of it—the house took her instead. At those times Mommy went away, and she was empty, like the black space in a closet.

Jason knew Daddy saw it, too—saw Mommy empty, knew she was empty—but Daddy didn't understand. He didn't understand like Jason understood, cuz Sara and Shelley had explained it to him. But Jason had no way to communicate his message.

Allison snapped one strap of the overall and wrestled him around to face the opposite direction.

Danger! The word pulsed across Jason's mind like the blood-red splash of light on the big truck that took mommy to the hos-spittle. A skull and crossbones. Danger. Not for Jason, but for her.

Allison struggled with the left snap.

The word flashed and was gone, leaving no meaning besides fear.

The house played with Jason, and sometimes, it played with Daddy and Adam. But it *wanted* Mommy! It wanted what grew inside her. The nasty thing, the slimy thing that would jump snarling from her tummy one of these days.

He had to tell her.

"It's a ba-a-ad place," he said, elongating the vowel, using the length of the sound to imply the severity of the blight. "Real bad."

"What are you talking about? What do you mean?"

Tucking his lip under his teeth, he gazed at the window seat. "The house is bad. It wants you."

Allison put him down on the floor, dropping to her knees. Her hands clasped the fragile shoulders, her fingers digging into the flabby, undeveloped muscles in his upper arm.

"You can't mean that, Jason. This is a perfectly lovely house."

He shrank away from her.

"The house is bad," he said in a small voice.

Allison shook him, as Scott had shaken her only a couple of nights ago. "Take it back," she shrieked into his face. "Take it back. The house is not bad!"

"Bad," Jason whispered, his pupils two pinpoints in the blue field of his iris as he peered over her shoulder.

"This house is not bad! Do . . . you . . . understand . . . me!"

William floated near the ceiling, motioning for Jason to come to him, and the warning that Jason had been about to deliver blew away. Gone without a second thought. Instead the toddler watched William circling above him, fascinated. Rapt, Jason stared. He wanted to fly like that!

With a disinterested glance at his mother Jason disentangled himself and pulled away. William darted through the wall to the hall. Talking to himself happily, Jason bolted through the door—everything else forgotten—leaving his mother kneeling on the floor staring at her own hands.

Another extravaganza in the parade of Saturday-morning cartoons pranced gaily across the television screen. Adam and Jason were splayed comfortably at her feet, draped over stuffed animals and Ninja chairs.

After having pulled his boots off, Scott walked in from the foyer, white bag in his hand.

"Doughnuts anyone?"

"Oh boy!" Adam and Jason grabbed at the bag simultaneously.

"There's enough for everyone," Scott said and he lifted the bag above their heads. "Who wants a jelly doughnut?"

"Me!" Jason jumped up. Scott handed him a doughnut and gave Allison several napkins. "I think you'll be needing these."

"Thanks." She accepted them with a wry grin at Jason. Her eyes held no warmth for Scott.

"And who wants a chocolate doughnut?" Scott said.

"Me!" Adam clamored.

Scott gave it to Adam and then passed the bag to Allison. After Allison had helped herself, he took the bag and flopped down on the recliner with a groan. Jason and Adam cheered on the Road Runner and Scott felt a twinge of pity for poor old Wile E. Coyote.

Selecting his favorite cream-filled pastry, leaning back in the chair, Scott observed his wife—the gray hair, the bruised eyes, the yellowing necklace around her throat, and the strained expression—and he wished he could make everything right. More than anything, he wished he could make it right again, but any attempt he had made to apologize was quickly rebuffed. After the other night, they had skirted each other like a couple of nervous dogs, and Scott wondered if she was right and he was taking this house thing too serious.

The house had not put those bruises around her neck or the wariness in her eyes. Allison had withdrawn from him, and he deserved it. She'd closed off completely—not only from him, but also the boys—and the house had the same empty feel, the blankness he had noticed before. She was gone.

He needed to jolt his family from their lethargy, but he realized they had received more than their share of jolts recently. Too many.

So Scott chose a more subtle approach. He only hoped it wasn't too little too late. Jelly squirted out the sides of Jason's roll, staining his cheeks and dribbling down his chin, some dripping onto his pajamas.

"Jason!" Allison took the doughnut from him. He pouted. Holding him at arm's length, she scrubbed at his cheek and only succeeded in spreading the jelly around from ear to ear.

Allison looked ruefully from the gooey napkins to Scott.

"Could you bring me a damp cloth?" She eyed Jason's shirt and added: "You'd better make that a big one."

Allison spit on the napkin, and Jason squirmed. He hated *that!*

"Sit still," she ordered. Scott returned with a sponge and a wet cloth, and Jason submitted his cheek reluctantly to her care.

"That reminds me," Scott said, standing up and heading through the foyer for the front door.

Allison and Adam watched him disappear. Jason contentedly chewed on his jelly-less jelly doughnut, eyes glued to the tube.

A minute later Scott entered, a K-Mart bag in hand.

"What we need is a new start. A fresh start for everyone. What with all the excitement lately, things have gotten a little out of control." He gestured around the room with a wave of his hand, but his eyes sought Allison's. It was to her he must apologize.

"Therefore"—Scott whipped the bag off the prizes to reveal two brand-new lunch buckets—"one for each of you."

Jason stood on the couch, and the doughnut fell to the floor with a splat. Allison winced, biting back her censure.

"For me!" Jason shouted.

"Yes, one for Jason and one for Adam," Scott explained. "We've been bickering a lot lately. There's been a lot going on. Well, I want you two to kiss and make up and promise not to fight anymore."

"Aw, Dad, do we hafta?"

"Uh-huh, you hafta."

"Okay," the boys groaned in unison. Jason slid away from Allison to hug his brother. He gave his sons the thumbs-up sign.

"Great." Scott clapped his hands together. "From here on things will be just like they were before."

Eyes downcast, he wandered over to stand next to Allison and gave her a wan smile.

"Oh, yes, and there's something else." He fished through his pockets, pulled out a small velvet box, and handed it to her. "It's not much . . ."

She took it and opened it. Inside highlighted by the black velvet, was a delicate gold chain with a floating heart. Her shoulders started to shake, her chest to heave as he knelt by her chair.

Weeping, she stepped into his embrace, letting his arms envelop her. They stood, and she lay her cheek upon his chest. His chin rested upon the top of her head—their two bodies molded into one.

The tangled knot of hard feelings dissolved, and they enjoyed a special communion as the boys looked on silently. Fear evaporated slowly, the gentle contact generating warmth between them.

The computer began to play tinny music, a barely disguised version of the *Star Wars* theme, which was meant to goad the player into another game. A son perched on each arm of his chair, Scott glanced down at the prompt. He keyed in Y for another game and waited. Allison's melodious halloo interrupted before Jason and Adam had a chance to engage in battle. His wife lumbered into the room, a sack in each hand.

"I didn't hear you coming. Where'd you materialize from?" Scott said.

"I snuck in. Can I get any of you big, strong men to help me with the groceries?" Allison passed two small sacks to Jason, who squared his shoulders and marched proudly from the room toward the kitchen.

"How much more, love?" Scott said.

"Not much. Just what's left is in the trunk."

Adam and Scott brushed past her, trooping through the front door and down to the car. Allison hurried and followed Jason to the kitchen. Allison pulled a box from the pantry, smiling cryptically. A muted mew shrilled from within the carton. Jason dropped the bags and rushed headlong toward her.

"Meow!"

Arrested by the sound, Jason halted, one foot raised, and stuck a finger in the corner of his mouth. Scott and Adam marched into the room.

"What's that?" Scott asked.

Allison opened the box, tilting it so they would see what scrabbled about inside "A kitty."

"Allison!"

"You started it this morning with the lunch boxes," Allison protested. "When I saw some kittens at the mall, I couldn't resist."

"Do you think that's wise?"

"You gave me the idea." Allison said. "Jason's so lonely now that Adam is in school. I thought maybe if he had something to play with . . . You're not the only one whose temper has been a little short lately. I kind of owe Jason an apology."

With a sharp inclination of his head, Scott remained silent. Two excited boys raced up to play with the terrified kitten and the creature scrambled out of the box and beat a hasty retreat through the door. Adam and Jason chased it into the living room. Her gaze returned to Scott. He stood with his arms crossed, leaning against the kitchen table.

"What if Jason gets scratched?" Scott queried.

"All little boys get scratched at some time or another. If it's not a cat or a dog, its a branch or a twig or something. I'll keep an eye on him."

A feline howl came from the living room, and Scott rolled his eyes toward the ceiling.

Allison cringed and gave him a wry smile. "Maybe I'd better go rescue the kitten."

With Adam in mandatory attendance and Jason in tow, Allison returned to the kitchen to lecture both boys on the proper method of holding cats. Scott gave her his best

I-told-you-so look and grinned before turning silently to put away the groceries. Kicking off her shoes, Allison plopped down on a chair. The kitten pounced on a shoelace. Allison removed the laces from her shoes, and she and the two children became engrossed in teasing the kitten with the string.

The dishwasher switched cycles with a heavy thunk. Both boys lay on the floor, sliding a gum wrapper back and forth between them. The kitten, dubbed Ralph, skittered after it, batting at the wadded foil. Scott watched television, occasionally glancing at his sons, still unsure about this new addition to the family, particularly after the incident with Adam at school. Allison, who was putting the finishing touches on the baby blanket, seemed content so he decided not to say anything.

Ralph clawed his way up the side of the couch. He stretched and yawned, arching his feline back, tail raised in the air. Adam clambered up after him.

Then the kitten squirreled into Adam's arms, kneading his lap. Adam frowned at Ralph. His motor ran in a loud rumbling purr. The claws dug deeper into his lap. Angry, Adam placed one hand on the fragile neck and began to squeeze . . . and squeeze . . . and squeeze.

The kitten hissed and spit. Adam squeezed some more.

"Stoppit!" Jason added his distressed wail to Ralph's and launched at his brother.

"Ow!" Adam said, pushing Jason away. The cat slid bonelessly to the floor.

Both Allison and Scott swung around to gaze at the boys. Adam held his bleeding finger in the air for them to see. "It scratched me."

Adam pointed at Ralph, who immediately took an ill-aimed swipe at the finger, and before either Allison or Scott could do anything Adam kicked at the cat. His blow struck the kitten full in the flank and Ralph sailed across the room to bounce off the wall. Jason's wailing echoed in the background.

Allison was out of her chair before she had time to remember she was clumsy with child. She hauled Adam to his feet, spun him around so his back faced her, and gave him a hard wallop on the bottom. Jason's howling came to gargling stop.

Her fingers loosened their grip, and her arm fell limply to her side. Adam turned slowly to stare at her with injured eyes, and she flinched away from his reproving stare. She looked at her hand as though it held the explanation for her action. She had never before struck one of her children.

Scott said nothing. His mouth formed a small O, and he blew forcefully through puffed cheeks. Horrified Allison stumbled back to grope for her chair. Ralph picked himself up, shook a few times, testing each appendage, and then lurched drunkenly away from the frozen group.

Scott cleared his throat. "Boys, I think you'd better go get ready for bed."

Adam and Jason scrambled for the door and cast a worried glance back at their mother before they departed, arguing loudly about who got to use the bathroom first. Scott scrutinized his wife as though he were seeing her for the first time, his expression tense.

"Ah, I'm so—"

"Don't worry about it; who am I to criticize?"

Dazed, Allison picked up her knitting and lowered herself gingerly into her chair, shaking her head. Things were falling apart.

21

The red-and-green-checked bedspread glowed, illuminating the room in Christmas colors. Beneath his makeshift tent, Adam trained his flashlight on his favorite monster comic book. A few weeks of school and the words his father had once read to him were starting to make sense. Adam was burrowed in this cozy habitat, scrunched safely under his covers, pleasantly warm. He relished this brief interlude of solitude and privacy.

His lips moved as he sounded out one of the bigger words from his book.

"A-a-b so . . . abso . . ." He gave up; he didn't want to know what that dumb old word was.

His mind reverberated with a crinkling crackle, as if a giant hand had crumpled paper next to his ear. Something moved overhead, and all the night's sounds became a single disturbing sizzle of static as his ears pricked to strain after the creaking movement.

His hand throbbed where he had been scratched, and Adam stared at the three red lines that extended from his wrist to his fingers. They stung.

That stupid old cat had hurt him, and his mother had hit him! It was all Ralph's fault. Ralph must be punished, just like Adam would be punished if he had hurt his little brother. He didn't even like cats, and Adam thought of the flaming streak in the cold winter night. Witches had cats, like the old witch across the street.

And he knew what to do with cats that didn't behave, didn't he?

Then he frowned, but he couldn't do that again, could he? The old woman must have found the lighter fluid because when he'd looked for it yesterday it was gone.

So what could he do about Ralph?

The wind blew around the house. The branch tapped and wood creaked . . . and creaked . . .

Picking at his pajamas, Adam again fixed on the long red lines on the back of his hand. Like thin strings. Like rope.

Creak.

Like a rope rubbing against wood.

Creak.

And the image of a noose formed in his mind.

Dumb old cat. All it knew how to do was make stinky messes in the box near the backdoor and scratch things.

Hiss, and the arthritic bough scraped against the window. Adam listened. *Rat-ta-tat-tat. S-C-R-E-E-E-CH!* There was a faint click, and the light that crept underneath the door was extinguished as his parents turned in for the night. Adam waited.

There was a splash as one of his parents settled in the water bed, a mumbled good night, and all was quiet.

Rat-ta-tat-tat.

"Yes, I know," Adam answered the tree, and he wondered where the cat was. In Jason's room? He moved quietly toward the door.

Holding his breath, Adam prayed to the golden girl that the door wouldn't squeak when he opened it. He turned the knob, wincing at the sound it made. Hugging the wall, he crept to Jason's door. In the night light's muted glow he could see that his brother slept. No round ball of fur cuddled at his feet.

Adam retreated, wondering what to do now. He looked around the hallway, stopping to study his parents' bedroom door. What if Ralph was in there, with them?

Shrugging, Adam descended to the first floor to continue his search. "Kitty, kitty, kitty."

"Mew."

Adam froze, pivoting to locate the source of the sound. "Here, Ralph, do you want a nice bowl of milk?"

"Mew."

The kitten rose from where it lay curled on the floor and walked toward Adam.

Confidently, Adam made his way to the kitchen. Ralph trailed along behind, taking swipes at Adam's bare feet. Sharp talons caught his heels, and Adam bit his lip to stifle a pained gasp. His fists clenched at his sides.

"Nice kitty," he said, his voice throaty and harsh. "Adam's going to give you a saucer of milk."

He opened the refrigerator, and the light falling over the arched kitten sent a shadow leaping across the floor. Ralph curled, wrapping himself around Adam's ankles, purring.

Adam grabbed a carton of milk and put it on the counter. Pulling a chair from the table, he dug out a bowl, which he filled and placed on the floor. Next he rummaged through the drawers until he found the sturdy twine Mom used for wrapping packages.

Ralph lapped contentedly at the milk while Adam carefully replaced the carton in the fridge, aligning the edge of the carton so it was precisely square to the wall. Leaving the door open, he watched the tabby in the narrow spear of illumination. When the kitten was finished, Adam scooped it from the floor, closing the refrigerator door as he did.

Naively it burrowed deeper into Adam's arms. Carrying the heavy string and the cat, he started up the steps. On the landing overlooking the foyer Adam set Ralph down. The kitten meowed.

He looped the twine over the rail and tied a square knot, just the way Dad had showed him. His fingers worked feverishly at the noose. Another trick Dad had taught him. Ralph skittered after the ball of string, but Adam caught him, slipping the noose over the cat's head and flinging it over the banister. The cat spit and yowled. Adam leaned over the rail, watching its frenzied, twitching dance in fascination. Hind legs tore at the string, ripping fur from flesh, tearing the tiny triangle ears, and Adam silently cheered—*dumb ol' cat*—as a hand closed upon his shoulder.

Adam jumped and swivelled to stare into his father's angry face.

The next morning, all but Adam, exiled again to his room, gathered on the porch for the funereal procession. Jason's eyes were bloodshot and swollen; they matched the red of his mittens. He stretched on tip-toe, reaching for the box. Ralph clambered around inside. His ragged ears drooped, and there was a distinct line around his neck where the fur had been torn away.

Jason wept. "No, mine! My kitty. Ralph."

Allison's cheeks were wet and Scott gulped, a lump forming in his throat. He felt sorry for Jason, but he could think of no other solution.

"Mamaaah!"

"I'm sorry, Jason, I'll bring you back another one." Scott stopped to pat the top of the boy's head. Shock registered in Allison's eyes, and Scott continued: "A nice stuffed one. What color do you want? Blue?"

"Don't want no other one." Jason snuffled. "Want Ralph."

Scott put the box in the backseat and then squatted down so he was on eye level with his son.

"Jason, we can't keep Ralph. He might get . . . uh, hurt. You don't want Ralph to get hurt, do you?"

Jason dug his toe into the snow. "No," he admitted reluctantly.

"I'm gonna take Ralph someplace where they can find a good home for him." Scott winced as he said the words, amazed that they couldn't make a home for a kitten.

He looked up at Allison pleadingly. Say something, he thought, anything, but she didn't meet his eyes. Her hand held onto the porch railing, knuckles white, as if she could find emotional support from the wood itself. Her breath came out in small, white clouds.

Jason whirled abruptly, scrambled up the stairs, and slammed into the house. Allison shrugged, tucking her head between raised shoulders, and winced an apology.

"What else can we do?" he asked Allison.

"Nothing, nothing at all," she said flatly.

Scott put his arms around her. She stiffened and pushed him away. "I'd better go see to the boys."

Later Scott bounded up the stairs, moved to Jason's door, and rapped lightly. "Jason, dinner."

Scott stepped into the room where his young son was curled into a tight little ball, sucking his thumb. He extracted Jason's thumb from his mouth, and then Scott paused, his eyes darting around the room. They were being watched. Scott shot a uneasy look over his shoulder and noticed the partially open closet door. He relaxed. He was getting as bad as Jason, scared of monsters in the closet.

Scott stroked the tousled head. "Wake up, Jason, dinnertime."

Jason stirred and stretched, both hands reaching overhead. "Daddy?"

"Yes, Jason, dinner's ready."

Jason slipped from the bed, putting a tiny fist in his father's hand. Scott smiled. "So when did my little man decide to start sucking his thumb?"

Jason blinked. "Do not! Only babies do that."

Bewildered, Scott stared down at his young son, one hand on his hip and his chin thrust out defiantly.

Scott led Jason to the door, hesitating on the threshold. *Smoke.* He stepped back into Jason's room and inhaled sharply through his nose. Yes, definitely smoke. Scott surveyed the room. It was just as it had been when he put Jason in bed, not a toy out of place.

"Daddy, hungry!"

"Okay, okay," Scott said. "How does McDonald's sound?"

Jason groaned, and Scott threw back his head and laughed. "Well, kid, you're stuck with it."

Jason sighed.

"Come on, let Daddy give you a piggy-back ride."

And Jason clambered onto his back. With him safely delivered, Scott returned to the second floor carrying Adam's tray. This time, he didn't knock but went right in.

The room was dark except for the pale illumination of the streetlight. Adam stood looking out the window. A branch tapped incessantly on the glass pane.

Scott turned on the lights. Adam swung slowly to stare up at him. Scott took an involuntary step backward when he saw his son's stricken expression.

"Why are you sitting in the dark?" Scott said nonchalantly as he set the tray on the desk. "Just because you have to stay in your room doesn't mean you can't play."

Adam remained quiet as he examined his father's face, looking for signs of forgiveness. The child's expression was pinched, bruised, his eyes two stony pebbles.

"Come here," Scott patted the chair in front of the desk. "Let's talk."

Adam's jaw tightened as he considered for a moment. Then with a shrug, Adam paced over to the small desk. Scott propped himself on the edge. "You know you've done a bad thing, don't you?"

Adam's lips pressed into a thin line. "Uh-uh."

"What?" Scott's voice went up a notch. "Are you trying to tell me that hanging Jason's kitten isn't bad?"

"Ralph?"

"Yes, Ralph. What other kittens have we had in this house recently?"

Adam's face jerked spasmodically and he burst into tears. "But, Daddy, I didn't. I didn't. I wouldn't hurt Ralph."

Scott dropped down to his knees and grabbed Adam's shoulders. "Adam, we saw you. Your mother, I, even Jason."

"No-o-o," he wailed.

Scott placed a hand on either side of Adam's face and forced him to look into his father's eyes. He searched his face carefully, all too familiar with the sudden withdrawal that would indicate a lie. Adam didn't flinch, merely gazed at him steadily with eyes huge and shadowed.

"You really don't remember, do you?" Scott whispered, more a statement than a question.

Adam shook his head no.

"What I don't understand is why you didn't tell me before now," Allison snapped. "How was I supposed to know?"

"I know, I should have told you. You were in the hospital when I was called in to talk to the teacher," Scott explained. "And when the teacher said that Adam had been caught torturing a dog, I didn't believe it. It didn't sound like our Adam. I suppose with everything else that was going on I didn't think it was important at the time."

"No, it doesn't sound like him," Allison said, averting her eyes, thinking about the old harpy and her cat. The woman had been so convinced that Adam had done something awful.

"That's what I thought then, but now . . ."

"He really didn't remember?" Allison spoke softly so Jason wouldn't hear.

"No, not at all. I'm sure of it. You know kids. When they lie they can't look you straight in the eye. They either look off to the side or at their feet, or if that's not possible, they withdraw and focus on your nose or your mouth. Anything but look you in the eye," Scott said, "and Adam wasn't lying."

"How is that possible?" Allison said.

"I don't know. Are you ready to concede that's something is wrong?"

Allison flared. "I never said that everything was rosy. All I've said is don't blame the house."

"I won't quibble with you about that, but what should we do about the kids?"

"I don't know. Take them to see someone, I suppose. I still think it's the stress."

"There's not all that much stress in moving," Scott argued. "Parents drag their children all over the United States, and they don't just self-destruct like ours have."

"Have you got any better explanation?"

Scott thought he did but didn't say anything.

Allison seemed to sense his train of thought because she stood up abruptly, saying: "I'll put Jason to bed."

22

A thin filament of smoke drifted through the keyhole. Allison jolted upright, watching as the slender wisp twisted and turned. She nudged the sleeping Scott—the words of warning caught in her throat—but he snored blithely on. She backed up to the headboard as the smoke coalesced, gaining mass, form, and shape. A little girl with sad eyes appeared before her, and Allison felt a sudden rush of relief and love . . .

. . . A single note held, warbled and quavered. The weeping sax held the wailing note, and then practiced fingers ran lightly up and down a minor scale, singing a sweet and sour song that sent chills up and down his spine. Scott sat in the study; the child stood in the doorway. The knowing look in her eyes belied the innocent, sweet face . . .

. . . The girl's face changed. Bones crumpled, skin splintering as though under the impact of a blow. One side of the childlike face drooped, molten, the eye a greasy smear across the cheek. Allison tried to pull her knees up to her chest to protect her stomach and the small child within, and the figure reformed, becoming whole again. The girl stared, imploring, and Allison was overwhelmed by the need to protect this child too. Sara—and Allison could put a name to the face—Sara drifted closer to the bed . . .

. . . The child took a step closer to Scott's chair. A grin spread across her face. Her expression was conspiratorial and proprietary. Scott felt the first stirrings of desire deep in the pit of his stomach, and the sax began to play a hot, throbbing melody that pulsed with the same rhythm as Scott's nascent lust . . .

. . . Allison clutched weakly at Scott's shoulder as the girl climbed onto the bed. He snorted and rolled over, and the girl's head imploded once more. Flesh and muscle stripped from shatter bone . . .

. . . Shelley grasped Scott's knees. Hungry hands stroked his thighs, his crotch, and Scott struggled against his desire. This was wrong! All wrong! The girl began to unzip his pants, and Scott succumbed. No fight left in him . . .

. . . Terror engulfed her as the figure reshaped and re-formed. A little boy. Clammy hands grabbed her ankles, pulling her flat against the bed. Allison writhed, movements slowed by the bulk of her undulating belly. The boy crawled over her, straddling her thighs. He smiled down at her and she watched spellbound as he clawed at her stomach . . .

. . . Flames danced gleefully in the background. His parents stared at him mournfully, their eyes full of rebuke. Scott could see them above her head where it lay in his lap. Lips and tongue teasing, tickling . . .

Smoke! Scott sat up and sniffed the air. He had smelled it before, quite often since he'd moved into this house, and usually it meant nothing. An olfactory hallucination.

His heart beat in his chest like voodoo drums. Scott threw the covers off and rolled from the bed with a muffled yelp. Allison mumbled something as she rode the crest of the wave caused by his exit.

Instinctively he headed first for Jason's room, listened to the child's even breathing before he padded to Adam's room. The rumpled bed was empty. Confused, Scott swung around to look at the bathroom. The door was open, the room dark. No, this time he definitely smelled something. He turned slowly, suddenly alert, and scanned the preternaturally quiet house.

Pulsing light emanated from the living room. A snaking thread of smoke drifted up the stairs, and he saw what his sleep-fogged consciousness had failed to register before. The blurred fuzziness of the air. Without a doubt it was smoke.

Taking the stairs two at a time, he was struck again by the silence that penetrated the pagan tattoo of his heart. Not even the steps creaked under his weight. Nearly tripping over his feet. He grabbed the wall to maintain his balance.

The crackly pop of flames splintered the stillness, and Scott threw caution to the wind, careening through the foyer and skidding into the living room to view Adam's limp figure before the blazing fire. The stuffed cat Scott had bought for Jason smoldered—its head consumed by leaping flames—and the smoke hung like a low-lying cloud over his son's body. Scott choked on the fumes.

"ADAM!"

The child coughed weakly, raising his hand to flutter in the air before it fell feebly to the floor and lay still. Scott grabbed his ankles and dragged Adam into the foyer, opening the front door to let in a blast of frigid, arctic air.

Returning to the living room, Scott wrenched the handle that regulated the damper. It slipped in his sweaty palms, and then it turned with a reluctant screech. The nearly stifled flames sparked at the renewed draft, and the smoldering toy flashed, burning brightly. Some of the smoke that drifted around the room was drawn up the chimney.

Scott went back to Adam and cradled the boy in his arms. His head flopped like the head of a dying flower. Supporting it with his hand, Scott propped him on his shoulder. A veteran of many late-night vigils with his son, Scott immediately realized that something was wrong. No warm, moist breath tickled the hair on his neck. Pushing the child away from him, Scott ignored the lolling neck and stared intently at Adam's chest.

It didn't move!

Icy air wafted around the room. He dropped to his knees. Propping the child's chest against his forearm, Scott rubbed Adam's back, lightly at first, and then with increasing pressure.

"Please, God, please. Please, God. Please, God," he intoned. "Breathe, dammit, breathe!"

Scott patted the tiny area between fragile shoulder blades. Adam gasped, gagged, and then started to wheeze. Scott hugged his son, nearly crushing him with relief, tears streaming down his face. Adam wiggled in his tight grasp as Allison hobbled down the stairs, a look of horror on her face.

"What happened?"

He said nothing, relinquishing Adam to her care.

In the living room the firelight danced with demonic frenzy. The stuffed toy lay half in and half out of the fireplace. So that a single spark swirling through the air to land on the sofa or the recliner and . . .

Scott plunged through the foyer back into the living room. He felt a helpless, mindless fury still rising, searching for outlet. Like a caged animal.

No! He would not succumb to it. Never again!

Grabbing the poker, Scott shoved the toy's charred and smoking remains back to the safety zone of the marble hearth. The wooden floor next to the fireplace was blackened and scorched. The caged anger paced within his skull, keeping time with his pulse and his throbbing head. He beat at the flames.

Suddenly his parents stared at him from behind the fiery wall. For the first time in his waking life he could see them, recognize them, their features well-loved and, at long last, remembered.

The image hit him like a fist, and the room reeled around him as he tottered backwards. Long repressed memories surfaced.

Fire! A cheap little tract home, not unlike the broken-down structure across the way, burning. His home. And it was on fire! Big red fire engines and flashing red lights. Ghostly figures clad in day-glo orange. Tramping feet and huge boots. Water, mud everywhere. Smoke-shrouded ghosts flitted in the conflagration.

His mother's face peering at him through the window, her mouth open in a scream. She beat at the window and he could see the blisters forming on the palms of her hands where they touched the glass.

He must help her. He ran, but a sooty hand grabbed him, yanking him back.

"Stay here, little boy!" the garbled voice ordered imperiously, and Scott shrank against the vibrating side of the fire truck.

Another figure appeared behind his mother, engulfed in flames.

His father!

Shrieking, Scott twisted out of the man's grasp and flung himself at the door, but the fireman caught him and held him.

"You stay here!" The smudged face looked frantically through the crowd. Seeing a woman in a tattered robe and, gargantuan fuzzy slippers, with pink rollers in her hair, the fireman threw the weeping child over his shoulder and carried Scott to the neighbor.

"Here." He shoved Scott at the woman. "Can you keep track of him?"

Nodding mutely, she took the young Scott and held him

against her side. Scott stopped struggling and allowed himself to be comforted.

When the house exploded, glass bursting outward, roof collapsing, Scott couldn't even hear the sound of his own screams. His hand hurt; something cut into his fingers. He opened his clenched fist and looked. A book of matches . . .

A single button eye gazed implacably at him, surrounded by a ring of flickering flames. Scott sat gracelessly on the floor. So hard, he bit his tongue and tasted the bitter, saline flavor of blood.

And everything coalesced. It all made sense. The gaps in his memory; his aunt's reticence and the frightened looks his cousins had cast in his direction when he first moved to the rundown farm; the dreams.

Sometimes Scott had wondered why he had no photographs, no mementos from his former home. The only pictures of his mother were Aunt Deirdre's and those were of the two of them as children. Even that made sense now. All the photos had burned up with his childhood home, with his family.

And he had killed them! He was sure of that now.

A choked puling noise came from his throat, and Scott couldn't breathe.

Other memories came flooding up in the wake of the first. No Leave-it-to-Beaver family, but parents who were little more than children themselves, who should never have had a child, and had never been able to cope with the small boy they had brought into the world.

Unsure what to do with a child, they denied him nothing, for it was easier to give in to him than to discipline him. No, they made no rules—except one: Do not play with matches.

Night after long, black night, they left him in the house alone because they couldn't afford a baby-sitter. The young Scott knew anger, rejection, and pain. *Abandoned and alone.* So when they came home one night, dead drunk, he had decided to punish them. To punish them in the only way he knew how. By breaking the one and only rule they gave him, and he had killed them.

Adam's coughing came to him from the foyer, and Scott realized that he and his young son weren't so different after all. Any anger he felt at his son's juvenile rebellion disappeared, and the crushing weight on his chest lifted just a bit. Yes, everything made sense now. The dark side of his character. His macabre fascination with death. The rage—rage at self, vented outward—and his overwhelming need for self-control.

"Scott?"

Brought back to the present, he turned to Allison. The button eye fell to the stone hearth with a tinny tinkle.

"Are you all right?"

"Fine," he said grimly. "Just fine."

23

Scott hustled the two boys into the car. Allison lumbered after, one hand resting on the small of her back. She ached all over. She tried to remember the last time she had gotten a good night's sleep. She had wanted to take Adam to the emergency room last night, but Scott had vetoed the idea, saying they would take both the boys to the doctor today and get the name of a good psychologist.

And she had acquiesced easily when she saw Scott's haggard expression. He looked for all the world like he had seen a ghost. She had tried to talk to him, but he had fled to his study, and she accepted that, too.

What was there to say? Things were falling apart. She could no longer deny it.

What was going on? The shell of habit—of polishing, cleaning, and cooking—into which she had retreated was broken—first a crack, then a fissure, and now it fell away, leaving her feeling naked and exposed. The house gleamed and shone while her family was falling apart.

Scott watched the road, his face a mask of concentration. She listened to her sons' quibbling behind her. Their voices grated—one plaintive, one querulous. And despite the revelations of the last few days, Allison found herself wanting to get away, to escape from them. She swung around to scold with a hand raised to strike. Jason choked back a sob, staring at her in wide-eyed astonishment, and both boys cringed. Allison stared at her upraised hand, and her gaze twitched to her husband. She let her hand drop to her lap, mind whirling.

This was crazy. She wanted her old life back.

Allison slumped against the car seat and wondered if their lives would ever be the normal again.

Jason perched on his hip, Scott walked into the clinic. Allison, Adam dangling from one arm, trailed him dully. Scott paused in front of a board to look for the office number. Allison bumped into him.

"What was the name of that pediatrician?"

"Farquar."

His finger drew an invisible line down the glass. "Here. He's in room 202."

Scott went to the elevator, punched a button, and waited for Allison and Adam to catch up with him. They wandered up the hall on the second floor, stopping to check the number on each door. Allison moved up to the receptionist's desk.

"Do you have an appointment?" The woman's voice was an obsequious drone.

"No, I'm afraid not. I'm Mrs. McDowell. I called this morning. The doctor said he'd squeeze us in. You see we had a . . . uh, little accident last night."

"Have you been here before?"

"Just to meet the doctor."

The receptionist got up and went to a large file cabinet.

"McDowell, Jason or Adam?" the woman called over her shoulder.

"Both." Scott spoke over her shoulder.

The woman, reading glasses perched on the end of her nose, glowered, clearly disapproving of the disruption to the routine flow of patients.

"Just a second, I'll speak with the doctor."

Scott sat Jason on the sterile white counter and made soft, soothing noises. Nestled safely in his father's loving grasp, Jason cooed to himself. Too young to have developed a fear of doctors, he happily began to play with his father's coat buttons. Adam leaned against Allison's side, quiet and subdued. He *didn't* like doctors; they gave shots and nasty-tasting medicines.

"Mrs. McDowell?"

Allison levered herself off the wall and faced the receptionist.

"Yes?" she said.

"What sort of accident?"

"Something caught fire, and Adam"—she placed her hand on the top of his head—"inhaled a lot of smoke."

The receptionist looked troubled, chewed on her lip, and spun, leaving Allison and Scott at the desk. A few minutes later a head poked through the open door.

"Doctor Farquar will see you now," the nurse informed them. The McDowells followed her down a long antiseptic-smelling hallway to the examination room.

The doctor's manner was crisp and efficient. He was the type of man to inspire confidence and quickly had Adam giggling as he poked, prodded, and tapped.

"This hurt?" Dr. Farquar asked.

"No, it tickles," Adam snickered as he tried to brush the doctor's hands away.

Farquar put the earpieces in his ears and placed the stethoscope's bell on Adam's chest.

Adam squirmed. "That's cold."

"Okay, son, take a deep breath."

Adam did as he was told.

"Another." The doctor listened for a moment. "Sounds

good. Now let's try the back. Lean forward a bit. That's good. Okay. Another deep, deep breath."

Farquar straightened and peered down at the boy, perplexed. The child followed his movements eagerly.

"I can't find anything wrong with him. His breathing is normal; it's not scratchy or rasping. There's no bubbling. His heartbeat's strong. All in all, I'd say you were very lucky. Especially if the smoke was thick enough to overcome him. We're all through. You can get down now, Adam."

"Now, young man, it's your turn." Farquar lifted Jason from Scott's arms and swung him to the examination table.

Clearing her throat, Allison nodded toward the door and said, "Adam and I will wait outside."

The parents exchanged significant glances over Adam's head.

The doctor noticed the look and turned to his patient. They played peek-a-boo with the pen light, and Jason seemed disappointed when the game ended. Then the stethoscope. Scott stared dully at the crayoned pictures on the wall.

"You wanna hear?" Farquar said to Jason.

"Yeth."

He pulled an alcohol-soaked cotton pad from a jar and cleaned the earpieces, which he passed to Jason.

"Now put these in your ears like you saw me do before. Gently," Farquar said. His fingers were palpating the tiny chest, feeling for the heartbeat. When he found it, he positioned the metal bell and turned to Scott.

Jason's mouth dropped open and he was quiet, awed by the sound of his own heartbeat.

"Gets 'em every time." Dr. Farquar winked at Scott, noting the father's harried appearance. Scott relaxed slightly and managed an insipid grin.

"Daddy listen," Jason shouted, drowning out the doctor's next words. Jason stuffed the earpieces in Scott's ears before the doctor could stop him.

"Do ya hear?" he said, still yelling.

Scott nodded. "Yes, Jason, I hear. No need to shout."

When Scott stood up to hand the stethoscope back to Farquar, the doctor continued: "As I was saying, both boys seem okay. Are you sure the older boy stopped breathing?"

"I would have sworn he did," Scott said.

"I'm surprised you didn't take him to the hospital."

Wincing, Scott said nothing.

"And he doesn't remember a thing, right?"

Scott inclined his head in affirmative.

"Sleepwalking, most likely. It's not uncommon, but damn frightening for the parents. You never know if he might wander out into the street." He pulled the chart and made a few notes on a piece of paper. "That's right, you're the one who bought the old Graves place."

Scott started and turned to stare at the doctor with shadowed eyes.

"That place has built up quite a reputation through the years," the doctor commented, indicating their address on the chart.

"I thought doctors weren't supposed to be superstitious," Scott said.

"I'm not, just cautious, and I can tell you I wouldn't move into that place—not with two kids." Farquar made another notation on the chart and signed it with a flourish. "You're a braver man than I am," he concluded.

Farquar stepped closer to the examination table, looping the stethoscope around his neck. Jason immediately yanked on the bell and brayed into it.

"Jason!"

"Don't worry, I've learned." Farquar pointed to the earpieces hooked safely around his neck. He extracted the bell from Jason's grasp, putting it in his pocket.

"Well, young man, put on your shirt. I'm all through with you unless you want to be tickled."

"Daddy!" Jason screeched, and stubby arms stretched out

for his father. Scott looped Jason's shirt over the toddler's arms and head, pulling it down over the soft, white stomach, and tucked it into his jeans.

"Well, Jason, want a lollipop for being such a good boy?" Farquar said. "And there's one for your brother too."

"Yeth," Jason said, and Scott raised a questioning eyebrow.

"Candy? Aren't you worried that it will rot his teeth?" Scott asked.

"Not at all. My cousin's a dentist," Farquar said with a wry grin.

The joke fell flat. Scott hefted Jason back to his hip. "Actually, there was something else we needed to talk to you about. You wouldn't happen to know a good psychologist, would you?"

"A psychologist? For the children? They look pretty normal and healthy to me. The oldest one's quiet, but that's not surprising; he's old enough to equate a visit to the doctor with vaccinations and other evil practices."

"Do you?" Scott persisted.

"Well, not a specialist. There's a family counselor here in the building. You're worried about him starting the fire?"

"Something like that."

"Don't be. All children go through that stage. Experimentation. Testing the limits of parental rules. Although, I admit your experience was pretty dramatic. I remember the first time I got caught playing with matches. My father really walloped me."

"All the same, we'd really like to talk to someone. Today, if possible."

"All right, I'll talk to my receptionist. See if she can set up an appointment."

With Adam safely—if belatedly—at school, Allison stalked through the house angrily. "Of all the pompous, officious . . ."

Watching her, Scott decided that he hadn't seen her this lively since they'd moved into the house.

"To think she had the audacity to blame us," she ranted.

"We should have expected it. It's something of a standard line in the industry."

Allison swung on him. "I don't buy it. Things have been a little rough lately, and we're no saints, but I don't think we're bad parents."

"No, I don't think we're bad parents either."

Allison walked over and hugged Scott. He clung to her, realizing that this was the first time she had initiated contact since before Thanksgiving, and he wondered how things could have gotten so bad, so out of control.

He lifted her chin with his index finger so he could look into her ice-blue eyes. It was good to have the old Allison back.

"Don't let it upset you," he said, patting her stomach. "Why don't you do some of your Lamaze exercises? They ought to calm you. The due date's not far away."

"I don't want to calm down."

"Honey, all it means is the psychologist can't help us. Maybe someone else can." And he thought of Sam.

Scott checked Allison and Jason one last time. They were propped on pillows, head to head, sprawled across the living room floor. Jason was helping Momma with her breathing exercises. Scott hid his smile behind his hand and left them both panting like puppies.

When he closed the study door behind him his smile dissolved to be replaced by a scowl. Pandora's box was open.

Fire!

A kaleidoscope of images burst into his mind. His mother's blistered palms, her screaming face. A house exploding. His father's mouth a dark circle rimmed in fire. Fire lapping toward Aldo's recumbent form. His hair caught, burning like a torch as the ruddy flesh bubbled and split.

Pushing away from the door, Scott shook himself soundly. He had no time for self-pity or introspection.

He crossed the room, sat at his desk, pulling the phone onto his lap, and dialed Sam's number. He listened to the mechanical clicks as the connection was made, and the not-so-mechanical hoots and hissing that plagued their line.

It took an eternity for Holloway to answer the phone. His boisterous voice turned old and tired when he realized who had called. With growing horror, Scott listened as Sam told him about his inquiries within the church.

Starting with his parish priest, Sam had doggedly worked his way up the hierarchy to the diocese offices and the chancellor. Without luck. They doubted the validity of the claims despite Sam's assurances. Allison's and Scott's religion, or the lack of it as lapsed Catholics, was held against them, and when they heard Scott's name they cut Sam off completely.

McDowell? The writer? What was this, some kind of publicity stunt?

Jokingly, Sam said he didn't know a priest could use such language. Scott found himself apologizing to Sam for his trouble and thanking him for his efforts.

When Scott replaced the receiver in the cradle, despair descended like a shroud. The room closed in around him. Rubbing his face with the back of his hand, he tried to comprehend the implication of the message.

No.

No help from psychology, from modern so-called science; no help from the church; no help anywhere.

With a happy howl Jason raced from the living room. He paused at the study door, pressed his ear against the wood for a moment, and listened. In the living room his mother was picking up the throw pillows from the floor. Turning from the door, he heard a squeak and muffled laughter.

"William?" he said hopefully.

A creak, and Jason turned terrified eyes on a decomposing Tommy Erwin dangling on the end of a noose that hung from the second floor landing.

Like Ralph.

The body swung in a lazy arc, back to the frightened toddler.

Creak! The sound of rope rubbing against wood. And it turned slowly to face Jason. A blackened tongue protruded from a pain-contorted face. Rocking gently back and forth, back and forth, back and forth. Hypnotic.

The eyes opened.

Dropping to his knees, Jason scampered up the stairs, eyes never leaving the creaking rope and its gruesome burden.

Jason and Allison napped. Scott, feeling a little foolish, wandered through the house carrying his precious burden, a small jar of holy water he had filched from the local Catholic church. He wondered if his means of obtaining it would ruin its potency.

But Scott had already tried legitimate means, hadn't he?

Now that he had it, what the hell was he going to do with it? He was no priest; he wasn't particularly religious. Neither had he ever been much of a believer in the supernatural, but—and he was echoing Sam's words—the house had made a believer out of him.

Pulling the jelly jar from his pocket, Scott headed for the basement. The game room remained unused. The boys avoided the place. Thinking about it, he realized that most of the incidents seemed to have occurred, or at least originated, in this area of the house—the accidents with the workmen, the sewage backup, the electrical problems. The strange shakings and rumblings all seemed to emanate from beneath the house; the same place where Sam said the child William had once been buried.

As he stood in the cellar, Scott wondered why he'd bought

the place. Holloway had done his best to dissuade him when he'd made the original offer, but Scott had shot his arguments down one by one. Sam had pointed to its history and the many deaths.

Yet when viewed singly, each incident seemed, if not innocent, at least explicable. The Van Clausens; the Graves. Each death, or series of deaths, were disassociated from the others, except by location. And the two incidents were separated by many decades so how could they be linked? Furthermore, there had been other residents in the intervening years. While, according to Sam, these renters had never stayed long, they had left apparently healthy and whole. Now, however, Scott wished he hadn't been so quick to dismiss Sam's arguments as superstition.

Yet he was a writer. Didn't he know how dissociated events could be manipulated to appear sinister? Was that not the warp and woof from which one wove plot? No, Scott—who had led many a reader down the garden path of subplot—saw the house only as a place of inspiration, a silent brooding house which its dark and dubious past enhanced. A place large enough for his growing family. A place made affordable by its history. And yes, the thought of publicity for his next book had crossed his mind.

Dipping his fingers into the jar Scott could have sworn he heard mocking laughter that came from somewhere beneath the house, and he froze, again feeling foolish. The only prayers he remembered were children's prayers.

Somehow he thought that running through the house chanting "Now I lay me down to sleep" wasn't going to be particularly effective.

Maybe he'd wait until he'd read a little more about the rites and rituals of exorcism. With that thought he replaced the cap on the jar and went hurriedly upstairs to get away from the maniacal laughter that rang in his ears.

The basement door closed with a click. The jar on the center of the pool table began to shimmy and shake. The water swirled, in a whirling vortex. The jar trembled, sliding over the surface of the table, and the water splashed, splattering across the deep green felt.

Harder, it shivered and shook. **Pop!** The jar exploded. The holy water seeped into the felt, turning the color of blood.

24

The smooth, unblemished landscape had become a uniformly dreary gray. The white marred by exhaust fumes and the once soft surface hardened by a thin crust. And so the scene remained until the sky belched forth a new coating of snow in nature's attempt to undo what man and pollution had done.

The town had climbed out from under its snow comforter, and a huge mound appeared at the end of the cul-de-sac, arising so quickly that it might have erupted from the earth itself. Any hill of such height and size should normally have been a playground, with children scampering up its side—to play king of the mountain or to slide down in a rump-chilling descent. But its sides were lumpy with the same abandoned, dirtied chunks with which it had been erected. No steps had been carved by juvenile feet. Neither runner tracks nor the curved indentation of many bottoms had been worn in the mound's graceless exterior.

Gray met gray in a horizonless, cheerless world—the sun refusing to put in an appearance. People defied the unrelenting gloom by putting up Christmas lights, but the character of the days was such that it devoured all their color, and the view remained as sodden and bleak as before.

The ceaseless winter and shortened days dragged at Allison's spirit. As the neighbors began to adorn their homes with the traditional lights or plastic Santas, Scott made noises about decorating the house and getting a tree—Allison would nod or grunt—but the house remained unadorned, as if winter had caught them and frozen them in place.

Standing at the window, cleaning and polishing the woodwork, Allison felt dull and apathetic, drained of energy and sapped of strength. Only in the sweet seduction of her dreams did she find solace, and even those had become menacing, although she could not have said how.

During her waking hours Allison was enervated only when she puttered around the house. It had developed an almost sterile, antiseptic look. She followed the boys, or Scott, from room to room erasing all trace of their existence. A fingermark here. A crumb there. And a cup ring somewhere else. Toys disappeared as soon as they were dropped, which elicited great hue and cry when their owners returned from the bathroom.

Since Adam's accident Allison had to force herself to move and drag herself around the house. She was immobilized, torn between two conflicting desires, one to protect her family and the other, equally strong, to retreat into her shell. Allison sensed danger in her apathy and malaise, but she couldn't seem to shake herself out of it. Her body dragged at her as though she were being drawn through the floor, and sometimes it felt as though some other being looked through her eyes, inhabited her body, as if she were possessed by it rather than being its possessor.

Dr. Greene was worried. She had lost weight and her mood was such that she did not care. Food had no taste, and she could see no real reason to eat except for the tiny life within. So she took the vitamins that the doctor gave her and choked down the protein supplement, which tasted of pure soy with a little sawdust thrown in to give it bulk. And she dwindled.

Waking up from a late afternoon nap, Allison felt *awful,* as if she hadn't rested at all but had spent the time wrestling her personal demon. She dreamt, she knew, but the images evaporated as soon as she opened her eyes.

With one ear cocked, Allison struggled out of bed. The boys' chiming voices drifted from downstairs. Allison padded to the door and plodded down the stairs to the living room where Scott refereed a rather lively game of Candy Land.

With a nod Allison went into the kitchen to fix herself some instant coffee, calling over her shoulder, "Can I get some help with dinner? I'm not feeling well."

"Sure." Scott followed her into the kitchen. "If you think I won't be doing more harm than good."

"We're having meat loaf. It's easy. I'll walk you through it. All you have to do is turn on the oven and watch the clock," she said as she hustled around the kitchen collecting the ingredients before her limited reserves of energy gave out.

Scott chuffed scornfully.

"Trust me," she said.

"Right. And the check is in the mail," he replied.

Unwrapping the hamburger, Allison dumped the meat into a bowl with a resounding plop and shambled back to the kitchen table.

"Now you add one raw egg." Allison lowered herself to the chair. "Some bread crumbs, parsley, and onion."

"I thought all I had to do was watch the clock." Scott pouted.

"Here, bring me everything. I'll mix it. You wrap the potatoes in aluminum foil and stab them."

"Stab them? What have the poor things done to me?"

Raising a brow, Allison surveyed Scott. His light banter was meant to cheer her, but his grim, concerned expression belied his humor. Allison wanted to tell him that she was all right, not depressed, only tired, but she couldn't find the words.

"It's not what they've done to you, but what they might do if you don't make little slits on the top," she explained. "They'll explode."

"The little devils." Scott shook his finger at the potatoes. The boys, who had followed their parents into the kitchen, sniggered. He brandished a fork like a sword and skewered each potato as instructed. Then Scott wrapped them in foil.

"Don't forget to turn the oven on."

With a potato in each hand Scott walked over to the stove, and time slowed. Electric current sang through her body, running along the nerve endings until she crackled with the energy that coursed down her arms. Allison's head snapped up to look at the light above her head. The bulb burned with a nice, steady glow. The even current hummed lazily. From there she spun to stare at the coffeepot.

His fingers grazed the control panel as Allison half rose from the chair. He grasped the knob firmly and turned. Even before she was fully upright, a hollow moan started in his chest, rocketing to his throat. All the breath rushed out of him, and his feet began to slide along the floor in a jerking, jittering dance. Arm rigid, he seemed to have become an extension of the stove, and his flesh, every visible inch of it, began to quiver with minute vibrations that rippled from his fingertips up his arm and down his body to his feet.

Jason clapped at his antics, and even Allison paused while she tried to decide if this was one of Scott's little jokes. Then she saw the hair on his arms, uncoiled and upright. His feet floated across the floor, barely touching the surface. The movement precipitated by a series of impossible little jumps, and then Allison realized that this was no trick.

"Oh, my God!" She sprang from her half-stooped posture as Adam too leapt up, and Jason had stopped clapping, suddenly aware that something was wrong.

Allison plowed through the boys to the pantry, sending them sprawling, and Jason began to cry. She grabbed the broom and ran back toward the stove, hesitating briefly, unsure of what she should do next.

Scott's feet continued to slide along the floor while his body twitched spasmodically, and, she thought crazily, he was doing a pretty damned good moonwalk. Allison thrust the broom between his hand and the stove's controls, wedging the wooden handle between his finger and the knob to break the connection.

And Scott let go and stood rigidly for a moment before he crumpled to the floor like a piece of limp cloth. Again she paused, torn between Scott's convulsing body and the need to disconnect the stove from the circuit. Adam scrambled for the plug.

"No!" she screamed.

Adam froze as she bolted into action. She swerved around him, the broom still in her hands, dropping it when she realized it was useless.

"Adam, a towel. Quick!" One eye was on her husband's ominously immobile body. The seizure had stopped, and there was no rise and fall of his chest. The other eye she kept on the snaking cord.

Adam handed her a towel, and she wrapped it around her hand. She clutched the cord and yanked, praying softly. It separated from the plug, so hot it had melted through. She could feel the heat through the towel. She flung it away from her, and the towel adhered to the molten plastic insulation. Then she dropped to her knees and crawled to Scott's side.

Adam stood protectively over his father. Allison placed her ear against his heart. Silence. Her hand hovered over his lips and mouth, waiting for the warm moisture of exhaled breath. Nothing.

Unable, Allison placed a tremulous hand on his chest, feeling for a heartbeat. No measured beat clattered against his ribs to her hand.

"Oh, God, please, no," she moaned. Allison rocked back on her heels, her cheeks wet with tears, and she saw that Adam wept, too. "Adam, quickly, call the police . . . the hospital . . . nine-one-one. Tell them it's your dad's heart. His heart. Give them our address, four-thirteen Elm."

Allison leaned back over to check again, hoping that the first time she had been wrong, and felt only taunting stillness.

"No, goddamn you, no." She reared up as far as she could and brought her fist crashing down on his chest. Jason, who had backed away to stand against the wall, wailed and threw himself on top of her. She shook him off. She didn't know what the hell she was doing, but she had to try.

Allison placed the heels of her palms on his breastbone, locked her arms, and then leaned into the movement. Rocking backward and forward, counting to five, she then covered his nose with her hand—pinching his nostrils shut—and his mouth with her lips and blew.

One. Two. Three. Four. Five. Blow!

One. Two. Three. Four. Five. Blow!

One. Two. Three. Four. Five. And blow!

Again!

Adam hung up the phone. "The phone's not working, Momma!"

One. Two. Three. Four . . .

"The neighbors," she gasped.

Five. Blow!

"Go," she roared.

Adam jumped, dragging Jason away from where he stood, pounding on his mother's back. "Come on, Jason," Adam mumbled. "Come with me."

One. Two. Three. Four. Five. Blow! One . . . One. Two. Three. Four. Five. Blow! One. Two. Three. Four. Five. And blow!

Allison threw her body into the movement, forgetting her abdomen, which rolled with each compression. The children returned, but she was only vaguely aware of them as they clung to each other and cried beside her.

One. Two. Three. Four. Five. Blow! She let the rhythm carry her—one, two, three, four, five—and the movement seemed to achieve a life of its own. One . . .

Her water-filled uterus propelled her forward as she swooped down to give him another breath. The blood rushed to her head, thundering past her temples, roaring into her brain. And the sound of laughter came from somewhere far away.

The clamor in her head was indistinguishable from the shrieking siren when the ambulance arrived, but she didn't stop. The motion carried her, beyond the fear, beyond the aching shoulders. And Allison didn't trust the sound, neither the laughter, the roar, nor the screaming siren.

One. Two. Three. Four. Five. Blow!

The ambulance crew poured into the kitchen, and the next thing Allison knew someone was pulling her off of Scott. She fought briefly until she saw the emergency emblem on the man's sleeve. He knelt down beside Scott and placed the stethoscope on his chest. Another man pushed cumbersome electronic gadgetry. He searched for an outlet, saw the broken cord in the corner, and stopped.

The first technician sat up. He looked at Allison and gave her a big grin. "You did it. He's alive and breathing. It's a good thing you knew CPR, or . . ." The man let the sentence drop.

Only then did Allison allow her self to exhale completely and collapse against the wall. Both boys were on top of her in an instant. She hugged them tightly, too numb to think, too numb to cry.

Driving into the cul-de-sac, Allison stared up at the house's leering exterior. Again she was struck by its resemblance to a human face, but its once-friendly grin looked more like a sneer. Unwilling to park the car in the garage,

Allison put the Saab into neutral and left it in position next to the back door, ready for a quick getaway.

The stiff wind pulled at her scarf and tugged at her winter coat. Allison bent to pick up Jason.

A shiver ran through her that had nothing to do with the cold, and she paused before putting her foot on the first riser, reluctant to make that first step that would take her into the house. Adam trailed behind, falling back when she hesitated.

Scott had nearly died; Adam had nearly died; she had nearly died. The peace had been a lie. Part of her resisted the thought. The house was safe; the house was secure, changeless. It was only a building, mortar, wood, stone; that's all, and yet . . . and yet . . .

The harder she clung to the lie, the more fate tried to wrest it from her grasp. Her first instinct had been not to hear, not to see, not to acknowledge what was happening around her. Such a thing could not happen; therefore, it didn't. Such a thing could not be; therefore, it wasn't. But in the spinning lunacy around her, reason and logic ceased, and she could no longer deny the obvious. Fear took over where reason failed, and fear told her not to go into the house. But where could she go?

"Mommy?" Jason said.

Allison glanced down at Jason. She ruffled his hair with her hand.

His eyes glittered unnaturally in the darkness. Heat radiated off him in waves. A fever!

"Damn," she muttered.

Clutching Jason's hand, Allison took the first step.

Beyond the reckoning of man and far beyond the scope of human comprehension—destroying with a thought, a slavering wish, the entity waited. From beyond time it had lived in its subterranean cell, part of the rock, part of the earth, but separate. Like a boil or a pustule deep beneath its surface. Walled off only by a thin skin of diseased tissue.

Humankind had given it many names: Demon, Satan, Lucifer, Beelzebub, Baal, Astaroth, Shiva the destroyer. But this power was no godling, no dark reflection of any puny mortal God. It was corruption itself. Abomination. Evil, nourished by the sound of death and dying, fortified by human fear and human greed.

From whence it came, and how it came to be, who could say? Perhaps it had formed with the earth, a bad gene, or it had sprung up later, like a cancerous growth. Some would say it was creation itself, the formlessness, the void, from which all came—Aeon—and in part, they would have been correct. For it was, in fact, self-creating. Forever changing, sloughing off parts of itself and recreating itself in its own image and likeness.

Yet it was without form and imprisoned, tied to the land, bound to this earthen form which gave it substance and without which its consciousness would have disappeared into nothingness. So the entity clung to its prison and despised it. Buried deep, geologists could not have found it—had they known to look—neither with seismic study nor core sample, for what in modern man's arsenal of scientific apparatus could measure pure evil?

In the distant past this being would occasionally escape for a brief respite into the body of a passing animal, reptilian in the age of reptiles, or a wolf when wolves still roamed in the unbroken woodland before the advent of man. Or as a crow, it soared through the heavens and viewed the world from hunter's eyes. During these times the entity knew envy of those things that walked abroad upon the face of the earth. Unfettered. Free. And its hatred grew—the sore festered—but the limitations of its animal host, with its animal intelligence, always drove it back to its underworld home to wait some more.

Then came man. First the tribes, a series of them as they were pressed westward by the arrival of white man. But linked as the natives were to the earth, to the very soil beneath their feet, they sensed the presence and avoided the small plot of land that had become its domicile. Later came the white man, a swaggering conqueror divorced from his environment, to rape and pillage a continent, and they had no such bonds, no such fears. Indeed the conqueror, the outsider, could not consider that the vanquished might bite back.

With the coming of those who knew too little to fear it, it had come to know the human soul, which could be manipulated, subjugated, even destroyed, but never ousted from its human host. For with the soul's destruction the host died.

So it waited still. Patiently.

The creature knew nothing of virtue, but it had patience. It had an eternity, and someday its vigil would end and that patience would be rewarded. The woman had come bringing the key, the small life pulsating within her womb, and it would have liked to have acted. Indeed, in its excitement, in its jubilation and glee, it had acted too soon, almost losing her and the precious burden she carried within. The woman was the vehicle through which it would find birth. She held the key. So it seduced her, nurtured her, caressed her, finding in her weakness and in her strength the lever it needed. In its way, it loved her. She was the creature's Madonna.

Bound to the bearer by an umbilicus, the fetus had shape and form, but no soul. It was an empty shell, a blank page awaiting imprint. The entity watched the growth of tiny limbs, fingers, and toes, delighted, and it flexed its mental fingers in anticipation.

The prescience felt the hum of the car's engine as it pulled into the drive. A thrill rippled through it as the woman set foot on the stair. It sent thoughts of its joy, its pleasure, to her and met . . . resistance . . . anger and confusion.

The key. The key. The key must not be lost.

Searching, questing . . . it reached for her and was repulsed.

No!

The key must not be lost. The child could survive without its parent host. Its time had come!

* * *

With Jason crushed to her breast Allison herded Adam before her into the kitchen. Dinner's abandoned ingredients sat on the kitchen table, roiling with maggots. Bile rose to her throat, and she swallowed, gently prodding the amazed Adam through to the living room.

"Mommy!" He pointed.

"I know, honey, I see."

Allison felt the prickling sensation, a faint tingle of nerve endings. They were being watched.

"Go away," she whispered, and daunting silence answered her.

Invisible hands plucked at her oversized sweatshirt with "Baby" and an arrow pointing down at her belly stamped on the chest.

Groaning, she squeezed Adam's shoulder. "Go ahead. I'm right behind you."

Her fingers found the switch and flipped on the living-room light. Arrested midstep, Adam blanched, mouth agape. Allison frantically searched the room, following his stricken gaze. Her eyes flicked to the mirror, where her reflection stood with a twisted, wrinkled fetus in her hands, the cord still attached, swinging from between her legs.

Without a skull, each infantile thought was revealed by a ripple of flesh that stretched over the unprotected forebrain. It struggled for life, for breath, and deformed as it was, the creature was losing the battle. And the Allison in the mirror bent her head to place her lips over the infant's lips—still wet from its journey through the vaginal canal—and blew the breath of life into his quivering breast.

Pressing Adam's face against her thigh, Allison hurried into the foyer.

A creak boomed loudly around the room, and Allison turned terrified eyes on Tommy Erwin hanging from the landing overhead. She inched closer to the stair. Jason beamed at her, feverish eyes sparkling in the dim light that came from the living room.

The rope twisted, and Tommy stared at her from empty sockets.

Her eyes fixed upon this swinging spectacle, Allison inched along the wall. In her fear, her grip on Adam had become a death hold. He pushed away from her. Jason peered curiously into his mother's eyes. Allison enveloped him in a big bear hug, crushing his face into her neck so that he, at least, wouldn't see the grim apparition.

He wiggled and squirmed, and Adam plunged, grabbing her legs and again hiding his face in her crotch.

Her feet slid out from underneath her, slipping upon impossible gore—bits of grey matter surrounded by white myelin sheath floating in puddled blood. Allison nearly dropped Jason as she caught the banister to slow her rushing descent to the floor. Adam fell with her. Still holding the toddler, Adam at her side, she managed a three-point crawl to the stair, ignoring the tacky slime that stuck to her hand, and sat on the bottom step until her legs would hold her once more.

Allison choked back a sob, hiding her eyes in her hands. She started to moan, rocking from side to side, an eerie ghastly keen. Jason wriggled out of her death grip and stared at her intently. He patted her shoulder, and she rocked on, moaning.

She wasn't going to make it. Not another minute. With Jason resting safely on her lap, she embraced Adam so he couldn't see the new obscenity. Jane Graves, the back of her head gone, sitting up on the foyer floor.

The wind howled along the eaves, tearing at shingles and battering the windows with driven snow. The branch beat a frenetic tattoo against the window in Adam's room. The sound penetrated to the master bedroom where they lay huddled together on the waterbed.

The storm had blown in soon after their arrival. The wind blew crystalline flakes in tornado whirls. Gust after gust sent icy snow against the wall of the house with a heavy patter. Yet Allison welcomed the noise. It covered the sound of movement in the attic and the piercing skree of the rope that held the phantom Erwin dangling above the foyer. Adam cowered at her side. Jason writhed upon the waterbed, and the mattress surged beneath them as she struggled to hold Jason's twitching body.

His face was a bright scarlet, even in the subdued glow of the bedside lamp. He was burning up! His shivering stilled briefly, and Allison cradled the rigid form in her arms. He jerked and then fell limply back into her lap.

Lowering him to the bed, Allison crept toward the telephone. Her fingers had scarcely grazed the receiver when Jason reared. His face contorted. A maniacal expression captured his cherubic features, and Allison halted, hand hovering over the receiver. His mouth opened, and his jaw unhinged as though he were going to swallow the sky.

"No," she whimpered and scrambled back toward the center of the bed.

His abdomen snaked sinuously as he started to heave. His shoulders shook with the strength of his retching, and Jason vomited a hurling, projectile stream.

Allison touched him, and he deflated like a pierced balloon. She crooned softly, inarticulate sounds of comfort and dismay. The wind rose again with a ferocious wail. Allison stared at the window pensively, and then turned back to Adam.

She stroked the hair away from Adam's face, looked intently into his eyes. "How are you feeling?"

"Okay, Momma," Adam said with a nervous sideways glance at his brother.

"Good. Can you stay with Jason while I go get something from the bathroom?"

He nodded.

Allison raced from the room, forgetting in her hurry to turn on the hall light. Blinded temporarily by the darkness, she felt her way along the wall. The air around her pulsed, and its tremor became a feeble, persistent murmur, a thread of sound. A not quite perceptible conversation rose and eddied around her. Allison's breath heaved, labored, and her heart batted against her ribs. The wall changed, darkening. Its surface boiled and bubbled and surged outward, clinging to her fingertips.

"No," she moaned, a choked noise that caught in her throat. Jason was sick and Scott was gone. Except for the two boys, she was alone.

The hallway gobbled Allison's protest and spat it back at her.

She gulped and flattened herself against the wall. It clung to her. She reeled, propelling herself toward the bathroom. Her hand struck the wooden door frame. Allison groped for the light switch.

With the sudden flood of light, Allison blinked a few times as she scuttled across the room to the medicine cabinet. She dug through the contents, brushing toothpaste, dental floss, and antacids out of the way. The overhead light flickered.

Once, twice, three times, and Allison held her breath. She located the thermometer and pocketed it in her robe.

The light flickered again, flared weakly, and darkness swallowed the light. Allison gasped, suppressing a rush of panic.

"Mommy, the light went out," Adam called from the bedroom, terror tangible in every syllable.

"I know, Adam, it went off in here too. I guess the electricity's out. They'll have it on in a few minutes, I'm sure."

Hah! Her mind shrieked at her. Her fingers fluttered over bottles and jars, their contents no longer distinguishable without light. A hand teased her neck and she jumped. Something made of glass fell, shattering in the sink. Allison stopped herself, counting to ten. Her eyes adjusted to the darkness. She started to pick up the broken glass and felt a sharp stab of pain.

Forget the glass, she told herself, and she squinted,

searching for the children's aspirin. Allison spied the bottle, and her fingers closed around it. A warm, tacky wetness slid from her fingertips down to her palm, the spreading stain only a black smear in the darkness. Blood.

Allison raced from the bathroom. Adam whimpered incoherently in the bedroom.

Why me? Why now? she thought as she careened into the hall at breakneck pace.

"Mommee!"

"Coming, Adam," she said—her voice quavered slightly—just as something laid heavy hands against her back and sent her plummeting down the stairs. Arms windmilling in the air, she didn't even recognize the sound of her own scream as the floor flew up to meet her. The last thing she remembered was her cheek crushed against cold wood. Her eyes wide open, memorizing each ripple in the wood grain.

A harsh blue-white light seared, burning through closed lids. Allison screwed up her face. Even without opening her eyes the world seemed to spin about her. A dull ache radiated outward from the base of her spine. Her head pulsed and throbbed, keeping time to . . .

Beep . . . beep . . . beep.

Allison opened a cautious eye to peer into the blank, computerized face of an IVAC. She recognized the device, which gave measured amounts of intravenous fluid, from her previous hospital stay. She followed the flimsy tubing to its source, noticing the Y-joint next to the solution bottle.

She lifted a tremulous hand to her head, trailing tubes. Something moved. With agonizing effort Allison raised her head from the pillow.

"Welcome back." The obstetrician, Dr. Greene, stared at her over a clipboard. "You and your family must like this place. You spend enough time here." He paused. "You took quite a nasty spill. Don't you know yet that pregnant women can't fly?"

Allison opened her mouth to protest, but the doctor

continued. "I've given orders to have this removed." He plucked at the plastic tube. "The baby is fine. No permanent damage done, just a few bruises to the mother."

"How's Jason?" Allison struggled to sit up, and Greene placed a hand on her shoulder.

"Your youngest? He's downstairs in Pediatrics. He's okay. Seems to have picked up some kind of bug, but he'll live. You'll have to ask Dr. Farquar if you want specifics."

"Adam?"

"In the waiting room. He rode in the ambulance with Jason and yourself. I'd say your Adam is quite a hero, got a good head on his shoulders. Not many kids his age would have had the wits to walk to the neighbors and call an ambulance, what with Daddy gone, Momma hurt, baby brother sick, and the phone out. He's one helluva kid."

"Is he all right?" Allison asked.

"A little scared, but he'll be okay once he's heard you're okay."

"Can I see him?"

"It's against hospital rules, but I think we can bend them a little bit in this case. After I'm through here, I'll go up and visit your husband. Any messages?"

"Just that I love him," Allison said weakly.

The doctor smiled and nodded. "He's not what you might call my typical patient. Both your husband and your son will probably be dismissed today. And you . . ." Greene's voice trailed off as he bent to listen to the fetal heart tones.

"I've got to be with my family. If they go home today, then I've got to go home too." She shuddered and looked nervously away.

The doctor frowned. "You're asking for trouble."

Her chin set stubbornly.

"I'll consider it. Look, I'll send your husband down as soon as he's processed. According to Farquar, Jason just had the flu. I'd say you got off lucky." Greene pointed at her. "You could have lost the baby."

He scratched his head. "I don't understand why you

didn't. How about if I go get your little boy? I know he'll be glad to see you. That's one worried little boy out there in the waiting room."

The door opened and closed, and Allison tried to get her turbulent emotions under control. Pushed, dammit, I was pushed, she thought.

25

On the way home Scott delivered his edict. "Well, that's it, we're going to move. Today. Tonight. I'll put you upstairs, you and the kids so you can rest. I want you to stay together. Safety in numbers. Then I'll start to pack, just what's necessary, nothing fancy. We can send a moving van back later."

Holding his breath, he waited for her to argue, but Allison said nothing.

Gaining confidence, he continued: "I don't know where we'll go." Scott faltered. He didn't like to think about that part. They didn't have the money to buy a new home, and he didn't think he could, in good conscience, sell the house to anyone else. "A motel, I suppose, until we can get settled elsewhere. Okay?" he added hopefully.

"Fine," she said.

With a quick glance in the rearview mirror at the boys who were draped over each other in the back seat, Scott turned to face her.

"I love you." He squeezed her hand.

"I love you, too." She gave him a wan smile. "I don't think I knew how much until yesterday."

"We'll be all right, I promise."

Allison gave him a long, appraising look. "Sure."

Rearing, it shrieked soundlessly. It whirled, spinning dizzily inward upon itself, like a snake devouring its tail.

So close! So close, only to fail.

Enraptured images of freedom and revenge dissolved. The screaming of a thousand nameless faces, aphrodisiacal, receded as its chances for escape retreated before it. Life beckoned. The creature boiled, seethed, and raged. In seducing it had been seduced. It had gentled her. It would be gentle no more. Longing and expectation denied. All its hatred converged on a single point. The woman must not be permitted to leave.

Its consciousness swept through its subterranean prison to create a living hell. It sensed their terror and reveled in it. There was pain and death in the air. Questions and doubts. It would use their fear, amplifying it and sending it back to them. The entity knew them; it knew their chinks, their quirks, their hopes, their desires, their fears . . .

A little past midnight, Scott sat at his desk. The polished oak of the foyer floor was bathed in the soft pastels of outdoor Christmas lights. A silvery crescent moon shone through the window. Scott paused, tilting his head to the side, a part of his consciousness seeking and finding Allison's old familiar presence. He breathed a sigh of relief.

Placing a manuscript in a box, Scott wondered where they were going to live and how they were going to make it. It didn't matter, nothing mattered, as long as they got away in one piece. He'd sell his body. He chuckled. Unlikely that he'd find any buyers. His soul—and he looked around at the room—or had he already done that when he bought this home? He'd burn the damn place down to get the insurance money if he had to. Scott snorted. Only a writer, or a very desperate man, would think of that solution, and he was both.

Scott recoiled from unwelcome memories, wreathed in

270

inferno's frame, and shook his head. He had no time for remorse or introspection. He had almost lost Allison, then Adam. His own near brush with death left him unmoved, but he wasn't going to take a chance with his family. If it took arson to get them free from this place, he'd do it.

Something scratched at the walls as if rats were trying to dig through them. Scott disregarded the sound, refusing to be distracted. He was almost finished here. The box was full, and Scott straightened. The computer would be a problem. He didn't have room for it in the car, along with their clothes and the kids' toys. At least he had the hard copy and the backup disks. He could start from scratch if something prevented him from returning to the house.

The frustrations, the failures of his life receded, and he was in control again. He'd get them out of this, and they'd start over. If that was what was necessary, so be it.

Something whickered softly in his ear. A sickly, sweet breath, and fatigue long denied wormed its way into his consciousness. His head started to droop. Scott hadn't slept much last night in the hospital despite the pills they gave him. He had been too worried about Allison and the boys. He hadn't thought then of leaving the hospital, although he should have. He should never have left them alone.

With a weary sigh Scott laid his head on the desk. He was so tired. He'd just rest his eyes for a few minutes . . .

Screaming, Sam clawed his way back to wakefulness. Body bathed in sweat, his mouth dry, as if someone had stuffed his mouth with cotton and taped his tongue to its roof. The dying shriek became garbled in his throat. His heart thundered in his chest. The nightmare dispersed, its images pushed aside by the pains that shot down his left arm, and for a moment Holloway was sure he was going to die.

His wife sat up in bed. "Are you all right?"

"The house, the house! Something's happening. I must call them, warn them," Sam wheezed, but all that came out was a strangulated squawk.

Holloway floundered in the bed, lurching under the two-ton weight someone had parked on his chest. The same joker that taped my tongue to the roof of my mouth, Sam thought inanely, and the room went black again.

Her children played in the hallway, all her children. Jason and Adam joined Sara, Shelley, and William. With clasped hands they formed a circle that went round and round.

Ring around the rosy, pockets full of posies.

Faster . . . faster . . . and faster, they whirled. The circle broke. Sara and William stepped aside. Shelley stood isolated from the rest. Shimmering, she flowed toward the stairs.

With a shiver of dread and excitement Scott waited. They were to be united for all eternity. Coupled in an . . . obscene embrace. Shelley floated outside the door, her hair forming a golden halo around her head. An alarm rang within his head, screaming that this was wrong. These thoughts, these desires, were alien. They belonged to someone else, not to Scott.

The saxophone trebled up the scale, and the thought was gone.

Union, reunion with those that he loved. She was his as he was hers. Revulsion battled with desire for supremacy. Scott left the safety of his desk and went to sit down in the rocker with a thrill of anticipation, but Shelley hung back.

"Please," he whispered, extending his arms in welcome, and the children smiled—a strangely feral smile. Still, Shelley hovered suspended inches above the floor at the study door.

"Please?"

A murmur of sound.

"Yes, yes," he promised. "Anything. Anything you ask."

Radiance trailed her as she drifted slowly forward. William and Sara closed in behind, smirking at some shared secret. Scott didn't notice, all his attention trained on the girl Shelley. She knelt at his feet. Teasing fingers kneaded his abdomen, his thighs, tearing huge rents in his clothes. Mentally paralyzed, his body was no longer his to command. Her touch burned, but an alien desire burst through him. His body reacted eagerly and Scott looked on, horrified. She stroked his loins, played with his zipper, and he moaned. Scott strained within the confines of his clothes, and she petted him until he couldn't stand it anymore. Hands he knew to be his yanked at the zipper and it stuck. Infuriated, he tore at his jeans, and the zipper broke.

R-r-i-p!

Release, succor. Scott wrapped his fingers around his own vibrating penis.

Panic, like bitter bile, rose to his throat. Then Scott felt a slight tickle at his neck. A sweet necrotic breath blew into his face, and he gulped.

Then she was in his lap. He penetrated her flesh. White hot, icy cold. He twitched, groin grinding upward. Deeper, deeper, deeper—until he was consumed by her.

"Ah, ah, ah, ah. *YES!*"

Shelley was gone, vanished, and with her the other children. His torn jeans halfway to his ankles, a sticky white mass coagulated on his legs.

A soft suspiration within his skull, and he listened to emptiness, stillness, staring at the blank space before the chair.

Empty, hollow, alone! As his hearing stretched, questing for sound, any sound, he sensed the blankness in the void. Allison was gone. While the house had kept him in the study, *it had gotten to Allison!*

Fury replaced shame as he was released from the spell and he could move.

Rat-ta-tat-tat. The twig worried at the window like a lost soul longing to come in from the cold. Adam shivered in the bed. The golden girl beckoned, waving at him from the hall.

There was something she wanted to show him. Adam slipped out of bed and went to join her.

The girl gestured, her movements sharp, swift, gaining urgency. She pointed down the stairs to the foyer. Adam followed, loping down the stairs, eager to participate in this new game. Each step he took was echoed by a leathery scrape, a creak of a rope against the wood rails.

At the base of the stairs he stopped. The girl hovered before him, her expression triumphant. Adam regarded her quizzically. What was it she was trying to show him? What did she want him to see?

Adam swung to face the study.

His father sprawled in the easy chair. Scott's pants were pulled down, his penis was painfully erect, as Adam's was in the morning and he had to pee *real bad*. Maybe Daddy had to pee.

A throaty chuckle came from somewhere. Lips pressed against his ear, speaking the unspeakable.

No! Adam's mind rejected what she said.

A shadow separated from the rest. Adam heard a soft rustle behind him. He looked down; Jason took his hand, and they both gazed into the study.

Scott's hips thrust upward, again and again. Then she was gone. Scott took his penis in his hands, and it turned ugly and red before it spit.

Adam's mouth dropped open. Jason whined, leaning against Adam's side for support, and Adam ran, hauling Jason with him, to the basement to hide.

Jason tossed and turned. He couldn't sleep. William had disappeared days ago. Maybe he was mad at Jason. Maybe William couldn't come. *It* wouldn't let him.

The closet door opened, and he peered hopefully into its inky recesses. Time to play hide and seek?

Two glowing red eyes glared back at him. The monster was back!

The closet door rattled on its hinges, and his gaze swerved

to face the beast. It was going to get him, eat him, gobble him up, and spit him out.

With a frightened gasp Jason plunged over the bedrails, escaping to the hall. Adam stood transfixed at the bottom of the stairs. William and Sara flanked him on either side. Jason heard a click, and he scampered down to the foyer to join his brother.

Hands, many hands, stroking her thighs, her belly, her breasts.

No! She struggled to sit up, to pull away from the hands and their profane caresses.

The ceiling above her head creaked, a continuous shrill squeal, as though legions cavorted within its confines.

Allison's eyes popped open. Elliot—a blue-black hole in his forehead like some obscene third eye—stood to one side. She knew without looking who would be opposite, and she didn't want to look it, but her eyes were drawn inexorably toward Jane. The wall was clearly visible through her open mouth. They bent over Allison, pinning her arms to the bed.

She kicked her feet, but they too were pinned. She peered over undulating belly at the twin apparitions of Sara and Shelley. As Allison watched, one side of Shelley's face began to droop, her features dissolving, melting. Her skin bubbled, blackened and charred; her hair shrivelled. Her lips twisted into a strange half-snarl. While a similar transformation took place on the smaller Sara. Her head crumpled, bones shattering, and the features crushed until all that was left was a grinning leer—and in their wounds they mimicked each other, even in death.

The boy William knelt between her legs, arms poised over her stomach, fingers twitching. Allison screwed her eyes shut just as the sharp talons ripped through her flesh, penetrating muscles into her uterus.

Agony washed through her in waves. *Contractions!*

She fought, thrashing, arching her back, trying to get

away, and suddenly it wasn't hands that held her but wires, copper wires like those that ran within the walls. They wrapped her in a metallic cocoon, and it wasn't hands that clawed at her, but sharp jagged strips of wiring that dug with independent life.

No! Outraged, Allison would not give up her child as long as there was one ounce of strength left within her. She opened her eyes again, this time to find Scott—not Elliot, not Jane—holding her shoulders.

He stared down on her with hollow eyes. His face distorted with bestial, inhuman emotions.

Behind Scott, Allison saw Jane's ragged skull, fractured into broken shards. Beyond her, Elliot. Then, Sara and Shelley. A small toddler with bulging eyes, and a young teenager his neck curiously awry. They collected around the bed, cavorting, capering with a strange lumbering gait. The child William drew sharp fingers across her belly.

The apparitions linked hands and danced around them, weaving in and out of the wall to make the circuit around the bed.

His grasp was light, and she threw herself upward. He pressed harder against her shoulders. Allison screamed, and finding superhuman strength from somewhere she broke. Scott's hands were flung wide, and the unseen wires dissolved. Allison floundered for a moment, and Scott made a move to push her against the bed.

"Scott!" she screeched, and she slapped him, her hand snaking out in a dizzying flash.

Smack! The ghostly visitors vanished, and the room was empty except for the two of them.

He placed a hand to his cheek—his expression hurt, confused. The air around him was alive with the sounds of rustling horror. Recognition registered in his eyes, and he moved, bending over to lift her from the bed.

"I'm all right," Scott said when she recoiled. "We've got to leave. Now! Can you walk?"

"Yes."

He placed her on her feet. "What about the boys?"

She shook her head as she stared at the broken zipper and the ripped, torn jeans.

"I'll go get them."

The words were barely out of his mouth when a shrill wail came to them from somewhere below their feet.

They hesitated, their eyes locked, and the sound came again. Twin howls, cries of fear and pain. Scott moved first, running for the bedroom door to leave Allison to struggle into her housecoat.

She heard the heavy thud of his feet as he bounded down the stairs, shouting the boys' names. Allison glanced nervously around her. The sudden disappearance of her tormenters was more daunting than any horror they had inflicted upon her.

Holding onto the banister with both hands, Allison moved cautiously down the stairs, waiting for an invisible hand to hurl her into space to land in a heap in the foyer, or to drag her down through the floor.

The air around her came alive as she placed a foot on the gore-spattered foyer floor. The house pulsed and vibrated, throbbing like a beating heart. The walls took up the sound and amplified it. Her son's cries became indistinct, obscured by the house—laughing.

Her uterus contracted, and Allison felt the pliable fetal skull pressing down against her cervix. She doubled over clenching her abdomen. This pain was real, no phantom-induced fantasy.

His cheek stung. Scott stared down at Allison, baffled. His palms itched to strike back, but he stayed his hand and helped her from the bed.

His son's screams pierced the night.

Reflex took over, and he was out the door plummeting headlong down the stairs to the foyer. Scott paused trying to orient himself.

"DADDEE-E!"

The call came from the basement. The house around him pulsed and throbbed. The walls became fluid, the floor molten under his feet. It surged upward, propelling him through the door toward the kitchen.

Their muffled cries overcame his fear. Scott sprinted through the living room, hitting the swinging door at a full run, ramming through to skid across the kitchen floor to the closed basement door. Scott seized the knob, and it spun uselessly in his sweaty hands. Again. The tumblers clicked. *Locked.*

Scott clenched the knob again, and the door burst open, slamming against the wall and dragging him with it into the basement. His arms flailed as he tried to maintain balance, and he flipped head over heels down the basement stairs. Momentarily stunned Scott simply lay—arms and legs akimbo—on the icy basement floor. Adam and Jason, huddled together along the far wall, were cut off from Scott by a sheet of flames and surrounded by ghostly apparitions.

One by one, the phantoms darted from their places in a large circle to bat at his sons. Each carried a weapon. William a stiffened rat. Jane a blue-black gun. The electricians copper wire. Shelley a burning match. First one then another moved forward, teasing at them like dogs at an ancient bear baiting or a pack of wolves around prey. With each contact the boys howled.

Something touched his flank. Scott cringed; the door above him slammed shut with a sound of finality. Allison was upstairs alone.

Torn, Scott spun, ready to race up the stairs, but Jason's frightened yelp stopped him, and he turned to leap through the leaping pyre toward his sons.

The specters attacked, and he was wading through an icy torrent, death's touch, fighting his way to their sides.

In a place beyond panic, beyond fear, Scott lunged. Picking up the boys and tucking one under each arms, he whirled. The walls bulged and drooped. The floor beneath his feet bucked and shimmied like a ship's deck on a storm-tossed sea while the illusion of flames danced around them.

Fighting for balance he teetered with his precious burdens toward the stairway. A crack appeared before his feet and widened into a chasm. He wasn't going to make it. He closed his eyes, praying for strength, and jumped to land with a teeth-jarring jolt.

Breathing a thanks to whatever god was listening, he hurled himself—a son under each arm—through the door. Allison was nowhere in sight. He stumbled for the back door, put the boys down, and fumbled with the knob. And the god who had helped them in the basement deserted them now. The door was stuck.

Without a second thought Scott shoved his fist through the window. Ignoring the pain and the blood, he batted at the jagged glass until none remained. Picking up Adam, Scott placed the simpering child on the back porch before he turned to Jason.

After passing the toddler through to his brother, he shouted at them: "Run! Get as far away from the house as you can."

Adam grabbed his brother's hand, and they scampered down the back steps to the driveway.

"Allison!"

Nothing.

Scott whirled and the floor bucked again. He landed on all fours and clambered across the kitchen floor, through Elliot's ghostly corpse, toward the living room.

In the foyer Allison was folded over upon herself, hands clamped protectively across her belly. She stared at him from pain-racked eyes, and he knew that labor had begun. She dropped to her knees.

Something grasped his ankle, and he kicked at it savagely. She started to crawl toward him and stopped.

"I can't. I can't. Go! Take the boys and get out of here."

"NO!"

With a surge of adrenaline he leapt through the living

room to scoop her up from the foyer floor, waiting for the oaken boards to open up beneath his feet and swallow them whole.

Staggering to the front door he drew his arm back, ready to break the glass, and the door flew open, nearly knocking him flat. The boys ran around from the side of the house to join them, and the McDowells fled into the snowy night.

26

Scott moved like a thundercloud through the hospital lobby. His face was pinched and his mouth drawn into a single, thin line. His jaw worked constantly as though he were chewing something indigestible. With fists clenched, shoulders bunched, and head thrust forward, Scott's long strides took him away from the elevator. People took one look at him and hastened to get out of his way.

Tumultuous alarms clanged within his brain. Alarms that told him he had long since been pushed past his breaking point. This time, however, was different. Before Scott had reacted instinctively, completely ruled by violent emotions, and his rage had been the color of red. Then it had been hot—tinged by passion and distorted with hate and a desire for revenge.

This time it was white, cold and pure. There was a clarity, a type of exultation. His rage had a crystalline structure, allowing him to think, to plot, to plan.

The first blast of frigid December air caused his pace to falter. Brought up short, he stood for a while pondering his next move. The boys were at the Holloways, and Allison slept after receiving a shot for pain.

The labor had been long and protracted, stretching from night to morning and into the afternoon. Scott didn't even know exactly how long she had been in the labor room. He only knew it had been night when he'd brought her here, and now an westerly sun shone weakly over fouled snow, providing no warmth.

The image of Allison, writhing on the hospital bed, caught in the throes of labor seared, feeding the white flame of rage. He stoked it until it burned brightly, blazing like a beacon to illuminate the path he must now tread.

The key. The key.

The idea had come to him as he held her hand, stroking dank hair from her damp face. Scott had realized then what he should have known before. The child, not Allison, was key. The small unborn life within her. And if that were the case, then she and it were still in danger until the babe was delivered.

They had emerged intact, barely, and he wanted to make sure that they stayed that way. And still more, he wanted to make sure no one else was ever hurt again. He must act swiftly, and then he could return to Allison's side, to caress, to hold, and watch the delivery.

Scanning the parking lot, Scott reviewed what he must do step by step. He tried to remember where he had seen a hardware store along the route to the hospital. He recalled a Tru Value and a Target in a strip center some miles down the main road. Both would have what he needed. The season was against him, but it was worth a shot.

He went to the car, ignoring the wind that pierced his shirt, the cold that penetrated his slippers, numbing his feet. Scott grappled with the key, letting himself into the Saab. He stared at himself in the rearview mirror. He looked like a lunatic, stark, raving mad. This would never do.

Scott opened the glove box and pulled out a comb. After straightening his hair he grabbed his boots from where they lay on the floor of the car, discarded and forgotten in the mad dash to the hospital, and shoved his feet into them, slippers and all. He tucked his shirt into his jeans, saw the broken zipper, and thought better of it. Muttering under his breath, he went to the trunk to extricate his long winter coat from one of the boxes. It would cover the tears. He looked presentable—not good, but presentable.

The Saab's engine purred, calming him more. He drove with measured movements. Neither a flicker nor a tremor betrayed his feelings. Scott stopped at Holloway's house to unload the boxes. Jason and Adam climbed all over him, and he held them to his breast, breathing their baby-soft smell, before pushing them away so he could memorize their features. Jason's so seraphic, rosy face and round, chubby cheeks; Adam's lean, intent face with its serious expression, thin lips, and straight nose.

Staying in the background, Sam waited. "Ah, anything I can do to help?"

"No, I'm going back to the house to get another load."

Dubious, Holloway said, "Are you sure that's wise?"

"I'll be okay." Scott extended a hand to Sam. "Thanks for taking care of the kids."

Before driving to the house, Scott went to the mall where he went from store to store, stripping the shelves of gas storage cans and lighter fluid. In Tru Value Scott picked up five gas cans; at Target, three. In Sears he found an additional two. At each store, Scott asked for charcoal fluid, and at each he was told that they didn't keep it stock during the winter.

Insistent, Scott asked them to check their back shelves, telling the incredulous clerk that he and Allison had a hibachi and wanted to cook a steak on the back porch. That yielded a meager few cans and more than a few suspicious looks as they rang up his purchase. Charcoal lighter fluid, lighter fluid for a zippo he didn't possess. Sterno, gasoline cans.

At a nearby mom-and-pop store the old woman behind

the counter was even more hesitant, although she had gone to the storeroom quickly enough and returned with a single container.

"Do you have any more?"

"Yes, we have another two or three," she said, nervously eyeing the box of lighter fluid and the three stacked gas cans. "What do you need it for?"

"We like steak—and hamburgers—and they just don't taste as good unless they're grilled," Scott replied, giving her his most charming grin.

"We-ell," she said as she contemplated the haggard, young man before her.

"If you're worried about running out . . ."

"It's not that, really." The old hag pointed at the empty storage containers. "It just that it looks like you are getting ready to start a fire someplace."

Something went click, and he struggled to hold onto his waning patience. She must have noticed a change, for she took a step back and started to stutter.

"Christmas presents," Scott said abruptly.

"Odd presents, aren't they?"

"Well, are you going to sell them to me, or not?"

"Ah, sure."

The woman retreated to the back of the store, returning a few moments later with four cans of charcoal lighter fluid hugged against a volumous breast. Scott paid with cash, although she tried to get him to pay by check.

No way, bitch, Scott thought, am I going to give you my address.

Chuckling, he carried the supplies to the car. As he drove away he noticed her talking furtively into the phone, and Scott hoped she hadn't bothered to get the license plate numbers.

Then he drove from gas station to gas station, filling no more than two cans at a time. By the time he was finished, the Saab reeked of gasoline and the cans rattled and sloshed every time he hit a bump or turned a corner.

Scott pulled up in front of the house and sat for a few minutes, trying to decide what to do next. He needed to empty the car, but he feared the reactions of the snooping neighbors, most of whom already thought he was deranged.

The windows, like blank eyes, gazed down on him implacably. The car's motor ticked, cooling. Scott surveyed the building with its palsied gingerbread trim, and his gaze fell on the garage. A cold calculating sneer spread across his face.

Scott started the car and put it into gear. He pushed the button on the remote, and the garage door rose on mechanized pulleys. He backed in and quickly unloaded the car. Scott pulled the Saab out, stopping when the passenger door was parallel with the back porch. Next to the car he paused, steeling himself for what he must do next—enter the house.

With a deep breath Scott silenced his mind. Reaching within himself, he found the crystalline kernel of his ire. He savored its pure beauty, its brilliance. He allowed it to fill his mind, his heart—indeed, his soul. The white rage would protect him. It was his armor and his shield.

Acting casual, Scott strolled up the wooden stairs to the screened-in porch. The door swung open. He smiled, accepting the silent invitation, and stepped inside.

Moving from room to room, he collected more toys and clothes, filling garbage sacks with shirts, shoes, and sweaters.

The house was quiet, curiously contemplating his activities. Its silence pregnant, palpable. Scott went straight to the study, and the house came to life around him. Every board in both floors and walls creaked simultaneously. As though buffeted by the winds, the house shook and thundered in protest. Without hesitation Scott unplugged the computer, breaking it down into separate components.

The house groaned in a loud lament. Muted whispers emanated from the walls. Senseless babbling. Voices without words, sounds without thoughts. It tested him. He shook it off, combating the white noise with static of his own, concentrating on the roiling fury within his brain.

Shapes rippled, quivering barely seen out of the corner of his eye. Incorporeal forms flickered, altering and shifting. Hypnotic and mesmerizing, it created a strobe effect, the rapid change from bright to dark distorting his vision, and Scott narrowed his line of sight as he neatly wrapped the cords around the corresponding computer parts.

Unseen hands began to tug at his clothing, and Scott felt the first tickle of fear at the base of his spine. He bit his tongue, tasting fresh blood. The hot flash of pain brought tears to his eyes. Fear ebbed, and anger returned. Scott turned to search through files and pull those he would need. Financial information, insurance policies, outlines for his next planned books. These he dumped in a disorganized jumble into a garbage sack, bank statements mixing with hand-scribbled notes.

Standing among the bags and boxes, Scott wondered how he was going to fit everything into the car when the floor lurched underneath, and he almost fell. Again he filled his mind with a picture of Allison as she lay in her hospital bed. Children darted into the study, and he saw one of them lift a bloody coat hanger, shrieking in triumph beside a misshappen fetus.

"No-o-o," he roared, and Scott grabbed two of the filled sacks and slammed out of the house. He raced to the car, opened the door to the backseat, and hurled the bags inside. Scott bounded up the stairs to repeat the process, and the back door shut with a bang. He twisted the knob, and it fell off in his hand. He climbed through the broken window.

Panting, he straddled a bag. An icy finger traced a circle on the back of his neck, and the bloody coat hanger twisted in his brain. Scott picked up another four bags, the smaller ones clenched tightly beneath his arms, and returned to the car, where he opened all the doors and the trunk.

Again Scott filled his arms, carrying as much as he could in a trip. Each time clammy hands touched him. Familiar apparitions appeared and solidified only to dissolve when he stepped over the threshold. Tommy Erwin hung suspended in the foyer, his legs kicking in a deathly dance. Jane, reclined in a puddle of blood at his feet while Elliot grappled with something unseen. A toddler battered at the front door.

Sara. Shelley. William. Floating, free-form, mobile, they dogged his footsteps, following him from room to room. Laughing. All rippled and vanished, winking in and out of sight, to reappear elsewhere.

And the house had also become crowded with small animals. Dogs, cats, squirrels, rabbits, even horses. All the animals that had died here through the years. The white terrier Scott had buried not long before circled, teeth sunk in its own haunch. Decomposed or decomposing, rarely intact. Sometimes the images merged and a squirrel would have a dog's head. A rabbit the tail of a racoon or the claws of a cat.

Their combined barks, brays, mewls, and howls reverberated off the walls. They clambered about Scott's feet, tripping him up. He swam through them as though swimming through thick molasses, feeling the cold chill of death as he passed through the ghostly images.

The back seat was crammed full, and the trunk would scarcely close. The front passenger seat remained empty, waiting for the computer. Only one or two more trips.

When he stumbled into the kitchen for the last time they had all gathered. All of them! Human and animal alike. Scott's pulse skittered erratically, and his legs turned rubbery. The skin of his balls began a slow creep. His blood rushed through his veins, throbbing like the drumbeat of doom, but he forced himself to continue. He snatched the computer from the kitchen counter. Juggling the keyboard and the VDT, Scott placed a testing foot in front of him.

Another step and something seized his ankle—something slimy, slippery. He opened his eyes with a stifled shriek and tried to shake the child William off. The boy clung, and Scott tried to jerked his leg away. The arm parted from the shoulder. William pointed a crooked finger at him and floated upward. Still Scott couldn't move; he was glued to the spot.

He looked down. The arm had grown into the floor, becoming an extension of the wood itself. Oaken fingers gripped his ankle, and their tips grew like fresh spring growth, wrapping sinewy wooden branches up his leg.

They cannot touch me, his mind bellowed, and the branches receded a bit. The new green growth blackened and died, and the hand itself began to dissolve, decompose.

Wrenching himself free, Scott bolted for the door. William's hand raked Scott's side, his arms, his back, and the others clustered around him. Poking, prodding, plucking at his clothes.

They cannot touch me; they cannot touch me; they cannot ... He intoned the words like a Gregorian chant. Claws shredded his shirt. Scott felt warm liquid dripping down his arms and torso as he burst through the door, gasping. The house shook as Scott, with all the restraint he could muster, gently placed the VDT on the passenger's seat.

Scott ran around the front of the car and climbed inside. All control gone, he wrenched the key in the ignition, rammed the stick shift into gear, and floored the gas. The Saab fishtailed down the slick driveway, tires spinning. It shot across the cul-de-sac and bumped over the curb, where it floundered in fresh snow.

Behind him the deserted house with its concave roof squatted, looking like a cat ready to pounce. Shouting, he gunned it, and the car plowed a weaving path through the yard and over a shrub before he steered it back onto the street. The old woman's face appeared at the window to see what the commotion was, and by the time Scott turned off Elm he was laughing hysterically.

At the end of the block Scott pulled over to the side of the road to assess the damages. Having put some distance between himself and the house, he was forced to acknowledge his injuries. So much for his idea that the house couldn't really touch him or hurt. That it was all in his mind, hallucinations.

Warm, sticky blood oozed from scratches he did not have when he entered the house. It had touched him.

Once again Scott had underestimated the place.

Shaking, Scott slumped over the steering wheel. Tonight he had to go back, and he didn't know if he had the strength to do it.

Wounds bandaged, Scott changed into the clean shirt and fresh jeans he had carried in from the car before returning to the maternity ward. The shot had worn off, and Allison was wide awake. Her grey-streaked hair was soaked through with perspiration. She gave a small cry of joy when he walked into the room.

"Where have you been?" she gasped between pains.

"The house."

"Scott, no, you've got to stay away from there!"

Scott sat on the side of the bed, and Allison clung to his arm.

"I just picked up a few things—more clothes for us and the boys—and the computer," he explained, slipping an aching arm underneath her neck, ready to support her during the next contraction.

"It'll be over soon. I promise," he said fiercely. "You'll never have to go into that house again."

"Promise me?" she said weakly. "No, I don't care about that. I *know* I won't ever set foot in that house again. Not voluntarily. Now promise me that *you* will never go into that house again. If anything were to happen to you, I couldn't go on."

Scott studied her for a moment, troubled, before he said: "I promise I won't do anything except protect you and the children." He lay a tender hand on her stomach.

Allison looked at him quizzically for a moment, trying to decide if she had extracted the promise she sought, when another contraction hit. Her fingers flexed, digging into a cut on his arm. Scott winced and lifted her, supporting her through the contraction.

A nurse entered as the slight gargling noise caught in the back of Allison's throat erupted in a scream. The nurse saw Scott, nodded, and began to monitor fetal heart tones. She checked Allison's pulse and bustled out the door.

Allison relaxed, collapsing back to the pillows. Her fingers released their hold, and her arm fell limply to the bed.

Scott winced as he saw her fingertips were red. He glanced down at his shirt. Blood had soaked through the sleeve in a growing red stain. Scott quickly grabbed the sport coat he had brought with him and put it on.

The nurse returned carrying a syringe. The doctor followed, calling Scott from the room, and the door closed behind him, shutting her from view.

"How's she doing?" Scott asked.

"She could be better. I never should have released her yesterday, but I don't think I could have kept her here unless I had tied her to the bed," the doctor said.

Chewing his lip, Scott stared at the closed door. "She does have a stubborn streak, doesn't she? Tell me, will the delivery be soon?"

The doctor shook his head. "I don't know. The nurse is checking the dilation now."

As though on cue the door opened, and the white-capped head poked out. It wagged from side to side. No. The doctor acknowledged her with a brief inclination of his head.

"It would appear she's not nearly dilated enough," the doctor said. "This may last a while yet."

"She's never had trouble in the past. Her deliveries were always quick," Scott said.

"You can't judge by past experience. Each delivery is new and different. I've seen some labors last for days. The infant's not in jeopardy, though. The fetal heart tones are good. We can wait a bit. As long as the heart tones are good and the mother can handle it, we'll do everything we can to avoid a C-section."

"Maybe you shouldn't wait." Scott cast another worried glance at the door.

"Cesarian section is major surgery. As difficult as this may seem, it's better for both mother and child if the delivery can be done naturally."

The nurse brushed past.

"We've given her another injection; she should rest for a while," the doctor said.

"Won't the drugs slow the process?"

"A little, maybe, but the medication will give her some relief from the pain."

The doctor patted him on the back. "Buck up, man. After this is over you'll have a healthy, squalling baby to take home with you."

Scott sighed as the doctor turned and walked away. Allison called to him, and he went back to hold her hand, through another contraction that came too slowly and stayed too long.

Eventually, she fell into an exhausted asleep.

The sun had sunk low in the sky, hovering above the town, and Scott tried to concentrate on the gentle colors of sunset as he drove. The speedometer's needle crept upward, thirty-five, forty, fifty—in a thirty mile per hour zone, and Scott forced himself to relax. Running over some little kid on the way wouldn't do anybody any good.

The sun dipped behind the treeline. Elongated skeletal shadows gave a last, dying wave as he turned onto Elm. Only a few bleached colors stained the western horizon. Stars winked slyly in the east. An occasional light twinkled on up and down Elm as he parked at the end of the block, well away from the house.

The Victorian loomed above its neighbors, at its most grim and foreboding. He had been wrong; a coat of paint had done nothing to relieve its formidable countenance. The western sky had turned from pale peach to a dusky maroon before he could rouse himself to action.

Scott let himself into the garage. He filled his pants pockets with the small cans of sterno and lighter fluid. He stuffed matches and additional lighter fluid into his shirt and jacket pockets. Then he hefted four of the gas cans— two in each hand—and headed for the back door.

They awaited him. All of them! Dogs with their heads cocked expectantly. Cats arched—their progress arrested as they clawed their way through the throng. Squirrels. Birds. Reptiles, small garden snakes, and even a few species Scott couldn't name.

Their human counterparts stood, unmoving, in their most frightening aspects. Mold traced a lacework over collapsed noses and empty eyes. Flesh stripped from bone. Motionless, they stared with sightless yet knowing eyes at the intruder—frozen as though in the last stages of rigor mortis and decay.

Nothing moved, but their eyes followed him as Scott stopped at the back door. His breath clapped against his ribs. He stepped noisily into the room, and they were released as if from some spell. The cats started clawing. The dogs bit. Forms shifted, snakes became birds, birds became mammalian. Shifting, ever shifting, unable to hold form and shape.

With a deep breath, Scott dove into the throng, wading in and through them. The humans trailed after performing their own strange metamorphosis—replaying the moments of their death.

Scott fled up the stairs. The weight of the cans dragged at him, pulling him down. They clanked and clattered. The house itself began to vibrate, and ghostly voices rose to a ferocious yammer.

William drifted behind Scott, unhurried, trailing him up the stairs—his skin a ghastly iridescent green. Conjured images erupted from shadow, and the flickering gloom filled the hall with changing shapes. Scott lost his footing and tripped, to land on hands and knees on the second-floor landing. Something swift and furtive skidded from his sprawling path.

Scott heard the predatory bark of a dog, the harsh caw of a crow, and the hiss of a whispered conversation. The phone began to ring, but he ignored it as it echoed along the height of the wall, and the wood took up the sound.

He clambered back onto his feet, leaving three of the cans lying on their side on the floor. He lurched into Jason's room to empty its contents into the closet.

Splash!

He squirted lighter fluid on the curtains.

Swoosh, and he emptied another container onto the mattress.

The wails vibrated in a single ear-splitting chord, as William landed on his back. Scott threw himself backward, hoping to smash the child into the wall. The force of the blow as his spine hit the rock-hard surface stunned him. Scott shook himself and moved on to the next room.

He sent fountains of foul-smelling gas and lighter fluid over furniture, curtains and walls until his precious supply was expended. Scott rushed to the stairs. His foot came down on an empty can, and he almost fell, catching himself just in time. Pulling himself upright, he limped for the garage.

Another load, pockets stuffed and bulging. Scott lumbered into the kitchen and darted down the stairs to the basement, and they came at him, flailing. Jane, Elliot, Erwin—his neck set at an improbable angle so that even as he attacked Scott the teenager looked at the ceiling.

Sometimes their touch was feather-light, cold fingers tugging at his garments—frightening, but harmless. Other times their contact sliced through his clothes and skin like a hot knife through soft butter. Still other times Scott found himself walking through some ghastly apparition, and this, he discovered, was the most disturbing of all.

Splash!

And he doused a pile of dirty clothes.

Splash!

And he poured gas on the old sofa.

Splash!

And he soaked the expensive pool table, with the broken baby food jar that still sat in the center.

Jungian beasts uncoiled, serpentine, from the depths of his unconscious, but he blotted them out by the sheer force of will. His motions were slowed as he struggled through a room peopled with phantasms. A mallet beat at his temples. It took an eternity to wade his way back up the stairs to the kitchen and then the garage.

Outside the brisk, clean air was tinged with the acid aroma of gasoline. Scott upended a can over the paint and cleaning supplies leftover from remodeling before he returned to the house.

Scott worked feverishly saturating walls and furniture.

Splash!

The drapes in the living room dripped.

Splash!

And the books in the study were soaked.

Splash! SPLASH!

And he sent the last of the pink liquid in a whirling cascade through the foyer.

Shapes rippled under the spray. Ghosts shrank, only to rise again. Ripping, tearing.

His heart fluttered wildly in his breast like a fly trapped between window and screen.

The hot stone of his own mortality weighed upon him, making his movements sluggish. He dragged himself up the stairs, pulling three cans of sterno from his pocket. He lit them one at a time and flung one into each room. Two flared darkly and went out, but the third caught, and he was hurled against the far wall by the force of the explosion.

BOOM!

Scott tumbling down the stairs, falling, but this time he

didn't resist it. He let himself somersault liquidly, rolling to his feet in the foyer. Fire cackled and danced, and he saw Aldo lumber toward him through the flames. Scott hurtled through the living room and kitchen to stand on the basement landing where he repeated the process, igniting a can of sterno and throwing it down the stairs.

It fizzled out before it hit the floor.

Again.

And the second can flamed, as did his arm. Scott shrieked his terror before heaving the burning can into the gloom, his arm a bright torch that he waved frantically and then tried to stifle between body and wall, only to ignite both the wall and his clothing.

KABOOM!

And the basement exploded. His entire body was encased in flames. A human candle, Scott ran blindly through the kitchen into the living room, igniting everything in his path. His hair sizzled and flashed as he burst into the foyer, falling to his knees. The landing above his head was an inferno.

A fiery apparition, Scott crawled across the foyer still trying to escape to the cold outdoors. To the snow where he could extinguish the flames. The house's many residents capered around him, their images mingling and leaping with the fire. His blackened fingertips brushed the front door and he let go, succumbing to the agony.

As consciousness ebbed Scott looked up. His parents appeared before him, surrounded by a golden glow. There were no ghostly house-sent apparitions, bubbled and charred. They stood intact and whole, perpetually young with laughing, happy eyes. They gathered him into their arms, crooning soft assurances and promises of love long delayed. He wallowed in their tender touch, and Scott knew he'd been forgiven.

Somewhere far away the sound of sirens split the night.

27

Standing outside the sterile chamber, Mrs. Dietrich explained the doctor's orders, but the oncoming nurse, Elaine Nelson, only half listened. Her attention was drawn through the glass to the lump of human flesh upon the bed.

The patient was one giant oozing sore. Only his feet and his scalp remained intact. His right arm was so badly burned that the fingers on that side were fused together, little more than stubby lumps. His face was almost entirely gone, with a large hole where the mouth should be and two smaller holes on a lump that had once been a nose. The lips had been burned off, and the eyes were seared shut.

The bed was like something out of a dream—or a nightmare—a great mechanized monster on a huge circular frame similar to a Ferris wheel. A second mattress suspended above the first permitted a nurse to turn a patient without touching him. Once the second mattress was clamped into place the nurse simply hit a switch. The electronics would do the rest. The bed would rotate with a great grinding of gears, flipping the patient from prone to supine position or vice versa.

The bed had been modified. A pneumatic pad—

something like an air mattress with continuous circulation —had been placed between the patient and the bed. IV tubes replaced vital fluids; an nasogastric tube permitted feeding, while chest tubes removed liquid that had collected in his lungs. A central venous probe monitored his heart rate. The jagged line displayed an irregular pattern.

Mrs. Dietrich handed her the chart, and Elaine wondered how the man had managed to survive debriding.

Dietrich pointed to the orders. "Silver sulfadazine applications q two hours. IV rate is one liter q hour and a half. Tagamet . . ."

Elaine looked up. "McDowell? The name sounds familiar."

"Yes, some kind of writer. Anyway, Doctor Greene's ordered standard aseptic procedures. I & O. Oh yes, and vital signs q half hour," Mrs. Dietrich said.

"Greene? But he's GYN," Elaine said.

"I know. The family just moved into town, and I gather they hadn't found a GP yet," Dietrich continued. "Pedal pulses are good. Thank God his feet are okay. Respirations are no problem. You should try to get an apical pulse at least once a shift. I've worked something out so it's not too painful for him."

"Is he conscious?"

The other nurse nodded. "Intermittently."

Dietrich led Elaine over to a small table. Several disposable syringes and a vial of procaine were arranged around a box of gauze pads. "Just withdraw a couple of cc's of procaine and squirt it onto the gauze. Place the soaked pad over the heart region, wait a couple of minutes, and then you can use a stethoscope without worrying about discomfort. The only thing he should feel is pressure, if that."

Nelson nodded.

"We should have a doctor's order for this, and I didn't think to get one when he was admitted. I had enough on my hands trying to get all this set up," Dietrich indicated the bed and pneumatic mattress. "Could you do that? I'm pretty sure Dr. Greene will be down as soon as he can break away from the wife. She's in labor right now. I understand it's been difficult and they're prepping her for a C-section."

Blowing air out of puffed cheeks, Elaine said, "That poor woman. Does she know about her husband?"

Dietrich shrugged. "I don't think so. Horrible, isn't it?"

Green-garbed, faceless figures flitted down the sterile corridor, pushing a gurney. They spoke in hushed, awed voices, as one might speak in a library or a cathedral. Grounded booties covered their shoes and muffled the sound of their rapid footsteps.

The woman on the cart, her belly moving visibly beneath the sheet, was prepped and ready for the C-section. Her face was a mask of exhaustion; her expression strained. Although she was drugged to the hilt, she fought to keep awake.

"My husband? Where is my husband?" Allison asked.

They pushed through the swinging operating room doors and pulled up next to the surgery table. The nurse snapped the wheel-locks into position and backed away from the table.

"Mrs. McDowell, we have to move you. Can you help us?" A second nurse took over, lowering the side rails. "Just scoot on over."

The anesthesiologist bent over to support the woman's back. The obstetric nurse helped with her hips. Between the three of them, they managed an awkward slide from cart to table. The OR nurse raised the rails, unlocked the wheels, and propelled the gurney back to the labor room nurse, who took it and fled back to the hall.

The anesthesiologist rechecked his math to make sure he had the proper dosage for her weight and height. Cesarian sections were always difficult. One had to think of the fetus. The OR nurse straightened the surgical implements on the tray, again, unwilling to look at the patient.

A claw-like hand clutched the anesthesiologist's arm. "We have to wait for my husband."

The two pairs of eyes snapped together, peering at each other over green masks. Simultaneously, they turned to the OB nurse. She shook her head from side to side. No, Mrs. McDowell had not been told yet.

Damn! The anesthesiologist thought, taking a moment to let this information sink in before he responded in what he hoped was a reassuring voice.

"Don't worry about your husband right now, Mrs. McDowell. You've had a long, hard labor. You just worry about yourself and having this baby," he said.

"But Scott should be here." Allison's fingers tensed around the man's arm, clinging, desperate to get her point across.

"Here in surgery? I'm sorry, Mrs. McDowell, that's against hospital regulations."

"Not in surgery, in the hospital. He was just going to check the boys," she said plaintively.

"In the hospital? Ah," he replied knowingly. Here was a question he could answer truthfully. "He is, Mrs. McDowell. I've heard from Dr. Greene that your husband is in the hospital at this very moment."

"He is?" Her voice rose, and she searched his eyes looking for the unspoken truth. The man glanced down at his feet.

Dr. Greene entered, hearing their exchange. He hissed a warning at the anesthesiologist. Allison tried to sit up, but the man's hands were on her shoulders, forcing her down.

"Mrs. McDowell, you have to lie still. I'm going to start the IV that will put you to sleep. You'll feel a little prick, and when I tell you, I want you to start counting backward starting from one hundred, okay?"

"Okay." Allison relented.

The doctor had moved out of her line of vision, but she turned her head and stared at him with accusing eyes. The anesthesiologist felt for a vein, found it, and adeptly inserted the needle. He moved swiftly back to the head of the table to sit next to large metal box with numerous dials, valves, gears, and switches.

With his thumb at the cutoff to regulate flow, he spoke: "Now, Mrs. McDowell, count."

"One hundred, ninety-nine, ninety-eight, ninety-seven, ninety-six, ninety-five, ninety-four, ninety-thr . . ."

The personnel swooped in as her droning voice faltered and faded. The nurse pulled the padded armboards from beneath the table, slid the metal pin into position to attach them and tightened the screws. When this maneuver was completed they strapped her arms to the boards. The second nurse removed the blanket, exposing the woman's stomach. With the drugs she had been given the contractions had finally slowed to a scarcely perceptible ripple.

Dr. Greene stepped up to the table, grimacing under his mask. No matter how many years he worked as a physician, he was always struck by the resemblance between the surgery table and the cross. Once strapped down, the patient looked like one prepared for a crucifixion.

He had never liked surgery, and he never felt completely comfortable in the operating theatre—although he had done his share of C-sections—but only as a last resort. Some nurses had accused him of waiting too long, but he had never lost a patient yet, and a few, whom other doctors would have operated on, ended up having normal deliveries.

This delivery would be anything but normal. The fetal heart—which had been beating quite happily and steadily, well within normal limits, for the entire twenty-some-odd hours of labor—had suddenly rose dangerously high sometime after Dr. Greene had admitted the father into Intensive Care. Almost as though the infant knew of his father's condition.

Dr. Greene bent over Mrs. McDowell's stomach. He pulled the special FHT stethoscope from his pocket. Similar to a regular stethoscope, except this device had an additional strip of metal which fitted snugly over the skull. The metal cap conducted sound to bone, allowing the doctor or nurse to hear the submerged fetal heartbeat.

"Let's hurry up about this," the doctor urged.

The OR nurse moved in quickly to paint the abdomen with an orangish mixture before putting the sterile drapes around the place where the incision would be made.

Greene watched the anesthesiologist intubate the woman and cover her nose with the black mask. He fiddled with the controls and when he was satisfied the doctor finally broke the silence. "You took one helluva a chance there, telling her he was in the hospital."

"It was the truth. What was I supposed to tell her?" the anesthesiologist said.

"She could've asked some pretty embarrassing questions."

"I didn't plan to give her the time to."

The doctor nodded tersely at the anesthesiologist. He didn't look forward to waking this particular patient up. Greene held out a rubber-gloved hand to the nurse standing beside him and said: "Right, let's get this show on the road."

The fire marshal stood on the dead brown grass before the burnt-out shell. The only full-time staff in an otherwise all-volunteer department, he was experienced and familiar with his job, but he had never seen anything quite like this. The place looked like it had been through a nuclear holocaust. Alex, close to retirement, had no desire to witness another inferno like this one.

The frozen earth nearest the dwelling had been turned into slick mud from the intensity of the blaze, and the snow in a hundred-yard radius had melted. The home had been a total write-off by the time they arrived. All they had been able to do once they had dragged the body away from the structure was try to contain the blaze to the one building.

Alex Bronsky had seen arson before, too, but this guy had been particularly thorough. The man had doused every room in the house. The smell of gasoline still wafted around the home when they arrived, despite the other mixed odors of burning rubber, insulation, sheetrock, wood, and smoke.

Not long after they pulled the body from the door, the porch had crumbled beneath them. Two firemen had been injured. The fire marshal himself had carried the man away from the conflagration. Alex had been amazed to see that the man still lived as he set him down in the melting snow before going to help the volunteers dig their cohorts from the debris.

The other firemen sifted through the wreckage, and neighbors lingered in the cul-de-sac. More townsfolk arrived periodically to gawk and stare. Their voices were a muted growl. The ugly crowd was held back by the yellow cordon that sectioned off the entire area.

Alex's second-in-command joined him, and they pondered the gaping hole where once there had been a house. One of two chimneys was still standing upright. The other had collapsed. The rubble of blackened bricks made a small mound in the center of the cellar. A fissure split the concrete so wide and deep that it seemed to go down to the bowels of the earth. Only a few of the main supports remained upright, and they had been all but destroyed, burned down to sharp ragged stumps that looked like jagged teeth around an open mouth. Wisps of smoke curled lazily from the basement, and the air had a greasy, choked, musky smell which would cling for several days. But for all practical purposes the fire was out.

"Well, what do ya think, Jack?" the marshal said, glancing at his aide.

"Arson, without a doubt."

"I know *that*. What I'm wanting to know is: should I report it?"

"What do ya mean?" Jack Gimble stared at his supervisor, amazed that he, a stickler for rules, would make such an unprecedented suggestion.

Alex Bronsky put a hand to his square jaw and rubbed at the stubble.

"Look at it this way. If I report it, the wife won't get the insurance money. She won't get insurance for the house

302

because her husband deliberately set the fire, and she won't get life insurance either. It could easily be misconstrued as some elaborate way to commit suicide," Alex said. "The way I see it, the family's screwed."

"Yeah," Jack agreed, and his eyes again swept the wasteland before him.

"I figure the family's suffered enough. I mean, something must have driven the guy to do it."

Both men shuddered.

"The poor woman. She's lost everything—her home, her husband. I'm reasonably sure that guy won't make it. Christ, he was cooked!" And he screwed up his face at the thought of the remembered image. "Just between you and me, I think he did this town a favor by burning this place down. There's the hole, but that can be filled up."

"Well, I won't tell if you won't, but what will we list as the cause?"

"How about the heater?"

"It's all right with me," Jack said.

"Good, 'cause you're the next person the insurance company'll talk to if I'm not around."

The fire marshal pulled off his hat and his hood to reveal a soot-stained face. "Let's see if we can get some of these people to go home."

Gimble and Bronsky had just started toward the crowd when an eerie cry rose from the debris. Little more than a moan at first, it grew louder—increasing in crescendo to a hair-raising shriek. The men spun back to stare in amazement at the basement. The moan became a high-pitched eldritch scream which contained all the agony of the universe within its vibrating, modulating chords. Human wails of pain. The howls of lost souls.

"Holy shit!" Jack shouted.

The ground beneath their feet picked up the sound and began to shake. Alex braced himself, knees flexed. Behind them the crowd muttered nervously and people leaned against their nearest neighbors in an attempt to stay upright.

The volume swelled, louder and louder, until both men were forced to put their fingers in their ears. Behind them, the observers cowered, crabwalking away from the wreckage and the uncanny wail. It continued for a minute, warbling triumphantly. Then the unearthly howl receded—not decreasing in volume as much as it grew more distant, as though the cry flew away from them on invisible wings.

Sweat broke out on Alex Bronsky's craggy face. "What the hell was that?"

He trotted forward and dropped to his knees next to the basement, looking for signs of life.

Jack simply shook his head and gulped.

Alex glanced quickly at his watch. "Look, it's eight-thirty-five. Why don't we go back to the station and finish those reports quickly? We can both use some sleep."

Elaine Nelson helped the staff distribute breakfast trays. After making sure all ICU patients were either eating or being fed, the nurse made her way into the small robing room. She scrubbed and then donned the requisite gown, cap, gloves, booties, and mask.

With a deep breath to steady herself the nurse opened the door and let herself into the room. The stertorous rasping breath was clearly audible over the multiple beeps of the regulated IV and monitors. She carried sterile sheets with her, positioning herself so she could look out the plate glass window and observe the other patients in the unit.

Suddenly confronted with the monstrous bed, Elaine wished she had paid more attention to Dietrich's instructions during report. She examined the many gears and pulleys and finally discovered the one that would lower the second mattress into place. Not a tall woman, Elaine had to stretch to reach it.

Her fingers had just grazed the black plastic knob when she heard the high-pitched squeal of the alarm. She knew without looking that he had died. Still she did what was expected, glancing from the flat line on the EKG monitor to the clock, and noted the time.

Elaine turned off the alarm and pressed the button on the intercom.

"You better call Dr. Greene," she said.

One of the staff nurses stared at her through the glass, motioned her acknowledgment, and picked up the receiver.

Elaine walked to the bedside table where they kept the chart, unable to do more until the doctor had pronounced McDowell officially dead. She stooped, picked up the pen, and wrote down the time the alarm had gone off: eight thirty-five a.m.

Dr. Greene completed the incision from *mons pubis* to sternum. He pulled back the flaps to expose the adipose tissue, the striated red muscle, white ligaments, and smooth pink uterine wall.

The fetus lay wrapped in its own umbilical cord and surrounded by a light membrane. He untangled the cord, lifted the infant from the womb, and placed it on Allison's chest. Then he clamped the cord, picking up the child to gently massage the feet. The baby gave its first thready cry and the doctor handed it over to the OB nurse to be bathed and tended.

Somewhere down the hall a telephone rang. The recovery room nurse poked her head through the door just when Greene was up to his elbows in McDowell's abdomen, feeling for the placenta.

"Doctor, it's ICU."

The doctor froze, staring over his mask at the woman.

"He's dead, sir."

"Damn!" He dug around in the woman's viscera for a moment, and his hand emerged with the still-pulsing placenta.

"I'll be right with you. Can you close for me?" He turned to the surgical nurse.

"Certainly, doctor."

The nurse began to sort through thread on the tray next to her as the doctor peeled off his gloves and hurried for the door. He paused briefly to look at the chart, noting the time when the child took its first breath.

It was eight thirty-five A.M.

28

The day was one to freeze a man's bones. A strong wind blew out of the north under a lowering sky. It teased the strands of hair from Allison's ponytail so they whipped wildly about her face. A car glided to the curb, unnoticed. Sam Holloway got out and went plowing through the crusty snow. Fresh accumulation covered the black, charred earth where the Graves's place had once stood.

He slumped further into his coat, trying to cover his ears with his upraised collar. With a loose-limbed gait he wandered up to the woman. In her arms she held a bundle, which she bounced with jerking, agitated motions.

Sam hesitated and then coughed apologetically into his hand, shocked by the white in the once jet-black hair.

"Hello, Sam," Allison said without turning her head.

"I'm surprised to see you out here today. I would've thought you'd wait until it got a bit warmer," Sam said.

"No time like the present," she said through clenched teeth.

Taken aback by her vehemence, Sam followed her gaze to the gaping hole across the cul-de-sac.

The chimneys had been knocked down, and the wood

cleared. All the debris had been piled into a heaping mound, which was covered with a sheet of clear plastic. Some snow clung to the translucent surface, softening its appearance. Equidistant from the chasm was another mound of fresh dirt.

She gave the bundle another sharp shake as the grease-stained and rusting hulk of a Caterpillar went a-chug, chug, chugging across the lot. It belched black fumes, and its engine revved, whining into a higher gear as the driver lowered the blade and pushed the earth into what had once been the basement.

"You don't have to supervise this, do you? They know what they're doing, I'm sure." Sam stuffed his hands in his pockets and began to do a shuffling hop from one foot to the other. "It's damn cold."

"Yes, it is; but I don't mind. I wanted to see this done. I wanted to make *sure* it's done. It's sort of like burying him twice." Her voice cracked on the last word.

"Are you going to be all right? I mean, what are you going to do now?"

"Well, Scott had insurance, and he had completed a second book. The contract was for five. Ira, Scott's agent, is going to help me to write those final books. Scott had outlines. I know what he had planned. I figure I can do it. I'm familiar with the topic." Allison took a deep breath. "Horror, that is."

Sam wanted to comfort her but didn't know what to say, so he changed the subject.

"Is this the newest?" Sam looked at the bundle.

Allison stared down at the swaddled infant in her arms. She rocked the baby rapidly back and forth, and Sam was surprised by the fact that the baby remained quiet. Usually infants picked up on their mother's anxiety, which she broadcast loudly.

"Yes, this is William," Allison said, lifting a tip of the blanket so the child's face was exposed.

"William!" Scott exclaimed, shocked, his voice rising to a squeak.

"William Scott," she explained. "William is a perfectly good name. It was my father's name. I thought of Scott, but couldn't do it. My heart would break everytime I call his name, and for some reason, the name William seemed appropriate."

The infant lifted its small head and stared straight at Sam. The movement seemed advanced for a baby at this stage of development. As Sam regarded the small babe he realized with a shock that the child was, without a doubt, looking at him—not with the fuzzy, unfocused look of a newborn, but with cunning intelligence and comprehension. The infant William held Sam's gaze with his own. The tiny jaw was gripped in an attitude of near defiance and the burning eyes blazed. Sam shivered involuntarily, totally unnerved, but could not look away.

Allison dropped a corner of the blanket over the child's eyes, and the spell was broken. As she continued to pat and swing the bundle frantically, Sam wondered if he had imagined it. Sam turned his attention to the young woman. Her eyes never left the bulldozer churning snow and muck across the way.

"Well, it's all over now," he said.

For the first time since he had walked up Allison turned red-rimmed eyes to gaze at him. The bulldozer sputtered, choked, and died.

"Are you so sure?" Allison whispered, and under the blanket the infant smiled.